I0603117

Brewery

Drake Wines, Volume 3

Chelle Pimblott

Published by Chelle Pimblott, 2021.

BREWERY

First edition. October 24, 2021.

Written by Chelle Pimblott.

Chapter One
CALEB

My siblings don't trust me and that hurts more than I can possibly explain. I know I've been a bit of a lazy screw up but they won't even give me a chance. They think they're the only ones who can do anything with the family business that our parents built, but I know I can bring a lot to the table. If only they'd let me.

I have this idea for a brewery and I think it would blend well with everything else in the business. Not to mention bring in a new crowd as well. I've got plans drawn up and everything, all I need now is to get a meeting with my siblings and convince them it's the right thing for us to do.

I know I've got a reputation for being a bit of a player and look, if I'm being honest, it's not totally untrue but I still think it's a bit of an unfair assessment. I like women, sue me. I'm always honest and upfront with them.

I know it hasn't always seemed like I take life too seriously, but I do. I did business studies at university and I didn't just pass the course, I blitzed the damned thing. I also know that my brother and sister, both older than me, have worked hard at Drake Wines. Their hard work helped put me through university and I will always be grateful for that. When our parents were killed by a drunk driver, we all looked after each other but being the baby of the family I know they both decided it was their responsibly to look after *me*. The truth is, I let them do it too, so I guess my current situation is just as much my fault as theirs but I'm still annoyed with them both. They keep putting me off. Every time I so much as ask them for a meeting to discuss some ideas I have for the business, they're suddenly busy.

It's also their fault I've spent so much time with Leila, the resident pastry chef and manager of Vines. I've been discussing my ideas and running things past her almost daily since the day she dropped off a hot coffee and a slice of my favourite chocolate cake and asked me what I was working on. It's been the highlight of my days recently because someone else knows about my idea. So, now I go into the bistro every day and drink coffee, while running over my plans, again and again. Determined to make them perfect so that when I eventually pin my siblings down, I have everything in order.

"Where are you going to plant this crop of yours Caleb? The property is already full of vines." She asks, not putting my idea down, just out of curiosity.

"The small plot of land next to the bistro and over the wall." I say, trying to sound confident. Her eyes widen in shock, as I rush on to explain myself. "Obviously with your approval but I've seen them grow up the side of a building before and it looks awesome. The vines grow up the wall and when they flower, it looks amazing. Obviously like crops of any kind, they have their season where they're dry and need trimming and replanting, but that will be my job. I'm not expecting anyone else to take the responsibilities on. No matter where they're planted."

"So, you're going to grow the crop here, next to my kitchen garden?" She asks me, surprised. "Are you going to brew it and then sell it here as well? All here, on Drake Wines?"

"Yes Leila, that's my plan." I admit, with a hell of a lot more confidence than I actually feel.

"You're not going to be able to go into this half-arsed, Caleb." I nod slowly, I know I'm going to have to prove to Logan and Kenna that I can do this and do it all myself. "Kenna and Logan are going to need to know and understand that this is your project. Your business, and you're going to take the reins."

"I know." Does she think she knows my siblings better than I do? I've lived with them for all of my twenty-four, almost twenty-five years. I know them better than they know themselves honestly. "I don't want them to think it's going to be another one of their responsibilities or projects. This is going to be my business."

"They're going to assume you'll flake on them and that one of them will have to take over when you decide you've had enough."

"Are you trying to talk to me *into* doing this or *out*?" I ask her, suspiciously.

"Honestly?" I nod yes, I want her honest opinion. We've been friends since she started here almost twelve months ago. Have we flirted with each other? Yes. Does she have a boyfriend? No, I don't think so but I don't want to risk her quitting because something happens between us and it goes bad! That will piss off my siblings. Again. So I've kept it light and teasing. Friendly. "I think it's a brilliant idea. Great concept and if you can sell your brother and sister on it, it will fit in here perfectly." I beam with pride. That's just what I wanted to hear. "But, you know you're going to have to prove yourself to them right? You've been a bit of a flake around here since I've been around. You've just been doing odd jobs and you haven't really had a job title. Everyone around here just says, 'Ohh yup Caleb, he'll fix that or organise for it to *be* fixed'. You're going to have to prove that you want this and you'll stick with it."

"I know but I've researched this. I know what I'm talking about and I think." I stop when Leila raises an eyebrow at me. "I *know* this can work. I can make this work and make a profit for Drake Wines. You forgot the cottages as well, I'm in charge of getting them fixed up and ready for guests."

"That's what I wanted to hear. You've got my full support. I'm behind you one hundred percent Caleb. I can see the passion and drive in your eyes when you talk about doing it, it's how I feel about baking." She gets up from the chair opposite mine and places her hand on my shoulder. "I hope they agree and you can have your own business next to your brother and sister. I know you can succeed if you're given the opportunity."

Before I can thank her, she's gone. Back into her kitchen to whip up some other delicious treat, that with any luck, I can taste test before anyone else. The joys of making friends with the best baker in town, I think as I take my first bite of the chocolate cake she brought over.

I moan, loudly and then open my eyes to see who else is actually sitting down to eat, but there's only a group of four Granny's sitting at a table laughing. I'm guessing they weren't listening to me so I'm safe to keep eating my cake.

Now that I've got Leila on board, all that's left is to get the rest of the Drake clan to see me for what I'm worth.

I SIT IN THE RESTAURANT until the last diner has left. The staff are cleaning up and then leaving for home, saying goodnight to me as they pass by.

"I'm planning on closing up now Caleb, are you leaving with the rest of us tonight?" Leila's voice envelopes me from behind as she speaks. I wish for what feels like the millionth time, that I was sitting here waiting to go home with *her* at the end of our days but I have to keep reminding myself that it just can't happen.

"Are you trying to get rid of me, Leila?" I ask, joking with her because it's safer than flirting.

"Well, today was a long day, Caleb and if I'm being honest I'm pretty tired." I really look at her face as she sits down in the chair next to me at the table as she says goodnight to the last waitress as she walks out the door. She looks exhausted, making me feel guilty for thinking she'd be more than happy to sit with me to hash out some more details for my Brewery. For all I know she's got someone waiting at home for her. Her phone vibrates in her bag just as my thoughts wander to the guy who might be wondering what time she's getting home.

"I'm sorry Leila, I didn't mean to keep you. I can lock up if you need to get home." I say, looking at her phone to make my point without actually asking the question that I really want to.

She looks at her phone, reading the text she received, not answering me right away. "Hmmmm?" she looks up and my heart stutters in my chest. Those beautiful, soulful pale blue eyes that seem to see deep into *my* soul every time she looks at me, tonight look even paler, displaying just how tired she really is. I can't help but wonder what shade they go when she's turned on. "Sorry, it was my Mum checking in to see if I've finished up for the night yet. She worries about me driving home late at night." Making me feel like an arsehole for not even considering she has a long drive home from here when I keep her late at night talking.

"How long is your drive home?" I ask.

"It only takes me a half an hour to get home this late at night." She says with a shrug. "She just worries about me. I guess it's a Mum thing." She continues, sending me a sad smile. It's sad, but I don't feel like she's sad because of my parents.

"Shit! I'm sorry Leila, why didn't you tell me? All the times I've kept you back here late at night discussing my stupid ideas and running things by you. I never should have done that." I say, gathering up my stuff. Closing my notebook, gathering up my pens and moving to stand up. Leila reaches over and places one slender, strong hand on mine, stilling my movements.

"It's OK Caleb, if I didn't want to stay, I wouldn't have. I just don't think I can keep my eyes open long enough tonight to be of any help to you." She explains, a yawn making her point for her.

"Well, you can't drive when you're this tired Leila." Shit. Kenna and Brady have the babies and they're as exhausted as new parents get when they're still getting used to be being parents. Logan and Jules have Savvy, so they're dealing with being parents as well as all of them having to adjust to Lori being gone all these months later, so I won't ask them. I've got a couple of the old farmhand cottages fixed up but they're both currently being used. One by Savvy's Aunt Jenni and the other by guests. There *is* a third one but it's nowhere close to being able to have anyone stay in it yet and asking her to stay with *me* would be out of the question. Right?

"I have no other choice Caleb." She says with a laugh. "I really should have taken Makenna and Logan up on their offer of staying onsite when they offered me the job but I wanted to have some separation from work in my spare time. I've been wishing lately that I had thought differently a year ago." She laughs again, quietly this time.

"Where were they going to let you live? In the main house some-where?" I know there are extra rooms in there, that back in the 'good old days' were where the house staff resided.

"No. They had plans to build some extra cottages like the farmhand one just up the hill here behind the bistro for accommodation for staff and guests. As you know, there are only two completed and let's face it, they've since had the wedding and other things to concentrate on." She answers sleepily, her cheek resting in her hand, as she rests her elbow on the table. She's almost asleep just sitting here, there's no way in hell I'm letting her drive the half an hour home!

"You're staying with me." I blurt out.

Her eyes widen in shock and she bolts upright in her seat, no longer sleepy. "No, I can't Caleb!"

"Why not?" I ask, but I don't give her the chance to answer. "I have a spare room and if you're worried about what other people will think, you can leave early in the morning and no-one will ever have to know." I'll know. I'm not sure if I imagine her shoulders slumping when I say that but I don't care. "You're not driving home Leila, I won't let you."

"I shouldn't stay, Caleb." She says quietly.

"I couldn't live with myself if I let you drive home and something happened to you, Leila. Please, stay?" I ask, just as quietly. I'm not above using my parents accident to get my way tonight.

"OK Caleb, I'll stay." She says with a sigh. "But I want you to know something."

"Hmmmm. What's that?" Not really wanting to hear her question.

"I don't care if people know I stayed over Caleb, I'm more worried about your reputation than mine." She says with a smirk.

"You're worried about *my* reputation?" I ask, placing my hand over my heart. "You mean, you don't care that people will talk about you sleeping over with the Drake playboy?"

"You're not a playboy Caleb." She lets out an even bigger sigh as she stands up. It feels good knowing that she doesn't think of me that way.

"That's what people think of me though Leila, and you'll be tarred with the same brush if anyone see's you leaving my place." I say sadly but Leila just shrugs her shoulders.

"Who cares? I've been called worse things, Caleb and we both know why I'm staying. You're a good man, who cares about his employees." She reaches up and pats my cheek with her small, warm hand, and then turns away from me to walk over to turn off the lights. "Let's get out of here before I fall down."

"OK. You can come with me and leave your car here. I'll bring you back up here in the morning before you go home."

"I can drive my car a few minutes to your place." She says, rolling her eyes.

"You can but you won't. " I place my hands on her shoulders and turn her to the front door. "Come on, let's get out of here." She lets me lead her to the door, we step outside and she locks up, leaving just the security lights on inside and out. I check the door is locked and lead her to my car, my hand resting lightly on her lower back. She has no idea how much I wish that this was how everyday ended, with me leading her home. Breathing in deeply to control my emotions, I direct her to my car, open the door for her and then close it after she's made herself comfortable. Walking around the front of my car to get in the driver's seat, I give myself a little pep talk about how she's just a friend staying over and I'm not allowed to touch her. Not the way I want to anyway. Nodding to myself, I reach out for the door handle and open the car door, putting myself behind the wheel.

"Everything OK Caleb? I can still drive myself home you know?" Leila says, I can hear how tired she is in her voice and when I look over to speak to her, I can see her eyes are already half closed.

"No you can't drive yourself home and yes, everything is perfectly fine."

"Why were you talking to yourself as you walked around the car then? You looked like you were telling yourself off, like you didn't really want me to stay with you tonight."

If only she knew just how much I wanted her to *stay* with me tonight! "There's absolutely no problem with you staying with me tonight Leila." I say taking a deep breath, I mumble, "No problem at all!"

"What was that mumble Cal?"

"Did you just call me Cal?" I ask, shocked.

"Oh yeah, I guess I did." She says, a lazy smile spreading across her face, even as her eyes start to close a little bit more. "Sorry about that, I didn't mean to shorten your name, I just don't have the energy to say the 'eb' as well." She giggles quietly. I've never heard Leila giggle before and if I'd ever been asked if I thought she *would* giggle, I would have said no, only full, big laughs for Leila Phillips.

"I liked it." I tell her, shocking myself and her, as her head snaps up and she looks at me to see if I'm joking or not, her eyes suddenly wide open. "I can't remember the last time someone called me Cal." I could but I didn't feel like sharing that with Leila tonight.

"OK." Is all she says, before relaxing back into her seat. Taking a very deep breath, I start the car, back out of the car park and drive the few minutes along the winding driveway to my house.

I pull my car into the garage, turn it off and open the door to get out, saying, "OK Leila we're here." When I don't get an answer, I look over to see her asleep in the passenger seat. She looks peaceful and sexy. So fucking sexy my breath catches in my chest.

Moving around the car, I open the door into my house and go back out to open her door. "Leila?"

"Mmmhmm."

"It's time to get out of the car gorgeous."

"OK, just one more minute?" It sounds like a question more than a statement, even as she squirms in the seat to get more comfortable. If I leave her in the car, she'll not only get a sore neck and back, but eventually she'll end up freezing cold as well. Not to mention I'm not that much of an arse-hole. I make a decision and I don't give myself a chance to talk myself out of what I'm about to do, I just do it. Sliding one arm under her legs, I slide the other one behind her shoulders and lift her out of the car.

"Caleb." She mumbles quietly while snuggling in close to my body, wrapping her arms around my neck and resting her cheek on my shoulder. Geezus, she's killing me. My cock jumps to attention.

"Fuck!" I mumble into her hair.

"Mmmm." Leila kind of moans, wiggles her butt in my hands and cuddles in closer. I'm pretty sure she's as close to me as she can get without me being inside her. Then it's my turn to groan because I shouldn't have thought about being *in* her gorgeous body.

I make quick work of getting from the garage door to my spare room. I think it's the fastest I've ever moved through my house but I *need* to get this woman out of my arms. Arms that want nothing more than to hold onto her forever.

Gently, I lay her down on the spare bed that Kenna made me buy because it was the 'grown up thing to do' for any friends staying over. My friends rarely come out here and they never stay over, I never let them. This is my sanctuary and I never bring women back here. Well, I never have before but tonight, I'm grateful for my sister's advice. I never would have allowed Leila to sleep on my couch and I don't think my back could have coped with *me* sleeping on my couch. I pull back the covers, remove her shoes and tuck her in. For a few seconds, I just stand there watching her sleep until I realise I'm being a real creeper and quietly walk out of the room, closing the door behind me. In the hallway, I lean back against the door and close my eyes while taking a deep breath to steady my heartbeat. After a minute, I push myself off the door and walk to my own room. Pushing my door closed so that I'm not tempted to walk back out again. I walk into the bathroom, stripping my clothes off as I walk and get straight into a cool shower. If I don't cool my body down, I'm going to do something we *both* might regret in the morning.

With my body back to normal, I start to wash the day away, but when I stroke myself just once to clean up, I start to get hard again and decide to turn off the shower and get out. I dry myself with my towel and tie it around my hips. I throw myself down on my bed and hope that sleep finds me quickly, because I don't want to lie here all night thinking about Leila being just a few feet away from me.

Sleeping.

Beautiful.

Not mine to touch!

Chapter Two
LEILA

Looking out the window connecting the kitchen to the dining room, I watch as Caleb Drake strolls into Vines, the bistro I run at Drake Wines. Vines started out as just a tasting room for the winery that Logan Drake, Caleb's older brother runs and they expanded it into the light lunch and dinner serving bistro it is today. We still have the wine tastings but now we've expanded our repertoire to include baked goods.

When I first started here just over a year ago, I was the manager and then, out of nowhere the pastry chef up and quit. She was only supposed to be part-time but it turned into a more time consuming position than first anticipated and I think she just cracked under the pressure. Makenna knew that I not only had a passion for baking but thanks to my resume, she also knew that I'd started on a path to become, you guessed it, a pastry chef. So, I agreed to take over the position until we could hire someone new.

That's how I became the pastry chef *and* manager of Vines!

People started coming in for the great coffee and cheese platters, then returned time after time for the cakes and other sweets that I created. Makenna promised me the freedom to create what I wanted *if* I stayed on as their pastry chef and then she took over a lot of the paperwork that I'd been doing so that I could concentrate on baking and making sure the day to day running of Vines was going well. I tried to explain that I hadn't completed more than a few months of my course but she didn't want to hear about it. She said, and I quote, 'Leila, I know you started and I know you didn't finish. I also know *why* you didn't finish that course. I've also tasted your food and I can't let you walk away from the fucking kitchen, please stay.'

I convinced her to install the porthole like window in the wall shared by the kitchen and the dining room so that I could keep an eye on the dining area. I'd already noted how often Caleb came in for a meals or a slice of cake. The joy I get from watching him walk in and out of the place, well I'm telling you, I needed a window right near my workbench so I can do just that. Makenna hasn't caught on to why I asked, just took me at my word and I kind of feel guilty about using her to stalk her little brother but my guilt doesn't last for long.

I watch one of the waitresses take his order over, flirting with him the entire time. He doesn't flirt back, he's nice to her but he doesn't flirt back. I can see the disappointment on her face from in the kitchen. He's got a reputation for being a bit of an easy going player that his siblings buy into, as well. I've never understood how they only see that side of him because I don't see it at all. Yes he's gorgeous and charming, but he was also top of his business studies class at university.

I realise he's finished eating, so I get the barista to make a latte, while I take out a slice of his favourite chocolate cake and put it on a plate. When the latte is ready, I take both over to his table and place them down in front of him.

"My favourite girl, with my favourite cake, what would I do without you Leila Phillips?" He asks with a charming smile on his face that makes me want to squirm under his attention and my underwear is slightly damper with his efforts.

"Cook your own meals and no doubt find some other sucker to make you chocolate cake." His eyes darken with something I can't explain before they start to sparkle with mischief again and I can't help but think I was seeing things.

"No-one else could ever give me cake as good as you darlin." I hear a long sigh to my left and realise Sara was in hearing distance of our conversation and she's swooning over him, again.

"Stop being so charming Caleb, I need my staff to be able to walk around and hold conversations, not melt into puddles around your smooth talk." My defence mechanism against my absolute attraction to this man is snark and sass. He'll never pick up on how desperate I am to tear his clothes off his body to lick and touch him all over, if he's too busy either laughing at me or trying to work out what the hell he did wrong. It's worked for me so far and it's been a year of longing to taste every fine inch of him. Right,

I have to stop right there otherwise I'm going to need clean underwear and he's watching me so closely as if he might actually be able to read my mind.

Instead, I ask him how his plans for the Brewery are coming along and when he doesn't sound very confident about being able to convince his siblings that he can make this work for them and *him*, I push back a little, demanding to know why he's suddenly lacking confidence. When he replies, "I *know* this can work. I can make this work and make a profit for Drake Wines." with absolute confidence, I'm happy because I have no doubt in his ability to make it work because he's passionate about it. Now he just needs to convince his siblings he won't flake out on them and leave it up to them to run the business when he gets bored.

"I'm behind you one hundred percent, Caleb. I can see the passion and drive in your eyes when you talk about it." I smile at him, hoping that he believes me. "I just hope your siblings can see it and give you the chance."

I don't give him the chance to answer me, I've got things to do in the kitchen and I don't want to hear him say he's thankful for my support or even worse, that he doesn't need it. I raise my hand to push on the swing door into the kitchen when I hear a low, rumbling moan and I turn around to see Caleb drawing the spoon out of his mouth, his eyes closed. Then his tongue flicks out to lick the chocolate frosting off his lips, I might just need that clean underwear after all!

That is until I hear the table of ladies old enough to be my grandmother, giggle, yes giggle and one says, "Holy crap! What I would give to be that chocolate *and* that spoon!" Making her friends laugh even louder.

"You're too old for him, Martha." Says Beryl but I think Martha is too busy drooling into her cappuccino while staring at Caleb, to listen to her friend.

"Oh to be forty years younger, hey Beryl?" Martha says to her friend telling her she's too old, never taking her eyes off of Caleb.

"Come on Martha, Beryl's right. You can look but you've got no chance and that's how it should be. You had your time with Harry, let the lovely Leila have her sexy young man to herself." Betty says but Martha doesn't answer her, she doesn't even glance her way.

"She's allowed to look and relive her youth Betty, but I think I know what I need for dessert today."

"Look but don't touch, is that your theory Edith?" Betty asks, a wicked smile on her face.

These older ladies are relentless and cougar worthy! I go to speak up, to tell them Caleb isn't mine, that he's a free agent but I stop myself, realising with a start that I would give anything to be that spoon and piece of chocolate myself. One of the waitresses goes over to clear up some of their plates and they all place orders for a slice of chocolate cake. I walk into the kitchen and get back to work. I need the distraction and baking always takes my mind of other things.

Including Caleb Drake.

It's also when I usually come up with some of my most sensual desserts. *Not* thinking about Caleb.

Sara, the waitress that served the group of Granny's and one of my best friends, comes into the kitchen with their empty plates, laughing. "Did you hear the language on those ladies? They just ordered a slice of your decadent chocolate cake each because apparently, 'Leila's young man found it orgasmic.' I can't wait to be their age and not care what anyone thinks of me." She laughs loudly as she walks out the door on the other side of the kitchen to get to the cake case. Her head pops back in and she says with a huge smile, "When did you and the youngest Drake become a couple anyway? I thought you weren't seeing anyone right now?"

"I'm not. We're not. Not that it's any of your business. Now get back to work." She laughs again and I can't help feeling a little annoyed. Is she teasing me because she knows it won't happen, or because she knows how much I *want* it to happen? "Give the ladies their cake before they decide jumping Mr Drake for his slice would be a good idea."

"Right, because we wouldn't want anyone jumping *Mr Drake* now would we?" Sara asks and then disappears, with any luck it's to do her job and leave Caleb eating his cake in peace.

For the next couple of hours I lose myself in preparing for the fresh bake that I do every morning. It keeps regulars, like the Granny's, coming back and new customers trying us out. The fact that they can also check out the wines available here is an added bonus. Soon we'll hopefully have beer for the guests to enjoy as well.

Drake Wines is out of the main town by about thirty minutes, so it's not an easy place to get to, but our reputation speaks for itself, for the wine and the food, and brings in tourists and locals alike.

Baking always clears my mind and before I know it, my staff are doing their end of night jobs, doing their part to help close up for the night. I'm grateful for everything they do but tonight I'm even more grateful because I'm exhausted.

"Hey boss, it's time to go home. Are you leaving with the rest of us tonight?" Sara asks, as she grabs her bag, ready to leave. I normally stay back for a while after everyone's gone to finish my prep for the morning but tonight I think I've got enough done, plus I'm just too tired to do anymore.

"Yeah, I'm done for the day. I might try to come in a little early in the morning."

Sara smiles at me, knowing I'll be the first one here in the morning. "You know, Caleb is still sitting out at his table." She pauses before asking, "Did you want me to see if he's leaving with the rest of us?" She knows we've been working on something, she just doesn't know what. I know she has her suspicions but they're mostly of the romantic kind. No matter how many times I try to tell her that we're not involved in any kind of way, she doesn't believe me.

"No, that's OK, I'll go talk to him." I reply, washing my hands and packing away the last of the doughs ready for the morning. "I'll just fill the dishwasher and then head out."

"Of course you will." She says with a smile. "I'll see you tomorrow, Leila. Have a good night."

"Good night Sara, enjoy your evening." I know what she's hinting at, I just don't have the energy tonight to try to convince her otherwise. So, instead I smile, fill the dishwasher, turn it on, then walk out to the dining room, finding Caleb exactly where I left him a couple of hours ago.

"I'm planning on closing up now Caleb, are you leaving with the rest of us tonight?" I ask as I walk over to him.

"Are you trying to get rid of me, Leila?" He asks, a sexy smirk on his face that I just want to kiss until he's no longer capable of smiling, just groaning. Instead, I tell him I'm exhausted side-stepping the why, because I really don't know why I feel so tired.

My phone vibrates in my hand and I look down to see it's my mum checking in on me. She worries about me driving home, alone late at night to an empty home. Caleb has a frown on his handsome face when he asks who I'm messaging. I feel like a teenager telling him it's my mummy checking up on me, I see him relax and my tired brain can't work out why he was tense in the first place.

What I *do* tell him is that I wish I'd taken Kenna up on her offer of staying on the property when they offered me the job, that way on nights like tonight, I wouldn't have to drive for half an hour to get home. At the time, Kenna and Logan were thinking about fixing up an old cottage for overnight accommodation or longer stays.

When Caleb offers to let me stay at his house for the night, even though my body is jumping at the chance and my mind isn't too far behind, I fight it. I know he's not offering a night between the sheets with the sexist man I've ever met *but* that's not going to stop my mind from wandering in that direction! In the end, I'm just too tired to fight him. The drive to his house takes less than five minutes but I can't keep my eyes open. His car is warm and I'm comfortable, both in the seat and with his company.

I hear him tell me we're at his house, but I just need another minute before I can get up and walk. The next thing I know he's lifting me up and carrying me into the house, then he's gently lowering me onto the softest bed and pillows ever! He takes my shoes off, covers me up, tucking me in tight. I sense that he's still standing there but I don't have the energy to ask him why, I just smile and drift off to sleep.

Waking up it takes me a few seconds to realise I'm not in my own bed. When I realise that I'm sleeping in Caleb's bed, my hand slides over to the other side of the bed, only to find it empty and I'm not sure whether that makes me happy or sad. I pull my phone out of my bag that's sitting on the beside drawer to check the time, 2.38am. I fling the covers off me, swing my legs over the side and go looking for the bathroom. Opening the bedroom door, I see a door on the opposite side of the hallway, slightly to the left of mine that's open. Walking as quietly as I can, I walk up to look into the room and sigh in relief when I find it is actually the bathroom, even if a small corner of my sex starved mind wishes I'd found Caleb's bedroom. I do what I need to do, then quietly make my way back into the bedroom, closing the door quietly behind me.

I look at the bed, then down over my body, while Caleb was the perfect gentleman and only took my shoes off, I know I won't be able to sleep if I go to bed fully clothed again. So I strip down to my underwear, removing my bra. No woman *ever* wants to sleep in her bra, she doesn't want to wear a bra unless she has to, full stop. Luckily, I put a singlet top on under my work shirt this morning, which means I can now sleep in that, along with my sexy cotton granny knickers. Don't judge me, they're comfy when I'm working in a hot kitchen all day! That being said, I'm damn lucky Caleb decided to be a gentleman tonight. I can't imagine what he would think of the unsexy, utilitarian underpants I have on today. The thought of Caleb's discovery of my less than sexy 'lingerie' while taking off my clothes last night makes me laugh.

I crawl back under the covers, still smiling to myself, wondering what Caleb would think about my choice of underwear. Suddenly, it hits me like a ton of bricks, that wouldn't be funny, we wouldn't laugh about it at all. For one, it was never going to happen, it wouldn't be right. For two, Caleb is used to women throwing themselves at him. I'm pretty sure they never wear cotton underwear when they're out looking to get laid. I'm betting he's used to the women wearing all kinds of sexy lingerie.

Why am I lying in bed thinking about Caleb, lingerie, and other women? Rolling over to my side and curling up in the soft bedding that I'm positive Kenna had a hand in purchasing and put Caleb and other women out of my mind.

Except that sleeping in sheets that shouldn't even smell like him but do, causes him to be the star of dreams that are even hotter than the usual ones he stars in home.

Chapter Three
CALEB

When my alarm goes off the next morning, I reach over and whack it to turn it off.

My first thoughts are of Leila, even as I rub the sleep from my eyes. The knowledge that she's asleep in my house, in my bed, does something to my insides. She's in my *spare* bed but still it's *my* bed. My *home*.

I take a deep breath, throw the covers off and swing my legs out of the bed. When my feet hit the soft carpet, I sigh and wonder if I should go wake her up or should I let her sleep? She looked so damned tired last night, I want to let her sleep, even though I made sure to set my alarm early because I know she needs to get to Vines pretty early. I hate to admit it but I have no idea what time she actually starts, I just know it's damned early! She's just always there when I get there and she leaves late with everyone else. It's one of the things I admire most about her, she's dedicated to baking and making everything perfect.

I also admire her legs, intelligence, dry sense of humour and her sassy comebacks. She keeps me on my toes and I love it!

Pulling on a pair of sweatpants, I stand up and reach for a t-shirt. I'm used to walking around with as few clothes on as I want but with Leila in my house I feel like I should cover up. For both of our sakes and not because I think she won't be able to resist me if she sees me naked, but more because of what *my* physical reaction could be.

I decide to go to the kitchen to start up the coffee machine before going in to wake Leila up. Yeah I know, I'm just putting off the inevitable. I can't decide if the reason I don't want to go in there is because I want her here for as long as I can have her or because I don't want to see her in my space.

I don't know if I can take it if she looks like she could belong here. Belong *with* me.

But I want her to belong here and *that's* the problem.

With that little revelation, I realise I've been standing in my kitchen, staring out the window at the vines that line our family property. I have to make this Brewery work first, that comes before anything else, especially my love life, which is sadly lacking these days. No matter what anyone else, including my siblings think. It's been a very long time since I've had the pleasure of female company that wasn't my sister or a friend. Leila is definitely someone I consider a friend, a good one at that.

Taking a deep breath, I make my feet move in the direction of the spare room. I stand at the closed door for a few seconds and knock quietly, before I open the door, letting myself into the room. I should have waited for her to yell out that it was OK to come in. Holy crap! I wasn't expecting to see a shapely leg hanging out of the covers, showing just a tiny bit of her pink underwear. Nor was I expecting to see her stretched out on her stomach, bare arms wrapped around the pillow and her silky dark red hair spread out across another pillow. When I put her to bed last night, she was fully dressed except for the shoes that I took off for her because let's face it, no-one wants to sleep while wearing shoes. I heard her get up and go to the bathroom around the 2am mark because I was hyper aware of her being in the house but I never thought that she might strip out of her clothes to make sleeping more comfortable.

She looks so comfortable and relaxed, I really don't want to wake her. Especially after seeing her so damned exhausted last night. The fact that she fell asleep in my car, when it takes less than five minutes to drive to my house from Vines, tells me just how tired she was.

I realise I've been leaning against the door frame just watching her sleep like a crazy man, when she rolls over to face me and stretches. I should have taken that as my cue to leave and wait for her to come out to the living room, instead I'm rooted to the spot just watching her, mesmerised by watching her stretch, her toned legs kicking the covers off. She's like watching a cat stretch in the sunlight.

I might have decided just now that I need to go adopt a cat.

A smile spreads across her face and she moans, causing a certain appendage to rise to the occasion. I'm grateful I've got sweatpants on, otherwise we could have an even more awkward situation happening here as her eyes slowly open and focus on my face. I can see the minute she remembers where she is and who is standing there watching her. Her eyes fly open so wide I'm afraid they might just pop out, then I watch as a sweet blush crawls up from her chest to her cheeks. A second later, she moves fast, covering her body back up with the white sheet.

"Good morning." I say, the roughness of sleep and speaking my first words for the day, still in my voice. At least, if asked, that's what my excuse would most definitely be. It's certainly not because of how much I'm turned on right now. Not at *all*.

"Good morning." She says, her voice still raspy from sleep as well. Geezus if she gets any sexier, I don't know if I can stop myself from kissing her. I would *never* force myself on a woman, ever but Leila makes me feel so out of control. The need I feel to kiss her, to touch her, is overwhelming some days.

"I just made coffee, do you want some?" I ask, because I need to stop thinking about crawling into the bed with her.

"Yes please, that would be amazing." She smiles at me and my heart skips a beat. I don't know why because she smiles at me more often than she frowns, so why is this morning any different?

"OK. I'll go make us one." I nod but my body isn't moving. She suddenly sits up, the sheet dropping down to her lap.

"What time is it?" She asks, clearly in a panic.

"It's seven thirty, I didn't want to wake you-" I don't get finish because she's talking over the top of me.

"In the morning? Ohhhh shit!" She reaches over to the bedside table for her phone and effectively uncovers the rest of her body without noticing she's done it. "Shit, shit, shit!" She mumbles as she opens her phone and starts doing something on there.

"I'm sorry I didn't want to wake you up too early because you needed the sleep but I also wasn't sure what time you needed to be up to get things started at -" Again, I don't get to finish what I'm saying.

"No, no it's OK. It's my fault really, I should have set an alarm on my phone. In fact, I thought I did when I got up to pee sometime early this morning." She mumbles, I'm pretty sure she's forgotten I'm even standing here. "There I did see!" She says, showing me the screen.

"Ummm yes you did but it's for six o'clock tonight Leila." I reply, trying not to laugh. Her face wrinkles up in confusion as she looks at her screen to see if I'm right. Hell, no-one should look that cute this early in the morning, or at our age to be honest but she does.

"Ahhh shit! Of course I messed it up." She says, slapping her forehead with her hand and shaking her head.

"Was there somewhere you needed to be that early today?"

"No." She says into the hand that's still covering her face. "I just. Shit! I wanted to go home for a shower and a change of clothes. I didn't want to inconvenience you any more than I already have."

"You're not an inconvenience Leila, ever." I walk over to the side of the bed and take her hand away from her face, place my finger under her chin and bring her eyes up to meet mine so she can see that I mean every word of what I'm about to say. "You being here, it's not a problem for me Leila. If it was, I wouldn't have offered you my bed." I cough to clear my throat because I know how that sounded. "I mean, you know, my *spare* bed. Anyway, it's no trouble at all that you stayed over or that you need to shower or have coffee and breakfast."

She pulls her face out of my hand and I instantly miss touching her. "Oh no, you don't need to feed me as well Caleb." She's shaking her head so vigorously that I'm afraid it might fall off.

"Don't be ridiculous Leila." Then a sudden thought hits me. "You don't think I can cook, do you?"

"I never said that Caleb." She squeaks.

"I know I come into the bistro for a lot my meals, probably too many but it's not because I can't cook darlin'." I laugh, if only she knew the real reason I eat close to every meal at Vines, it's not for the food, even though it's brilliant.

"Then why *are* you in so often then?" Suddenly she's back to being sassy, confident Leila and I like it, a little too much but do I dare tell her the truth?

"Do you have any idea how boring it is to cook for one person? To eat almost every meal on your own?" I can't believe I'm telling her this, it's a half-truth but that's all I'm willing to share with her today. She nods her head in agreement and it makes me feel like an arsehole to be happy that she knows what it's like to eat alone. "I'm a social kind of guy Leila. I like talking to people and having company. I like noise and chatter, so I come in because there's always people, movement, noise and music. I enjoy the company of the people who work there too." I smile at her, hoping that she realises that I mean *her* company, not someone else.

"Yes, well Sara has a way of making everyone feel at home." She says and while she sounds serious I can see the hint of a smirk on her lips. "So does the rest of the crew. I mean, it's why we hired them, after all." She nods thoughtfully but her lips are twitching.

"That they do but that's not who I meant, and I think you know that." I don't give her a chance to respond, I barely register the shock on her face. "Now, get yourself into the shower and before you say you've got nothing to change into, Kenna has some clothes stored in the closet, so feel free to look through those to see if something will work for you today." I say, pointing at the closet in the room, just to clarify.

"Why does Kenna have clothes stored at your house?" Her confusion is fucking adorable.

"Probably because she doesn't have enough space up at the house *or* she doesn't want Brady to see *all* of the clothes she has." The look on her face tells me that doesn't answer the question she really wants to ask. "Is there something else you want to ask me Leila?" Her head whips up and she looks me in the eye. There is a minute of silence, neither of us move, keeping eye contact, until she quietly asks the question she really wants answered.

"Are you sure they're all your sister's clothes?"

"Who else do *you* think would be leaving clothes here, Leila?" I want to hear her say that she thinks I have women here all the time that might actually leave their clothes here. I *need* to know if that's what she *really* thinks I am.

"Well, you know." She mumbles.

"No, I don't. Please explain it to me like I'm stupid because the only woman leaving clothes around my house is my sister." I say, a little more sharply than I intended but I can't regret it when I see a spark of defiance light up in her eyes and I know I'm in for one hell of a comeback.

"You *do* know what I mean Caleb Drake *but* if you need me to spell it out for you, here goes. I *mean* are you sure it's not one of your one night stands that left something behind as an excuse to come back and see *you* again?" There's a bite in her voice that I can't help hoping is jealousy and doesn't that just make me a sick bastard?

"Kenna is the only one who has left clothes here, Leila." I say, pissed off that she actually *does* believe all the gossip about me. "Wear the clothes or don't wear the clothes, it doesn't bother me either way." I reply, turning abruptly and leaving the bedroom before she can say anything else. I don't want to hear what she thinks about me and the 'women' that don't exist.

A few minutes later I hear movement and assume I'll be seeing Leila out here any second asking to be taken to her car so that she can go home to get changed in her unsullied by me, home. Instead, I hear the shower start up and I can't help the smile that spreads across my face. Thinking about her in my shower, using my towels, shampoo and soap has my cock hardening. To take my mind off the video running through my brain, I get busy cooking us up some breakfast.

Breakfast works so well to distract me, that I don't hear the shower turn off or Leila walk out to join me in the kitchen. I turn around to face the island, only to find her sitting on one of the stools on the opposite side, smiling at me.

"Holy shit! I didn't hear you come out from the bedroom." My voice changes an octave or two with the surprise of finding her sitting there watching me.

"Sorry, I didn't mean to scare you." She says, smirking.

"You didn't *scare* me, Leila, I just wasn't expecting you to be there. I was concentrating on what I was doing and I didn't hear you walk in the room." I say, a little too defensively. "I'm not used to having anyone around here, that's all."

"Not even Kenna, Brady, Logan and Jules?" She asks, not looking at me.

"Very rarely. Kenna's only ever here to grab or leave more clothes *or* she's coming to check up on me and probably give me a lecture of some kind or other. She thinks I've made poor decisions as well and wasted my life." I turn back to the stove top to turn it off so that I can dish up our food.

"That's not what I said, nor is it what I meant, Caleb. I just wanted to know whose clothes I would be putting on. It's my body you know and I'm kinda fussy about what goes on it and in it." My dick jumps in my sweatpants a little because we're thinking about *being in* Leila's body now.

"Here you go, I made you some breakfast." My voice is rough, I must almost sound angry to her but when she mentions being *in her body, my* body goes into overdrive.

"Thank you Caleb." She says quietly, as we both sit at the bench eating quietly.

It's not really what I would call an awkward silence but it's also not really too comfortable either. I know I should say something, anything to break the tension but I don't know where to start. Do I explain that I don't *bring* women *here*, ever? What will she make of that? I don't want it to sound like I've put her in the friend zone because as much as I want to get to know and be her friend, I want *so* much more than that. Right now though, it feels way beyond my reach, my past seems to be catching up with me in the most inconvenient way.

We're both lost in our own thoughts and we both jump, muttering a few choice words when my phone rings and vibrates across the benchtop.

"Are you going to answer that?" Leila asks me.

I pick up my phone and look at the screen. It's Brian, he could potentially be my hops supplier but he's making a few weird demands, making me think he's a little eccentric and potentially hard to deal with. I push the answer button, hoping I haven't left him waiting for too long.

"Good morning Brian. How are you today?"

"Good morning Caleb, I didn't wake you up, did I?" He chuckles.

"No, of course you didn't. I'm just eating my breakfast and I didn't want to answer with my mouth full." Leila snorts, trying to hold back her laughter, earning her a dirty look from me. She pulls her lips into her mouth and ducks her head.

"I'm sorry, do you have company? I can call back later if you're busy, Caleb." He says it like he's being generous but he's fishing to see who I have here and we both know it.

"No, this is a good time to talk Brian." I reply, trying to sound like I'm not annoyed with him because truthfully I'm not. A little frustrated perhaps but not annoyed.

"I just have a couple of things I want to clarify before we meet up on the weekend."

Ahhh yes, the dinner party. The one I'm invited to and expected to bring a date to but not just any date, no I'm supposed to bring *the one*.

"What did you need to know?" I ask, not wanting to ask him and *really* not wanting his answers. I know what's coming and I still don't have an answer for him, well, not the one he wants to hear anyway.

"You're staying with us for the weekend right?"

"I sure am, Brian."

"The full three days? You know, I do understand you've got a business to run there and need to be on the farm, so if you don't want to come up Friday afternoon, I understand."

"No, I'll be there for the whole weekend. I cleared it with Logan and Makenna." Although, they think I'm going away with some friends for the weekend because I haven't told them about my Brewery plans yet but Brian doesn't need to know that.

"Fantastic. I'm glad they can see the benefits of us doing business." He says and my guilt rises.

"Me too. They're both very supportive."

"Also, Mary wants to know if you're bringing someone for the weekend. She needs to finalise numbers and asked me to check in with you." He pauses and then adds, "It would be nice to see you with a young lady Caleb. A wife and family really settles a man and makes him work harder to succeed. You need your business to succeed when you have others that are relying on you and that makes you more determined to win."

"I have every intention of making a success of the Brewery Brian, make no mistake about it." Leila coughs to get my attention and mouths that she's going to walk up to Vines. "Brian, can you excuse me for a minute, please?" I don't give him much opportunity to say no but I hear him hum and say sure as I pull the phone away from my ear.

"No, this won't take long Leila. I'll take you up in a few minutes." When she hesitates I say, "Please, finish your breakfast and then we can both go up to Vines." She hesitates for a second and then nods, sitting back down on the stool to finish the breakfast I cooked for her. I can't help but wonder how many times someone else has cooked for *her*. Then, I wonder whether she's worrying about someone seeing us together, of her walking out of my house so early in the morning and people talking.

"Sorry Brian, what were you saying?" I ask, distracted by thoughts of Leila not wanting to be seen with me. The Drake playboy.

"I knew you had someone there. You must bring her this weekend." He sounds so excited. "You will make Mary incredibly happy if you bring a nice young lady with you. She worries about you, you know? So, who is she? What's her name?"

I can't help it, before I have time to consider them, the words are out of my mouth. My brain not catching up with my mouth until I hear Leila gasp.

"That's Leila, my fiancée." Leila's eyes widen in shock and I know I've got some explaining to do.

Chapter Four
LEILA

What the hell did Caleb just say?!

I can't think, I can't move. I'm frozen half on, half off the stool.

"Yes, I'll talk to Leila and let you know for sure later today, if we can make it Friday or not. I'll have to check if she can get away from work early enough." There's silence as we stare at each other. "Yes, the engagement is brand new. No, we've been together for quite a while but I decided to propose on the weekend because I knew I couldn't live without her." There's more silence as he listens to 'Brian', but neither of us have moved. "Of course. I'll talk to you soon. Goodbye Brian." Then he hangs up.

It's so quiet in the house, you could hear a pin drop and still neither one of us have moved. I'm still half on and half off the stool and Caleb is just standing there, looking like he's as shocked as I am at this turn of events.

"Did you just tell Brian we're engaged?" I ask, my voice a little high-pitched.

"Ummm look, let me explain." Caleb starts but I can't.

We speak at the same time, which is funny considering how quiet we've both been for at least a few minutes now.

"Can you let me explain the situation to you, please Leila?" He pleads warily, closing his eyes briefly.

"Oh please, go ahead. I can't wait to hear this explanation. I'm kind of intrigued to see how this one plays out and what your thought process was. Very interested for sure." I say, trying not to sound like a wench but finding it hard to keep my emotions under control. I feel like he's backed me into a corner that only he can get me out of or explain it.

"OK. So, to answer your question, yes. Yes I *did* just tell Brian we're engaged but hear me out. OK?" The pleading in his voice makes me sit my butt back down on the stool and I wave my hand for him to keep going.

"Go ahead. This should be good." Honestly, I can't wait to hear what the hell made him think this was a good idea.

"Where do I start?" He asks himself in a mumble.

"The beginning is generally the right place when someone needs to start explaining themselves Caleb." I say dryly.

"Very helpful Leila." He scowls at me, until I raise an eyebrow at him, then he coughs and tries again to explain our predicament because it is *our* predicament now. "Well, as you know, I'm trying to get all my ducks in a row for the Brewery *before* I take my business proposal to Logan and Makenna." I nod yes, so he knows I understand. "And you've met Brian, the man I plan on getting my hops from?"

"Yes Caleb, I get all of that. Can we get to the reason as to why we're suddenly engaged, please?" My irritation levels are starting to climb a little too high and he's about to find out what angry Leila looks like. Guess we should get to know each other better seeing as we're getting married and there's no better time like the present.

"Brian is a family guy in a *very* big way and while he understands that I lost my parents a few years ago, he knows that I have family, they're 'only' siblings and therefore they don't make me settled and to him that makes me a risk. He thinks that people who are settled and have a reason to succeed, like supporting a family, are the best people to do business with. You heard that conversation, he's having a huge gathering at his family's main residence and yes I did say *main residence*. My invitation included a plus one but Brian has made it very clear without actually saying the words, that the invitation for the plus one was only for the woman that I'm planning a life, a future, with. Just now, he mentioned his wife and how interested she was in whether I was bringing someone with me." He takes a deep breath like he's steeling himself to say the rest, I don't say a word, I just let him get it all out. "Mary is the sweetest woman you could ever meet, honestly but she seems to have made me her special project. She wants to see me settled and happy. She thinks of me as a sad, lonely and tragic orphan. If I don't take someone this weekend and I mean someone *special*, she'll start trying to set me up with her socialite friends daughters and granddaughters again. I just can't stand it again." He shudders. "It's not as fun as it might sound, believe me and Brian, well he's holding back from agreeing to sell to me because he still feels like I'm too big of a risk because I'm not settled enough." Caleb takes a deep breath, his eyes are already closed, he closed them when he explained about Mary trying to set him up. I'm guessing he didn't really enjoy of the dates she set him up on.

"Well, technically, you *are* an orphan but you're not without a family Caleb. Haven't you explained that to them?" I ask, curious. I can't believe people still think like that!

"Of course I have!" His voice is raised but he's not yelling, he's just full of frustration. "I'm sorry, I didn't mean to yell but do you really think I haven't tried to explain that to them? I have my brother and sister, they're my family and the family business is my focus. You would think that alone would help him to believe that I'm serious and less of a risk but apparently not." I watch as the frustration defeats him and his shoulders slump.

"I can see why Brian wants you to be less of a risk but I don't understand how you being engaged helps the situation."

"Me either honestly but it's how Brian does business."

"Isn't there someone, somewhere else you can get the hops from?"

"Yes there are, plenty but I've invested a lot of time and effort with Brian and honestly?"

"Of course."

"He's got the best hops, his prices are fair and reasonable. He also has the hops I want."

"Right." I say thoughtfully, knowing my answer already. In fact, I knew the minute he told Brian I was his fiancé, well as soon as I got over the shock of it anyway. "So, what you're saying is, this is the way you want to go and to move forward, you need a fake fiancé?"

"Yes." He closes his eyes again, mumbles something to himself and then to me he says, "Look, it's OK. I'll find someone else."

"But I've already met Brian, won't he remember me?"

"Maybe but I can make up an excuse of some kind. I guess. It's not like he comes out here very often anyway."

I've asked him a lot of questions because I want to know how much thought he's put into this and how much he wants this brewery. I think I already know the answers but I need to make sure before I jump into this quagmire with him.

My answer was always going to be, yes. An absolute resounding, without reservation, yes! But, giving in to him easily was never going to happen. I mean, I had to make him work for it, otherwise he might actually catch on to how I really feel about him and I'm not ready for the fallout from that just yet. The fact that I'm wildly attracted to him and have been more than a little in love with him since the day we met, has no influence whatsoever on all the time I spend with the him, or how eager I am to do this for him either.

Nope.

It's not like he's even noticed me as more than a friend and employee but helping him with his idea for the brewery has helped make me fall for him even more. If that's possible. The fact that said brewery will be right next to the bistro, Vines, that I run for the Drakes is just the cream on top.

If it means I get to know him better and spend some extra time with him by being his fake fiancé, then count me in! Now I just have to hope that I can keep my heart intact in the process and not have to walk away from the best job I've had.

Caleb stands in front of me, I don't know when we managed to move so close to each other but we did because I can reach out and touch him if I want to and boy do I want to.

"Did we just get engaged Caleb Drake?" I ask, a smile stretching across my face.

"If that's your way of accepting my proposal then I guess, we did?" He asks, searching my face for clues to my answer.

"Are you asking me Caleb or are you not interested anymore?" I ask, slightly annoyed. I know it's not a real proposal but a little more confidence and happiness that I've accepted would be nice.

"I'm all in, Leila." His smile lights up his face.

"I'm all in too, Caleb."

"So, yes, we're doing this?"

"Yes, we're doing this." I laugh.

"You'll come away with me this weekend?" I nod yes and Caleb starts talking a million miles a minute. "Do you think you could get away Friday or would you rather not make it a 3 day weekend away? Can you take that time off? Do you have someone who can cover for you?"

"Caleb, stop. One question at a time, OK?"

"Sorry, you're right, I'm just so happy you said yes." Then his face wrinkles up in thoughtfully. "Oh and I have to go buy you a ring. I've got the perfect one in mind. It will be perfect for you." A smile spreads across his handsome face again. "Do you want to come with me, or do you want it to be a surprise?"

I'm sure my face is full of shock because, shit he's going to buy me an engagement ring! "Ummm I don't think I can take the extra time off." I pause because I see the disappointment on his face. "Are we telling everyone? Like your brother and sister? The guys at Vines? My mum?" My hands fly to my mouth. "Oh. My. God! My *mum*! We can't tell her Caleb, she'll believe it even though it's quick and she'll expect a wedding, a marriage and a honeymoon and kids. Oh my god, she'll want grandkids!" I start to hyperventilate and Caleb moves to my side so that he can rub my back.

"So you *don't* want to tell everyone then?" He asks, letting me decide how this is going to work.

"I don't think so. I mean it's not real and that's just going to hurt everyone in the end. If you tell Makenna and Logan about us, then you have to tell them about the brewery and you're not ready for that yet. We both know that Caleb, so no, this stays between the two of us and the Weavers, of course."

"OK."

"That's it? Just OK?" I mimic his voice as I say OK. I don't know what I was expecting him to say. Was I expecting him to say no, I want to shout it from the rooftops because here's the truth Lei, I'm in love with you and this is my dream come true. How stupid and dreamy can I be? I take a step back from his touch.

"You're right. If we tell everyone then we're exposed. We'd either have to be in this for real or we'd have tell them that we're faking it and Kenna and Logan will want to know why. It's for three days, we can keep this between us and the Weavers. Plus their guests." He says, thinking out loud, making me start at the idea of there being a lot of people gathered there this weekend and he must see the panic in my eyes. "I'm sure there won't be too many, I mean their house isn't *that* big. It might house fifty or so people." I feel my eyes bug out of my head and he realises what he just said and starts to backtrack, the jerk. "But I'm sure the house won't be filled to the brim like that, they don't like having *all* the rooms filled."

"I can do this. We can do this." I open my eyes that I hadn't realise I'd closed, to look at Caleb and repeat my mantra again. "I can do this. We can do this."

"Come on, I'm not that bad am I? Surely you can stand spending the weekend with me and having some fun. I'll be a perfect gentleman, you can trust me Leila." He says the last part so softly, I want to grab his face in my hands and kiss him but I can't, even if we *are* engaged now.

"OK."

"That's it? Just OK?" He asks, laughing. I guess he thinks he's really clever throwing my words back at me like that.

"Yes that's it, OK." I reply, trying not to smile at the jerk.

"OK. We can put some ground rules in place if you want. You know, what is and isn't acceptable in the touching and all that kind of stuff. I'm not a monster, I won't do anything that makes you uncomfortable. Well, apart from telling a prospective supplier that you're my fiancé, anyway."

While his grin spreads across his face, he is still kind of hesitant and while I'm feeling slightly panicked at the idea of trying to pull this whole thing off without getting hurt, I laugh at his ridiculous attempt to make me feel more at ease about the situation. "Yeah, please don't do or say anything to put me in a weird position like pretending to marry you." Then without warning, I absolutely lose it. Tears are pouring down my cheeks and I can't breathe properly, I'm laughing so hard.

"Ahhhh it's not that funny is it darlin'? I mean, I'm not that ugly or horrible that you couldn't even imagine wanting to spend your life with me. Am I?" Damn it, now he sounds hurt, like I've wounded his pride but this thing was *his* idea and it's *pretend*!

Controlling my laughter and sucking in some deep breaths, I say, "No! That's not what I was laughing at, I'm sorry Caleb. You're the most handsome man I know, you make me laugh and I enjoy your company." Without realising it, I've stepped up close to him and my hands are holding his face so that I can make him look at me so that he can see that I'm telling the truth. Hell, if only he understood just how much truth there was in my words, he would abort this little pretence and run for miles. "I was laughing because you promised not to put me in any *more* weird positions, like being engaged to you isn't weird."

"It's not?" He asks, adorably confused.

"Well OK, it is but now that I'm thinking about it, maybe I'm the one who should be slightly offended that you think it's so weird."

"That's not what I meant. I didn't mean to say that I thought you weren't good enough for me or that *you* were weird. I only meant that the situation was weird." His hands take hold of my wrists and that's when I realise that I'm still holding his face in my hands and try to pull away but he puts just enough pressure on my wrists to keep my hands where they are. "Any guy would be proud to be engaged to you. You're amazing, smart, beautiful and you make the most amazing chocolate cake."

WOW! Just, wow!

We stand there, my hands on his cheeks, his hands on my wrists, for I don't know how long, until there's a noise outside and then knocking on the door. Jumping apart, Caleb walks away to answer the door.

"Good morning Caleb, what are you up to?"

"I was having a conversation actually, if you wouldn't mind coming back later or calling me, that would be great." Caleb says in a fast jumble of words.

"Good morning Makenna." I say as she blasts into the kitchen without noticing me. I figure I might as well get in before she spots me and then the questions start. Might as well jump in with both feet and fight it head on.

"Oh, good morning Leila. I wasn't expecting to see you here." She looks back at Caleb, who's still standing at the door, although he did manage to close it. "I wasn't expecting to see anyone actually."

"Well, why are you here if you weren't expecting me to be home, Kenna?" Caleb asks, seemingly suddenly by my side. I swear one minute he was still at the door, now he's standing next to me.

"You know what I mean Caleb. I meant I wasn't expecting anyone other than you to be here. There's never anyone but you here." Righto then, that wasn't subtle at all.

"I'm going to get my things so that I can walk up to Vines." I say and start to leave the room, they've obviously got things to talk about and they don't need me in the room to do it. I've only taken a few steps when I feel Caleb's hand gently take hold of my hand.

"Don't walk, OK? Wait and I'll take you. I promise we won't be long." I don't answer him, I just nod and pull my hand out of his and walk to the spare room.

"Did Leila stay here last night, Caleb?"

"Yes Makenna. She slept in the spare room because she was exhausted and I didn't want her to drive home. You know just as well as I do how dangerous it is to drive when you're ready to drop from exhaustion, Makenna. I was looking after a friend."

"Is that all you were doing Caleb, looking out for a friend?"

"Yes." He answers her in exasperation.

I know I shouldn't be listening, so I force myself to give them the privacy they deserve and do what I said I was going to do. I go into the spare room, close the door, gather up my clothes, fold them and put them as neatly as I can manage, into to my handbag so I don't have to carry them out of the house in an obvious show of the fact that I stayed here last night.

About five minutes later, there's a gentle knock on the door. Yes I know how long it's been because I have my phone in my hand. I've been scanning social media waiting for Makenna and Caleb to finish their talk.

"Leila, you can come out now, Kenna's gone." Caleb's voice is muffled through the thickness of the door.

I stand up, shift my handbag onto my shoulder and open the door. Oh my lord! Opening that door makes my heart stop beating for a second. Why you might ask, the reason being because Caleb Drake is leaning against the doorframe, one ankle crossed over the other one, one hand stuffed in his sweatpants pocket and the other hand resting on the other side of the doorframe to hold his balance. I've never seen anything more magnificent in my life. I am well and truly screwed with our little arrangement. It won't matter that it's only going to last for the weekend, I'm going to fall even more for this man when I'm allowed to touch him whenever I want.

"Are you ready to go?" He asks, oblivious to the thoughts running through my head.

"Yeah, sure but I can walk Caleb, it's not that far you know."

"I know you *can* but I want to take you. I'm allowed to take care of my fake fiancé aren't I?" He asks, with a glint in his eyes and gorgeous smirk on his face.

I whack him in the stomach as I duck under his stretched out arm to get out of the room and far away from *him*. I shouldn't have touched him at all thought because all I could feel under my hand were the hard, defined plains of his abs and I want to run my nails over them, to feel every dip and all the hardness. I quickly pull my hand away, before I can embarrass myself by caressing his chest and abs.

This weekend is going to be fucking torture of the most delicious kind!

Chapter Five
CALEB

Makenna has the worst timing in the world. I swear she can tell when there's a woman within twenty feet of me that I might actually be interested in.

What she said in front of Leila was true though, I haven't had a woman here at the house since I've moved back home. Moving back and working in the family business, I knew I had to grow up and get my shit together. I know I need to prove to them that I meant business that my education wasn't wasted and that I'm going to be an asset here.

"I'm sorry if I upset Leila, that wasn't my intention. I have to admit, Caleb I'm surprised that you had someone else here, especially a woman."

"I understand that Kenna but there was no reason to be rude to Leila."

"You're right and I'll apologise to her later but I'm worried, Caleb. She's a very valuable employee, I'm not sure what we'd do at Vines if she left. It would be difficult to find someone to fill her exceptionally talented shoes. Logan and I spent a lot of time interviewing people and getting the right person to run the bistro for us, I don't want to see her leave." And there it is, she doesn't trust me not to fuck things up.

"Leila and I are friends, Makenna. I stopped in there last night and had dinner while working on something. I was still there when they closed up and Leila and I were talking. She was so tired she almost fell asleep where she was sitting, Kenna. When she told me she had to drive half an hour to get home, I was worried about her and convinced her to stay here. In the spare room. You know, the room *you* made me set up for *your* husband! I was looking out for a *friend* and someone I know that you care about as well. I'm sorry that you don't trust me to keep my hands to myself or to not screw shit up." My sister is standing there, her mouth hanging open, her shock obvious. "If all you wanted was to let me know how much of a screw up I am this morning, then can we finish this up now, because I've got other things to do? If that's OK with you, *boss*."

Kenna takes a few steps closer to me but I take a few steps away from her. I don't want her to touch me or try to placate me like she always does, I've had enough. Her hand drops to her side and a sadness drifts across her face.

"I'm sorry, Caleb. I didn't realise I was making you feel like that *but* I can tell you that's not what I meant. I just meant that if you *do* take things further with Leila, it could affect other things. Things you might not have thought about."

"Yeah because I never think of the future, the business or any consequences, right? I only ever think about the here and now, along with my own selfish needs. I get it." I'm beyond angry with my sister now, I want her out of my house. There are certain disadvantages to making your home so close to your family and this morning's little performance is definitely one of the biggest ones.

"That's not what I meant either, Caleb but I can see that I won't be able to convince you of that, not this morning anyway." She gives me a sad smile and for some reason that just pisses me off even more. "I'm going to go now, I'll talk to you later."

"What did you come here for this morning Kenna?" I ask, curious as to why she chose this morning, of all mornings to pop by for a visit.

"Nothing that can't wait Caleb. I can see you've got other things that need your attention, so I'll talk to you later about what I came over for." She holds up her hand to stop me from talking as I open my mouth. "No, honestly, Caleb it can wait." She walks up to me, kisses me on the cheek while patting my shoulder like she's done ever since I can remember and goes to leave. As she reaches the door she turns back to me and says, "And before you think I only showed up here this morning because I knew you had someone here, I didn't. I didn't even realise you had another person here and I certainly wasn't expecting to find Leila, or any other woman for that matter."

"Okayyyyy." I say, I'm not sure whether I believe her or not, but I guess I have to.

"It's the truth. Look after yourself and Leila, I'll find you somewhere around the place today and we'll talk. I love you Caleb."

"I love you too Makenna." Without another word she's gone and I'm left standing in the middle of my living room wondering what's true and what's not. Instead of wasting energy on wondering what my sister needed from me so early in the morning, I walk over to the spare room and knock lightly on the door. I don't want to startle Leila and I sure as hell don't plan on just walking into the room without knocking at all.

I wait for her to answer the door as I lean my shoulder against the door-frame, stretching one arm over to the other side of the frame to hold myself steady. As the door opens, I realise I'm already over the day and it's barely begun. I shove my other hand in my pocket, I don't want to be tempted to reach out and touch my fake fiancé as she opens the door looking sexy as always.

I can't believe she actually said yes.

I can't help but think this is the craziest scheme I've ever had in my life. I know it is but I'm not annoyed with myself, not if it means I get to spend some time alone with Leila away from here. Away from prying eyes and I get to pretend she's mine, even if it is just for a few days.

"Are you ready to go?" I ask, not really wanting her to leave, I kind of like her being here, in my space.

"Yeah, sure but I can walk Caleb, it's not that far you know." We both know what she's says is true, we also both know that she waited for me anyway. The fact that the reason she waited probably had more to do with her giving Kenna and I the privacy to talk but she still waited.

"I know you *can* but I want to take you. What kind of *fake fiancé* would I be if I didn't take care of my cuddly bear?" I ask, trying to get us back into a carefree and light mood. Then she touches me. Her hand lands in what I suspect she meant as a smack but ends up being more of a caress. I've never been more grateful for my workout sessions and days of physical labour than right this second because the quick intake of breath hopefully means she likes what she feels. I *know* I'm enjoying the feeling of her hand on me, even if skin isn't touching skin, then she pulls her hand away like she's been zapped by a bolt of electricity and the moment is over. For now.

There and then, I decide we're going to have to put in some hard and fast rules in place of what is and isn't acceptable but even with them, this weekend is going to be sweet fucking torture.

Leila swiftly walks by me, managing to not touch me at all after that unintentional grope. I guess I'm not the only who felt something when her hand touched my stomach. I could have sworn I was firmly placed in the friend zone, with little hope of getting out of it any time soon but that reaction of hers makes me not so sure I'm as stuck as I thought.

I don't have the time to analyse her actions though because I hear the front door open, followed by her footsteps crunching on the stones of my driveway. Luckily, I put on my socks and shoes while I was talking to Kenna, hoping she'd get the hint and leave. I grab my keys off the rack next to the door, make sure said door is locked when I close it and rush to my car, opening the passenger side door a millisecond before Leila can do it for herself.

"Thank you Caleb but it's hardly necessary." She doesn't have any bite in her words but I sense the tension still in her stiff body next to me. Is she stressed because Kenna knows she stayed over? Is it our fake fiancé arrangement? Maybe it's spending the long weekend alone with me? Or maybe, like me, she can still feel the spark that ignited between us when she touched me? Let me assure you the touch of her hand on my body is burned into my flesh, I'm sure of it! I wish I was still *feeling* it for real and not just the ghost of the memory.

"You're welcome, Leila." I say, with a smile that I hope is charming. "Just making sure that my beautiful fiancé is treated properly."

"*Fake* fiancé." She mutters.

I feel her body stiffen as I lean in to whisper in her ear, "Fake or not, you deserve to be treated with respect and affection, so that's what I'm doing." Before she can respond, I kiss her lightly on the cheek, guide her into the seat and close the door. Walking around the back of the car to get in the driver's seat, I decide we definitely need some ground rules, guidelines if you will, that both of us find acceptable for this weekend we're spending together.

Sliding into the driver's seat, I start the engine without looking in Leila's direction, even though I can feel her eyes boring into the side of my head.

She's got something to say but she's holding back. She doesn't usually hold back, so I take a deep breath and let out a long sigh, not because of Leila but the situation we've found ourselves in. That I *did*.

"Look, Leila if you've changed your mind and this is just too much for you to take on, I understand. I didn't drag you into my mess on purpose, I swear. I can go on my own and just explain to Brian and Mary that I'm an idiot. I mean, I may not be in a serious relationship but I *do* have family that I'm determined not to let down. If he doesn't want to do business with me after that, then I guess I'll find another supplier and move on."

"What? You don't want me to come away with you this weekend now?" She asks, sounding offended and a little pissed off.

"That's not what I'm saying, Leila. I'm saying *if* this is just too ridiculous for *you,* then you are free to say so and I will understand. No hard feelings at all and we can stay friends." I frown, not having considered that I could ruin our friendship over the course of this stupid weekend. "Friends either way, whether you go through with being my fake fiancé or not."

"I'm not having seconds thoughts, Caleb but if you are, if *you'd* rather someone else to play the part, all you have to do is say so." There's hurt lacing her voice now, fuck it!

"No. I don't want anyone else to come away with me, I'm just giving you an out if you've changed your mind. This is my problem after all, I can go alone and explain myself, consequences be damned."

"No, I'm good for the weekend." She sighs and looks out the side window before continuing. "I do think we need to make some rules though, I mean I don't want to ruin our friendship over this, do you?"

"You're right. In fact, I was just thinking we need to lay some ground rules so that we know what each other's boundaries are." She nods her agreement, so I tell her my idea. "I was thinking that you could use today and tonight to think about it and write a list. Then we can get together like usual at Vines and I'll write a list of my own, then we can compare and agree on the rules. What do you think?"

"That's a great idea. Then we both know what the other expects and we can agree on the boundaries together. You've got yourself a deal, Mr Drake." She says, smiling and holding her hand out for me to shake. I don't like her making this sound like a business transaction but I guess that's exactly what it is and I would be stupid to think of it any of other way. So, I take her hand in mine and shake it. Feeling her palm in mine, that spark I felt earlier fires up again and I don't want to let go. Turning away from her face that now has a beautiful blush on her cheeks, I put my car in gear, I drive us out of my driveway and up to Vines. The radio is playing quietly and thankfully, there's no tension between us anymore. We're both quiet, no doubt we're both in our own heads, already thinking about the boundaries we're going to put up to keep this weekend in the friend zone.

I hate the fucking friend zone. I fucking hate boundaries.

When we get to Vines, we sit in the idling car and look at each other.

"I don't want things to be awkward between us, Leila. I want us to be friends."

"We always will be." She says, smiling at me. "Aren't you coming in?"

"Well, we just had breakfast." I laugh as I watch that fact register on her gorgeous face. "Nice to know my cooking and company are that forgettable, it does the ego real good darlin'."

"I didn't mean it like that and you know it, Caleb. I just forgot because of everything else that happened this morning. I'm barely awake and I've got a fiancé, a trip away for the weekend and I'm not wearing underwear. Something I'm about to rectify, then get to work so that I *can* go away with you for the weekend. I still have to talk to your sister about having the weekend off as well. I mean, what are we going to tell them we're doing, Caleb if you don't want to tell them about the engagement?"

"You're not wearing underwear?" Look, I heard everything else she said and I know we need to discuss all of those details but I can't get my mind to wander too far away from this gorgeous woman in front me not having anything on under those clothes. She's commando?

"Geezus, Caleb you're such a man!" She hits me again, this time on my shoulder like she's trying to keep her hands off the rest of me.

"Umm yeah, did you miss that memo? I know I had it circulated around the staff. Maybe it was before you started but I am definitely a man Leila Phillips. All man." I can't help myself, her dig at me being a man brings out my inner caveman and I slowly peruse her gorgeous, curvy body. What I wouldn't give to be able to run my hands and lips all over those luscious curves of hers.

"Oh no, I must have missed that one. It definitely must have been before I started." She says, with a laugh, as she gets out of my car to walk over to her car. "See you later, Caleb."

"Are you dismissing me darlin'?" I ask, surprised by her reaction.

"I have to get to work and I do believe you have a job to get to as well, Mr Drake. I think it's best if we get to it, if we want the weekend off. Together." She looks at me from over the open door of her car and smiles. It's a cute smile full of sunshine and sarcasm. I swear she winks at me as well but that could be my mind playing tricks on me. She's right though, if I want to get away this weekend, I need to get my shit together and sort out a few last details.

"You're lucky you're cute and I'm an awesome fiancé because you're right. We need to talk to Kenna as well." Thinking about what I've got to get done today, I say, "I'll come by for a slice of my favourite chocolate cake and we can decide what we're going to tell her."

"Deal. I'll save you a piece of cake *and* I'll have a latte ready for you."

"See, look at that. You're a good fiancé too. We're a perfect match." Leaving her with that parting shot, I put my car in gear and take off, careful not to kick up too much dirt when I leave.

Wouldn't want to piss off the little woman before we've even begun.

I drive to my workshop slash office laughing loudly at my own joke.

Well no one else was around to enjoy it and I have to amuse myself most days.

Chapter Six
LEILA

When Caleb drops me off at Vines, the first thing I do is go to my car and throw yesterday's clothes in a bag I've got in there. My mother taught me to always have a change of clothes or at the very least clean underwear, in the car. While I don't have a full change of clothes, I do actually have some fresh underwear in there, which I am relieved about. Wearing Makenna's clothes is one thing but I was never going to wear another woman's underwear. Ever. No matter who they belong to. So yes, I'm commando and I really enjoyed letting Caleb know as much.

The look on his face was priceless. Although, I wasn't quite expecting the heat that flooded his eyes, or the tease of him telling me he's *all* man. I've felt how manly he is pressed up against me before and I have to agree, he *is* a whole lot of *man!*

Grabbing my handbag, I shove my clean underwear in there, not that there's anyone around to see what I'm doing, I'm not up for showing my underwear around though. Smiling broadly, I walk to the front door to open up Vines just like any other morning. The difference this morning is, that I'm not usually grinning like a lunatic when I do it. I shake my head, laughing at myself. I may have Caleb as my fiancé but I would be doing myself a great disservice to believe that any of this is real. Including the heat in his eyes that I saw earlier. It's a means to an end, for both of us.

I make my way to the staff locker room which also has a couple of toilet cubicles and duck into a cubicle to put on my underwear. It's not like anyone else can get in the door because I locked it behind me and no one else has a key. Well, unless a Drake decides to walk in the door anyway. Oh crap, that prospect wipes the huge goofy smile off my face. I don't know what I'd do if Caleb's brother or sister caught me quickly changing my underwear in the staff bathroom!

Pulling myself together, I shove my bag into my locker and get my butt moving out to the kitchen, play music on my phone and get to work on the rest of my early morning prep and cooking that I need to do.

"Good morning, boss! Look at you go! What time did you get here this morning?"

I jump a mile, almost needing to be scraped of the damned ceiling when Sara speaks loud enough to be heard over the music and interrupting my peace.

"Bloody hell Sara!" I exclaim just as loudly. "Are you *trying* to give me a freaking heart attack or what?" I ask, as I turn the volume down on my music, I was really enjoying those tunes this morning too.

"Sorry Leila." She says, but I can hear the laughter in her voice. "You did seem to be enjoying your tunes this morning. Wouldn't happen to have anything to do with a certain Drake sibling would it?"

"What do you mean? Why would you say that?" I ask, all my words rolling in together to make one very strange word instead of two separate questions. "Hey, how the heck did you get in here anyway? I know I locked the door when I came in, I always do." I know I was distracted this morning, but not *that* distracted. When I'm here alone, I'm always much more aware of security and my safety.

Sara laughs at me, obviously amused by my sudden realisation and confusion. "I was wondering when you were going wonder how that happened." I looked at her, waving my hand for her to continue and waiting for her explanation. "One of the Drakes let me in. Can you guess which one might be here this early, working away and waiting for coffee and a slice of his favourite cake? I wonder who *that* could be, hmmmmmm?" She ponders, tapping her bottom lip with the tip of her index finger, her grin spreading across her face and her sparkling with mischief and excitement.

"Which Drake is out there, Sara?" I ask, pleading with her and the gods and whoever might listen, that it's Logan sitting out there waiting for a coffee and his apple danish. Please let it be Logan *or* Makenna. I don't want it to be Caleb, not yet. I haven't thought things through, even though he's the only thing I've been able to think about since I left his car earlier.

"Which one do you *think* it is, boss lady?" She says, still smiling until she looks at my face properly and recognising the panic on my face as just that, not lust. "What's wrong? What happened last night? Did he do something he shouldn't have? I *knew* I shouldn't have left you here alone with Caleb Drake. He's got a reputation for a reason, you know? But I thought you could handle yourself. I thought you could handle *him*. Damn it, Leila I'm so fucking sorry! Do you want me to go out there and ask him to leave? Can I do that? I mean he *is* part owner of the place. Ohhh fuck does that mean you're going to have to leave? Do you want me to get Mrs Harris for you?" She takes a breath and I use the break to my advantage.

"Sara! Oh my god, stop talking for a few seconds would you?" I yell just to be heard over her constant questions. "You don't need to do *anything*! Nothing happened after you left, alright? Calm the hell down!" I close my eyes and take a deep breath myself. Then I hear his voice and I almost wish I didn't have to open my eyes to talk to him.

"Hey Darlin', everything OK in here? I thought it would be OK if I let Sara in seeing as I was just sitting at my table waiting for my latte and chocolate cake and working. I'm sorry if I did something wrong darlin'." Damn I wish he'd stop calling me Darlin'. Where hell did that come from anyway? Does he think he's in Texas?

"Darlin'?" Sara mouth at me in silent question behind Caleb's back, her eyes wide in shock.

"Everything's fine, Caleb." I say, rubbing a hand over the back of my neck. "I just didn't realise anyone else was in the bistro, that's all and I wasn't expecting a voice behind me."

He nods, then says, "Yeah I'm not surprised you didn't hear us. Do you always have music that loud when you're working? I mean, how do you manage to hear when Sara and the others show up for work?" He asks, genuinely concerned but before I can answer, Sara does it for me.

"Ohhh normally I would have messaged or called her. Both of them cut into the music and it annoys her enough to look at her phone." She says, shrugging like it's the most normal thing in the world to have to call your boss to be let into you place of work.

"I'd be surprised if she could hear anything over her music." Caleb chuckles and his damned dimple pops out and winks at me. Damn it! Why is he so adorable? "It's nice to know what you think of me though Sara." Sara has the good grace to blush, I guess there's a first time for everything.

"I'm so sorry you heard that." I have to laugh, at least she's honest. "I didn't mean to offend you, it's just that you *do* kind of have a reputation for being a bit of a lady killer, Mr Drake." She says with a genuine smile and I can see that Caleb actually isn't offended. He looks more amused than anything else.

"I appreciate your honesty, Sara." He says with a chuckle. "I also appreciate you looking out for Leila but you don't have to worry about me when it comes to your boss. She's safe when I'm around, I'll always protect her. Even from my womanising, lecherous ways." He winks and leaves us alone in the kitchen again.

"Oh my god! Did I just do that?" Sara asks, the mortification all over her face, suddenly her face morphs into this insane looking grin. "Did he just say he would protect you, *always*? That's very possessive and boyfriend like there Leila Phillips. What the hell happened here last night?"

"Nothing happened last night Sara." She crosses her arms over her chest and raises an eyebrow at me, making it obvious that she doesn't believe a word I'm saying. "Fine! I'll tell you but if you say anything to anyone, if this gets out Sara, I swear to all that is holy I will hunt you down and murder you. Do you understand me?" I whisper yell at her. Sara has become a valued friend and confidante since I started working here, always trying to get me to go out with her circle of friends but I can't. I get up too early to go out partying and I need the money this job pays. She nods her head vigorously in answer to my question and leans forward to hear me better. "Nothing happened! I stayed at his house last night, *in his spare room* because I almost fell asleep at the table trying to get him to leave last night. He insisted that I shouldn't drive home, that if his parents accident had taught him anything, it was to look after his family and friends. He didn't want me to drive all the way home exhausted."

"Awwwww that is *so* sweet. He cares about you!" Sara swoons and yes, that is the *only* way to describe what she's doing in front of me right now.

"Cut it out you idiot." I say, slapping her on the arm as she bats her eyes at me. "Get the man his slice of cake and his latte would you? I don't even know how long he's been waiting out there for his coffee."

"You know he prefers it when *you* make his latte for him. He always remarks that it tastes better when you do it for him."

"He does not." I blush, I can't help myself because I've heard him say that every single time I make it for him, even when he has no clue that it was me, he manages to get it right every time.

"Just let me go dump my bag and stuff, then I'll come take over for you while you fix up Mr '*I'll always look after her*,' treats." Before I can think of a retort, she's gone and I'm left standing alone in the kitchen wondering what the hell just happened.

"Are you OK? Did I overstep?" Caleb's voice is quiet and full of concern behind me. I don't jump this time, instead I find his voice to be comforting and I know I have to stop these feelings dead in their tracks.

"Everything's fine. Sara was just worried about me and she's well, let's just say everything Sara does, she's very enthusiastic about." I laugh, as I turn around to face him. Big mistake. "I'm sorry you overhead what she said about you, I know none of it's true." I say quietly.

"Well, actually, she didn't say anything that wasn't true at one point. I have to live with that, it's my past and I can't change it. Honestly, I don't want to." He says with a shrug. "I haven't been like that for a long time though, Leila. I promise."

I don't know why it should matter to me but it does. That being said though, I have no idea how to answer that, so I don't. I look at the hallway because I can hear Sara's footsteps getting close again.

"I promise darlin'." Caleb whispers in my ear as he walks past me to make his way to the staff bathrooms.

"I really am sorry about what I said Mr Drake." Sara starts again but Caleb waves her away.

"It wasn't anything that wasn't true at one point, Sara, don't worry about it." He tells her with another wave of his hand and a shake of his head. "It's Caleb, Sara, please. Mr Drake is my dad or my brother, not me."

"OK Caleb." She says with a smile. He gives her an absolutely winning smile and walks away from us. "My god Leila, if you don't want him, I think I might try and see if I can win him over. He is one very fine specimen of male hotness."

"You will *not* hit on Caleb, Sara." I growl. Damn, I've never heard that noise come out of me before.

"That's what I thought. Now go make him his coffee and get him a slice of your fresh chocolate cake that he loves so much." She says, shoving me out of her way and towards the huge coffee machine.

"I didn't mean it like *that* Sara, I meant because he's your *boss*. I mean he's *my* boss as well you know." I make the effort to correct her assumption because I don't want anyone getting the wrong idea. They're all going to know we're heading out of here for the weekend together soon enough and that's going to raise enough eyebrows as it is, I don't want to add fuel to the fire.

"Just give the man what he wants." Sara says, her smile so wide I'm scared her face might actually split in two if she holds it like that for too much longer.

"I agree, give the man what he wants and what he wants right now is the best latte he's ever tasted and some of the best chocolate cake this side of, well anywhere really. I don't know what you do differently to cakes and food here Leila, but you sure do it well. Really damned well, if you ask me and seeing as though you're not, I'm just going to tell you anyway, cause that's the kind of guy I am. I'm sweet like that you know?" Then he winks, he damn well *winks* at me! Who the hell does that? Yeah I know the answer. Caleb bloody Drake, that's who!

Shaking my head because with the two of them agreeing, there's no way I've got a chance of winning a thing, I face the coffee machine and turn it on. "You're going to have to wait a few minutes while I turn the machine on and warm it up, OK?"

"I'm sure with you turning it on and warming it up, I won't have to wait for long at all, darlin'." He says, sending me another damned wink and heading back to 'his' table. No-one else ever sits there, it seems to be permanently reserved for Caleb without it ever being said out loud by anyone.

"Yeah, you're right, Leila, he doesn't have a thing for you at all. He wasn't flirting with you over a *coffee machine*. Not at all." Sara singsongs in my ear.

"Oh shut up and get to work would you? You think because we're friends I'm going to let you slack off?" I ask her, annoyed with both of us and Caleb.

"Oh no, trust me I know that means you'll be harder on me. We all understand that boss lady." She salutes me and wanders back over to where I was working before Caleb and Sara interrupted me, easily picking up where I left off. I sigh in relief, knowing that I can leave the bistro in her more than capable hands for the weekend while I help Caleb out.

That's makes me snort. Help Caleb out. Helping him out would be to help him move house, pack up boxes, decorate his house or even go over his plans for the brewery. I'm not sure what I would call pretending to be his fiancé for an entire weekend. What the hell was I thinking? I wasn't, that's the simple answer.

I wasn't thinking. It sounded good because it was Caleb asking me. He needed my help, so I gave it, simple as that. I shake my head, clearing it of all thoughts of Caleb because if I don't, I won't concentrate on this monster machine and I'll screw something up, then Kenna will be mad at me and threaten to get rid of it again! I like Ted, we've got an understanding, he works and I don't let Kenna sell him for scrap. Yes, we named the coffee machine, actually Sara did.

Ted warms up nicely without too many strange noises. Usually there's a few bangs and whines before he gets going. This morning he was pretty quiet, so I feel like I'm already winning this today and I smile. I beat Ted this morning and that makes for a great day ahead.

I make Caleb's latte and myself a macchiato because I need the coffee. Sara wasn't wrong when she turned up this morning, I am very much ahead of where I usually am at this hour in the mornings, so I'm going to take a break and have a chat with Caleb. No-one else is here, so I think it's the best time to do this.

Slicing off a larger piece of chocolate cake, I grab two spoons without thinking and place them on the tray along with the coffees and walk over to where my fake fiancé is sitting, concentrating on the spreadsheet in front of him. I take a second to enjoy looking at him, before I cough quietly letting him know I'm standing there with hot drinks.

"Oh, thanks Leila. You're an absolute angel with perfect timing." He smiles at me and as I bend over to place his coffee and the cake on the table in front of him, he reaches out and kisses me. He kisses me! In public! Where I work! At his family business! Like it's nothing at all and he has every right to touch me like that. I don't remember giving him permission to take whatever he wants, wherever he wants. Luckily, no-one else has arrived yet because not only am I stunned from feeling his lips on my cheek but I'm also stunned he did it so openly.

What the hell did I get myself into? I ask myself as I sit down opposite him with my own coffee, without even saying a word.

Shit! I think I'm screwed.

Chapter Seven
CALEB

I hadn't planned on going to Vines to work today, well not this early but when I knew that Leila was commando I just couldn't shake the idea from my mind, it made me want to see her for as long as I could. It's insane just how much time I spend in here, I have my own office and everyone knows it, still I spend hours sitting in here at what has become 'my table' doing business. I used to wonder what her staff thought about my presence, what the staff think wouldn't stop me from doing my work here but I didn't want it to affect how they see Leila. I've been doing it for so long now though, I think they've just accepted that I'm here.

Which is why I don't think Sara was too surprised to see me this morning when I unlocked the door for her instead of Leila. I'd been here for about half an hour or so already without interrupting Leila's work in the kitchen. I could hear and see her working away in there and I didn't want to break into her easy flow. She was truly magical to watch in the kitchen. I don't know what the hell she does differently in there because all I see are ingredients mixing together like I've seen other people do, including Makenna and our Mum, Leila has this touch that makes cakes lighter, frosting fluffier and chocolate tastier.

So, instead of letting her know I was there, like I knew I should have, I let her get on with her work and I got to watch her in her element. She had the music so loud she didn't hear me come in and that worries me because I could have been anyone coming in but I also know there are only four people with the keys to get in here and none of us are going to hurt her. Still, I don't like the idea of her being here alone for so long in the mornings.

The squeal that comes out of the kitchen when Sara goes in to say hello could have woken the fucking dead and I'm surprised it didn't bring one, if not both, of my siblings running! I knew that both women were relatively safe in there but I still wanted to check that Sara scaring the shit out Leila hadn't caused her to cut herself or something similar.

I'm not sure whether I'm glad or pissed that I walked in, just in time to hear Sara warn Leila about my bad reputation. I know what everyone says about it and I'm not going to deny that I've lived life pretty freely but the minute I walked back onto Drake Wines, I've taken my job and life deadly serious. I'm not saying that I've lived like a monk but when I met Leila something happened to me and I haven't been out on a date since we started having our meetings to help me with my brewery idea almost a year ago. She's been with me every step of the way and I've enjoyed every second. So, while I'm happy her friend is looking out for her, I'm a little pissed off that my past is trying to kill off anything we could possibly have together. I don't let them see how much it annoys me though, like I said, Sara didn't say anything that wasn't true. It's behind me but it's still the truth.

I'm bought out of my thoughts as Leila sets down a larger than usual slice of cake, my latte, and a coffee for herself on the table. "Oh, thanks Leila. You're an absolute angel with perfect timing." I say with a smile and then, before she can sit down, I act on impulse and kiss her. It's probably way more than it should be but once I get my lips on her, I can't hold back. I don't leave a big, sloppy kiss on her cheek but it lingers longer than a friendly peck should. She seems surprised for a second but doesn't pull away, making me a happy man. Nothing gives you a hit to your ego quite like a woman turning her nose up to a kiss from you.

Pulling back from the kiss, I smile at her, hoping that I can soothe any uneasiness she might be feeling after that amazing kiss. "Is everything OK?" I ask, as she drops down into her chair in a daze. I feel like I've asked that question a hundred times already this morning. I know I've asked her to do me a massive favour and put her on the spot with Sara this morning but she can choose to say no to anything and everything, at any time.

"Hmmm?" She looks up at me from her coffee that she was staring into, a little confused, then she shakes her head, as if clearing it and says, "Oh, yes. Everything's fine. Why?" She brings her hands that were resting in her lap up to take a hold of her coffee, only to discover it's still too hot to touch.

"You look a little dazed and confused, that's all." I say, trying to hide my smirk behind my coffee cup and not really succeeding. "Did you get enough sleep last night? I mean, I know you get up early to get here and set everything up but I wanted to let you sleep for as long as possible seeing as how you didn't have a commute this morning."

"I slept just *fine* last night, thank you, Caleb." She answers with a little more violence than I feel is necessary.

"I was just asking." I say, holding my hands up in surrender. I've seen Leila get tough on customers and staff alike but I've never had that look directed my way before. I don't think I like it and I know I'm going to do everything in my power to never see it directed my way again.

We sit there silently, watching each other over the edges of our coffee cups. I'm not sure what she's thinking and I'm almost too scared to ask. Normally, I can read women, as my reputation tells you, I've known a few in my time and it's always helpful to be able to read a situation so as to *not* get a knee or fist to the balls. Leila, as much as I've observed her in Vines and taking into consideration how often we've sat at this very table and talked, is still quite a mystery to me.

"You shouldn't have done that." She says so quietly, I almost miss it. I know what she's talking about but I feign innocence and ask her what she means anyway.

"Shouldn't have done what? What did I do?" I raise my eyebrows at her in question over my cup.

"You know." She says, still speaking quietly. I shake my head answering her no. "Kiss me. You shouldn't have kissed me in public like that." So, it's not the kiss itself she objects to, it's the location and the possibility of witnesses that she finds uncomfortable. Interesting.

"I just couldn't resist and I thought we could get in some practice for the weekend." I say with a shrug, slowly putting my coffee down on the table. "You're right though and I'm sorry Leila. It was an impulse that I didn't really put too much thought into. This is your workplace and I shouldn't have put you in a situation that might make you uncomfortable."

"Thank you." She says, sitting up a little straighter, twirling her ponytail through her fingers.

"But there wasn't anyone here except the three us and Sara is busy in the kitchen. I did look over there before I kissed you to make sure she wouldn't see it." I guess it wasn't as impulsive as I first thought.

"You said it was an impulse, Caleb, it can't have been too impulsive if you were checking to see if Sara would notice." I know I shouldn't be turned on by the fact that she called me out on my behaviour but I've never claimed to be a perfect man.

"You got me again." I say with a shrug of my shoulder and a smirk that I hope makes my dimple a little more noticeable. It's gotten me out of more trouble, both serious and not so serious, more times than I can count. When I see her roll her eyes, I know I might get lucky this time too. Well, not *lucky*, lucky but you know, out of trouble. "In the instant that I knew what I wanted, I quickly looked over to make sure Sara was too busy working to watch what we were doing."

"Uhuh, sure you did." She says, obviously not believing me but I'm saved from further discussions by a loud knock on the door and couple of the staff standing there looking in. I look at my phone to check the time and I'm surprised to see that they're right on time. Well, OK I don't mean that I'm surprised they're on time, I mean I didn't realise so much time had passed since I got here. Leila jumps in surprise as well, it probably doesn't help that she's got her back to the door and didn't see movement before she heard the knock. "I have to go let my staff in but this conversation is not over Caleb." She warns me and I kinda like stern Leila, it's a real turn on. Geezus, who am I kidding? Everything about this woman is a fucking turn on for me.

"Yes ma'am." I say, with a salute that she shakes her head at. I don't know why I said that or followed it with the salute but I'll own it.

"You're an idiot." She says it like she means it but she's laughing as she walks away to open the door to let the guys in.

There's a chorus of 'good morning Caleb' and good morning Mr Drake', as a few of the staff file by the table. I correct, for what feels like the hundredth time the couple that call me Mr Drake and tell them to call me Caleb. They nod like they're understanding but I know I won't change their minds and I can't explain how frustrating that is. I have no desire to be thought of as 'Mr Drake' around here.

"I don't have a lot of time to talk now, Caleb, is there anything that we urgently need to talk about?" Leila asks, as she sits back down at the table, taking a sip of her coffee. Selfishly, I want to keep her here, sitting at the table with me for the rest of the day but I know she has a million other things she needs to get done so that we can go away for a long weekend together.

"We really just need to agree what we'll tell people, namely my siblings, about what's going on this weekend." She nods and takes another sip of her coffee. "I was thinking we could tell them what effectively would be mostly the truth. You want to go visit your Mum because she's not doing well and it's been a while since you've seen her." She nods and takes another sip of her coffee, at this rate she's going to be finished before I can think about drinking mine.

"And you? Why are you heading into the big city for the weekend?"

"I thought I would tell them a half truth."

"What would that be exactly?"

"I'm going into the city for a business meeting and catching up with some friends. I won't have to elaborate on the meeting and they'll assume, thanks to my reputation, that I'm going out to paint the town red, so to speak."

"Hmmmm." She says, looking at me like I'm an art exhibition. Guess she didn't think I had the brains to think this thing through, that makes her like everyone else, they underestimate me. "That's a great plan, I was thinking of something similar myself. Good. Good." She nods some more.

"I'm glad you agree. I'm glad it wasn't a stupid idea." I say, unnecessarily grumpy. Leila has never, not once, given me a reason to believe that she thinks I'm stupid. She reaches over and rests her hand on mine.

"You're not stupid and it's a great idea." Her voice is soft, reassuring.

"Thank you." It's all I can say because I know she's not being kind to make me happy. She's told me off many times in the past for my self-loathing ways.

"Right." She coughs, pulling her hand from mine and I wish I could ask her not to. To stay here with me but I can't. "Let me go talk to the staff, get a few things sorted and then we can go see Makenna together if you want?"

"Sounds like a plan." I agree. "Do you mind if I stay here and work? I promise I won't take your staff away from their jobs at all."

Standing up, she collects her coffee and picks up a spoon, then smiles at me. It's such a broad, happy smile I wish I could see it all day, every day. "You can stay here for as long as you like, Caleb, it's your business remember?" Before I can answer, or realise what she's doing, she drags that spoon through the chocolate cake sitting in front of me and takes a giant chunk out of it. I watch, entranced, as she puts the spoon in her mouth, sucks the cake off it and moans. Loudly and erotically, with her eyes shut, totally enjoying the pleasure of her delicious cake. Trust me, I know just how delightful this cake is. Her eyes flick open and she bounces the spoon up and down in my direction a few times before exclaiming, "You're right, Caleb, that *is* the most delicious thing I've ever had in my mouth!"

She disappears before I can recover my senses, her loud laughter following her. When my senses finally *do* return to me I laugh as well. A full belly laugh because she got me. She absolutely beat me at my own game and I loved every god damned minute of it. I know everyone but Leila is looking at me, wondering if I've finally lost the plot but I don't care, let them think what they want.

Sara swings by my table about twenty minutes later and clears up my dishes. "Thanks Sara." I say, knowing I'm a special kind of pain in the arse for them taking up a table that a paying customer could be sitting at.

"No worries." She smiles and starts to move away but she hesitates to look back at me like she's trying to sort out a puzzle.

"What is it Sara? Spit it out so that we can both get on with what we need to do." I like Sara because of her no bullshit personality, you always know where you stand with her.

"I just want to say." She hesitates again, so I wait for her to gather her thoughts and start again. "I just wanted to ask you to be careful and take care of her, you know? She's special and I think she's been hurt before. Like really *hurt* and I don't want to see her hurt. Ever. I won't hesitate to kick you in the balls if you hurt her. Boss or not, you don't get to treat that woman like shit, not on my watch. You understand me?"

I don't doubt for one second, that Sara would follow through on her threat, so even though the thought terrifies the fuck out of me, I'm also extremely happy that Leila has someone on her side that will fight so furiously for her.

"Of course, I understand you completely, Sara, and believe me, I have no intention of hurting your boss because just between you and me, I quite like her myself."

"Yeah well, anyone with eyeballs can see *that*! Just take care of her is all I'm saying." Without giving me a chance to respond, she's gone. What is it with women walking away from me this morning without letting me defend myself? The truth is, I didn't need to defend myself with Leila, I just need to pick my jaw up off the floor long enough to be able to speak.

Sara? She's a different matter altogether. Sara scares the shit out of me and my balls ache just from the thought of her threat. A shiver of dread runs down my spine and I have to wiggle around to adjust myself in my pants, discreetly of course. I don't want anyone thinking I've got a hard-on sitting here but I need to reassure my balls that they're OK.

An hour later, another latte and an apple danish are placed down in front of me. "Oh thanks, but I didn't order anything." I say looking up to see who is delivering me fresh snacks.

"I know you didn't but the boss sent them over and I'm not arguing with her. So you have a fresh latte and one of her fresh pastries, enjoy!" Quickly I look at the name badge on the pocket of her uniform.

"Thank you Debbie." I smile brightly at her because of course this isn't an issue and if it was, it's not *her* issue. "Tell the boss lady I said thanks, too."

"You're welcome." She smiles, then leaves. I look up searching for Leila so that I can say thank you but I'm interrupted.

"Do I *need* to ask who you're looking for?"

"Good morning *again,* Makenna. How are you this fine morning?"

"Aren't you a happy camper this morning? It wouldn't have anything to do with your overnight guest, would it?" She asks, while raising an eyebrow at me and sitting down opposite me. The eyebrow raise was a trick she learnt when we were kids, it's something she's always done to try and scare me into telling her the truth. It doesn't work on adult me but she keeps trying it out.

"Yes and no. Nothing happened last night Kenna. I told her she was staying over because she was almost falling asleep sitting here at this very table last night before she locked up. I didn't want her driving in that state, so I insisted she stay."

"Fair enough." I knew she would agree, we all feel that way ever since the car accident that took our parents. "Did she *really* need to stay in *your* spare room though?"

"Where would you have liked me to let her stay, Kenna?" I ask, irritated. "At Logan's so she could deal with his grumpy arse? He's got Jules and Savvy there as well, they're dealing with enough, don't you think, without me dumping an unexpected guest on them? Or perhaps I could have deposited her on *your* doorstep unannounced, where you and Brady are still having sleepless night with the babies? I'm sure Leila would have *really* enjoyed that with how tired she was." I snort. "It was late, I didn't want her to drive and yes I care about her, so I insisted she stay with me."

"What about one of the cottages?"

I shake my head. "They're still getting work done on them or they're occupied, but Leila is the first staff member that gets offered one of those cottages. Agreed?" I stare her down, I can see her thinking, wondering why I'm fighting for this but I don't really care. Those cottages were for staff back in the dark ages and if that's what they're going to be for again, then Leila deserves to get first dibs, she spends way too much time here to not live on the property. "Look, Kenna, I know you think I'm a playboy or whatever but I can assure I am not. I don't bring women back here and I never have."

"I never said that Caleb and I'm sorry if you think that's how I see you, because I truly don't."

"Well, it's always nice to hear. Thank you, Kenna." We're both silent as another member of staff drops by the table leaving a caramel latte and an apple cinnamon muffin in front of my sister. Kenna thanks her and she disappears again. "What is it in here? How do they know what you want?"

"She knows what I want because I order the same thing every day, at the same time. The only difference is today I came in to get it rather than someone delivering it to my office." She smiles and waves at someone behind me and I follow her eyeline to find Leila standing there, a beautiful smile on her face and waving back at my sister. I decide now is as a good a time as any to ask Kenna about this weekend and not ask her why she ventured out of her office this particular morning for her morning snack.

"So, I have something to ask you." I start, then take a deep breath. "Is it OK with you if Leila takes the weekend off? Now before you say no, I want you to know that she's already organised someone to take over the responsibilities for the weekend and Leila will be contactable on her phone all weekend. She's not falling off the edge of the world or anything and let's face it, she's allowed to have time off."

"I was going to say yes, Caleb. I've been trying to get her take some time off for a few months now." Kenna says, her eyebrows do that drawn down and wrinkly thing they do when she's thinking. "Why are you so worried about her getting the time off?"

"Because she's my friend Kenna and she needs this. Her mum isn't well and she needs to go see her. Her car won't make the trip and if it does by some miracle, I doubt it could make the trip back."

"So, how is she getting there then?" She asks as she takes a sip of her coffee, although I get the feeling she already knows the answer. I hate it when my sister does this to me.

"I offered to drive her into the city and then back out here late Sunday. I have to go into the city for a business meeting anyway and I'm meeting some friends as well. So, I figured we may as well kill two birds with one stone and all that." I say, trying my hardest to look and sound innocent but my sister has always been able to read me like a book.

"Uhuh." Is all Kenna says and if I know my sister like I think I do, she's thinking all the possibilities through and when she barks out a laugh, I guess she's come to a conclusion that's pretty close to the truth. "What's the meeting about?"

"Oh, just something I'm looking into. I'll let you know after this meeting, if things can work out how I want them to. "

"Geez, that was vague. That's so unlike you, Caleb, I actually think I should be worried."

"There's nothing to be worried about, Kenna." I say, rolling my eyes at her.

"You're not planning on planting a cannabis crop are you Caleb?" Now it's my turn to bark out a laugh.

"No, I'm not. Geezus Makenna! I may be a lot of things but a drug deal-er isn't one of them." I'm sure the disappointment, mixed with anger is ob-vious in my voice.

"I'm sorry Caleb, that wasn't what I meant. You're just a little, shall we say, unconventional and I thought perhaps you were wanting to broaden your horizons out here on the property." She says, with more uncertainty than I've ever heard in her voice before. Even when our parents died, she was strong and capable. "I just got you back, I don't want you to move back to the city."

She thinks my meeting in the city means I'm looking for a job out there? "I'm not looking to move back to the city Kenna. The meeting is about a crop I'm thinking of growing out here, just not dope!" I laugh.

"So, you're not going back to the city?"

"Not permanently, no, this is my home. Well, at least until you or Lo-gan kick me out anyway."

"It will never happen, Caleb. We're all finally back together again and that's the way it's going to stay if I have any say in it."

I wasn't serious about them kicking me out but it's nice to know they don't have plans to. Well, Kenna doesn't have any plans to, Logan is a dif-ferent story all together.

"Ummm guys, I hate to interrupt but could I have a moment please, Makenna?" Leila asks from beside the table. I didn't even realise she was standing there until she spoke and normally my body tells me when she's nearby.

"Of course we can talk. Have a seat." Makenna says, motioning to the chair between us for her to sit on.

"Oh, thanks." Leila sits, then fiddles with the paper napkin that was placed on the table with my danish. "I won't take up too much of your time, I just wanted to ask if you were OK with me taking the weekend off? I've al-ready arranged for Sara to take over all of my usual jobs and I promise she'll do a great job. She helps me out a lot, so she knows what needs to be done and she can do all the cooking as well."

"Yes, that's fine with me." Makenna smiles at her but Leila doesn't take any notice whatsoever, she keeps talking, explaining why she wants the time off and that we're going together. I just sit there and smile at her because she's nervous and it looks adorable on her.

Chapter Eight
LEILA

I finish up the last few things I needed to do for the morning, before making my way over to his table to finish, or perhaps start, the chat we were meant to have earlier. Getting there is a bit of a challenge because a few customers stop me to say hello and compliment me on the food. Which means, I'm floating on a cloud as I reach Caleb's table and I don't notice Makenna sitting at the table as well. I suppose I should have guessed when the order for a caramel latte and apple cinnamon muffin came in but Makenna usually asks for it be delivered to her office. It's pretty rare that she eats her morning tea in here.

When I drop into a chair and interrupt them to ask if I can have the weekend off, I stumble over my words and kind of ramble. I didn't even stop to think about whether Caleb might have already mentioned the weekend to his sister, so when she answers me, I just roll over the top of her, assuming that she's said no or asked me why I'm giving her such short notice.

"Yes, that's fine with me." Makenna answers while smiling brightly at me.

"I'm sorry about the late notice but my mum hasn't been doing too well lately and my car, well it's a bit of a bomb and I'm not sure it would get me there and back. So, when Caleb offered to take me to the city with him and make himself available to bring me back on Sunday, it just seemed like a perfect opportunity." I take a breath and look at Caleb who is just sitting there smiling at me like a damned lunatic. "Oh crap, did you tell Makenna you were going into the city this weekend? I'm sorry I just kind of barged into your conversation without really knowing what you were talking about and bulldozed right over it, didn't I?" I rest my elbows on the table and drop my face in my hands. God damn it! I'm making a complete arse of myself and a mess of the whole situation.

I feel a gentle hand rest on my arm and Makenna says, "Relax Leila, Caleb, already told me about his plans and yours." She chuckles quietly, as I peek at her through my fingers. I'm supposed to be an adult, a trusted employee who runs this business for her and she's laughing because I've become a bumbling idiot! "If you're comfortable letting this knucklehead drive and spending some time alone with him, who am I to argue? I've been trying to get you to have some time off anyway, had I known your Mum wasn't doing well, I would have insisted *much* earlier that you go and see her. Family should be cherished while we have them, Leila." She squeezes my arm and a silence settles around us for about a minute until Caleb talks.

"You know, I'm not that bad. I drive pretty well thank you very much and those defensive driving courses you guys *insisted* I do, did their jobs too!" He looks at me and rolls his eyes. "Yes, they made me take multiple defensive driving courses *before* I got my license. Leila will be safe in my hands on the weekend."

Makenna takes her hand off my arm and reaches over to rest it on Caleb's hand. "I know that Caleb, I didn't really mean anything by it, I'm sorry." She tells him quietly.

"I know, Makenna." Caleb says to his sister in a quiet, almost sad voice and I feel like I'm interrupting more than a simple conversation. I feel uncomfortable and start to excuse myself, before I can, Caleb speaks again, his normal cheekiness back in place.

"So, see you'll be safe in my hands Leila, Makenna told you so." He winks at me and I get the double meaning he's mentioned twice now and I just hope like hell Makenna didn't catch either the wink or his double meaning. Otherwise, we might be in trouble. Well, I might be in trouble. I don't know how my boss would feel about me dating, even if it *is* fake dating, her little brother.

"I never thought for a second I wouldn't be Caleb." I smile at him and rest my hand on top of his, the same one Makenna just released. Even knowing that his sister is watching us intently, I don't want Caleb to think that I believe he would hurt me in any way, so you know what? Bad luck. If Makenna doesn't like it, if she doesn't want to see the friendly affection that her brother and I have for each other, as *friends*, then that's her issue. I understand that if I no longer have a job, that it becomes my issue but I'm willing to take that chance.

"I never said she wouldn't be safe with you, Caleb." Makenna says, her eyes staring at our joined hands on the table. I go to pull away but Caleb catches my pinkie finger with his and stops me.

"I know but it becomes a little tedious when you're constantly reminded that you're not quite up to the standards expected from your family." He says quietly but his words definitely have some intensity to them.

Makenna's eyes dart from our hands to look her brother directly in the eyes. "Oh no, Caleb, that's definitely not what I meant. I was just teasing you, it's what we do but if it hurts you I'll stop. I promise." Her eyes dart up to look at me and she takes a deep breath, like she's trying to decide if she should speak in front of me or not.

"I should go." I say, starting to lift my butt out of the chair so that they can have whatever conversation it looks like they want to have without me present. I don't get very far though because Caleb doesn't let go of my hand, making it difficult to actually leave the table, so I park my butt back in the chair and look at our hands that are now joined together, with our fingers twisted together.

"Just spit it out, Kenna. Leila knows me better than most people, so I doubt you could say anything that I wouldn't tell her later anyway." Well, I guess that was one way of telling her we're maybe a little more than just friends. I can feel Makenna's eyes on me and even though I really don't want to look up and see whatever is on my boss' face, I'm not going to back down from supporting Caleb either. I don't want to choose between my job and Caleb but I know I will if I have to. Makenna might be surprised by my choice too.

Makenna looks at me, her eyes darting between mine and she obviously sees whatever she needs to because she speaks again and this time, she barely holds back.

"Look, Caleb, we don't mean any harm OK? You're the baby and Logan and I have kind of stepped up in place of our parents." She holds her hand up to stop him from speaking and he snaps his mouth shut. "I know we can't and won't ever replace our parents, Caleb but for better or worse, we have taken on those roles without really thinking. We've obviously made you feel like you're not an equal member of the family and for that I'm sorry and I know Logan would be too." She looks my way again, her eyes dipping to our still joined hands and then back to her brother. "That being said, I'm glad you've got such a good *friend* here in Leila. Look after each other this weekend. Head out whenever you need to as long as Sara has everything under control. Let me know when you get there, please?" Without another word, she stands up and kisses Caleb on the cheek and gives me a one-armed hug.

"OK, Kenna." Caleb says with a nod and then Makenna is gone, and I feel like I can breathe again!

"Well, that went better and yet kind of worse than I was expecting." I say with a sigh, while trying to pull my hand back but he doesn't let go. "At least she said I could have the weekend off." I say, smiling at Caleb, trying to ease the tension I can feel in his body.

"At least." He says, his eyes cast down, staring at our joined hands. His entire demeanour screams defeated and I don't think I've ever seen Caleb look anything other than smart, a little cocky and confident. I want to say something, anything that will bring that cheeky, gorgeous smile back to his face but I can't think of a thing right now with my hand in his.

"Caleb, I don't think." I don't get to finish because he speaks over me.

"Don't, please, Leila?" He looks up to meet my eyes and I can see the sadness there. At least I think I did for a minute but his demeanour changes in an instant, as he flashes me that gorgeous smile, the dimple in his cheek popping. "So, you heard the boss, we can get out of dodge whenever we like. Are you packed?" He asks, and I feel his hope in the middle of my chest.

"No, Caleb, I haven't packed yet, we're not leaving until tomorrow."

"Oh yeah, right."

"We only made the decision to go this morning and I haven't been home yet, just in case you forgot." I nudge my shoulder into his, not wanting to let go of his hand any sooner than I have to. One, because I'm enjoying touching him and holding his hand like I'm entitled to and two, because I feel like he *needs* the comfort of *my* touch.

"Of course! You're right and I stupidly didn't think once again." He mumbles and that distant look returns to his face.

"You're not an idiot, Caleb, you just forgot. I forget stuff all the damned time and feel like an idiot too but the fact is, there's just a lot of stuff on my mind and too many things to think about. Once in a while, forgetting one of those things is normal, not stupid. That being said, I'm a little disappointed my stay at your place was so unremarkable that you've forgotten about it already." I say, bumping my shoulder into his again, trying to lighten the mood.

"You're absolutely right." He says, squeezing my hand but not letting it go, his smile shining once again. "I was thinking."

"What exactly were you thinking, Mr Drake?" I say, moving to sit a little closer to him, not recognising my own voice because it's a little huskier than usual. Caleb scrubs his hand over his face before he speaks again.

"I was thinking that maybe we could go early, you know, if you want to? You could leave your car here. We can go back to my place and I can pack what I need for the weekend and then we can drive to your place, you can pack what you'll need, and we can head out from there. We can go and see your mum tomorrow and spend the whole day with her before we have to be at the Weavers."

"Ummm. You want to meet my mum?" I ask, surprised as hell.

"Yeah." He says with a shrug of his shoulders. "Why not? I mean we're going out there together anyway and how else were you going to go see her?"

"I kind of figured I could get a taxi or Uber to her place and be back in time to go the Weavers.' I answer him.

"Oh, right. Of course you didn't plan on introducing me to your family. Right, I wasn't thinking, once again." He sighs.

"That's not it at all, Caleb. I just didn't want you to think that I expected you to run me around everywhere." I rest my hand on top of his again and continue. "As for my car, I just figured that I could drive home and start packing while you were packing whatever you needed and that way we could get on the road earlier in the morning?" I see the disappointment roll across his face like a wave. "But, if you want to head out today, then we can easily do that. I mean, it's not like I don't want you in my house or anything. You can easily look up where I live on the employee records. It's not like it's a secret or anything." Bloody hell! Now I'm talking nonsense and stumbling over my words.

"I would never do that Leila! I would never invade yours or anyone else's privacy like that. I know I have access to that information but I would never, ever, take advantage of that."

I sigh because damn it, I'm not helping this situation at all today. "I know that Caleb and I wasn't accusing you of doing it either." I close my eyes and sigh again, before looking him directly in the eyes. "Yes, Caleb, if it's not too much trouble, I would really appreciate you driving me to my house and waiting for me to pack for our weekend away. Believe me, taking you to meet my mum will be my pleasure, thank you. Just don't forget that *you* asked to meet her, OK?" I laugh.

"I can't wait to meet her Darlin'. I'm sure she's an amazing person, I mean look at you!" He says with that charmingly, irresistible, sexy smile of his.

"What does that mean, Mr Drake?" I ask, in a serious tone.

"Well, that means she can't be all bad, she brought you up and you're pretty amazing." I can't help the blush that blooms across my cheeks. Could this man be any more charming? He's going to have my mum eating out of his hands! "Fantastic! Can you leave now, or do you have things that you still have to do before you can leave?"

"Can you give me an hour or so? It's only late morning, Caleb, we have plenty of time and I just need to check a few things. I also want to have a chat with Sarah before I leave but I promise, we should be ready to go after that." I smile at him. "I should probably also let my Mum know we're coming."

"Of course! Take as much time as you need. It will give me time to finish off my coffee and go over a few things I need for my meeting with Brian." The enthusiasm is back in his voice, happiness shining in his eyes again.

"You mean the now *cold* coffee in front you?" I laugh, watching him pick it up and take a swig out of it to prove me wrong and then pull a face that can't disguise how horrible his now cold coffee tastes.

"Oh hell! That's disgusting! I didn't realise I'd left it sitting there untouched for so long. Sorry Leila." He says, looking embarrassed and I can't help laughing.

"It's OK, Caleb, there were other things going on and it won't be the first or the last coffee to go cold. I'll get Georgie to make you a fresh cup and bring it over."

"You don't have to do that, Leila, I let the drink go cold. It's my own fault."

"I know I don't *have* to, Caleb, I want to. So, why don't you just let me do something for you and then I can go do what I need to so that we can get out of here and enjoy our weekend. How does that sound?"

"Perfect. That's sounds perfect Leila."

I nod and move to get up from my chair but I don't get too far because Caleb doesn't let go of my hand. I look down at our joined hands and then to Caleb, opening my mouth to speak but he beats me to it.

"Thank you, Leila." He says quietly.

"It's just a coffee, Caleb." I laugh just as quietly, deliberately misinterpreting his words.

"That wasn't what I was referring to and you know it, but thank you for that too."

"Any time, Caleb." I say, pulling my hand from his and taking the cold coffee from his other hand. "I'll have a fresh one sent out in a few minutes." He nods, dropping his gaze from mine and down to the papers in front of him. It's not until then that I realise that Makenna didn't even notice the papers he had sitting right in front of him earlier. She had the perfect opportunity to notice her younger brother's plans and ask him all about them but she didn't. She doesn't even know what he has planned and she wasn't even interested enough to ask what he was working on. That just makes me sad.

I leave Caleb to his work and on my way to take his cold coffee to the kitchen and empty it, I pass by Georgie and ask her to make a fresh one and take it out to him.

"Caleb?" She asks, confused.

"Yes, Drake. Caleb Drake? You know, your boss?" I ask her, not understanding why she's so confused. After all, he's in here almost every day, I thought everyone who worked here knew who he was.

"Oh, the *cute* Mr Drake. No worries, I'll take it out there as soon as I can, Leila." She says with a smile.

"I'm not sure you should refer to your boss that way, Georgie." I frown at her.

"You're right, Leila, I'm sorry it won't happen again." She says with a small, nervous smile. "I'll get a fresh coffee out to Mr Drake as soon as I can."

"Thanks, Georgie." I say with a smile, leaving her to it. I turn to walk into the kitchen, only to find Sara standing there leaning against the doorframe. "Haven't you got anything to better to do than stand there holding up the wall?" I ask, only half joking.

"I was just watching my boss harass her staff for calling her boss *cute*." She raises an eyebrow at me in question. "Did I really just hear you *admonish* Georgie for calling Caleb *cute*?"

"No." I say a little too quickly. "I was just reminding my staff to show their bosses some respect. Caleb doesn't need to walk in on his staff gossiping about him."

"Right. So it had nothing to do with the way you two were holding hands out there and making goo goo eyes at each other then?" Sara asks, with another quirk of her eyebrow.

"No." I say, shaking my head as I walk around her to get into the kitchen.

"Are you sure about that?"

"Very. We weren't holding hands."

"You weren't?"

"No, we weren't." I say, starting to become annoyed. Sara may be my friend but I'm still her boss when we're at Vines.

"What were you doing then? Because it sure looked like you were holding hands from here." She says with a smirk.

"Well, we weren't." I say with a huff. "Doesn't anyone around here have any work to do? Do I need to start laying people off because there isn't enough work to go around?" I ask, loudly enough that everyone in the kitchen can hear me and they all suddenly bury their heads in the job at hand, rather than listening to Sara bombard me with questions. "I was reassuring him that's all Sara." I wasn't going to share with her what I was reassuring him about, that's his business, I don't have permission to share it with anyone else.

"Sure. Were you letting him know that you think he's as handsome as always?" She asks me, laughing.

"You know what Sara? We may be friends but when we're at Vines, I'm your boss and Caleb Drake is *my* boss. Which in turn makes him *your* boss and everyone else's boss in this kitchen. I think he deserves a little more respect for that alone. His private business is exactly that!" I say to her, irritated. "Now, if you've stopped gossiping, can we go through all the things I'm going to need you to do for me this weekend, please? By the way, I'm leaving for the weekend as soon as we're finished, if you can't work late tonight, just shut a little earlier."

"No I'm good, I can stay tonight boss." She says with a tight smile. "Let's go through all the things."

"OK." I nod and we start finalising all the plans for the weekend and making sure she'll have enough staff working to cover herself not being available for a few things. When we're done she heads off for a break and I finish up the couple of doughs I started for the morning.

Everyone is working, laughing and chatting but stuff is getting done. I'm placing the last batch of dough in the warming cupboard when Sara walks up behind me and whispers in my ear, "But he was still calling you Darlin', right?" I close my eyes to stop myself from rolling them at her and take a deep breath. "You're going to have to come up with a cute nickname for him this weekend, you know that, right?" I let out another sigh because little does she know I already have one. "Oh my word, you have one already don't you?"

I haven't even opened my eyes, how the hell can she possibly *know* anything that I'm thinking? I know I didn't say it out loud. "Sara." I grind out, trying my hardest not to lose my shit at her.

"You know you want him and I suspect the feeling is very much mutual." She says quietly in my ear. Loud enough that the rest of the room can hear her, she says, "Off you go boss. Go have your weekend off and see your family. Us ragtag bunch of losers can hold down the fort while you're gone. Don't you worry about a thing."

There's a chorus of, 'hey who you calling losers?' and 'what do you mean ragtag', mixed with variation of, 'have a good weekend away Leila, see you

Monday,' all through the kitchen, as Sara not so gently pushes me out the door.

"Go get him cougar." She says quietly.

"I think you mean tiger, that's the saying."

"Nope, I'm pretty sure I said what I meant. Have fun *boss* lady. Don't do anything I wouldn't do." She says with one final shove.

"Well, that leaves the weekend wide open doesn't it?"

"Yes, yes it does. Now scram. Get out of here before you find something else to do." Sara demands, flinging her hands at me, shooing me away.

I laugh, shaking my head as I walk towards Caleb's table. I'm happy to see him occupied with whatever paperwork he's got in front of him, hopefully that means he didn't catch any of the mucking around from Sara. When I'm right behind him, I gently put my hand on his shoulder and say, "Hey handsome, are you ready to get out of here?" The smile I'm rewarded with as he looks at me is devasting. Devastatingly handsome and successful in making me melt into a puddle. He looks so happy to see me and to be getting out of here. Let's hope he still feels that way by the end of the weekend and we've spent all day and night together.

That's when it hits me. I'll be spending my nights with Caleb Drake! The next three in fact because he managed to add an extra night on to the trip by going today.

Nights. With Caleb. In his bed.

I am in *so* much fucking trouble!

Chapter Nine
CALEB

There's a light touch as a hand comes to rest on my shoulder and I know without looking that it's Leila. "Hey handsome, are you ready to get out of here?" I'm tempted to tell her the truth. I've been ready to get out of here since she said that we could leave today.

"Absolutely. Just let me finish this one thing, then I'll pack everything up and we can go." I smile up at her still standing behind me. I see something like panic flash across her beautiful face but it's gone so quickly I don't know if I imagined it or not, so I don't say anything.

"While you finish up, I'll take these empty coffee cups up." She grabs the two empty cups and hesitates. "Did you have a second cup?"

"Umm yeah. You were gone a little longer than I was expecting, so I asked Georgie for another cup. Is that OK?" I ask, wondering why she's frowning.

"Of course it is, you're allowed to have as much coffee or whatever you like in here. It's your bistro after all but Georgie should have cleared off the other cup when she brought over the fresh, that's all."

"Oh, right. That would be my fault." I say sheepishly.

"How on earth could that be your fault, Caleb?"

"Because I asked her to leave it behind?"

"Is that a question or an answer?"

"An answer. I told her I would bring them both up when I was done but I got distracted playing around with some figures in my presentation and I forgot."

"It's not your job to take the empty dishes to the kitchen Caleb."

"I know but I'd planned on coming into the kitchen to see what you were up to and how long you were going to be. So, like I said, my bad."

She laughs, shaking her head, which is exactly what I was hoping she'd do. I don't want to get any of the staff in here getting in trouble on my account. Leila might say this is *my* business, or our family's business but she's the one running the place and that makes it her business in my books.

"You don't need an excuse to come into the kitchen, ever, Caleb. Just don't make it a habit to scare me when you do, otherwise one of us is going to end up injured, then I really will have Makenna and Logan on my arse."

"No more sneaking up on you, promise. Not that I did last time but from now on, I promise to yell out and let you know I'm here before just popping up in your kitchen. Do we have a deal?"

"Yes, we do, thank you, Caleb." She says, smiling broadly at me before walking away, taking the dirty dishes into the kitchen to be washed.

I really prefer it when she calls me handsome but we can work on that over the weekend. I have a feeling the more I call her darlin', the more likely I am to be called handsome. At least I hope so.

My mood is back to my usual happiness after my conversation with Makenna put me in a mood, as I pack up my laptop and paperwork. Just as I'm about ready to leave, I hear a voice that puts me right back into a foul mood. I really don't want to have to deal with him right now. Surely it was enough that I had to talk with our sister earlier?

"Packing up early today, Caleb?" The king of grumpiness asks.

"Good afternoon to you too, Logan. How are you today?" My voice as sweet as I can possibly get it. You'd think that he would be less grumpy now that he and Jules kissed and made up, but nope, it seems his sunny disposition is just how he was made. I don't know *why* Jules married my brother but I'm glad he did.

"I'm great, Caleb, thanks for asking. Busy as usual." I get what he's saying but I'm just not going to bite today.

"How are Jules and Savvy?" I ask, hoping that I can divert the conversation away from what he really wants to say.

"They're perfect." The smile that spreads across his face says more than words could explain, just how happy the both of them make my brother. I'm happy for them, happy for Logan. He deserves to be happy after everything he's struggled with. "They're absolutely perfect. Savannah keeps asking when you're going to come visit. It's been a while since we've seen you at the house." I understand the underlying question, 'where have you been Caleb?'

"Tell Savvy I'll come see her either Sunday night or Monday afternoon. I have to go away this weekend but I promise to bring her back something from my trip." I smile at him.

"Where are you going for the weekend?"

"Just into the city. I have some things I need to take care of. A few people to see." I answer him cryptically, as I feel a light touch on my arm.

"Are you ready to go?" Leila's voice says beside me. "Oh, good afternoon Logan how are? How are Julian and Savannah? I haven't seen either of them in here for a few days, I hope they're both OK? They normally come in for a treat after school at least a few times a week." She says with a bright smile.

"That would explain why Savannah doesn't always eat all of her dinner some nights." Logan says with a loud laugh, catching at least half of the customers sitting at the surrounding tables attention. "They're both fit and healthy, thanks for asking Leila, we've all just been a little busy. Jules had to go out of town for the night earlier in the week, so we've been cuddling up at home making up for lost time. He works from home a lot these days so that we can take it in turns to pick Savvy up and look after her. We're all still a work in progress." Logan looks between the two of us and his eyes settle on Leila's hand still resting on my arm and she slides it down my arm to settle on my wrist as he watches. "So, where are you two off to this weekend then?"

"Didn't Makenna tell you?" I ask, not really sure why I've bought our sister into the mix.

"Yes, she mentioned you were both going to be unavailable for the weekend, I just didn't realise she meant you were going to be together." He raises an eyebrow at me in question as Leila's hand tightens around my wrist and I fight the urge to take her hand in mine.

"Yes, Caleb offered to drive me into the city so that I can visit with my Mum after he found out my car would most likely not make it there and back. He's going that way to catch up with some friends and sweet talk some people into doing business with Drake Wines."

"Well, he is a sweet talker, so you be careful Leila." He tells her with a wink. "I hope your Mum is OK? I know you said she wasn't well the last time we spoke."

"She's OK, thanks Logan but I really want to check in on her and my brother. He's doing well at university but I haven't seen them for a while."

"If I had known you hadn't seen your Mum for a while I would have made you take some time off. I remember Makenna telling me you were well overdue for a break. Why didn't you say something sooner?" He asks, frowning at Leila. "Is her health improving?"

"I don't think her health will ever improve, Logan but she's doing OK. I just don't want the majority of the worry and her care to be on my brother, he has a life to live." She sighs and I can hear the sadness in her voice. "Caleb heard me telling Sara that I couldn't go visit because I wasn't sure that my car would make it there and back again, so he offered to take me with him on his trip. Makenna said it was OK for me to have the time off, I hope that isn't a problem?" She asks my brother, while squeezing my wrist in reassurance.

"Of course it isn't a problem, Leila. Like I said, you should have said something sooner and we could have arranged for you to visit your mum before now. I'm glad that Caleb can help you out this time. Just ask one of us for help in the future, OK?" Logan lectures her and I watch as she rolls her eyes and I can't help the loud laugh that escapes me. I've never seen anyone roll their eyes at my big brother after he's scolded them, even with good humour and survive it. He looks my way, then much to my surprise, looks back at Leila and says, "You'll keep young lady. Now you two get out of here before I find something I need help with."

Without thinking I take Leila's hand in mine to pull her out of Vines door, yelling behind me, "See ya later Logan."

"See you Sunday Caleb and have a great weekend." He calls back. Just as I open the door he calls out, "Hey Leila."

We pause at the door, without dropping my hand, she turns back to look at my brother. "Yes Logan?"

"Look after him, OK?"

"Will do." A huge smile spreading across her face.

"Tell your Mum I said hi and guys? Can you send us a message to let us know you got there in one piece, please?"

"Will do, Logan." I promise, then I pull Leila out the door towards my car, before anyone else can stop us. I open the passenger door for her and gesture for her to get in.

"Why, thank you, Handsome!" And I'm back to being called handsome. I love it when she calls me that, I can feel my blood warming in my veins. A smile spreads across my face, making me look like a madman.

"You're very welcome, Darlin'." I say, closing the door gently as she settles into the seat.

I walk around the car to the driver's side door, I look up because I can feel eyes on me. I see Logan watching us with a smile. I wave in his general direction and see his returning wave out of the corner of my eye as I get in the car and close the door. Reaching behind us, I put my bag on the floor behind Leila's seat.

"Caleb?"

"Yes?" I answer, my arm still stretched behind her seat, I look up to see her watching me.

"Thank you for taking me to see my Mum, I really appreciate it."

"Any time darlin', you just have to ask. I'd rather you didn't drive your car that far." I would suggest we look at getting her a new car but I get the feeling I might just be on the receiving end of quite a mouthful of how far out of line I've stepped. So, instead, I'll offer to take her any time she wants to go *and* bide my time until I can suggest looking into getting her another, safer car, without getting my balls taken off.

She doesn't answer me, just gives me a slight nod of her head in acknowledgement. What's most important is that she's still smiling.

Pulling out of the car park, we drive by Logan who is still standing in front of Vines, watching us. Leila waves as we reach him, I salute him without looking his way and take us to my place. Which means bypassing both the main house *and* Logan's house. I smile when I see a flash of yellow and then blue running around the yard, knowing that means Savannah has Jules chasing her and no doubt that dog of hers, around.

"It makes me so happy to see those three smiling and relaxed. It warms me to see them happy as a family, especially knowing everything that they've all been through. It can't have been easy for any of them." Leila says beside me.

"You're right, it's been tough, but everything's settled down now. I think they're going to be all right, the three of them, together. Sorry, the *four* of them, together. Savvy would kill me if she knew I was leaving her precious pup out of the equation." I say, shaking my head, but smiling. "I'm still not sure how she managed to convince my anal retentively clean brother to get a dog but the evidence jumps up and gets me in the balls every time I visit."

"I'd think she might be able to convince Logan and Julian to agree to just about anything right now." Leila laughs, and it's music to my ears. "They're all still finding their feet, their situation was a surprise to everyone, all be it a happy surprise I'm sure but it's going to take time for them all to get used to it. I'm sure somewhere around Savannah graduating high school they'll be able to say no."

"I think you're right." I say laughing, as we pull into the garage at my house. "Come on, let's go inside, get a drink and you can advise me on what clothes you think I should take for this shindig."

"You need clothing advice? Is that the real reason you wanted me to come over and not go home first?" She jokes, as we walk from the garage into the house.

"A second opinion never hurts, Leila and I trust you to give me very solid, honest advice." I turn to look at her response and she doesn't fail me. She throws her head back, letting out a loud, raucous laugh.

"You. Think." She's trying to breathe between her words and her laughter, while holding on to her stomach but she's struggling. "You. Can't. Honestly. Believe."

"Are you OK, Leila?" I ask, a smile almost splitting my face because I love, beyond belief, that I can make her laugh this hard but I don't want her laughing if it's at her own expense.

She holds her hand up, asking me to wait for a minute until she can speak. With a hand resting on her chest, the fingers on her other hand swipe at the tears sitting just under her eyes. "Sorry. Did you assume that I would be able to give you fashion advice?" Still dragging in large breaths and holding her stomach lightly.

"Why wouldn't I?" I ask, confused as fuck.

"Why wouldn't you? You see what I wear to work, right?"

"Yes, your uniform." I answer, still confused.

"Have you ever seen me in anything else, Caleb?" I know what I'd like to see her in, nothing but she does make me think.

"Well, no but that doesn't mean you don't know what to wear *or* what you like a guy to wear." She's watching with wide eyes and a little bit of, dare I hope, heat. "You know what you find attractive and what you don't. Am I right?"

She swallows deeply. "Yes, you're right but that doesn't mean it's the right thing to wear."

"If you like it, that's all that matters to me." I say, as I start to walk into my bedroom. "Are you coming?"

"Ahh what?" Oh that blush deepens and I realise what I said. I can't help chuckling quietly.

"You'll need to come into my bedroom so that you can see my clothes. You know, to help me choose some and pack them?"

"Yeah, right, of course!" Her voice is a little higher pitched than usual, making me happy. It means that I'm not the only one affected by the thought of her being in my bedroom. She was in the spare room last night and we shared a wall, but she hasn't be *in* my bedroom. Quietly and quickly she walks up to me and I lead the rest of the way.

We're quiet, not quite awkward but we're both definitely assessing the situation and how we feel about it, as soon as we enter my room.

"This is my room." I say, stupidly. "Why don't you sit here and I'll go pull out some clothes for you to look at, then you can tell me what you think of them. How does that sound?"

"Perfect." She says, her voice still higher pitched than usual, as she sits on the bench seat at the foot of my bed. I've never been more grateful to Makenna for forcing my hand on getting some 'decorative pieces' for the house. I don't think either of us could have done this if Leila had to sit on my *bed*. As it is, I can't help imagining what she would look like all spread out in the middle of my king sized bed, among the grey fluffy and very warm, comforter.

Shaking my head to clear it, I get down to business and by business I mean packing a bag for the weekend, not any other kind of business, as much as I might *want* that kind of business.

"Give me a few minutes and I'll bring out some clothes." Nodding, she smiles at me. I walk into my wardrobe and stand there looking around. I honestly don't know where to start. When I built this house, Makenna demanded to have a say in some of the design and she made sure that the master bedroom had a huge walk in robe. I never could understand why because I don't *have* a lot of clothes and there's a lot of empty space. At the time, she made me believe I needed it. Her reasoning was that in the future, my *wife* would enjoy the space. I let her have her way because it was easier than actually fighting her over these small things that made no difference to me but seemed to make Kenna *very* happy!

"Hey, do you need some help in here?" Leila asks quietly, with her hand resting lightly on my bicep.

"Hmmm?" I didn't realise I'd been standing here for very long but I guess it must have been a few minutes for Leila to have followed me in here. "Yes. Please."

"It's pretty impressive in here. You've got every woman's dream wardrobe, except that it's pretty damned empty Caleb."

"Is this *your* idea of a dream, Leila?" I can't help asking.

"Yes and no." I raise my eyebrow at her in question, hoping she'll explain herself. "Let me explain."

"Please do because I was told this was pretty much every woman's dream."

"It is because there's just so much *space* for *everything*!" Sighing as she walks in a small circle looking at all the empty space. "That's also the problem. There's so much *space*! I mean, I would feel like I had to fill it all up, otherwise that would be a waste but I'm not a shopper. Not of clothes anyway and it seems silly to buy clothes just to fill a wardrobe."

"Is that why you think you shouldn't be giving me advice on what clothes to take this weekend because you don't buy yourself many clothes?"

"Yes and no." Her quiet laugh tickles something inside me, when I raise another eyebrow at her in confusion.

"You are a walking contradiction you know that, right?"

"Yes, I do." Her laughter fills the not so small space. "The fact is, Caleb, I'm not into fashion like Makenna or Sara. I wear clothes to be comfortable and hopefully they look good. I don't really go out anywhere that I need to dress up, so I've never bothered. I spent a lot of time at school wearing jackets and aprons. I was working and learning when everyone else was out partying and drinking. I worked hard to get to where I am and dressing up, taking notice of fashion just hasn't been on my radar. Not for a very long time." She looks embarrassed but I admire the dedication and commitment she needed to get her to where she is today. Running Vines perfectly, delivering up pastries that are beyond delicious. "You would probably be better off asking Makenna or Sara for their opinions. Better yet, ask Julian, I'm sure he'd be *more* than happy to help you out."

I laugh. "The thing is though, I don't care what they think. I want *your* opinion, not theirs. So, will you help a guy out?"

"If you insist, sure, let's get to it then. Time's a wasting Mr Drake." Now, normally I don't like it when people call me Mr Drake. It makes me think of my father *or* it refers to Logan, not me but that name rolling off Leila's tongue? That I think I could get used to!

"Let's have at it, Darlin'."

For the next twenty minutes, we forage through my suits, jeans and shirts. Leila picks out all her favourite ones, then we narrow those down to the handful I'm going to need for this weekend at the Weaver's.

"I think we're done Darlin'." A goofy, happy grin on my face. I usually hate packing for anything, even a one night trip but with Leila helping me it wasn't so bad. "Do you mind if I have a quick shower?" I know I had one this morning but I'd love to freshen up before we get in the car and drive for a couple of hours to meet her Mum.

"No, of course not. Go for it, I'll just wait out here." An awkward smile spreads across her face.

"Where else would you want to wait, Leila?" I ask, because I just can't resist seeing that blush creep up her cheeks again.

"Nowhere else." She says on a cough. "Nowhere else at all. Off you go, go have your shower." She waves me away.

"Fine, I'm going."

"Umm, Caleb?"

"Yes?" Wondering what I could have possibly missed.

"Don't forget to pack some underwear, OK?"

"Oh crap, you're right! You don't want to help me with that? You can choose whichever ones you like." I offer in my most serious voice.

"You might need some socks too." She offers, as she walks out of my bedroom, ignoring me.

I can't think of anything else to say that won't make me sound like the horny bastard that I am, so I turn on my heel and head to my bathroom. Is it wrong for me to hope that she might follow me in and ask if she can join me?

It's wrong, I know it is but you can't fault a man for having dreams. Can you?

Chapter Ten
LEILA

I leave Caleb's bedroom as fast as my legs can take me. There's no way I'm waiting around in there to see if he's going to undress in his room or wait until he's in the bathroom. I *want* to watch him strip off every stitch of clothing but I know that can't happen. It shouldn't happen.

So, instead of following him into the shower, I go into his kitchen and go in search of coffee. I really need something to do right now. Something to occupy my thoughts *and* my hands, coffee seems like just the thing. I search through his cupboards and find two travel mugs because I assume we'll have it to go, just as soon as he gets out of the shower. There I go, thinking about him naked. Wet and *naked* in the god damned shower, again. I fan my face which I can feel heating all over again.

"Is everything OK Leila?" I hear his voice behind me. I didn't realise that he'd finished his shower. I couldn't have been out here looking for coffee long enough for him to have had a shower. Surely?

"Just thought we could do with some coffee for the trip." Not turning around to look at him when I answer. My cheeks are burning and I'd really rather I didn't have to explain why.

"We'd be better off taking the travel mugs to Vines on the way out to get them filled Darlin." He says with a chuckle. "Didn't you notice I didn't offer you coffee this morning with breakfast?"

"You didn't?" Thinking back to breakfast this morning I realise that we didn't have coffee, although I do remember him having one at Vines. "Then why do you have coffee and travel mugs if you don't have coffee here? I know you drink coffee because you have one or more, every day at Vines. What's the deal, Caleb?"

"The truth?' He looks like he's trying hard not to laugh when he asks, my answer is a nod of my head. "The truth is, I'm not a fan." His admits with a shrug of his shoulder, it hits me like a brick.

"What the hell are you talking about? You drink a mug or two every day at least at Vines. You have a latte with whatever pastry you decide to try for the day. What do you mean you're *not a fan*?" I can't decide if I'm confused or angry. Perhaps a mixture of both? Not sure why I'd be angry though, except that I feel like he's been lying to me.

"I mean exactly what I said. I'm not a huge fan of coffee and the only coffee machine I have here in the house is one of those pod ones. I don't have a coffee maker per se. I *do* have a kettle but Kenna refuses to drink instant coffee when she visits, so she bought the pod coffee maker and I hide it in a cupboard."

"You don't like coffee?"

"Well, I don't *not* like, it's just not my hot beverage of choice." He answers, looking like he's not going to like what I say next.

"So, what hot beverage *do* you prefer, then?" That's the next logical question, right? By the looks of it, he was waiting for it too and he's fighting himself about answering it honestly. "If we're engaged, don't you think I should know these things, Caleb? Any self-respecting girlfriend or *fiancé* would, right? I mean, you already know that I'm addicted to coffee, so it only seems fair."

"Tea. Black." His voice is strong. Unfaltering in his admission even though I get the feeling that it's taken a lot for him to make it.

"Black tea?"

"Yup."

"So, why don't you just order that at Vines? It's not like we don't have it on offer on the menu, among all kinds of other hot drinks, including hot chocolate. I don't understand why you would drink something you don't really like when the thing that you *do* enjoy is on offer as well."

"I order lattes because all the milk takes some of the bitterness away from the coffee."

"OK, but why do you drink coffee at all if you don't like it?" I'm trying hard to understand his logic behind drinking something he doesn't enjoy.

"I drink it because it stops others giving me grief about it. In University, the guys gave me a hard time about being a 'tea drinker' and women thought it was strange." He explains. "The look on your face doesn't give me any reason to believe you feel any differently." He sounds pretty annoyed and slightly embarrassed.

"I'm shocked, yes but not for the reason you think. I can't imagine eating or drinking anything that I didn't like or even remotely enjoy. If you don't like coffee, don't drink it, Caleb. I think it's strange that you would stay away from your preferred beverage to keep others happy. Kenna proved people will always adjust and make space for what they want. You need to think about doing that for yourself." I nod like that's just the way things are, Caleb appears to be a little speechless. Almost like he wasn't expecting me to react like this. "So, do you want me to make some tea for the travel mugs then?"

"You want one too?" His voice full of surprise, making me even more determined to make sure he understands that I don't care.

"Yes. I don't mind a cup of tea but I'll have some sugar in mine please."

"But you want a black tea?"

"I do. Thank you." He takes the mugs that I've been holding over to the bench, where he rolls up a cupboard door that I hadn't noticed earlier. It hides not just the kettle and tea bags but the coffee pod machine. Without looking my way, he fills the kettle and flicks it on. Then he makes himself busy putting sugar and tea bags in the mugs, then just casually watches the kettle waiting for the water boil. All without looking at me so I keep quiet, letting him get over whatever issues he has about not being a coffee drinker. Like it's a crime or something.

"I don't know why you kept this a secret. This isn't anything to be ashamed of." I keep my voice quiet, not wanting to startle him because I can see that he's deep in thought.

"Most people are coffee addicts, Leila, yourself included. I just found it easier to enjoy one type of coffee and not get hassled about my preference for tea. It's not like it's my shameful secret or anything, it's just not something I advertise. All the people that mean something to me know about it. Kenna and Logan know about it. So does Jules and a few other people. Including you." Does that mean I *mean* something to him now that I know? That my opinion of him matters?

"Georgie. She knows doesn't she? She brought you over a tea when I wasn't looking and that's the real reason you had two cups on the table earlier?" I ask, trying to not focus on the fact that he told me his 'secret'.

"She doesn't *know*. I just asked her for a black tea after I finished the latte you sent out for me. No big deal, she didn't even bat an eyelid." He says, with another shrug of his shoulders. The kettle has done its thing and I watch as he pours the water into the travel mugs. He takes a deep breath, then turns around to look me in the eyes as the tea brews for a few minutes. "The truth is, I learned early on that people think it's weird that I don't drink coffee. It's like growing up and still living on a vineyard but not particularly liking wine." He smiles at me, I already knew he wasn't a fan of wine, hence the brewery idea. "But even stranger because others just can't understand my aversion to coffee. I've just never been a fan. I couldn't get used to the smell or the taste, that's why I always make it sweet to cover the bitterness. I still get ribbed for drinking my coffee so sweet but at least it's coffee."

"People are stupid, I think we can agree on that, can't we? We're allowed to like different things and I think it's amazing that you can get through your day without coffee." I laugh, hoping to ease his tension.

"Geez thanks, Leila." He says, turning his back to me to throw out the tea bags and screw the lids onto the mugs. I rest my hand lightly on his back, then slide it around his side, I curl my body into his other side and I can feel it in every god damned pore. I can hear his blood pumping through his body as his pulse speeds up and I'm happy to know that I'm not the only one affected by our closeness.

"I didn't mean to make fun of you, Caleb. I meant to offer you support for your choices. You don't have to drink coffee around me, I'm no coffee snob. I don't care if you don't want a hot drink at all, just don't stop me from drinking my coffee in the mornings unless you want a grumpy fake fiancé on your hands."

We stand there, just like that for a few minutes, neither one of us daring to move. I don't want to burst the bubble of contentment we're in. With my body cuddled into his side, my arms wrapped around his waist, it feels more like we're actually together for real, not faking it.

"I'll be sure to remember that every morning from now on, fake fiancé." He says, and I can tell he's trying to keep things light but my body and heart are feeling all kinds of things in this moment and I don't know how the hell I'm supposed to deal with them.

"We should probably get going huh?" I ask, but I don't make a move to step away from him. I'm pretty comfortable right where I am. At least I am until I look up to see Jules looking in the kitchen window with a huge smile on his face. Shit! I pull away from Caleb and he follows my line of sight to see what I see. Julian smiling like a loon and Savannah pulling on his sleeve, urging him to keep moving. I'm with the kid, keep moving along Julian, nothing to see here.

"Right. Let's get moving before we get to your Mum's too late for me to get to know her and talk to her." He says, louder than necessary, causing us both to jump a little, which in turn causes us to separate. "I can't wait to talk your Mum into showing me all your most embarrassing childhood photos and tell me stories so that I can get to know my fiancé better."

"I really wish I'd had more notice for this trip so that I could get some dirt on you from Logan and Makenna." I groan, knowing that my Mum is going to just *love* Caleb and take even greater joy in telling him stories and showing him photos. This may not have been my best idea to be honest, I'm kind of nervous about the two of them meeting.

"Oh come on, you've had more than enough time. I know for a fact that Logan and Kenna have taken great joy in telling you stories of my youthful antics. I know for a fact that you've seen more than enough photos of me naked." He says, a smile on his handsome face and twinkle in his eyes.

"Wh-what?" I stumble over that one word as he directs me back out of the car, with his hand on my lower back and locks the door from the garage into the house.

"You know, the obligatory baby in the bath photos." He raises his free hand to his chest in what can only be described as mock shock. "What did you think I meant Miss Phillips? What kind of man do you think I am? I would never allow my siblings to take naked photos of me and I sure wouldn't allow them to show them to anyone. Even if she *is* my fiancé!"

"Whatever." I shake my head at his antics, I'd give him a shove, except I'm the one that ended up carrying both travel mugs to the car because he has his bag in one hand and his keys in the other.

Taking a sip of my tea before I make my way to the passenger side of the car, I pause as I feel his body come up right behind me. He leans down to whisper in my ear, "But if my fiancé asked me nicely, I'd definitely send her a pic or two for when we can't be together, so she doesn't forget what she has." The deep tone of his voice vibrates through my body, his breath whispers over the shell of my ear, causing a rather large shiver to run through me from head to damned toe.

Then, without touching me or saying another word, he leaves me standing there, trying to catch my breath, to throw his bag in the back and get in the driver's seat.

"You getting in or do you need another minute Darlin'?" He asks through the window he's opened and I swear I could smack the pleased look off his face and be really damned happy right now.

"Here, take your tea and shut up." I say, as a I shove his travel mug in the window causing him to pull his head back in, taking that sexy smirk of his with it. I shouldn't let him get to me like that and I wouldn't if my body didn't react to him.

I get into the car, place my mug into the holder and buckle my seatbelt before I even look Caleb's way. I actually take a deep breath before looking at him because I know he's waiting for me. So, I take my time, not truly ready to look in his eyes. I'm not sure what I want to see there, heat or coolness. When I look up to meet his eyes, I don't find either. What I find almost does me in.

"Darlin', I get the feeling you want me to apologise but I'm not going to. Do you want to know why?" I nod yes, because I really want the answer to that question but I don't think I can speak. "Because *if* you *were* mine, I would be more than willing to you send any picture you wanted. If you were *mine*, I would get off on knowing that you were getting off looking at pictures of me when we couldn't be together." His eyes stay on mine as he continues. "But mainly, I just love the way your body reacts to mine. When you're ready, *if* you're ever ready, all you have to do is ask, Leila."

I don't know what to say, so I respond the only way I can, while hoping my voice sounds stronger than it actually feels. "OK."

His eyes dart between mine a few times, he must find whatever he was looking for because he nods just once. "OK." He responds, before opening the garage door, putting the car in reverse and pulling out onto the dusty track that leads us off the Drake Wines property and out onto the highway. Neither of us saying a word the entire time but not before seeing a few people along the way. People I would have thought he would rather avoid and people who had better things to do than watch what we were doing, but apparently not.

Although, seeing Savannah and Jules and talking to them for a few minutes certainly wasn't a chore, even though Jules kept giving me funny, kind of knowing looks. I had a feeling I was going to be in for some serious questioning the next time I saw him. That was something to look forward, hopefully he brings Savannah in with him and I can distract them both. Somehow, I'm not sure that's going to work but it's worth a try.

Caleb takes all of the stops in his stride, even waving to Sara as we drive back past Vines on our way off the property. He doesn't stop though and I'm more than happy to just wave at her as we go by. She'll be expecting a complete update when I get back but I won't be surprised if I get a few messages while we're gone as well.

"You've gone quiet. You haven't changed your mind about the whole thing, have you?" He asks, reaching over to gently take my hand in his. It's such a small, yet sweet gesture, I can't help squeezing his hand a little before answering him.

"No. No second thoughts, I'm just thinking about what I'm going to need to pack. I don't want you waiting around too long for me to organise myself."

"You take as long as you need to take." He replies with a smile. "I can always help you pick out some clothes if you want, just like you helped me. I'm not as adverse to looking at your underwear like you were about looking at mine, just so you know." His smile spreads across his face.

I try to pull my hand from his but he holds on tighter to it for a second before finally letting it go. I find I don't want to pull it back too far, just in case he might feel the need to hold it again. So, I leave it sitting close to the

centre console and flick on the radio to combat the easy silence that's settled between us.

Chapter Eleven
CALEB

Leila seems nervous about letting me into her home, so nervous that I almost offer to wait in the car. Almost, except that I'm curious to see where she is when she's not at Drake Wines. So, I don't offer because I'm pretty sure she'd take me up on it.

"Are you coming in?" Leila asks, her hand poised on the door handle.

"Of course I am!" Does she think I'm giving up this opportunity. She nods as she pushes her door fully open and walks inside, turning to hold the door open for me and waving me in.

"It's not much but it's home." She speaks so quickly I look over to see if she's OK, only to see red spotting her cheeks.

"It's home to you, you've made it comfortable and pretty much you. It's what I was expecting it to be honestly, Leila."

"So, you were expecting me to live in a dingy, two bedroom, tiny house that looks like a second-hand store threw up in it? Great. At least I know what you think of your fake fiancé. Why did you even choose me, Caleb? Surely you could have chosen any number of girls that you've dated to do this for you. Maybe I was just convenient because I was there when Brian called." She sounds embarrassed and ashamed but I don't see anything in her home to be embarrassed about.

"That's not what I meant. I see you in every part of this place, Leila. From the kitchen, it's all ordered and clean, as industrial as you can get in a domestic setting and well used. You can smell the baking that you've done. You can sense all the recipes you've tried out in here. The love you have for creating them and the joy when you make it work." I see the shock cross her face and I know I've gotten it right. "I see your determination to make this work for you."

"I can't imagine you ever living in a place like this." The way she says it, so sure of her assumption that I laugh. Loudly. Which earns me a dirty look and a growl. Fuck me if I don't want to make her growl at me again, only I'd rather it be in bed, with her legs around my head!

"You think because I grew up in the house that Kenna and Brady live in now that I've lived a charmed life, is that it?" The laugh that comes out of me sounds bitter, even to me.

"Well, that's not quite what I meant. I know the last few years haven't been easy on any of you, Caleb."

"No, they haven't but that's not what *I* meant either, Leila. That house didn't always look like that. We didn't always live that way. My Dad built that house with his own hands, while he was getting the Vineyard up and running, trying to make a name for himself. The original house was made of stone and was full of holes. My Mum made the most of it, especially in the hot summers and damned cold winters. The house only started looking like it does now when Logan was eight, maybe nine. So, believe me when I say, we know how lucky we are. My parents both worked hard for everything they had and we inherited everything when they died. Logan and I built our houses so that Kenna and Brady could have the main house. We knew they'd get married and start a family before either of us did. None of us wanted to be living under each other's feet but none of us wanted to be too far away from the others either."

"You don't have to explain anything to me, Caleb. I'm sorry I assumed you've always had what you have now. I guess it's the opposite of what I accused you of doing to me."

"I guess we all assume things until we know better." I tell her honestly with a shrug. "Believe me when I say, I did not live like a king at University. I lived in a dorm and it wasn't pretty. Four young men, in what was effectively one room and no grownups around. Trust me, it wasn't great." There's honestly nothing wrong with Leila's house. It's clean, it's neat, there aren't any holes in the walls or stains on the carpets. She has nothing to be worried about. "Come on, let's get you packed so we can go see your Mum before it gets dark."

I gesture to the doorway that I assume leads to her bedroom and the rest of the house because I can only see the kitchen, dining and living rooms out here. She starts to walk that way and I follow behind her. At least I do, until she stops abruptly and turns around, she moves so fast that I only *just* manage avoiding crashing into her.

"You don't need to come in to help me." Her hand is resting on my chest to stop herself from crashing into me. I can't explain how much I like having her hand on me and that's why it takes a few too many seconds for it to register what she's said.

My eyes dart from her hand to her eyes. "It's only fair Darlin.'" I smile, before taking her hand in mine, spinning her around and gently nudging her to get her moving forward.

I struggle to hold in my laughter when she mumbles, '*Such a pushy bastard*,' under her breath. She doesn't even know the half of it but I plan on her one day finding out. One day really soon with any luck, she's going to find out just how bossy I can be.

When we reach the door to her bedroom, she stops again but doesn't turn around. "You know, you really don't have to come into my bedroom and help me pick out clothes. I'm a girl, I've got this covered you know?"

"Are you messy, Leila, is that why you don't want me in your room? Are you a closet messy girl?" I ask, leaning in to whisper just behind the shell of her ear. "Cause I don't mind mess, Darlin.'"

"Holy shit!" She mutters, as shivers travel down her back and I take note that Leila Phillips really doesn't mind some dirty talk, which suits me just fine! "No!" She says louder, this time I can't hold in my laughter, earning me a dirty look from the woman standing in front of me, still hesitant about letting me in her room. If she's not messy, then what other possible reason could she have for not wanting me in there. Oh, I guess she might want some privacy.

"I didn't think you were, Leila, honestly." I drop her hand and hold both of mine up in surrender. I don't want her to think that I'll push into something she doesn't want. "I'll just wait out here then, take your time."

She rolls her eyes, her body half twisted to look back at me as I retreat back into the living room.

"Fine! Come on then, let's get this packing done. I guess I need you to tell me what the Weavers are expecting of me this weekend. Just don't make me embarrass myself Drake, otherwise I'll take tea off the menu at Vines and I'll make everyone serve you strong black coffee from now on."

With my hands still held up in surrender, I promise to help her make good choices in clothing for the weekend, and we get down to the business of packing a million choices for three days.

"So, do I get to help with your underwear choices as well? I'm definitely willing to lend a hand." My lips quirk up and I hope it wins her over and for a second, I think I have.

Her lips twist, making me wonder if she's trying to hide a smile or a grimace. When she rolls her eyes, I figure she's trying to hide a smile. "I bet you would like to help me choose my underwear. Let me guess, something lacy and barely there?" She pauses for a second and I open my mouth to answer but I don't get the chance before she holds up her hand to stop me. "No, I'm betting you're the, *don't wear anything darlin' cause that'll give me easier access*', kind of guy. Am I right? I'm right, aren't I?" She shakes her head. I'm not sure if she's amazed at my brilliance, of which I haven't even admitted to yet, or she thinks I'm just so stereotypical that I can't have an original thought in my pretty little head. I start to speak only for her cut me off, again. "For your information buster, most women don't wear lingerie to please a man. *Most* women wear it because it makes *them* feel sexy and confident. Let me ask you this, are you a thong or briefs man?"

"I'm a whatever you want to wear kind of man." I answer honestly. The truth is, I don't care what she is or isn't wearing, only that I'm allowed to touch her naked skin.

"How convenient. Of course that's what you'd say!" She says, placing her hands on my chest, not quite gently pushing me backwards out the door. "I bet you say that to all the girls you call Darlin." Then the door closes in my face. I'm not even sure how she managed to push me out of the room but here I am. I guess I was too busy imagining her in lace, silk, or nothing to notice that we were moving.

Bracing one arm on the doorframe, I lean my forehead against the wood of the door. "You're the only one I call Darlin." I say, quietly to the closed door. She's also the only woman I've ever said I didn't care what they were wearing under their clothes too and one hundred percent meant it.

I'm not gonna lie, I've been known to say whatever I needed to, to get into a woman's pants but not recently. Never with Leila.

With one quiet thunk of my head on the closed door, I take a deep breath and push off the door frame. If I don't walk away now, I'm worried I might do something we'll both regret. Well, maybe *I* won't regret it but I don't want Leila to regret anything about us. That is, *if* anything ever happens between us.

Instead of making my way back into Leila's bedroom uninvited, I walk into her kitchen. Looking in her fridge for a bottle of water I see lots of nothing and I'm hoping that she mostly eats at Vines, otherwise we're going to have to have a talk about her not looking after herself. I'm searching for a glass when I hear a cough behind me and I slam my head into the open cupboard door above me.

"Fuck!" It comes out as more a growl that an actual word but it means the same thing and I rub the top of my head.

"Oh shit, sorry." The next thing I know her hand is on my head and she's pulling it down so that she can have a look at the damage.

"Stop it, Leila. There's no damage other than a bump. No blood, no cut, I'll be fine." I say, trying to push her hands away from my head and stand up straight.

"I just wanted to check the damage for myself." She says, huffing and crossing her arms, wrapping them around her body. "I didn't mean for you to hurt yourself, I was just wondering why you were snooping through my kitchen cupboards."

"I was just looking for a glass so that I could get a drink of water."

"They're in the only cupboard you haven't opened yet." A sexy smirk forms on her lips. Those are lip I wouldn't mind kissing right now. Or any time really. Not for the first time today, I wonder what the hell I've gotten myself into this weekend?

"That's OK, if you're ready to go, I'll just drink the bottle I've got in the car." I mumble, still rubbing the top of my head.

"Are you sure you're OK?" She asks taking a small step towards me and starting to raise her hands. "Can I please just have a look? I want to make sure there's no damage. It will make *me* feel better." She looks so concerned that I can't help taking my hand away and bending down so that she can see the top of my head. As her fingers tangle themselves in my hair and push it around looking for any marks, bumps, or cuts, I can feel her touch in every part of my body. My whole body is on high alert. When she starts running her hand through my hair and scraping her nails along my scalp, I can't hide the shiver that runs through my body. I don't move a muscle and she keeps running her fingers though my hair. I don't know how long we stand there, in her kitchen like that but I know if I don't stop her soon, I'm going to do something neither one of us is ready for yet. So, instead of allowing her to continue to touch me like I've been hoping she would, I stand up straight and watch the disappointment spread across her face, as her hands drop loosely to her sides. I hate that I put that look on her face.

Taking a step towards her, I make it so that we're so close, her breasts are almost touching my chest. If we were naked, her nipples would be grazing the hair *just* below my own nipples. I hold her face in my hands, so that she has to look me in the eyes when I answer her question from earlier and tell her *exactly* why I chose her to come with me this weekend. "Earlier. You asked me why I chose you for this weekend and not someone else I've dated before. The answer is simple really, I wanted you to come with me. Another truth is that I haven't been out on a date for quite a long time, Leila. You weren't just convenient because you were standing in front of me. I want you."

Without giving her the chance to ask me any more questions, I drop my hands and take her bags out of her hands and walk out of her house. I throw them into the back with mine and jump in the car, starting the engine without looking to see if she followed me. I know I've surprised her, I surprised myself with my admission.

The passenger door opens, Leila falls into the seat and puts on her seatbelt.

"Did you lock up?"

"Of course Caleb, I'm not an idiot."

"I didn't mean that, I just. I'm sorry."

"OK."

"I was checking. I don't want anything to happen while we're away."

"There's nothing in there anyone would want to steal, Caleb." The snort that comes out of her has my mouth tipping up at the corners.

"Well, you never know and they don't always break in to steal stuff you know. Sometimes they just get a sick joy out of messing shit up and breaking shit." The look she gives me could kill the most hardened criminals, I swear!

"Are you supposed to be making me feel better or worse, Caleb? Because I can tell you, if that was meant to make me feel better about going away for a long weekend, it didn't. Not for a second. What it does have me wondering though, is if I should go away with you at all."

"Sorry." The smile I give her is supposed to be reassuring but I don't know if it works at all. Without saying another word, I back out of her driveway, so that she doesn't have the option of changing her mind and getting out of the car and not coming with me.

For the next ten minutes we drive in silence. I know which town we're heading to, so I don't need to ask her for directions. Yet.

"Are you OK?" My voice is quiet so that I don't startle her after the extended silence. When she looks over at me, I feel my heart clench. The look in her eyes is sad and tired.

"I'm just a little tired. I didn't sleep very well last night." Her voice is so soft I almost miss her speaking.

"You didn't find my bed comfortable?" My question is an attempt at getting her to smile, even if it's just a little smile. I'm rewarded with a roll of her eyes and the tiniest lift on the corners of her mouth. "I'll have to let Kenna know that her purchase wasn't as great as she thinks."

"Your *spare* bed and no! Don't tell Makenna anything of the sort." Her hand lands on my bicep and she's smiling. "Don't you dare tell Makenna that I don't like the bed she bought! Geezus Caleb, are you *trying* to get me fired?"

"Of course I'm not. Who else is going to bake the best chocolate cake I've ever tasted?"

"Or send out black tea for you to drink?"

"Exactly." I smile at her, glad that the tension from earlier has been mostly lifted. "Why don't you try to get some shut eye now then? I'll wake you when we get closer to town and then you can give me directions to your Mum's."

"That sounds like a great idea, if you don't mind?"

"Here." I say, while reaching behind her chair and then hand her a small pillow. "Use this to get comfortable."

"Why do you have a pillow in your car, Caleb?"

"You've obviously never travelled anywhere with my sister because if you had, you would know that it's in everyone's best interest to make sure that woman is happy on an even slightly long drive." I laugh, but Makenna is a nightmare to travel with and I don't know how Brady managed when they went on their honeymoon. Also, I'm never going to ask because there are some things a brother doesn't want to hear about and one of them is how his brother in law distracts his wife on a long arsed flight like that. Some things are better left unknown.

"I bet I can tell you how Brady distracts Makenna on long drives and flights." She offers, mischief in her voice as she gets comfortable with the pillow.

"Thank you for the kind offer but I think I would be much more comfortable not knowing any of the details." I groan, not wanting to have this conversation, now or any other time.

"Oh, I'm not saying I know for sure but I think I might be able to take an educated guess."

"I'm pretty sure I know exactly *how* he does it too, which is why this conversation is done. Finished. Over, Miss Phillips. I don't need to be thinking about my sister and Brady in any way other than that they're my family, my siblings. That's all!" I shiver, totally grossed out thinking about any kind of sexual escapades those two get up to. "Brady may be one of my best friends but there has to be a line drawn somewhere and that's it right there."

"What about Jules and Logan?" She asks, all sweet and innocent, her head resting back on the pillow, her eyes closed already.

"What about them?" I ask, before I can stop myself. "No. Just no, Leila." I wave one hand in her direction, motioning for her to cut it the hell out. I cut my eyes from the road to her and back to the road a few times. She's resting back, eyes closed, arms crossed over her chest and I can see her body shaking from laughter. "They're *family*, Leila! You don't think of your family like *that*! Imagine *your* Mum or *brother* 'distracting' the special someone in their lives and I bet you won't be laughing anymore."

Oh yeah. *That* killed the laughter in her and wiped the smirk off her face.

"That's just wrong, Caleb!" I watch as she shudders but she still doesn't open her eyes.

"See, not so funny when the shoes on the other foot now, is it?" I laugh, while I turn the radio up a bit so that I can hear it better but not so loud it will keep Leila from being able to sleep. "Get some sleep. I'll wake you up when we get into town and you can direct me to your Mum's place."

"You know, I could just put the address into your GPS and then I could just sleep." She sounds like she's already about ninety percent there.

"You could but then you'd be sleepy when we get there and I'm sure you'd rather be awake when you see your mum."

I get a mumbled 'mmmmm', so I guess she really is tired and already nodding off.

I lean over and turn the radio up a little bit more and when she doesn't stir, I try for a little more volume. When she shifts in the seat, I decide I've probably pushed my luck and leave it there. Every now and then, I look over to watch her for a few seconds before I pull my eyes back to the road. I can't resist looking at her. She's relaxed and beautiful. She's always beautiful but she's so relaxed asleep. She looks comfortable and I'm grateful that she trusts me and she's comfortable enough with me to sleep while I drive. It makes me feel things I shouldn't. Then again, perhaps she's just really fucking tired and she's one of those people who can sleep anywhere.

I really hate people who can fall asleep at the drop of a hat, anywhere they want to, whenever they want to. I have to calm my mind before I can sleep, and it drives me *insane*!

Chapter Twelve
LEILA

"Leila. Darlin', you have to wake up." I swear I can hear Caleb Drake telling me to wake up but we've never slept together, I *know* I would remember that! He's never even been in my bedroom, not that I don't want him to join me in there though.

"Caleb?" His name is out of my mouth before I can think about what I'm saying. I know I'm waking up and confused about who's speaking. "Hey handsome." I smile.

"Yeah Darlin', it's me. We're almost at your Mum's, it's time for you to wake up." His voice is so gentle, like he doesn't really want to wake me up, that thought makes me smile. I have to be honest, I don't want to open my eyes when I have Caleb talking all low and gentle to me. "I'm sorry Darlin', I didn't realise just how much sleep you didn't get last night. If I had I wouldn't have pushed you to leave this afternoon."

Now it's all coming back to me. I'm sleeping in Caleb's car, on our way to my Mum's before we head to the Weaver's party weekend tomorrow.

"I'm awake, it's OK." I sit up abruptly to look out the windscreen, only to discover that we're parked in the car park of the main playground in town.

"Hey, Darlin' relax. You're allowed to take a few minutes to wake up." Obviously, he doesn't know where my mind wandered to as he gently woke me up, so he thinks I'm in a dazed panic *because* I'm waking and *not* because he's the one doing the waking.

"No, I can't. We can't stay parked here like this." I can hear the panic in my voice, I must sound insane to him but I can't help it. "Someone will see us." As soon as the words leave my lips, I realise how they must have sounded to him. I turn to face him, to explain, apologise, until I see the hurt settle on his face as he pulls away from me.

"Well, OK, I understand." He says it with such a sharp nod, thinking that he understands what I mean.

"No!" I reach out and pull him back to me, as much as I can in the car with the centre console between us. "Don't, please." I beg him, placing my palm to his cheek. "You misunderstood what I meant. If someone spots me sitting here, it will be all over town that I'm here with a man." I tell him, closing my eyes, trying with everything in me to wake up properly so that I can explain it correctly.

"I don't understand Darlin'. Please explain why I shouldn't be confused and a little annoyed right now."

"Look, this town still has a small town mentality. It's not small anymore but everyone likes to know what everyone else is doing. Especially the people who have lived here forever, grown up here. It's infuriating, yet comforting all at the same time." I swallow roughly, then look back out the window to see who is walking around this afternoon. It looks pretty clear for now. "I didn't tell my Mum you were driving me to see her today and her finding out from someone else before we get there, well, it won't go down very well, at all."

"So, let me get this straight. She knows *you're* visiting, she just doesn't know that I'm with you. Is that right?" I can't speak, so I look over at him and nod, he nods right along with me. "My next question then would be, why? Why didn't you tell her I would be with you? Are you embarrassed to be seen with me?"

"What?! Oh my god, no! No, that's not even *close* to being the reason I didn't tell her!" I blurt out. "Shit, I'm screwing this up!"

"Explain it to me then, Darlin'." His voice is soft, gentle, and yet demanding an explanation.

"Well, I had two choices." I tell him, ticking them off on my fingers as I speak. "One, was to be honest and tell her I was bringing a boy home."

"Man." He growls.

"Sorry." I nod, no-one could describe Caleb Drake as a boy anymore, so he's completely right to correct me. "Man. I *could* have told her I was bringing a man home. Or two, I could just show up with said man and explain why you were here."

He nods slowly and all I can think of is the time we're sitting here out in the open while I explain this to him, someone is likely to spot me, even in a car that isn't mine. *Especially* because I'm in a car that isn't mine or local! With a man no-one in town knows.

"Are we explaining the engagement to your Mum?"

"No." I shake my head vigorously. "We cannot do that under any circumstance. Do you understand me, Caleb? She will get all these ideas, wrong ideas, about us and tell the world. Then, when the inevitable break up happens, she's going to be heartbroken."

"But you won't be?"

"I won't be what?" I ask, confused.

"Heartbroken?"

"Well, we'll still be friends, Caleb. It's not like this is a real engagement or relationship. So no, I don't think I'm going to be heartbroken when we eventually break up." I say, trying to convince myself as much as him that this is all just fantastic. "We'll still have our friendship. Right?"

"Right." He nods, sharply and moves away from me to sit properly in his seat again, starting the car up. "Direct me to your Mum's house so we can get this party started then."

As I direct Caleb to my Mum's house, I can't help feeling the tension in the car. I know I didn't explain myself properly and I'm still trying to work out how to do just that. I decide that he's about to find out when he meets my beautifully strange Mum, so I don't say a thing. The closer we get to the house, the more my mind wanders to how he's going to view my childhood home. I know he's told me about his house and its humble beginnings but my Mum's place really doesn't compare in the slightest to what his Dad managed to build. There wasn't a Dad to make it better, or build anything for his family. Not for a long time anyway.

I take a shaky deep breath when I direct him to pull into her driveway and we stop. I try to look at the house from his point of view, from an outsiders perspective and I can't help the sigh that escapes me.

"I'm not here to judge Darlin' and if *you* think I'm that kind of a guy, perhaps this engagement, fake or not, isn't the best idea. I can leave you here with your Mum for the weekend and tell Brian either you couldn't get away or we broke up. Whichever one is easier for you." Caleb speaks so quietly beside me, that I have strain to hear him, the rejection is clear though.

"It's not what you're thinking that's the problem, Caleb, it's me. I'm so used to being out at Drake Wines, that coming home makes me realise that I don't *actually* live in that world. My Mum, she's fought hard to give us everything, it hasn't always been easy for her though. I know now that it wasn't always easy for your folks either but that doesn't stop *me* from feeling less than. Kids can be pretty fucking cruel to other kids and adults aren't a whole lot better."

"But you said it's still a small town. Surely everyone understood the situation and they were kinder to your family?" Ahh I love his innocence and kindness.

"You would think so, wouldn't you, but no, the fact that they knew exactly what had happened was even worse than my Mum just showing up one day without anyone knowing our history. When people know everything about you, it's a lot harder to escape it." Caleb reaches over and takes my hand gently in his and even though I don't want to need his kindness, I take it. "I know you don't look at anyone like that, Caleb, it's just where my mind goes." He pulls our joined hands to his lips and kisses my knuckles in a move that can only be described as fucking hot.

"I really don't, Leila. Your Mum has worked hard to give you and your brother everything, I think she did a pretty amazing job. Just saying." He says with a shrug of his shoulders. "I evaluate people on the way they treat others and how they behave in difficult circumstances. I do believe that you pass with flying fucking colours, Darlin.'"

"Thank you, Caleb." I say sincerely, while wishing there wasn't a blush creeping up my cheeks. Why can't I just take a compliment without making it a big deal? "We should get out of the car and head inside, otherwise my Mum is going to burst out that door, then the entire neighbourhood will know I'm home." We both step out of the car and reach for our bags.

"And that would be a bad thing?" I can hear the curiosity in his voice.

"Not normally, no, but having you with me will have everyone even more curious than usual and there will be people 'popping in for a quick visit', who haven't been here in months." I roll my eyes, letting him know that it's just plain annoying and predictable.

"So, you're not trying to hide because you're ashamed to be seen with me then?" Caleb asks, his face the picture of innocence and I can't help laughing at him. The man sure knows how to lay it on thick. He's far from innocent, that I am certain about. He grabs our bags in one hand and closes the door. I reach to take mine off him but he shrugs me off. "I've got them."

I'm not going to argue with him over bags, I could have taken mine out of his hand, just as much as he could have handed it over but that's Caleb for you. He's a gentleman.

I walk to the front door and just as I raise my hand to knock, it flies open. "Leila! You're here!" I brace myself for the body that will be attached to mine in less than a second. "It's damned good to see you, Sweetheart. It's been too long since your last visit. They're working you too hard over at that new place of yours. I swear, if I could get up there, I'd give them a piece of my mind for working my baby too hard."

"Mum!" I sigh, closing my eyes for a second in embarrassment. "They're not working me to the bone, they're looking after me, OK?" As she steps back from me, she nods her agreement, but I can see in her eyes she doesn't agree at all. That's when she notices Caleb standing behind me. I don't need to look over my shoulder to know that his smile is wide and his eyes are gleaming with amusement.

Before my Mum can ask, I introduce them.

"Mum, this is Caleb. Caleb *Drake*." I emphasize his last name so that maybe, just maybe, she might make the connection between Caleb and my workplace. "Caleb, this is my Mum, Kim Phillips."

"Good afternoon ma'am, how are you today? It's a real pleasure to meet you." My Mum's gaze darts between Caleb and myself for the next minute, I see the exact second she understands that this man is part of the family that runs Vines.

"Let's get inside before the gossips notice there's a handsome young man in my house and they all decide they need to come over to get a peek." She ushers us into the house, looking around the street and then quickly shutting the door behind us. "Call me Kim. None of this ma'am or Mrs

Phillips rubbish, you hear me?" Caleb has the good sense to nod his agreement.

"Agreed ma'am, I mean Kim. Thank you." That smirk of his that I love, spreads across his face and my mum doesn't stand a damned chance.

"You're welcome." She smiles with an ease I haven't seen in a while, back at him. "Now, have you kids eaten yet, or can I whip something up for you? I can't cook anything as fancy as Leila here but I don't do a bad job, even if I do say so myself."

"You do perfectly fine Mum, where do you think I learnt all my skills from?" I ask her.

"While you were training as a pastry chef, obviously." She says, without even hesitating but we both know that my lessons started right here, in this kitchen. Just about everything we ate was made from scratch, we couldn't afford much else.

"Of course, Ma. You don't mind if we stay for the night do you?" Before she can answer, Caleb speaks up.

"It's OK if you don't want me to stay Mrs Phillips." She sends him a glare. "Sorry, Kim. I can go find myself a hotel room for the night." It's then that I notice that he actually didn't bring his bag inside. I think I fall for him a little bit more just because he didn't assume that he could stay the night.

"Don't be silly, Caleb. Any friend of Leila's is absolutely welcome to stay in my house." She turns her back to us and starts to pull a rather large pot out of the fridge. "Give me a hand would you, Love?" She asks me but before I can move, Caleb sweeps in like a damned action hero and takes the pot out of her hands, placing it on the stove top. "Thank you, Sweetheart."

"Wow! You're doing OK for yourself here, Caleb. A term of endearment already from you, Ma? That's got to be a record of some kind, doesn't it?" I can't help joking with her. None of the other guys I've bought home have managed to earn anything close to that, even after months and in some cases a year or more.

"They didn't deserve it. Caleb here, he does. Isn't that right Sweetie?"

"Control yourself Ma. That's two in a matter of minutes and the second one was a shortened version of the first. Control yourself woman!" I laugh as she swats at me with the tea towel she's holding.

"Go on, take your stuff to your room." Her smile is big, I think they can see it from the moon!

"OK. Caleb can put his stuff in Matt's room. He's not coming back tonight, is he?" Ma smiles as she turns her back to me. What she says next almost kills me.

"No, Matt isn't coming home tonight but Caleb can't use that room either, sorry, Leila."

"Why not, Ma?" I'm suddenly feeling very suspicious.

"The room is full of stuff and there's no room for anyone to sleep in there." There's never any clutter in this house. Not for as long as I can remember.

"What are you talking about, Ma?"

"I'm sure you two won't be too bothered about sharing your old bed, Leila. Your mother isn't as old and tired as you'd like to believe. I realise you kids sleep together before marriage and all that stuff these days. It's not like it was unheard of even back in the Dark Ages when I was young." She laughs. My mother laughs at her own silly joke like she thinks Caleb and I are going to fuck each other's brains out the minute we're left alone.

"Caleb and I, we aren't together, Mum." She chooses to ignore me and focus on Caleb instead.

Turning to him, she says, "There's a Queen size bed in Leila's old room, I'm sure you two can share all that space, don't you agree with me, Caleb?" I drop my head into my hands to hide my embarrassment and shake my head. I'm going to kill her. I swear to the heavens above, she's going to take her last breath tonight for doing this to me.

"You know Mrs, I'm sorry I mean, Kim, I think you're absolutely right. There should be more than enough space for the two of us on a bed that size. What do you think Darlin'?" I think I might take them both out tonight. I can manage that, I'm almost positive I could. "I'll go out to the car and grab my bag so that I have my pajamas." Then he's gone.

"Damn it, Mum! What the hell are you up to? Is Matt's room really unusable tonight?"

"I'm not up to anything. You didn't tell me you were bringing someone with you. Perhaps if you'd given me a little bit of notice I would have made the effort to clean out Matt's room a little, as it stands, I didn't." She says with a huff and I can't argue with her, she's not wrong. "I don't think it's going to be a hardship sleeping next to that gorgeous young man anyway. Believe me when I tell you that he doesn't think it's a bad idea at all either." Before I can tell her that she's completely off the mark, Caleb walks back in.

"Do you want to show me to our room so that I can drop the bags in there?" That smirk is back, it's like he knows that the idea of sleeping next to him, in the same bed, has thrown me for a loop and he likes it.

"Sure, follow me." I know when I've been defeated. With these two teaming up on me, I'll never win.

"Dinner will be ready when you get back. It's simple but it will fill you." She pauses for a minute. "You're not a vegetarian are you, Caleb?"

"Not a chance, Kim." Caleb replies, at the same time as I groan out a "Mum!"

"Well, you can't be too careful these days. I don't want anyone suing me because I fed them chicken when they only want food without eyes. You know that means they can't eat potatoes? You know, because they have eyes." I roll my eyes and keep walking towards the other end of the house, Caleb chuckling as he follows behind me.

"Don't laugh. You'll only encourage her bad jokes and bad behaviour." I admonish him.

"I think she's adorable."

"Thank you Sweetie." She yells from the kitchen, causing Caleb to let out a very loud laugh.

"You're welcome." He yells back. Yeah, I think I can definitely take the two of them out and dig a hole in the backyard for them. "Does your Mum hear everything?"

"It's a Mum thing, especially when you do it on your own." I answer him with a shrug. "Here, you can put the bags in here." I say, opening the door to my childhood room and gesturing inside.

"Where are you going?"

"To see if Matt's room really is overtaken with crap, so I know if she's toying with us." I inform him.

"Does your Mum do that often?" He asks, as he drops the bags just inside the door and follows me. "Tell you untruths, just to mess with you?"

"They're lies, Caleb, not untruths and no. She very rarely lies about anything to me and that's why I want to check if what she said is true because that woman doesn't hoard *anything*." I say as I open the door to my brother's room and gasp in shock. "Holy fuck! She was telling the truth. How the hell does she even get in here to move stuff around and where the hell does Matt sleep when he comes home?"

"He doesn't because he rarely comes home anymore, Leila." I jump, surprised by her voice. "I knew you'd have to come in and check if it was true."

"What do you mean he rarely comes home anymore?"

"Exactly that, Sweetheart. It's pretty rare and when he does, he doesn't stay overnight. He comes for dinner, sometimes he stays for a movie but he's always gone before it's time for bed." I'll kill him, he's closer than I am and he's supposed to be checking up on her and making sure everything's OK. "He does check up on me, Leila, so don't go getting your knickers in a twist. He just doesn't want to stay the night with his Mum and I can understand that."

"So, you took revenge and took over his room?"

"Yeah, something like that." She laughs wickedly. "Come on now. I warmed up some chicken soup and warmed up the bread I made this morning. You don't want either one to get cold."

Caleb steps aside to let my Mum and myself go first, then he follows up behind me. "Your Mum makes her own bread?" He whispers into the back of my ear.

"Yes, I do Sweetie and it's delicious." Mum says without turning around to look at him and I can't help smiling. "Just fair warning Caleb, there isn't much that happens in this house that I don't hear. Do we understand each other?" This time she does turn around to look at him and even I kind of shrink back from her glare, but not Caleb, he stands his ground.

"Yes ma'am." He answers her, reverting to not using her first name, as I say, "Ma we're adults."

"I know you're adults but that doesn't mean I can't lay down the law around here, it is still my house you know, Leila."

"I know that Ma but seriously? We're in our twenties, we're not teenagers!" I roll my eyes at her. "Not to mention, your room is at the other end of the house, you won't hear a thing."

"There won't be anything to hear Kim, I promise." Caleb shines that gorgeous smile of his on my Mum and I can see her physically melt, feeling almost relieved by his confession.

"Thank you, Caleb." She smiles at him in answer. A second later her eyes skip past him to me and she scowls.

"Give us a few minutes to clean up, Ma and then we'll come into the kitchen so that you can feed us, OK?" She huffs and then leaves us alone.

"I see where you get that spitfire streak of yours." Caleb says, laughing as he heads back to my bedroom. Our bedroom for the night, I guess.

I walk into the room behind him and look up just as he rips his t-shirt up over his head, throwing it onto the bed, then he bends over to pick up his bag. I'm still standing in the doorway, mouth open and quite frankly, enjoying the scene in front of me. That thought pulls me out of my daydream. "What the hell are you doing?" I squeak out.

"Getting cleaned up to sit down to a meal with your Mum." He says it more like a question than a statement, like he's not sure about what he's doing now that I've questioned him. "I'm sorry. Did you want to have the first shower?" He asks as he sits on my bed, half naked!

Shower? What? "No. I'm good." I turn to walk away but then I turn back to him. "Didn't you have a shower before we left? Do you really need another one now?"

He smirks. "You know, you're right. I can wait until the morning for another one."

I turn and start to walk away as he pulls his t-shirt back over his head and lets it drop down his body. I don't want to watch that progress, OK I know I'm lying to myself, so I keep walking, knowing that he can catch me up in a couple of long strides. "To the right just here is the bathroom. You saw Matt's bedroom. This is the spare room." I pause for a second at that door, wondering why Caleb can't sleep in there and then I remember she took the bed out to make room for all the different hobbies she's taken up in the last few years to try and keep her mind busy. "This is, of course, the living room and you've already been in the kitchen and dining room. Through that door there is Mums bedroom and her own bathroom." It's a short and sweet tour of the house, there's nothing else to see.

"Ahhh there you two are."

"We were only gone for about five minutes Ma, if that." I say rolling my eyes at her.

"Well, dinner is ready, so sit at the table and I'll bring it over for you." She smiles, and I can see it in her eyes. She's up to something and it's not going to be a good something for me.

I turn towards the dining table, that's when I see what she's up to and I groan. "Oh my." I don't get to finish speaking because Caleb talks over me.

"What's all of this, Kim?" His voice is full of excitement, like he already knows exactly what she's done and he can't wait for her to confirm it for him.

"Oh that? That's just some old photos of Leila that I thought you might like to have a look at. You know, for some fun."

"Mum! This isn't fun! Caleb doesn't need to see any of my old baby photos and what not." I cry.

"Oh but I do, Darlin'." Caleb says. He's already sitting at the table flipping through an old photo album.

"Why Mum? Just why?" I whine at her smiling face.

"Because I thought your boyfriend would love to see some photos of when you were younger." Is her answer.

"We're not." I start, but Caleb interrupts me.

"Her *boyfriend* very much appreciates your thoughtfulness, Kim." Damn it, there's that sexy smirk again. Sighing I sit down at the table to eat the chicken and vegetable soup that my traitorous mother made, along with her delicious bread. I've missed eating with her but this move of hers, showing Caleb these old pictures and telling him stories for the next few hours is as awkward as it is humorous.

Watching Caleb relax and have fun, laughing even if it is at my expense most of the time and telling his own tales from his childhood, without the sadness of his parents' deaths marring his happiness, is something else. I have my Mum to thank for that. She has this amazing ability to make people relax and just enjoy.

"Well kids, I think I need to head to bed." Looking my way, she says, "You're OK with sorting everything that you two need for the night, right?"

"Of course Ma. Do you need anything before we go to bed?"

"No Sweetheart, I'm good but thank you." She hugs me tight. "Do you two need to get up early so you can head out in the morning?" She asks, as she pulls out of my embrace.

"No Kim, you've got us for the morning if that's OK?" Caleb smiles at her.

"I'll let you two sleep. Honestly, I sleep until I wake these days. No alarms required, it's an amazing feeling after all these years." Caleb gets to his feet and pulls her into a hug. They whisper something to each other and then the hug gets a little tighter, before they step away from each other. "Night Leila, Caleb. Sleep well, I'll see you both in the morning."

"Night Kim." Caleb says as I say, "Night Ma, love you."

"Love you too, Sweetie." Then she's gone and I turn to find Caleb stacking the albums in neat piles.

"Leave those Caleb, Mum will put them away in some specific order tomorrow when she gets up." I tell him, resting my hand on his arm to still his movements, and he nods, then follows me to the bedroom.

"Which side do you want?" It's a simple question and one I know he's waiting for me to answer. I can't speak as I stand at the foot of the bed, just staring at it. It still has the same comforter on it from my late teens and I feel a bit weird sleeping in it with Caleb. "Leila?"

"Hmmmm?" Is all I manage in reply.

"I can sleep on the floor if you're more comfortable with that?"

"What? No! No, you don't need to do that. Don't be ridiculous. It's just a bed. We're just going to sleep in it."

"Exactly." He agrees. "I'm tired and I just want to sleep, so which side do you want Darlin'?" Damn it! I wish he hadn't called me Darlin', I was just starting to get my thoughts back in order.

I look up to find him looking at me curiously. "Left. I'll take the left side."

"So, the closest to the door or the window?" He asks to clarify.

"Door. Closest to the door, please." I shake my head to get my brain in working order and look him in the eyes. "Do you want to use the bathroom first?"

"Sure." Is his simple reply, then he's gone. I take the opportunity to pull out my pajamas. A few very short minutes later, he's back and I realise he never took anything to change into.

"Your turn." He says with a smile.

"Thanks." I turn and go to the bathroom, do my business, and get changed. When I get back to the bedroom, Caleb is already in bed and he's looks cosy in there. Almost like he belongs. If only teenage me could see the boy that ends up in her bed, she might not feel so out of place in the world. Then I remind myself that he's not in my bed, *in my bed*, he's just sharing it for the night and the next few nights as well.

I jump into bed, careful not to touch him, then turn off the light.

"Goodnight, Leila." His deep voice says quietly.

"Goodnight, Caleb." I say just as quietly, trying not to disturb the peace. Peace is a strong word because I don't feel very peaceful with Caleb Drake lying next to me.

"Sleep well, Darlin'."

"You too, Handsome." I whisper, pretty sure that he didn't hear me. He rolls over, his back to mine and I lie there for I don't know how long trying not to enjoy the heat radiating off his gorgeous body. That's how I fall asleep, eventually anyway, very aware of the man lying behind me while trying not to touch him. I wonder if he's making the same efforts not to touch me?

The next morning, I wake up feeling rested. I'm warm, comfy because my body is wrapped around a nice warm, hard body. I snuggle in closer, enjoying that warmth and comfort, until I remember this isn't a dream and I know exactly who I'm snuggling up to!

"Crap! I'm so sorry Caleb!" I say, trying to jump away from him but his arm tightens around me to hold me where I am. Unfortunately, my leg that was resting over his jumps up a little too high and grazes against his hard cock. Geezus! I freeze, not sure where to go from here.

"Morning wood." He says with a shrug of his shoulder, pulling me impossibly closer to his half naked body, like there's nothing unusual going on here and well, perhaps for him there isn't but it's been a hell of a long time since I've woken up wrapped around another human being.

Did he just say morning wood? Is that his answer? For real? Guess that knocks any and all fantasies that he finds me even remotely attractive out the door. It was just a natural reaction to waking up, not me being wrapped around him at all. Great! Fucking brilliant!

Chapter Thirteen
CALEB

I wake up hot. My body over-heated and I can't work out why, until I open my eyes. Even then, it takes me a minute or two to recall where I am. When my memory kicks in and I realise I'm in Kim Phillips home and that the heat is coming from the body draped over mine, I smile happily.

Leila Phillips body is draped over mine and I'm going to enjoy every fucking minute of the feeling as I can.

Slowly, I stretch out from lying slightly on my side, so that I'm completely on my back and it's a relief when Leila moves with me. I move my right arm to rest it behind my head, while my left arm wraps around her waist, holding her tightly to me. One of her legs lies across the both of mine, her ankle rests between my legs, just above my ankles and she's got a hand resting in the middle of my chest.

If there's a better position to wake up in, I've never been in it and I doubt it exists.

I relax and close my eyes. I don't want to wake Leila up and spoil this cuddlefest we've got going on. Call me a pussy, or whatever else you want but when you've got the woman that you've been dreaming about for just on a year wrapped around your body, you enjoy every fucking second you can before she wakes and realises what she's doing.

"Caleb?" She says my name so quietly, I almost miss it falling from her sleepy lips. I smile knowing that I'm the man she's thinking about as she drifts of out sleep and into consciousness.

"Yes Darlin." I answer her quietly, trying not to freak her which doesn't work so well.

"Crap! I'm so sorry, Caleb!" Leila yells, trying to jump away from me as fast as she can now that she's awake. I don't let her get too far away from me though as I tighten my grip around waist to hold her tight up against me. Unfortunately, the leg that was lying over mine jumps with the rest of her and her knee grazes my balls and dick. My entire body reacts to the lightest of touches as though it was hit by a lightning bolt, by stiffening. Honestly, she could have touched me with a feather and I'd have had the same reaction. Look, I'm not a young guy but I'm not exactly old yet either, so when a person of the opposite sex, one of whom I'm exceptionally attracted to, touches me in the general area of my cock, it's going to react.

"Morning wood." I say with a shrug of my shoulder, trying to pull her impossibly closer to me like there's nothing for her to worry about and there isn't, it's perfectly natural, human response.

"Of course that's all it is." She responds, barely relaxing. Guess I fucked that one up hey?

I move my head down so that my lips are resting on the top of her head and drop a light kiss there. Her body stiffens and I get the feeling she's trying to work out how to get her head off my chest. I let her untangle our bodies so that she can get out of here but she's not going to get very far until I can clear this up.

"It's morning wood combined with a beautiful woman touching me." She's wriggling around as I speak, trying to get away from me, while I'm not holding her down, I'm not really ready to let her go yet either. "Relax Leila. Please?" I ask her, moving my hand from behind my head to rest it on hers that is on my chest still, over my rapidly beating heart. My naked chest. "Let's just enjoy the moment and wake up properly before we go getting all self-conscious, OK?"

"Sure." Her answer is quiet but she relaxes and cuddles back into my side. Luckily, the room, as well as the rest of the house, are very quiet. I don't even know what time it is. but I'm not moving to check my phone. I get the feeling the minute I move in any way, she's going to take the opportunity to bolt. I just want to enjoy having Leila in my arms without any pressure. Not pressure of a relationship, fake or real, or sex or our friendship. Just relaxing, together.

So, I lie there, my eyes closed and just breathe, without pulling my arms away from holding her but they're also relaxed enough that she could get away, if that's what she wanted to do. After a minute or two, I feel Leila's body relaxing beside me. Lying there for the next ten minutes just feels right. It feels like this is where she belongs. It's where I belong.

"We should probably get up before Mum comes in looking for us." She mumbles into my chest.

"I thought she said she'd let us sleep in this morning?" I mumble onto the top of her head, where my chin has been resting.

She lets out this cute little snort and says, "She doesn't know how to sleep in and I haven't even checked the time yet."

"Me either, but it's not like we stayed up late, so it should be reasonably early. Right?" I can't remember the last time I slept past 8am. "I haven't checked yet either." I admit.

"I'm too comfortable to move." Her admission makes me happier than it should.

"Me too." After agreeing neither of us wants to move, we lie in comfortable silence for a few more minutes. I don't know about Leila but I'm savouring every minute of this morning.

"We should at least check the time." She mumbles.

"Uhuh." Then we continue lying there in comfortable silence for a few more minutes. It would seem that I'm not the only one hoping to draw this out for as long as Kim will let us.

"No really we should."

"Then why aren't you moving, Darlin'?"

"Why aren't you moving, Handsome?" The arm wrapped around her waist pulls her a little closer to me when she calls me that.

"I'm not moving because you're not moving."

"Well that's just an excuse, Caleb." She laughs.

"You're using me as a pillow, I don't think it's an excuse Darlin'." I say laughing until I feel her starting to pull away that is. "Where are you going?"

"Well, I'm using you as a pillow, so I thought I'd move off you. You know, so you can get up and get this day started." She pushes against my arm and in this position I won't be able to hold her forever but I'm not going to give up easily.

"I didn't say it because I'm uncomfortable or trying to get you off." I pause, knowing that the last part had a double meaning, it was unintentional, honestly. "I was simply explaining why I hadn't moved yet, not saying that I wanted to get moving. I'm enjoying the peace."

"OK." She says quietly. "I guess we can stay like this a little bit longer."

"Well, I wouldn't want to put you out or anything Darlin', maybe we *should* get moving." I make a move like I'm going to move her off me and sit up but she's not having it and pushes her weight down on me to stop me from moving. I smile, happy that my fake out worked. Sometimes having older siblings is helpful in the world outside of your own family.

"A few more minutes won't hurt, right?" She mumbles.

"Absolutely not." I reassure her. Abso-fucking-lutely not. In fact, I think another hour lying here wouldn't hurt a soul. It sure wouldn't hurt my soul, my heart maybe in the end but I'm not willing to think that far ahead, yet.

Keeping my eyes closed, I lie there, holding her close to me, enjoying the weight of her body pushing into my side and listen to her breathing slow down. It makes me happy to know that she's comfortable enough with me to relax like this. It's so nice, I wish we could stay here in this cocoon forever.

We both jump slightly when there's a light knock on the door.

"Are you kids awake yet?" There's silence for a few seconds and I hope that Kim has walked away when we didn't answer her. No such luck for me and I can't help sighing when she continues. "I hope I'm not interrupting anything but I think you really should make a start to the day."

"Ma!" Leila draws out the word, mumbled into my chest but apparently she's loud enough for her Mum to hear her.

"Nice to know you're still hard to get out of bed, Leila Phillips." Kim grumbles through the closed door. "Are you as difficult to wake up, Caleb?"

"No, I'm up, Kim." My whole body is shaking with laughter, making Leila's body bounce up and down with it. She slaps me hard on the stomach and I 'oomph' so loudly from the hit, that her Mum comments.

"Stop hitting the man and get your butt out here to help me make breakfast young lady." There's a beat of silence as I try to control my laughter, even with the death glare Leila's sending my way doing crazy things to me. I know, I'm a sick, twisted man. "I'm serious, Leila. Move. Your. Butt. Now!"

"Yeah, come on, Leila, move that cute butt of yours and go make me breakfast!" I smack her on said amazing butt and she jumps up to a sitting position within 2.5 seconds, making me laugh again, especially when I hear her chuckling as she walks away!

"Did you? You didn't? Did you?" She stutters out, the grin I know I shouldn't have, spreads across my face.

"Are you asking if I just smacked your arse? Cause Darlin', if you need to ask, then I need to work on my technique!" Her jaw drops open, her eyes widen in shock and she keeps making these squeaking noises, like she's trying to get words but she just can't. "I'm think I'm going to go have that shower now, if you don't mind?" I throw the covers off, revealing the form-fitting boxer briefs that I wore to bed last night. I must thank Jules for putting me onto this brand because he was right, they *are* very comfortable *and* they show off a guys assets quite nicely.

"You. You can't leave the room like *that*!" The words fall out of her mouth as she waves her hand up and down my body.

"Like what?" I ask innocently. I have no intention of walking around her mother's home in just my underwear but she doesn't know that, obviously.

"That!" Her head nods my way, as her hand waves up and down still, indicating all of me. I turn to face her, until that point, she'd only seen me from an angle that showed her my hip and one cheek but now, now she gets the full frontal view and her gasp builds up my ego. I'm not hard, well not fully anyway, I'm only half-mast but she doesn't know that. "Oh my god!" She covers her mouth with her hand, trying to hide the fact that her mouth is hanging open in shock. I'm not the biggest guy, I've seen bigger in changerooms but I'm no slouch in the cock department either.

"Like, this, you mean?" I wave my hands out to the side, like I'm on a stupid game show, barely holding in a grin.

"You'll give my Mum a heart attack, Caleb!" Her voice is barely a squeak that I'm starting to think my underwear aren't as flattering as I first thought.

"I think your Mum has seen a cock or two in her time, Leila, she has a son after all and this one is covered, so I think she'll survive."

"Caleb." She actually *growls* my name and I have to turn away from her as my cock takes notice of that growl and tries his hardest to pop out the top of the band of my boxers to see what's going on.

"Don't worry, Leila. I wouldn't *dare* embarrass or shame you." I announce as I pull on my sweatpants and t-shirt, before finding my toiletries and walking out of the room, leaving her trying to find some words.

"There's clean towels on the bench, Caleb." Kim yells from the kitchen, making me wonder just how much of our conversation she actually heard.

"Thank you, Kim." I yell back, even though I'm pretty fucking sure she'd have heard me even if I'd whispered my thanks. She might have even heard it if I'd simply thought it, who knows, mums are magical beings.

Making my way into the bathroom, I close the door quietly behind me, not wanting to scare either of them because I'm annoyed. I've seen girls at university who walked on eggshells because they never knew how their boyfriend or guy 'friend' was going to react to something and I *never* want to be *that* guy.

I strip out of my clothes as the water heats up, then I step under the steamy water. I'd love to take my time but I don't know how long the hot water lasts here and I know that Leila will want a shower before we head out today. You can call me a lot of things and I'll accept them but selfish, whether I'm making love or saving you some hot water, I am not.

I step out of the shower, dry off and wrap the towel around my waist. Picking up my clothes, I think about what Leila said about giving Kim a heart attack, so I pull my t-shirt over my head as well before leaving the bathroom and heading back to the bedroom to get dressed.

I close the door behind me, not wanting either of the women in the house to walk in on me naked. OK, so I wouldn't *mind* Leila catching an eyeful but not in Kim's house where I can't do anything about it.

I pull off my t-shirt, dropping it back into my duffel bag but just as I drop the towel, there's a light knock on the door and before I can say a word or make a move, the door flies open and Leila walks in the room, just as I pull on my underwear.

"Fuck!"

"Mum wanted me to let you know – oh! Oh! Oh. My God! I am *so* sorry Caleb, I should have waited for an answer before I barged in here." She *says* she's sorry but she isn't making any effort whatsoever to look away or cover her eyes and while I know I *should* make the effort to cover myself up, *she's* the one who walked in here without waiting, so she gets what she gets. The fact is, she caught me half bent over to grab my jeans out of my bag and I'm still frozen in that spot, I can't seem to move and apparently, neither can Leila.

"What was it that Kim wanted me to know?" I ask, as I finish bending down to grab my jeans out of the bag.

"What?" Leila asks and I look over to see her staring at my butt, so of course, I flex my cheeks a little and I'm rewarded with a quiet gasp.

"Kim? What did she want you to tell me?" I ask again, as I step into said jeans, pulling them up over the area that her eyes seem to be glued to. "Leila. Leila." I repeat her name to get her attention. "My eyes are up here, Darlin'." I say with a chuckle and I know that'll grab her attention.

"I know that!" She snaps, as her eyes meet mine and I watch as a beautiful blush creeps up her neck, over her cheeks. I want desperately to follow that blush with my lips. "Kim, I mean Mum, wanted me to let you know that breakfast will be ready in a few minutes. In fact, it's probably ready now."

"OK, well I'll get dressed and meet you ladies in the kitchen." When Leila doesn't move to leave, I have to ask her something even though I know I'm poking the bear. "If that's OK with you, of course? I mean, do we give Kim that heart attack or do you want me to wear some clothes?" I can't resist smirking at her as I see the fire lighting up her eyes. I love it when she gets all sassy and bites back, it's fucking sexy as hell.

"Put some clothes on Caleb." She says with a huff as she spins on her heels and storms out the door.

"As you wish, Darlin', as you wish." I call after her and she flips me the bird as she closes the door with some force behind her.

Damn it, my snap decision when Brian called me yesterday might have been my biggest mistake yet. I can't get through this weekend without wanting to get closer to her physically. I can't pretend to be in love with her, touch her, kiss her for show and not *feel* it with every part of my soul.

To put it mildly, I'm fucked because I'm pretty sure it won't be pretend for me, I just wish I knew if it will be for her. I could ask, I know that but where does that leave us all weekend if she says she's just doing a friend a favour? Awkward, awkward as fuck *that's* where that leaves us and our friendship means the world to me, so I won't screw it up.

Chapter Fourteen
LEILA

I didn't *mean* to walk in on Caleb half naked. Not really , I didn't! I'm not going to deny it wasn't a damned nice sight to see, nor am I going to say that I regret it, I don't. What I *am* saying is that it was a mistake, in more ways than one, honestly.

"Ma!" I yell as I walk back into the kitchen looking for the woman who is supposed to love me more than anything else in the world, even my brother! "Mother, where did you run off to?"

"Stop yelling, Leila! I just went to my bedroom, I didn't abandon you!" She waves me off like she didn't just send me into that room on purpose just now.

"You did that on purpose, Ma! You knew! You *knew* he'd just gotten out of the shower." I whisper yell, hoping that Caleb isn't on his way up the hallway yet.

"Of course I knew he was out of the shower! Just like you did, we *both* heard the water turn off, don't pretend you didn't." She huffs at me, as she checks on the food cooking on the stove.

"Don't you act all innocent with me, Ma, I *know* what you did. I *know* you can hear *everything* in this house." My eyes dart to the doorway to check if Caleb is close. "You *knew* he didn't have enough time to be dressed yet and you *still* sent me in there to get him!" I accuse her, still whisper yelling.

"Now, you listen to me young lady. If you went barging into that room, knowing that young man had just gotten out of the shower, without knocking or waiting for him to answer your knock, then that's on *you*! I brought you up with better manners than that and we both know it!" She sends a glare my way and I know she's not impressed with my accusation but I *know* she did it on purpose. "Now, if you did walk in there and saw that young man naked, or even *half* naked, I don't see the issue with it. I mean you slept with him last night, Leila, I assumed you two were already pretty *close*."

"You assumed wrong, Ma and you know you did!" I hiss again.

"I know nothing of the sort."

"Good morning ladies, how are we this morning?" Caleb says louder than necessary from the doorway as he enters the kitchen. "Something smells delicious Mrs ... sorry, Kim." He walks over and leaves a light kiss on her cheek and she blushes. My *mother* blushes as Caleb steps back and looks towards me.

She pats him on the cheek before telling him to sit himself at the table and we'll bring over the food. When he offers to help, she shoos him away as he laughs at her antics and she giggles. My *mother* giggles! I've never heard that noise come out of my mother before, to be fair though, I get it because he's flashing her that lopsided grin that most people would call a cocky smirk, except on Caleb, it's so damned endearing it's almost sickening!

"Ma." She ignores me and laughs at something else that Caleb says, quietly and only to her. Are they flirting? Is Caleb *flirting with my mother?* "Caleb." Neither of them hear me so I speak louder. "*Caleb!*"

"What can I do for you, Leila?" He looks at me and there's a twinkle of mischief in his eyes. He knows exactly what he's doing! "Here, can you take the plates and cutlery please?"

"Caleb, why don't you sit down and relax." Ma says, sending me a dirty look.

"That's OK, Kim, I don't mind helping out. I'm not here for a free lunch, or breakfast, as the case may be, Leila knows I like to pay my way." He smiles at me warmly as he takes the plates and cutlery from my hands, fingers brushing mine and I fight the shiver threatening to run through my body at just that light touch.

"That's very sweet of you, Caleb." Ma's smile is so big I think her face just might split in half if she's not careful. It gets even bigger when Caleb winks at her again.

He sets everything on the table, setting up three places for us, as Ma starts taking a few plates over to the table.

"Come and sit down, Leila." Ma gives me a look I can't interpret with her invitation.

"Come sit next to me, Darlin'." Caleb pats the seat next to him as he speaks, winking at *me* this time.

Instead of following his command, I take a seat next to Ma, which causes Caleb to chuckle loudly.

"That wasn't very nice, Leila." Ma says, even as Caleb passes the plate and cutlery he has set next to him over to me.

"That's OK, Kim, I understand why she would want to sit next to you. She misses you and believe me, if I could sit next to my mum for another breakfast, I'd jump at the chance." He smiles but it's sad and my heart melts a little more for this man who has shown his vulnerable, soft underbelly to me on more than one occasion. Ma pats his hand and says something comforting that I should listen to so that I have some chance of being able to repeat it the next time one of the Drakes mention the loss of their parents but my attention is stuck on Caleb. Watching him talk, laugh and joke with my mum as if he's known her forever, I can see that he's just enjoying her company. The company of a mum, something that he's been missing for quite some time.

We eat and I'm pretty quiet, speaking only really when spoken to, my mind drifting to all the times that Caleb has spoken fondly of his parents. As I watch him with my mum, I see now that what I thought was flirting before, is simply him soaking in being in a mums presence. He misses it.

"Leila and I will clean up, won't we?"

"What?" I look up at them both and realise we've all finished eating. I don't even remember eating the delicious, scrambled eggs, bacon and chunky homemade bread, toasted to perfection, but it's all gone. "Of course. Why don't you go do whatever you were going to do before I said we were coming yesterday."

"You don't want me to do that." She mumbles. "That's OK, I'll get another coffee and go sit outside to relax for a while."

"Sure." I kiss her on the cheek as she quickly pours herself another coffee, as Caleb collects up all the dishes and puts them in the sink. I watch as Ma walks out the back door and sits herself on the egg chair that I bought for her last year.

"Is she OK?" I start at Caleb's voice in my ear. He's closer that I thought. "Sorry Darlin', I didn't mean to startle you."

"She'll be OK, right?" I ask no-one in particular, I mean it's not like Caleb can answer that one for me.

"You know I can't tell you that, Darlin' and I don't think you want me to." Gently, he turns me around and gathers me into his arms. In this space, in his arms, I feel warm, safe and cared for, for the first time in a long time, I feel like I don't have to do things on my own. I enjoy that feeling for exactly sixty seconds longer before sighing and pulling away. I want to stay right there, in the safe cocoon of his arms but I can't. I can't start relying on Caleb to be there for me, to help me deal with things because once this week is over, so are we.

"I know but thank you." I sigh and move to the sink. "Let's get these done." I put my hands in the water, a second later, Caleb's hand grip my wrists lightly and he pulls them out of the water, dripping with suds.

"Why don't *you* go have a shower?" He suggests as he dries off my hand with a towel.

"No, you've already helped out here more than you should have. You're a guest, Caleb." I protest, simply because it's instinct not to allow him to care for me, I'm the one who cares for everyone else. Plus, like I said, I can't get used to this.

"Leila." When I don't respond or look at him, he places a finger under my chin and pushes up until my eyes meet his. "Leila, let someone look after *you* for a change. Let *me* look after you, please? You're not a burden, you're no trouble and these are just dishes. Dishes that I helped create and dishes that I'm more than willing to wash up. I've washed up more than this small batch by hand before. Please?" He's almost begging to let him help me, how am I supposed to resist *that*?

"OK." He leans down and drops a light kiss to my forehead, it feels like it lingers a little longer than perhaps it should but I close my eyes for those few seconds and drink it in. It's nice to feel his lips on me, even if it *is* just my forehead.

"Now, go have that shower." He spins me suddenly, smacks my butt, then with a gentle push, directs me out of the kitchen. "I can smell you from here Darlin'." My step falters and without turning around, I flip him the bird because I can't say what I want to, without my mum hearing me. I can hear his full-throated laughter all the way to the bedroom and even as I shut the bathroom door, his laughter is still travelling up the hallway.

I do my best to put his laughter and the touch of his lips out of my head as I shower. I can't but I sure as hell try. My hands running over my body, slick with soap isn't helping at *all.* My imagination runs wild with the possibility that Caleb might join me under the water and it would be his hands soaping up my body, making it slick in more ways than one.

Until my mum's laughter trickles into my conscious from down the hallway and my hands stop, I can't relieve the tension in my body in my mother's house! Most definitely not when she's in the kitchen with the object of attraction, laughing and joking. More frustrated than when I started my shower, I wash off and step out. There's a light knock on the door as I wrap a towel around myself.

"Yes?" Hoping that it's my mum but when the deep timbre of his voice comes from the other side of the door, I can't help the shiver that runs through my body and thankfully, I'm free to let it run its course for a change because no-one can see me.

"Ummm I'm sorry but we're going to have to get going soon if we want to make it before dark to the Weavers."

"Oh, OK. I didn't realise we'd had to leave so soon."

"There's no hurry, honestly. I just wanted to let you know that we'd have to get going soon, I wouldn't want you to miss spending time with your Mum." Damn it, why does he have to be so thoughtful? "I was just packing up the few things I got out of my bag so that I can throw it back in the car, so I thought I'd let you know." He hesitates for a second. "I'm also going to go for a walk around the block or something, to give you time alone with your Mum."

"You don't have to do that." I open the door, having gotten myself dressed as he spoke.

'It's OK, I won't let anyone know I'm here. With you."

"That's not what I meant." I start.

"Maybe I'll tell them I'm Kim's toyboy, that sounds like fun to me!" He taps his fingers on his chin like he's thinking about it and I can't help it, I stamp my foot, then I smack his arm until he drops his hand to his side.

"You'll do no such thing, Caleb Drake! My mother has to live here after you've left and I have to return, you won't make any mischief or create any trouble for her, do you hear me?" There's a flash of something in his eyes that I can't quite read and then he smiles, but it's a kind of sad smile.

"I promise to behave myself in your town, Leila, no-one will ever know that I'm visiting the Phillips ladies, I swear. I won't embarrass you." He swings the bag I didn't see sitting at his feet, up onto his shoulder and then he's gone.

"Shit!" I hurry into the bedroom and put on my socks and shoes, ready to rush out the door and chase him down. Explain to him what I meant.

"What did you say to Caleb?" Mum asks from the doorway, blocking my exit. "He looked rather unhappy when he left just now."

"It was a misunderstanding. He took something I said the wrong way." I try to get by her but she doesn't budge. "So, if you could please move to the side so that I can get by, I will chase him down and explain myself properly."

"No."

"I'm sorry, what?"

"I said no, Leila. Let him go for his walk, he needs the space."

"What the hell is that supposed to mean?"

"He needs some air Lei, give it to him."

"You mean he needs to get away from *me*, right?" I'm getting angry and I don't want to direct that at her.

"Yes and no. Before you start to argue with me and try to follow him, let me explain." When I don't make a move to get by her again, she continues. "My sweet, darling girl, that man is in love with you and he hasn't realised it yet."

"No, Ma, he's not. I told you, we're not dating, we're not together, there is no 'us'. We're friends, that's all."

"And you're in love with him as well." She says it so matter of factly that I'm sure I didn't hear her correctly. "I just hope the two of you can see it before something keeps you apart." This time she turns and walks away before I can say anything in my own defence.

I take a few steps backwards until I feel the backs of my knees hit the edge of the bed, then I let myself fall down and sit.

She's wrong. Isn't she?

I'll give her a partial credit, I *do* like Caleb and I am *very* attracted to him and not just physically, although he does have a pretty amazing body. I'm also attracted to *him,* he's smart, funny, kind and very generous.

She might have a point and if she does, I know that after this weekend, I'm going to have to put some distance between myself and Caleb.

Damn it! This is why you shouldn't get involved, even unofficially, with people you work *with* or *for*!

Chapter Fifteen
CALEB

I throw my bag in the car and walk down the driveway, look both ways and decide left will do. It's not like I know where I am anyway but if I walk in a big square of some kind, I should be able to make it back to Kim's home.

What I do know is, I don't want to spend another minute in that house with Leila. I know she didn't *mean* to upset me and that's the reason I didn't respond to her little dig but that doesn't mean it didn't hurt. If I hadn't already heard her telling her mum earlier that we were nothing more than friends and that Kim had it all wrong, perhaps what she just said in her room wouldn't have annoyed me so much. The fact is though, I overheard most of their conversation and I'm starting to wish that I hadn't lied to Brian. If I'd just told him the truth, I wouldn't have put either Leila or myself in this situation where we have to lie to people. It's not fair on her and it's sure as fuck not fair on me, either.

"Good morning." I'm startled out of my thoughts by a chipper voice almost right beside me. Luckily, they're on the other side of a front fence but I still can't believe I was so stuck in my thoughts that I was completely unaware of my surroundings.

"Good morning." I smile and keep walking.

"You're visiting with Kim Phillips I see." The question that is more of a statement, makes me stumble over my next step but I don't stop. "It's nice to see young Leila bringing home a nice young man." She smiles at me but it doesn't look all that friendly.

"Kim and Leila are both very kind, friendly and amazing women. They inspire loyalty from those who know them, at least the people that I *know* and being that Leila works for my family, I'm guessing that I know a few.

She's respected by everyone, so yes, I guess you're right, it *is* nice that Leila and Kim *both* have such great friends."

"Oh come now, no young man would come and stay at Kim's house if he wasn't interested in her daughter." The woman laughs, it's not friendly at all and I suddenly understand what Leila was talking about when she warned me about this place.

"I think anyone who judges anyone else for their home or life should probably have a perfect version of themselves and being that we're *all* human and make mistakes or have bad things happen to us, I don't think *anyone* should judge another person for how their life is. You're judging me simply by my look this morning and I'm telling you, I've been judged more harshly than either of the Phillips ladies and yet neither of them have judged *me* in anything but a favourable manner. I wish I could say the same about everyone I meet."

"Well, of course no one is perfect." The woman starts, trying to back track on her not so friendly assessment of the two women that, for the most part, have accepted me for who I am and not my past behaviour.

"You're right, so whether I am a friend of Leila's or her boyfriend, you should probably keep your opinions about the Phillips women to yourself, don't you think? Because I can assure you, no man, no *person,* worth a damn would let you put down someone that they cared about in *any* way." I take a breath but barrel on because this woman has pissed me off and she's now copping the brunt of my annoyance with Leila as well. "Perhaps next time you're looking for any kind of gossip, you should think twice about the source you're asking because anyone close enough to give you the real answer wouldn't tell you about it and if they're not close enough, then they're telling you bullshit." I turn on my heel and start to walk back towards Kim's house, only to stop halfway there when I see Leila standing there.

"Did you just tell Mrs Francis to mind her own business?"

"Yes."

"Did you just defend us to her?"

"Yes." I move towards her without thinking about it and when I reach her, I go to reach out for her hand but I remember what she said about this town and after my experience with Mrs Francis, I get it, so I don't touch her. "I'm sorry Darlin', did I do something wrong?" I ask when I get close enough to see the tears in her eyes.

"No."

"I'm sorry, I just saw red. I couldn't let her talk like that about you and your mum. She was looking for a story, some gossip to tell everyone and I really dislike people like that." This time, I don't think about it, I place my hand on her cheek and use my thumb to wipe away her tears. "I'm sorry, I didn't mean to upset you."

"You didn't. You haven't." I raise an eyebrow at her in question because, hello, tears! She laughs even as she sniffles. "I'm just. It's been a long time since anyone defended us, that's all. Anyone that didn't have Phillips as their last name, anyway." She sounds so sad, I just don't know what to do with that information, promising her that it stops right here and now, won't do much, so I pull her into my arms for a hug, onlookers be damned.

"After that encounter, if I thought your mum would let me, I'd pack her up and move her out to Drake Wines." Leila stiffens in my arms but I hold her tighter so she can't pull away from me. "That would give them all something to talk about, wouldn't it? Why are moving vans in Kim Phillips driveway? Where is she moving to after all these years? I could have her out there by the end of the weekend and they wouldn't even know what hit them."

"You can't Caleb." Leila protest is muffled in my chest.

"I *can,* Leila, I just won't because your mum wouldn't move anyway."

"We're not even going to *be* there this weekend!" Her voice isn't quite as muffled this time because she's moved her head to the side.

"You really think that means I couldn't get this done?" I pull back to look in her eyes. "You saw how fast we moved Lori, Jenni and Savvy into a cottage, didn't you? Do you really think I couldn't make one phone call and have Logan, Jules and Brady here within hours?" I ask her, already knowing the answer. My siblings and their husbands might annoy the absolute fuck out of me almost every day, that doesn't meant that I know without a doubt that they have my back. They'd annoy me about it but they would have my back and they would totally have Leila and her mums backs too.

"Oh I saw, it was pretty amazing but they're family Caleb." This time, I rest my hands on her shoulders and push her back so that she can see my face and I wait until she's looking me in the eyes.

"You think you're not?" I ask, surprised.

"I know I'm not Caleb. I know I like Makenna and Logan and we get along pretty well but they're my bosses, not my friends and they're certainly not family." No mention of me or where I stand I notice.

"I think they would beg to differ, Leila. In fact, I know they would. Why else do you think Logan keeps warning me to keep my hands to myself? Why do you think Makenna warned me to behave myself this weekend, even though she thinks we'll be spending a majority of it apart?"

"That's because they don't want to lose an employee they value and they think, unreasonably, that you're some kind of reckless playboy. Which we both know that you're not." Their beliefs aren't unfounded about my recklessness and I know she knows that and I *am* grateful that she never seems to judge me on it though, unlike my siblings.

"That's not true and you know it. If you needed them, any of them, they would be there in a heartbeat." I pause, searching her eyes for something that even I don't even know the answer to. "And so would I. I hope you know that Leila."

"That doesn't make me family, Caleb, that just means you're all good people." She pulls out of my arms completely and turns back to her mum's driveway.

When she's almost at the door, I ask just loud enough for her to hear me, "So, where does that leave me, Leila? Am I your employer? Am I your friend? Have I taken advantage of you for this weekend away? Do you feel like you *have* to be here to keep your job? Because if that's the case, you can stay here with your mum all weekend and I'll go to the Weavers on my own." It's an offer I don't want her to take up but I need to offer her an out any way.

"You don't want me to come with you now?" She stops, her hand on the handle of the front door. I take a minute to think about how best to answer her question, even though there's no question in my mind about whether I still want her with me this weekend. Before I can put a sentence together, she's opening the door, letting herself back in the house. "That's OK, Caleb, I understand."

"I don't think you do." I've never moved faster in my life than I do in that moment. I've gotten down the driveway, moved by the car and gotten to her before she's even managed to get in the door! "Leila, stop."

"It's OK, Caleb, I get that you've had second thoughts. That you realise you jumped into this arrangement of ours with both feet without thinking and now, well you've changed your mind."

"But I haven't." My hand is resting on hers on the door handle and I squeeze her hand, hoping that it feels reassuring more than it might be hurting her in any way. "I admit I jumped in feet first without thinking, Leila. I'll admit that I shouldn't have told Brian a lie. I'll admit that perhaps neither one of those things are ideal but you? Spending the weekend with you? That isn't a mistake nor is it something that I've changed my mind about. Unless you have, changed your mind that is."

"Oh my god!" Kim's voice shouts in frustration as she whips open the door. "I have no damned clue what's going on between you two this weekend or what kind of 'agreement' you have between you for the weekend and as long as you don't hurt my girl and she's OK with said arrangement, I won't have to string you up by your balls, young man. That being said, you two need to stop this bullshit! Stop dancing around each other and whatever is going on. Leila, do you *want* to go away with Caleb this weekend?"

"Ma, the neighbours!" Leila whisper yells.

"I don't give a fuck about the neighbours and what they think. You hear me Janice Francis? Let them think whatever the hell they want, they always have before! If that's what's worrying you, then get yourselves inside. Now!"

We both walk by her into the house and she herds us in to the living room.

"I'm sorry, Kim, I didn't mean to upset you or Leila. I think it might be time for me to leave."

"No! Sit your handsome butt in the chair, you don't get to leave until I say so."

"Ma!"

"Don't you 'Ma' me, young lady. Just answer the damned question. *Do* you want to go away with Caleb this weekend?" Leila gives her mum a dirty look and they're staring each other down, making me feel like I should excuse myself but I'm a little afraid that Kim will yell at me again, so I stay put. "Leila, answer me."

"Yes." The answer is quiet, I only *just* hear it.

"A little louder please, I'm getting old, my hearing isn't what it used to be." Kim demands.

"Yes! Yes, I want to spend the weekend with, Caleb! Are you happy now?"

"No, not yet." She turns her attention to me, I haven't been on the receiving of a mother's glare like that in years. Makenna attempts it and while she's really good at it, I know she's my sister, not my mother, therefore it doesn't work as well. I *know* that Kim isn't *my* mother either but damn she's scary as fuck as she stares me down. "Do *you* want to spend the weekend with my daughter? No, don't look at her, I want an honest answer." Kim says as I start to look to Leila for some kind of support, making my head snap back to her.

"Yes." My voice is strong, sure and I'm confident with my answer. I look Kim in the eyes so that she knows that I'm being honest. One quick, sharp nod at me and I know she gets it.

"Good. Now I don't know what's going on between you two but you need to sort it out. Either enjoy this weekend trip as friends or, well you both know what I mean but don't skirt around each other like that again. It's annoying and frustrating for the rest of us around you."

"We're friends." Leila says without any conviction in her voice.

"That's right, we are and we always will be. Leila agreed to help me out this weekend and I'm grateful. I don't want her to be uncomfortable though, so I thought I'd give her the chance to change her mind and stay here with you."

"Nonsense." Kim shakes her head. "Not that I don't want you here Lei, you know that but if you've packed up you guys should get going."

"I'll go get my bag." Leila says and disappears to her room. There's a silence between Kim and I that I wouldn't quite call uncomfortable but it isn't easy either.

"Thank you for having me, Kim. I appreciate you letting me stay here."

"You're always welcome, Caleb." I stand up and pull her into a hug just as Leila re-enters the room.

"I'll wait for you in the car." I take her bag off her after a small tug of war and leave them to say their goodbyes.

I haven't been sitting in the car for long when they emerge from the house and Leila slides silently into the car. We both wave to Kim as I back out of the driveway, as we drive through town, the car is still silent.

I get onto the highway that leads out of her home town and then ask the question that's been begging me to ask it.

"So, if Logan and Makenna aren't family or friends, they're just your employers, what does that make me? Us?" I can't look her way because I have to concentrate on the traffic but I do hear a sharp intake of breath and I get the feeling I know exactly where this is going and it's going to hurt like hell.

Kenna and Logan were worried about *me* hurting Leila! The potential for her hurting me this weekend in a way that I can't repair, almost seems inevitable.

Chapter Sixteen
LEILA

Where *does* that leave Caleb?

How the hell am I supposed to answer that without telling him everything? I don't see him as my boss, Logan and Makenna employed me and Makenna offered the baker position to me. They're definitely my bosses. Caleb?

How do I explain what he is to me without telling him *exactly* what he means to me?

"Friends?"

"Are you answering my question or asking me another one?" I can hear the slight irritation in his voice and I can't say I blame him but why should I have to be the one who owns up to their feelings first? If what my mum said is right, then he's just fishing to make sure *he* won't get hurt.

"We're friends, Caleb. At least, I think we are." He doesn't look at me, he's concentrating on the road and I'm kind of grateful because it gives me the chance to observe him. I see him shake his head but it's so slight, that if I hadn't been watching him out of the corner of my eye, I wouldn't have noticed at all.

"I guess we should create some ground rules for this weekend then." His words and his jaw tense.

"Like what?"

"I don't know, I've never done this before, Leila, despite what everyone thinks of me." I knew I'd pissed him off earlier when I said I didn't want him to go for a walk but he took it completely the wrong way.

"I didn't mean that you had, Caleb but I've never done anything like this before either, so I have no idea what kind of lines we need to draw." I throw my hands up in exasperation.

"Well, what are you comfortable with?" He asks, never taking his eyes off the road ahead.

"In what way?"

"You know what I mean, Leila."

"You mean ... touching?"

"Yes." He sighs and I can see his hard chest rise and fall.

"What do you think?" I want to know how much *he* wants to touch *me* without flat out asking him and well, he started this conversation.

"It's not up to me, Leila, it's up to *you* how much you're comfortable with. Not everyone likes public displays of affection, some like more and being that we're only *friends*, there are no doubt some lines that shouldn't be crossed."

"Well, we have to behave like we're in love, right? I mean, you told him we're engaged, so we can't *not* touch each other, that would be ridiculous." He nods but doesn't say anything. "What I mean to say is, we *have* to touch each other. Hold hands, kiss, that kind of thing."

"And you're comfortable with that?"

"Why wouldn't I be? I trust you, Caleb."

"Thank you." His voice is so damned soft I almost miss it.

"Of course. I trust you more than most of the people I know and I know, without a doubt, you're not going to hurt me or let me get hurt. Not if you can help it, anyway."

"I wouldn't hurt you, ever, Leila. Never on purpose." His eyes dart away from the road for a second to meet mine and I see the sincerity in them.

"I know that Caleb." I reach out to touch his hand on the steering wheel and almost immediately wish that I hadn't. The air in the car is electric already but touching him, does something to my insides and it always has. I pull my hand away after a minute and place them both in my lap, clasped tight between my thighs. "So, normal touching and kissing, like we're *in* a relationship."

"Like we're in a relationship." He repeats, I'm not sure whether it's to check that's what I mean or whether he's telling himself the rules.

"Exactly." We drive in silence for the next half an hour, the only sound in the car is the radio and it's not up loud enough to drown out my thoughts.

Thoughts that are running rampant, thoughts of his hands running over body, uninhibited touching as we're pretending to be in a relationship where we're supposed to be madly in love. I don't know how we're going to be able to pull *that* off when the mood in the car has taken a nosedive. If Brian and his wife, Mary, could see us now, they'd never believe that we're getting married any time soon.

"I'm sorry." Caleb starts but I cut him off.

"You have nothing to be sorry about, Caleb. Nothing at all. You were just trying to create some clear boundaries and make me comfortable."

"No, I mean I'm sorry that I got us into this situation to start with." He glances at me, before returning to concentrate on the road ahead of us. "If I hadn't felt backed into a corner, if you hadn't been sitting at my kitchen bench you wouldn't have been dragged into this mess with me. For that, I truly am sorry."

"So, if any other woman had been sitting at your kitchen bench, they would have been dragged into it instead? If it had been Makenna sitting there, would you have said her name instead? Or are you trying to say, that any woman would do and I just happened to be there, so it was my name that you said? Because I have to say, none of that is making me feel any better, Caleb!"

"Damn it!" He scrubs a hand across his face, before speaking again. "I'm not saying this right and we're both annoyed and this just isn't working."

"Turn around and take me back to my Mum's, I'll get Sara to come get me in the morning for work." I'm angry, I'm hurt and it all seems so damned irrational but I can't help it.

"No."

"No! What do you mean, no? You *said* that if I changed my mind at any time, you would be fine with that and I could call it all off. I'm calling it off, Caleb. This is mortifying! Knowing that you don't want me here with you, that any woman would have done, is just mortifying and embarrassing. I can't take it, Caleb. I can't."

"I'm not taking you back to your Mum's because I *want* you with me. I *never* would have asked anyone else, not even Makenna. *Especially* not Makenna, she's my *sister!* You are not just someone who was convenient."

"It sure feels like it." I mumble.

"Well, I'm not explaining myself very well right now but the fact is I want *you* here with me this weekend. I don't want anyone else and had you not been sitting at my kitchen bench, I doubt I would have named anyone, least of all called them my damned fiancé."

"Then why *did* you say my name, Caleb? Why did you call me your fiancé? Why couldn't you just say girlfriend, wouldn't that have been easier?" I'm sure it would have been easier to have put the girlfriend label on me, rather than fiancé. "I mean, I get that Brian is a family man and he only wants to deal with men who have families and are settled but you *have* a family. An *amazing* family that already run an amazing business, so I don't understand why he was pushing this so hard."

"I don't understand it either, Leila." He mumbles but I'm not sure which part he doesn't understand.

"I don't understand why you would want to jump through these kinds of hoops for a business deal. For hops to brew beer. I mean sure, I don't like beer, in fact I hate the taste of it, so therefore I just don't understand the attraction to it. Which means, I also don't understand the hold this guy has on you and the hops that you want to buy. Surely, *surely,* there are other suppliers. Suppliers that you wouldn't have to jump through all these silly hoops for?"

I take a breath, not realising that I've just spent that last few minutes ranting at Caleb about his brewery, hops and choice of supplier until I stop. Then, I realise I've almost done exactly what he's expecting Logan and Makenna to do, pick holes in everything he's chosen to do with the brewery idea of his but before I can think about apologising, he speaks, offering to explain it all to me.

"I can explain it all to you, if you want?" He sounds so hesitant.

"All of it?" I look at the side of his face but he doesn't try to look at me. "Even why I'm here and not someone else?"

"You want the truth?" He asks and the tone of his voice makes me hesitate for just a second but he notices. "Honestly, Leila. If you want to hear the truth, just say the word."

"Yes."

Chapter Seventeen
CALEB

"Which one do you want the answer to first?" I need to put an end to all this back and forth between us, without giving her a full on admission of my true feelings for her because I'm not ready to go there. Yet.

"Why do you need Brian so much?" Ahhh, so she doesn't want to deal with emotional part either.

"OK, so the truth is, you're right. I *could* get hops from someone else and to someone who dislikes beer, I can see how you wouldn't understand what the difference is between hops but it's the same differences between grapes and vines. They have different levels of bitterness and different aromas, just like grapes."

"Does that mean that you'll grow different kinds, to make different beers?" Her forehead crinkles as she asks and it's so cute, I almost pull the car over, simply because I want to look at her.

"To start with, no. I think I'll concentrate on this one kind and see what I can create with it."

"And Brian is the only supplier of the type that you want?"

"Well, no but I've spent so much time researching and looking at different crops and Brian has helped me learn the differences and what will grow here, that I feel like I would be stepping backwards if I go elsewhere." I take a deep breath because I really want her to understand but I don't know if I'm explaining it as well as I could. "Brian and his wife, Mary, have been very welcoming and kind. I get how weird this looks from the outside, I do and I don't feel trapped or like I'm being forced into this friendship with him. What I'm trying to explain is, I've already got a relationship with Brian and it may look strange from the outside but he's really been a mentor to

138

me. I know, without a doubt, that if I decided to go in another direction he would be fine with it. He would be hurt in a way that relates to our friendship but not in a business sense."

"Brian and Mary have kind of stepped in for your parents."

"No!" I'm probably sound angrier than I actually am.

"I don't mean to imply that you've replaced your parents, Caleb, I wouldn't ever do that and I know how much you love them. What I meant is that, as a mentor, his opinion means something to you."

"That and Mary trying to set me up with every single young woman they know drives me *insane*!" I smile at her, trying to deflect my true feelings, even though I know she's reading my mind in some weird way that she has when she nods slightly, letting me get away with my light-heartedness when she probably shouldn't.

"I can see how that would be annoying. I mean what guy doesn't like having a parade of beautiful women offered to him like a moving buffet?" She sounds little snarky but I can see the smile she's fighting. "I mean, let's be honest, I wouldn't mind it if someone decided to parade a collection of hunky guys for my perusal. Actually, that kind of sounds like a *lot* of fun. I bet I could get Sara to join in with that kind of fun." I can't stop the low growl that rumbles out of me at just the thought of her having a smorgasbord of guys vying for her attention.

Staring at the road ahead of us, I hear her laughter bubble up and then she bursts out laughing. My head snaps to the side to look at her, then back to the road. I look back and forth a few times in quick succession, which causes her to laugh even harder. She's holding her stomach and she has tears rolling down her cheeks, leaving me struggling to understand what the hell was so damned funny!

"What's so funny, Leila?" My eyes still darting back and forth between the road and looking at her.

"What's. So. Funny?" She asks between gasps of breath. "Your. Face."

"Well, geez, thanks for the compliment!" I decide concentrating on the windy road ahead of us is a better idea than trying to look at Leila to work out what I said.

"Oh, Caleb!" She's found a tissue in her handbag and she's wiping the tears from her eyes. "Your reaction to *me* having a parade of guys to choose from was ridiculous! For one, I would never be in that kind of situation. Two, I doubt you could find enough guys to make a parade that were attracted to me. Three, I don't *want* to be in that situation, even though I'm sure Sara would enjoy it, especially if it *was* me in the spotlight. Last but not least, even though Ma wants me to settle down, she would never do that to me and I don't know anyone, other than Sara of course, that cares that much about my sex life."

"I'd be in that line in a heartbeat." I mumble.

"What was that?" She asks and I can feel her eyes on the side of my face.

"I was just wondering what you meant about not finding enough guys. You're attractive, cute, funny, smart, kind *and* you can cook, who wouldn't want you?"

"Plenty, Caleb, plenty of guys wouldn't want me." Before I can say anything to object, she keeps talking. "Do you know how many guys don't want to deal with the hours I have to work? I have to be up early, therefore I can't stay out late because I need sleep. I work six days a week and even though I love it and I don't want to change that, most guys can't deal with it. If I'm home, I'm sleeping and while you *say* one of my best qualities is that I can cook, when I'm home I don't always feel like cooking and most guys can't deal with *that* either! I mean, just once, it would be nice if someone cooked for *me,* you know? I mean, it's exhausting working at Vines, I'm on my feet all day and mixing, kneading, proving, cutting, chopping and cooking *all* day. Just *once* it would be nice to come home and someone has cooked a meal for *me*!" I'm not sure if she took a breath that entire time but it does feel like she told me something she doesn't share with many, if any, other people.

"I'd cook for you." I say, darting a look her way, only to see shock on her face. "I mean, if you were mine, if we were *together.*"

"That's easy for you to say, Caleb, we're *not* together." She sighs.

"I know but if we were, I would cook for you. I know how hard you work at Vines, I see it every day." There's a quiet between us for a few minutes that I think means we're both thinking about what was just said. For my part, I'm wishing she *was* mine and that I *could* look after her and cook for her, often.

"That's nice of you to say, Caleb." She says quietly and I can't help wondering, hoping really, that she's thinking about us being together, in a real relationship.

"I already told you I can cook, Leila, I just choose not to because cooking for one is kind of boring. Not to mention, my Mum taught me how to cook and she didn't *know* how to cook for just one person, she always cooked for a group of people readying for a feast." I smile at the memories flooding my mind. "She *always* had more food than we could possibly eat, which meant we always had people in the house to share it. The workers on the vines, in the winery, anyone who was on their own always got at least one hot meal a week in the Drake household." I laugh quietly at the memories of the loud dinners we'd have when we were kids.

"Sounds like a lot of fun."

"There were always people around." I nod smiling. "Sometimes I wished they would all go away so that we could just have a family dinner but those rare occasions where it *was* just the five of us or later the six of us when Brady started being here more often, it was quiet and kind of boring. Before our parents died, those big family and friends dinners had kind of died out. Logan had gone off to University and gotten a job in the city, Kenna and Brady were at University and I was the only one left at home. They still had the odd worker come in for a meal here and there but things around Drake Wines had already started to change a bit. There were less people working on the property and more machinery doing the jobs instead. Vines, however, was Mum's dream and Dad was trying to get it up and running when they were in the accident."

"Do you miss it?" She asks and I'm grateful she asked about the gatherings and not my parents. I don't talk about them to very many people because people mostly respond with uncomfortable sympathy or are completely over the top with their sympathy, and I hate either one. Girls tripping over themselves to 'comfort' me is weird and happened way too often in my first year at university.

"We still have family dinner most Sunday nights at Kenna and Brady's. Although these days, Jules and Logan do a lot of the cooking so that Kenna doesn't have to do so much since the babies arrived. With every addition to the family, the dinners become more alive."

"Every Sunday? No exceptions?"

"Kenna almost needs a signed confession of illness if you don't show up." I laugh.

"She's trying to keep the tradition alive. She misses it and your parents as much as you do, as much as Logan does and this helps you *all* feel like they're still here in some way." She's not wrong. "And now with the kids here, Savannah, Anna and Beau, it must make it feel more like it was back when you guys were kids."

"I love having those kids around. It makes me feels happy again that there's love, laughter and kids running around the place again."

"You can see how much you love your nieces and nephew, Caleb. You're always the first one to help with any of them, including the twins. I've never seen you hesitate to take Anna or Beau off Makenna's hands to help her out."

"I never want her to feel overwhelmed with them and think that she can't ask for help if she needs it." I explain. "I know it can be hard with one kid, two must make it even harder. I know they're not getting much sleep or time together but I also know they wouldn't change it for the world. They went through hell to get those babies and I know they will love them with everything they have."

"You love them."

"The twins? Hell yes. I will do everything I can for them and Savvy."

"Weren't you shocked when Lori and Savannah showed up?"

"Yes but that didn't mean I wouldn't embrace them and Jenni." I admit. "Savannah is Logan's kid, that makes her family which makes Lori family. I just wish I'd had more time to get to know Lori because she did an amazing job with Savvy before she left us."

"She was a lovely woman and Savannah is a beautiful girl. I'm sure, in fact I have no doubt, that Logan and Julian will do an amazing job of bringing her up now but you're right, Lori did an amazing job."

The rest of the car ride is silent both of us lost in thought. I don't know what Leila is thinking about but I'm thinking about Leila joining us at those family dinners, by my side, perhaps as my fiancé for real.

Not for the first time, I realise I've screwed myself over this weekend because while I'm pretending that I'm in love with this woman, I just might actually wind up hurting us both. I don't know if I can go back to the easy friendship that we had before we left Drake Wines yesterday.

Chapter Eighteen
LEILA

I'm sure Caleb is lost in the memories of the family dinners he had when he was kid with his parents. Me? I'm lost in the daydream that I could join him at those family dinners at Makenna and Brady's.

Who am I kidding? Caleb Drake is firmly placed in the friends only zone.

"We're here." Caleb's voice breaks through my daydreaming and I look up to see where exactly we've arrived and I can't help the gasp that falls out of my gaping mouth.

"I've never seen anything like this before Caleb!" I hear him chuckle beside me but I don't take any notice, I'm too busy taking in the mansion and the estate we're driving onto. "This is insane!"

"It's pretty impressive." He chuckles again.

"You could have warned me." I say, my voice barely above a whisper.

"I did! I told you it was an estate with a guest wing and a family wing."

"OK, but I didn't think it was anything like *this*! I could never fit in here Caleb, it's too fancy." I realise something as I say that and I turn to him, hoping he's catching the glare that I'm sending him. "Nothing I packed is suitable for a casual dinner here, Caleb. It sure as hell isn't suitable for a 'fancy dinner', as you called it, tomorrow night!"

"It's fine. You're perfect, Leila." He says, taking my hand in his and squeezing it reassuringly. Which works until I see the elegant man and woman standing on the front step, grinning ear to ear as we pull up.

"Is that Brian and Mary?" I ask, searching his eyes for the answer to a question I'm not sure I'll ever ask.

"Smile, gorgeous and they're going to love you." He raises our joined hands to his lips and leave a light kiss in the back of my hand. "Take a deep breath. I promise to not leave your side all weekend. I will never leave you alone to deal with any of this without me. OK?"

"Promise?"

"I promise, Darlin'." The use of his nickname for me, relaxes me enough that I move to get out of the car.

"Wait for me, please?"

"What?" I ask, but he's already out of the car and moving around to my side, a wide smile spread across his face.

"Darlin'." He says, when he opens my door and holds his hand out for me to take. I can't help the smile that spreads across my face at his chivalrous behaviour. I wonder briefly if it's just for show but only briefly, simply because I know this man. We've become friends over the past year and a half, and I won't believe he's putting on a show for the Weavers.

"Thank you, Handsome." I return the beaming smile he's giving me.

"Hello there, Caleb, how are you? We didn't think you were going to make it before it got dark!" Brian's booming voice greets us as he walks towards us, his wife by his side.

"We left a little earlier than I was expecting and the traffic was really light for a change." Caleb takes Brian's hand in his firmly, then he smiles that smile that has women eating out his hand at Mary, who wraps her arms around him, pulling him into a tight hug. It's obvious that these people adore Caleb.

When Mary releases him, Caleb tugs lightly on my hand that he's managed somehow to keep a hold of, pulling me into his side. Before he can speak, Mary does.

"This must be the lucky, Leila." It's my turn to be pulled into a tight hug but still, Caleb doesn't let go of my hand.

"Yes, it's nice to meet you, Mrs Weaver." I say as I step out of her embrace and am pulled back into Caleb's side.

"Oh please, any friend of Caleb's is a friend of ours sweetie, call me Mary and this oaf is my husband, Brian." She introduces him with a laugh when he huffs out his pretend annoyance, the smile on his face giving him away as enjoying his wife's ribbing.

"Fiancée." Brian corrects her as he pulls me into another hug, not quite as tight as his wife's though.

"Oh, that's right! How could I forget that you're completely off the market now?" Mary chuckles.

"Well, to be fair, even if she was my girlfriend, I would *still* be completely off the market Mary." Caleb says, smiling but I can see the annoyance on his face and can't help wondering if the older couple can too.

"Of course, you know what I mean, Caleb. You're getting married, therefore, you're off limits." She smiles and loops her arm through Caleb's arm that isn't holding on to me. "Can I see the ring?" She looks at my hand, the one that Caleb just happens to be holding, looking for the sparkler that should be there and coming up empty and panic to surges through me. We didn't even get that far because we only got fake engaged yesterday, we haven't even had time to think about a ring. I'm about to answer her but Caleb beats me to it.

"Leila was working in the kitchen yesterday and neither of us want her wearing it in there in case it gets caught or lost somewhere." He smiles so easily at the older couple that I can't help wondering how damned often he lies to me in a day but then I'm jolted out of my thoughts by his question directed my way. "It's in your bag, isn't it Darlin'?" His eyes are boring into mine, begging me to go along with his lie.

"Absolutely. I don't like to wear it at work. I use all kinds of machinery that it could easily get caught in." I smile easily at them, even as the guilt for lying starts to sit heavily in my stomach.

"Leave the kids alone, Mary, let's get them settled into their room and you can ask your questions later at dinner." He takes his wife's hand and gently pulls her away from Caleb and towards the front door. "Don't worry, it's a very casual affair tonight, Leila. We only arrived ourselves yesterday and we were only expecting you pair and two other couples today. Unfortunately, one of the other couples won't be here until tomorrow, so it's just the six of us for dinner this evening."

"Don't forget Francine and her daughter are here already as well." Mary reminds him as we follow them inside and I hear Caleb groan quietly beside me. When I look over to see if he's OK, he leans in and whispers in my ear, "I'll explain later in private." I nod my head, so slightly that no-one else would notice but Caleb does and he smiles at me.

"Your room is this way and don't worry Caleb, I convinced Mary to put Francine and Anita on our side of the house." Brian adds with a chuckle and I feel Caleb shiver slightly beside me.

"Thank you, Brian, I appreciate you thinking of it."

"Not a problem, son." Brian says with a quick glance behind him to look at me, so I try to look like I understand the issue, even though I have no freaking clue what's going on here.

"Oh stop it you two, they're not that bad and they're dear friends. You shouldn't speak like that about friends, Brian." Mary admonishes her husband but he just snorts at her.

"Those two are not our friends, Mary and you know it!" Before she can respond we've followed them to a door that is open, revealing the most amazing room I have ever seen!

"Oh my! This is gorgeous!" I say, as they lead us into the room and give a small tour.

"Thank you, Leila, I'm very proud of the way we decorated the rooms here. We hope to make our guests feel comfortable and at home." Mary informs me with a beaming smile.

"Well, I think you've probably out done yourself." I smile warmly back at her. The honest truth is, I've never even been in a hotel that looks as amazing as this room. Although, it's more of a suite than a room.

"You have your own private bathroom, no sharing with other couples here. There's also a small kitchenette if you need anything and as you can see, you have your own living area, complete with a comfy couch and big screen TV for those times when you need some time alone. We hope those times are few and far between." Mary smiles at us both and Caleb chuckles.

"Your only obligations to us this weekend though, are dinner tonight if you don't mind, after your afternoon of travelling and then dinner and the function tomorrow night, of course. The rest, is up to you." Brian informs us and as Caleb is thanking him, there's a knock at the open door and our bags are brought in for us. I didn't even know that Caleb had given the keys to anyone!

"Thank you." Caleb nods to the guy who quietly places our bags on the floor close to the door and slips back out into the hallway.

"We'll leave you lovebirds to settle in and freshen up." Brian says as he guides Mary out of the door. "I'm sure they don't need us hanging around until dinner, Love. Plus we have plenty of things to do to keep us busy. Dinner tonight is at half past six, it's not an exact science but if you could be down stairs around then, we would appreciate it." He informs us with a warm smile. I don't know if either Brian or Mary can do anything else *but* smile warmly to be honest.

The silence in the room stretches for a few minutes after the door shuts behind our hosts for the weekend, as we take in the surroundings.

"This place is amazing, Caleb! And Mary and Brian are the sweetest! I mean they have a real soft spot for you! I think I better watch out this weekend, I feel like I might be getting assessed as to whether I'm good enough for you!" My words all run into each other, proving just how nervous I really am about actually, finally being here. I also really feel like Mary and Brian will definitely be assessing my ability to make Caleb happy in the future. In fact, I'm one hundred percent certain that Mary will find a way to get me alone with her, just so that she can politely question me.

"I don't think they're that invested in my life, Leila. I think they're just a little protective but once this weekend is over, they'll be fine." He nods like he's trying to convince himself as much as he's convincing me and I can't help laughing. That is, until it hits me that we don't have the *one* thing that Mary insists on seeing.

"Caleb, we don't have a ring. What are we going to do?"

"Yes, we do."

"No, we don't, Caleb and I don't just carry a spare engagement ring in my handbag as you suggested outside!" I start to pace the living area of the suite, thinking about how we can get this ring without them noticing. "We're going to have to head out to find a shop and seeing as how we just got here, they're going to notice that we're already leaving again."

"No, we won't." He insists but I know I don't have a ring stashed in my luggage anywhere and let's face it, this engagement only happened yesterday, there's no possible way he could have a ring available for us to use. Not unless he already had one and that would mean I would be wearing a ring meant for another woman and even though this is *fake,* I can't do that!

"Yes, we will. Unless you're going to tell me that you actually *have* a ring in your pocket." I laugh at the absurdity, until he drops to one knee with a sexy smirk on his face, a twinkle in his eyes and small velvet box in his hand!

Chapter Nineteen
CALEB

Instead of listening to Leila argue with me about whether we need to sneak out to buy her a ring or not, I decide to prove to her that we don't *need* one. So, as she rattles off all the reasons we have to try and sneak off the Weaver's estate, while pacing the living area of the suite, I drop to one knee and hold up the open ring box for her to see.

"Fuck!" She whispers, throwing her hands up to cover her now rosy, red cheeks.

"Leila Rose Phillips, will you do me the honour of becoming my fiancée?" I smile at the woman who will soon be wearing my ring and hope that this was the right way to do it.

"Caleb." My name is a kind of hoarse, sexy, whisper. One that makes my cock stir to life and I know if I stand up right now, she's going to see exactly how she affects me.

"What do you say, Leila?" My grin gets wider as she walks quickly over to me, taking my hand in both of hers and she tries to pull me up to my feet and I let her.

"You mean, fake fiancée, right?" She whispers again and I'm not sure if it's because she doesn't want anyone to hear us or because she's feeling like she wishes this was real, just like I am.

"Sure, if you want to split hairs, Leila, we can put the word fake before fiancée but you're going to have to stop using it at some point or everyone is going to know that we're lying to them."

"Oh." She looks like she didn't even consider that before now and I can't help laughing.

"Darlin', you can't call me your fake fiancée when we're with other people, so you might as well get used to calling me your fiancée here and now."

I smile. "So, Leila Rose Phillips, will you marry me?" My heart skips a beat when I ask her and I can hear the blood pounding in my ears as she says yes.

"Yes, Caleb, I'll be your fiancée."

"Thank you." I tell her as I slide that ring on her finger and look at it sitting there, twinkling in the dwindling sunlight.

"Oh my god Caleb, it's gorgeous."

"Nothing but the best for my fiancée you know." I smile but I feel a little sad as well. Perhaps I shouldn't have used this particular ring because I won't be able to use it in the future if I don't admit my real feelings to this woman sometime in the future but too bad.

"How on earth did you get one so quickly." She pauses, looks at me. "You didn't buy this ring for someone else did you because I don't want it if it was meant for another woman. Not that I have any rights to demand my *own* ring for obvious reasons but I still don't want something you bought for someone else."

"I didn't buy it for anyone else, OK? It's a family heirloom, I guess you'd call it. Please, just wear the ring, you like it don't you?"

"I do, I love it, it's absolutely gorgeous, Caleb."

"Good, I'm glad. Now, why don't you go have a shower and freshen up before dinner." I put my hand up to stop her from protesting. "And no, I'm not saying you smell or anything like that, I just thought you might like to freshen up after the drive. I'm going to have a quick shower too and change my clothes, so I figured you might want to as well."

"Thank you, Caleb, I think I will." Her smile is beautiful, her cheeks are still a little rosy from all the excitement and I'm grateful that she's not questioning me any further about the ring.

"Let me just put our bags in the bedroom and then, I'll leave you to it."

"I *can* carry my own bag, Caleb." She laughs, as she follows me into the bedroom. I look up from placing the bags at the foot of the bed when I hear her gasp behind me.

"Holy shit, this place is amazing."

"Wait until you see the bathroom." I chuckle, waiting for her to find the door to said bathroom and open it. I know the minute she sees what I was hoping was in this room, I know it was in the rooms I stayed in before when I visited.

"Oh Caleb, have you *seen* this bathtub?"

"I have, yes. Why don't you have one? I'm sure that Mary has left some oils or salts or similar in there for that very thing." I chuckle, knowing that without a doubt she's spotted the clawfoot tub in the centre of the room, it's pretty hard to miss to be fair. I had a dream last night that we shared a bubble bath that smelled like lemons and vanilla.

"Do I have time?"

"Of course you do, Darlin." I walk into the bathroom and turn on the taps over the tub, then start opening the doors in the cabinet, looking for the salts and oils. "Here you go. I knew Mary would have a selection in here somewhere." I say, pulling out a basket full of bottles and jars.

"Have you stayed here before, Caleb?"

"A few times but they've recently updated everything, so even though I knew the tubs were in a few rooms, I wasn't sure there would be one in this one. They *do* however have the *most* magnificent showers, so I'm looking forward to having one after you're done."

"You should have a shower before I lie around in the tub for ages." She starts to leave the room and the sudden vision of her naked, wet and lying back in that tub is something that knocks the breath out of me.

"No! You should stay and relax for a while. I have to call Makenna and let her know that we arrived safely before she starts calling the police and hospitals to see if we were in an accident." I rush by her and out of the room, closing the door behind me.

I hear her mumble something behind the closed door but I don't stop to check what it was. If she needs me, for *anything* she'll call out to me, not mumble.

As I walk out of the bedroom, I pull my phone out of my pocket, there's already a message there from Kenna asking if we're OK! Instead of answering her text, I pull up the call screen and tap her number.

"Caleb? Are you OK?" Kenna sounds slightly panicked.

"Of course we're OK, Kenna, I was just about to call and let you know I arrived in the city."

"There was some big accident and when none of us had heard from you, I got worried." I can hear the emotion in her voice and I wonder if any of us will ever not stress out over this.

"Sorry, Makenna, I was driving and my phone was on silent. I just got in the house and thought I'd give you a call."

"Is he OK?" I hear Brady's voice in the background and other mumbling voices that I know are Logan and Jules.

"Yeah, he's OK." She tells them and I hear them all sigh, which is impressive when you consider I'm on the phone! "Do you know if Leila is OK?"

"Yeah, she's fine." I say without hesitation because obviously, I know she's in the bath. Getting warm and hot. The silence on the other end of the phone hints at the fact that Kenna thinks that there's more to my answer than she knows. "She stayed with her Mum, remember?"

"Uhuh, sure she did." Kenna says, her tone now changed to a teasing one. "We believe you, Caleb, of course we do."

"Well, you should because I dropped her off at her mum's last night." I say, just as a beautiful voice calls out from the other room and I want to slap my forehead at her timing.

"You weren't wrong about that bathtub, Caleb! It's all yours now."

"So, who's that then?" Kenna asks, laughter in her voice and I'm happy that she's no longer stressed but only half happy.

"Caleb?" Leila pops her head out of the bedroom door that I'd closed behind me. "Oh, sorry I didn't know you were on the phone." She whispers.

"That, Kenna, is my friend's girlfriend and it appears it is now my turn for a shower." I say to Kenna but my eyes don't leave Leila's and her mouth drops open with the realisation of what's just happened. "So, I'm going to have to go now."

"Your friend's girlfriend needed to be told that the shower was amazing? Surely she knows what his shower is like? Not to mention, she sounds a *lot* like Leila. Did you forget that I talk to her every day, Caleb?"

"No, *Makenna,* I did not forget you talk to Leila every day and I think you heard Leila's voice because you think she's with me, which of course, she's not because I dropped her off with Kim yesterday."

"Kim?"

"Yes, Kim Phillips, her mum." I roll my eyes but when I finish Leila's shaking her head.

"I didn't know that was her mum's name, Caleb." The gleeful tone in my sisters voice, like she's caught me out on a lie, is so fucking annoying!

"Well, I needed the bathroom when we stopped yesterday and Mrs Phillips, *Kim,* was kind enough to let me use hers. We had a cup of tea, a chat and I was on my way again."

"But you just said that 'we' had just arrived. Why didn't you call me last night?" Fuck!

"He messaged me and I forgot to tell you, sorry Kenna." Logan says from somewhere behind Kenna. Damn it! Now I owe Logan and I know he's going to want to know the truth about my feelings for Leila in exchange for him lying to our sister for me and *then* I'm going to get a lecture.

"He did? Why didn't you tell me?"

"I forgot. We've been a little busy Kenna."

"You're right, I'm sorry." Kenna says and it kind of hurts that she accepts his explanation so easily, even though I know how much they've all been through lately, it still sucks balls. Big hairy ones.

"Right, now that you two have that and my life all sorted, can I go have that shower now? I need to get ready for dinner."

"Where are you going?" Kenna asks and before I can answer, Brady speaks.

"Kenna, sweetheart, leave the man alone. He's an adult, he's fine, now let him live his life. Goodnight, Caleb, enjoy your weekend."

"Thanks man."

"No problem." He says and when he pulls the phone away from either Kenna's mouth or his, I'm not sure, I hear her speak.

"Call us when you're coming home!" I roll my eyes again but I know I'll send them a group text just so they know what time we *should* be back at Drake Wines.

Chapter Twenty

LEILA

"**I**'m sorry, Caleb, I didn't know you were on the phone, I wouldn't have called out to you otherwise."

"That's OK, no harm done."

"Don't you hate lying to them?"

"I do but we agreed to keep this between us. This weekend and well, you know." He glances down at my finger, which makes me look at it too, only to see the gorgeous ring glistening in the glow of the overhead light. It makes me feel giddy that I have Caleb's ring on my finger.

"You're right, of course." In a few long strides, he's standing right in front of me. He places a finger under my chin, guiding my eyes up to meet his.

"If you were really *mine*, Leila, believe me, the world would know about it, including my family and they wouldn't be able to persuade me otherwise." His eyes search mine and I just can't bring myself to look away. "No man would come near you because he would understand from one look. You. Are. Mine."

"OK." I swallow deeply.

"And for this weekend at least, that's *exactly* what they're going to see." He drops a kiss to my forehead, takes his hand from my face and walks towards the bathroom. "My turn for that shower, right?"

"Uhuh." I breathe out because that's the only way I can think to explain what that noise was. It was an exhale that happened to have something that sounded like a word in it.

I'm frozen in the doorway for a minute or two after he's gone because the combination of his words, his touch and that look. Holy. Fuck!

I'm honestly not sure if I'm turned on by that display of dominance or pissed off at it. The more I think about it, the more turned on I am and that kind pisses me off even more. I'm not *his* property! I'm no-one's fucking property but when he looks at me like that I feel like I'm loved and cared for. That being said, I'm also well aware of the fact that there's a fine line between loving possession and serious issues possession.

I don't doubt that Caleb would let me or any woman that he's with, have their own life and earn a living. I don't think he's possessive in the sense that he wants to lock me, or anyone else, up in a house and keep them there, away from family and friends. I think he's simply saying that his love would be unconditional and he wouldn't let any guy or girl, think that they had a chance with me. With either of us for that matter.

I shake my head because I'm crazy! Who thinks that way? Plus, why am I justifying that kind of behaviour like I'm *talking* myself into being someone's *possession*. Been there, done that, got the postcard and I am *not* going back. Ever!

"Are you OK, Leila?" Caleb's voice snaps me out of my thoughts and I realise that I've gotten dressed without even thinking about it. As I turn to answer him, I also realise that I forgot that he just stepped out of the bathroom. "Leila?"

"Hmmm? Oh yes, I'm fine. Sorry I was just lost in thought." The words tumble out of my mouth, as I try not to study him in just a towel but I lose when a single drop of water drips from his hair, to the front of his shoulder and travels down over a very well defined pec and starts to make its way to his well-defined abs.

"Leila?"

"Hmmmm?"

"My eyes are up here, Darlin'." He chuckles and my eyes snap up to meet his. "I asked if you're OK? You looked like you were thinking some pretty serious thoughts a few minutes ago. Is everything OK with Kim?"

"Kim? Oh, yes Mum's fine. Well, as far as I know anyway." I shake my head, breaking our connection and making it easier for me to think. "In fact, I should message her and let her know we got here in one piece as well. I'm surprised she hasn't messaged or called just like Kenna did." I turn my back to him and search for my phone.

"As long as you're OK."

"Yes, yes, fine. Peachy." His quiet chuckle behind me makes me think he doesn't quite believe me but that's his choice, isn't it? "I'm just going to go call Mum, let her know we're good." I tell him, before walking out the door without waiting for his reply.

Closing the bedroom door behind me I let out a breath I didn't even know I was holding, lean back on the door and close my eyes for a second to get my brain working again. I push off the door and walk over to the large windows that look out over the backyard of the property. If you can *call* it a backyard, it's more of a garden in a town centre but it sure is beautiful.

Putting my phone to my ear, I wait for my mum to pick up. It takes longer than it should and I start to panic.

"Hello daughter of mine, what can I do for you? Shouldn't you be enjoying your weekend away with a handsome man?" Her voice is kind of sing-song and it's very strange.

"Mum? Are you OK?" I feel like that word has been spoken more in the last few minutes than it has in a long time!

"Of course Darling, what can I do for you?" I can *hear* the smile on her face and there's a joy in her voice as well.

"Are you sure there's nothing wrong?"

"Of course, Leila!" There's a slight amount of exasperation in there that makes me feel a bit better.

"You kind of sound like you're being held captive and trying to tell me without alerting the people who are holding you."

"Don't be ridiculous, Leila." She sighs and I'm relieved because she sounds much more like her wonderful self. "If you *must* know, I'm busy. I have company and I'm busy."

"Oh, sorry I didn't know you had friends over. I just wanted to let you know that we made it here and this place is *amazing*! It's like something off a TV show, Mum!"

"That's fantastic, Leila. I look forward to seeing some pictures if the two of you pop in here on your way home. If not, I'll see them next time or you can send them to me."

"Wow."

"What? I told you, I have company and I think it's rude to be on the phone for too long, Leila."

"I'll take a photo of the view from our room and send it to you then."

"I look forward to it. Enjoy your evening, Leila. Give Caleb my love. Bye now." Then she ends the call.

"Wow!" I say as I stare at the screen on my phone. "Just, wow!"

"What's wow? Is everything good with your Mum?" Caleb's voice startles me, making me jump a little. "Sorry, I thought you heard me, obviously not." I turn to look at him and damn! Dark blue denim jeans and a black button up shirt, with one sleeve already rolled up to just below his elbow, while he's working on the other, has never looked so damned good! My mouth goes dry and I've forgotten what we were talking about for a second. Strange. Oh that's right, my strange mother!

"No worries. She hung up on me after telling me to enjoy my evening and sending you her love."

"Aww she's sweet." His smile holds genuine affection for my mum and it's adorable. "So, what's wrong then?"

"Well, when she first answered, she sounded almost like she was being held hostage and was trying to send me the signal, you know?"

"No, no I have no idea what you mean with that, Darlin'." He shakes his head, a frown crinkling his forehead.

"You know, when they act different on the phone but the kidnappers don't *know* that they're being weird and it's so that the person on the phone that *does* know them, knows that something is wrong."

"Right." He draws the word out and I know he still doesn't get it.

"Whatever don't bother. You obviously don't watch crime dramas or cop dramas like I do." I shake my head and turn back to the window, my phone clasped in my hand still.

"You're right, I don't but if you're worried we can head back to your mums right now." He's standing in the gap between the window and myself.

"You would do that? This weekend means so much to you that we're fake engaged but you would leave just like that?"

"Yes." He takes my shoulders firmly in his hands and searches my eyes. "Now, tell me exactly what Kim said and we'll try to work out if she's safe or not."

"Not much, she just said that she had company and that she thought it was rude to stay on the phone for too long. Then she told me to just send her pictures of this place and she'd look at them later." I look down at the phone in my hand and sigh. "I thought she'd like to hear about this place. We used to watch all those stupid shows on TV that showed big celebrity mansion like this and dream."

"She did say she wants to see the photos, Leila."

"Yeah, I guess. I shouldn't be so upset, should I? I mean, she's allowed to have friends over for drinks or whatever they do."

"Did she say she had friends over, Leila?"

"She said she had company, so I'm guessing that she has some friends over."

"Did she tell you it was friends or *company?*"

"Why is that important, Caleb? I told you she said company." He starts laughing. "What?"

"Did she tell you any of her friends names?"

"No, I didn't think to ask, I know most of them."

"Leila, Darlin', I'm sorry to be the one to tell you this but your mum doesn't have her girlfriends over."

"What are you talking about, Caleb? Of course she does, what other kind of company could she have over?" He raises his eyebrow at me, his eyes twinkling with the mischievousness I see all too often and a smirk on his face.

"She has *company,* Leila." His eyes are searching mine again but I still have no clue what he's on about. "*Male company,* Darlin.'"

I feel my eyes widen as the realisation of what he's just said sinks in. It must look quite comical because he drops his hands to his knees and is bent over, laughing hysterically.

Chapter Twenty-one
CALEB

I can't help laughing as she understands what I'm trying to tell her without saying the words and the shock registers on her face. It's the most adorable, yet funniest thing I've seen in a very long time. There isn't too much that this woman does that I *don't* find adorable but that doesn't count right now.

"Are you saying? Do you mean?" She sucks in a breath and I force myself to stop laughing because I can see the absolute horror on her face. "You can't. No. No!"

"Do you need me to spell it out to you, Darlin'?" I ask, seriously.

"I just. No. Maybe."

"Oh, Darlin'. I think you'll find that your mum had a gentleman caller."

"Oh my god!" I pull her into my arms because she looks like she's about to burst in to tears. "How do you know?"

"Well, think about it, even though I know you'd rather not." I say, quietly just above her ear. "When she has her friends over, does she tell you exactly that?" She nods. "Does she mention them by name? Does she tell you, for example, that Margaret and Simone are over for drinks and a movie?"

"Yes." She whispers, her breath ghosting over the skin on my neck as she rests her chin on the front my shoulder.

"So, do you think that in fact, she *was* talking code just not kidnapping code?"

"Code?" She hasn't moved, except to wrap her arms tightly around my waist.

"She said she had *company*, Leila, not friends. Company usually means, people that you're attracted to, not friendship."

"Argghhh." Is all she grumbles and all I can feel, is her breath caressing the side of my neck and I am struggling to keep my hands on her waist. "Why wouldn't she just tell me, Caleb? I mean, I wouldn't mind at all if she had a new man in her life. She deserves happiness just as much as anyone else, more I might say."

"I'm guessing your reaction right now might have been one of the reasons, Darlin'." Her body stiffens in my arms and I know she's about to pull away, so I rush on. "I'm not saying you did anything wrong but going by the look of disgust and horror on your face just now when I told you, I don't think your mum *really* wanted or *needed* to see it as well."

"Oh god, I'm a terrible child aren't I? I'm an adult and so is she and deserves to be happy. She's been through so much already and spent most of our childhood alone, bringing Matt and I up. I should be happy for her, not freaked out by it."

"I think it's understandable, Leila. None of us, even as adults, want to think of our parents having sex or intimate relationships, even when they've been married for a hundred years. This one kind of snuck up on you and I think it was more shock, than true disgust at the thought of your mum having a companion of the male variety." I nudge her shoulder with mine, which is a little difficult in the tight embrace I'm not ready to move out of yet. "You never know, maybe it's a companion of the female variety!" My joke earns me an exceptionally dirty look and even though I know I shouldn't, I can't help laughing again because I've never seen that look on her face before. It's something Kenna would be very proud of to be honest.

"Look, I don't really care as long as she's happy but really, Caleb? I just found out she's seeing someone and felt like she couldn't tell me." Her voice is little whiny and that makes me laugh as well because I have *never* heard her behave like a child before. Ever. She's a smart, capable, intelligent human being and a great manager. We've kept the same staff since she was put in charge of Vines and it's not because my brother is easy to deal with, let me tell you!

"Leila, maybe it's new, maybe it's not. Maybe she's just having fun and therefore didn't want to tell you."

"Are you telling me my *mum* has a booty call or friends with benefits kind of arrangement?" She interrupts me.

"No because I truly have no idea what she's got going on." She steps out of my arms, takes a few steps away from me and crosses her arms over her chest. I miss touching her the second she's out of my arms and I know I'm in deep. When she raises an eyebrow at me, I have to pull my lips into my mouth and hold them there with my teeth to stop from laughing again.

"Really? I think you're protesting too much. You have information, don't you? You two got pretty chummy in a few short hours. She *told* you, didn't she?" It's an accusation and one I can firmly deny.

"We didn't get *chummy,* as you put it pretty quickly. I like your mum and we have an understanding but no, no she did not tell me she has a gentleman, or lady, friend with or without benefits, so no I can't answer that for you. I do not have confirmation at all." I know I sound even more ridiculous and like I've got something to hide but I don't. She can't get more information out of me when I don't actually have it.

"What kind of understanding?" Her question is quiet, unsure. I take two large steps towards her and take her hands in mine.

"To protect you and not be an idiot and hurt you." I smile the cheeky smile that normally gets me out of all kinds of trouble *and* I know she likes it too.

"Don't pull out that smile."

"What smile?" I raise my eyes and try to pull off looking innocent.

"You know which one." I cock my head to the side and bat my eyes. "Cut it out! You *know* the smile, the one you use to charm people, women specifically. It gets you out of trouble almost every time."

"It does?" I place a hand on my chest, let my mouth drop open and my eyes widen in mock shock.

"It does and you know it! Don't play the innocent act with me." She laughs and that's what I wanted, so now I'm happy.

"Well, it made you smile and that's all that matters to me." I say taking her hand in mine and running my thumb over the ring she's wearing. My ring. "Are you ready to head down for dinner? They're probably waiting for us." I pull my phone out of my jeans pocket to check the time and find a message from Brian there.

Brian: *Don't forget, dinner is at half past six, don't be late*
Me: *We're on our way*

"Are *you* ready?" Leila asks me, it's her turn to raise an eyebrow at me.

"Yeah, sorry. I was checking the time but there was a message from Brian reminding us to not be late for dinner."

"Let's go then." She says with a smile, pulling on my hand to walk with her and the fact that she doesn't drop my hand makes me even happier. What can I say? I'm easy to please.

"Do you want to take a picture to send to Kim, first?"

"You know what? It can wait until tomorrow, she's obviously busy and doesn't need me interrupting her *and* we have our own plans."

"Alright then, let's get this show on the road, Darlin'." The smile she gives me, my lord! It warms my heart completely and I know that the affection will not be fake when people look at us.

I lead her out of our suite and she closes the door behind us. We're laughing and joking, so I don't notice the couple walking up behind us until it's too late.

"Caleb Drake! How are you my darling?" I close my eyes and take a deep breath because this, *this* is not going to be a lot of fun and not just because I'm going to have to introduce Leila to this mother and daughter pair but because I have to talk to them as well. I give Leila a look that I *hope* like hell says, 'please fucking forgive me but I'm about to lay it on thick,' because otherwise, we won't even be fake friends, much less fake engaged!

"Anita. Francine." I say through gritted teeth that I hope I'm hiding reasonably well. Leila notices though because she stiffens slightly beside me, obviously recognising the names from our earlier conversation with Brian and Mary. Instead of moving away from me though like I expected, she moves close and wraps her arm around my waist. I can't help the smile that spreads across my face, even in the face of these two women, Leila makes me beyond happy.

"And who is this?" Anita's smile isn't friendly, it's almost predatory but my girl, she doesn't even flinch.

"Leila, this is Anita and Francine Roberts, friends of Brian and Mary." I introduce Leila to them, rather than the other way around because I know Anita will take it the way it was meant. "Ladies, this is my fiancée, Leila Phillips."

"Your, *fiancée*?" Anita squeals in some horrendously high pitched voice and both Leila and I flinch from the noise. Anita reaches over and grips on to her mother's arm, who in turn wraps her arms around her daughter's shoulders.

"Yes, we're engaged." Leila, the beautiful woman that she is, flashes them the ring on her finger and flashes *me* the most amazing smile, causing one of my own to spread across my face, even as she presses a kiss to my cheek. "We haven't picked a date yet but we're not really in any hurry. I mean, both his brother and sister got married recently, so we figured people wouldn't mind a break."

I pull this magnificent woman in closer to me, as she rests her hand on my chest, displaying more than just that ring on her finger and I leave a kiss of my own on her cheek, a little closer to her lips than she got to mine and when she doesn't pull away, I smile even larger.

"Well, congratulations." Francine says, he teeth clenched tight. "To you both. That is a truly beautiful ring, Caleb. You must be so happy, Lola."

"Leila." I correct, before my *fiancée* can even take a breath. "It's Leila, don't forget it, she's going to be my wife as soon as we can get a date organised."

"I am happy, *Francine* but not because of the ring, as gorgeous as it is. I'm happy because I get to marry my best friend and the kindest, sweetest man I know." She emphases the woman's name and I wonder if it's her way of letting the women know she knows who they are and they don't matter. Or it could just be that she's letting them know that she's a nicer person than they are because she remembers their names. Either way, my heart pounds with pride.

Anita hasn't said a word, she's recovering from the news that I'm getting married and that makes this whole weekend worth it.

"Shall we continue heading on down to dinner? You know Brian will start looking for us if we take too much longer."

"Of course." Francine replies.

"Why don't you ladies lead the way? We wouldn't want you to witness anything that might offend you." I wave them by us and I can feel Leila's body shaking slightly with laughter beside me. I lean over and kiss her on the temple so that I can whisper close to her ear without looking like I'm whispering *in* her ear, "Stop it or we'll both be laughing and that's not good."

She rolls her lips between her teeth to stop the smile and pulls herself together, giving me a slight nod. I pull back from her but don't remove myself from her side and start following the women to the dining room.

It would be wrong to tell her I love her, wouldn't it? Because there is no doubt in my mind, that in this minute, I love Leila fucking Phillips.

Chapter Twenty-two
LEILA

I thought poor Anita was going to pass out when Caleb introduced me as his fiancée and I struggled not to laugh. Although, I feel that I'm going to bear witness to women having this same reaction over the weekend and I can tell you, *that* is a sobering thought!

I knew that he was popular with the ladies but this takes it to a whole new level, truly. I'm also starting to understand why he wanted a fake fiancée and not a girlfriend. Mary's reaction earlier when we got here was something else and then, we have Anita. Even her mother, Francine, had quite a reaction. I'm guessing she was hoping for a joining of two families but I can't imagine Caleb with anyone like her daughter, with or without me in the picture.

Having Caleb call her out on calling me the wrong name was kind of delightful and heart-warming as well. He held me closer and defended me in a weird way, in front of these two women, letting them know that I meant something to him.

"There you are." Mary says, by way of greeting and walks by the mother and daughter pair without sparing them a glance, causing Caleb's smile to grow. When she reaches us, she takes Caleb in a warm embrace but he manages to keep hold of my hand. He's forced to drop my hand though when she embraces me in a hug that I wasn't expecting, almost knocking me off my feet, forcing me to let go of his hand to hold on to her so that we both don't go down in a heap on the floor.

"We weren't gone *that* long, Mary." Caleb chuckles behind us somewhere.

"Why did you four come in together? Did you meet in the hallway?" Brian's booming voice asks from somewhere behind his wife. I think.

"Yes." The two other women chime as Caleb says, "No."

"Which is it then?" Brian asks, while I'm still being tightly held by his wife.

"They met us in the hallway just outside our room." Caleb explains, his voice tight with annoyance and Brian grunts, I assume that he's just as annoyed but I can't see his face yet.

"I thought I told you ladies that you were to stick to the main areas of the house and the wing where your suite is located?" Brain asks them, his voice quite cold.

"We were unaware that we were banned from moving freely around the house, Brian." Anita says snottily to our hosts.

"No-one said you weren't free to walk the grounds, Anita but you were specially told to stay away from that wing of the house. There are plenty of other areas that you *are* free to use." Brian says, as Mary finally lets me go.

"We got lost." Francine explains with a smile. "It won't happen again, we promise." She's smiling but it's tight and I don't know about the others but I'm feeling pretty uncomfortable.

"You didn't get lost, Francine and we all know it. You know this house almost as well as I do!" Mary scoffs as Caleb pulls me into his side once again. "Now, I think we can all agree that we know *why* you decided to go over there and we can all agree that you need to *not* do it again."

"I don't know what you're implying." Anita starts but her mother knocks her hip into her daughters, obviously trying to get the other woman to shut the hell up. I would be doing the same if I were her because the look on Mary's face scares the hell out of me and I think she's as sweet as pie.

"OK, I'll spell it out for you then." Brian says, anger lacing his voice. "You went looking for Caleb here because you either saw him arrive or saw his car. I think none of us, except poor Miss Leila perhaps, are under any illusions as to why you went looking for him. I know that Mary and I have been part of the problem, trying to find him someone to share his life with but that stops now. He is engaged to be married and that's all there is to it. I will not take any more of these shenanigans this weekend, Francine, Anita. Do you understand me?"

"We're not children you know, Brian and I think we can handle walking anywhere on the property we like." Anita scowls at him, pulling herself up and pulling her shoulders back in defiance. She looks like a child who is having a tantrum, while rebelling against her father.

"Anita." Francine scolds her daughter. "We're sorry, Brian." She at least has the decency to look embarrassed by her daughter's behaviour.

"There will be no harassment of Caleb or Leila this weekend." Mary looks between the two women, I find myself withering a little under that look myself and it isn't even directed at me! "I know that this is partially my fault, I have introduced Caleb as an eligible bachelor previously *and* I've participated in setting him up on many dates but it stops now. He's with Leila now and they have plans to marry. If I see or hear of any misdeeds, then I will not hesitate in asking for you to be escorted off the property."

"We promise there won't be any issues, Mary." Francine promises. "Don't we, Anita." She nudges her daughter, prompting her to drag her eyes away from Caleb and back to Mary.

"Sure." She answers begrudgingly, with a smile that we can all see is less than sincere.

"With that out of the way, let's move into the dining room and enjoy our dinner." Mary says with a smile, waving for the two women to go ahead of her.

"Let's hope that it isn't cold by now." Brian grumbles beside Caleb, who laughs at his friend and mentor.

"I have no doubt in your chef's skills, Brian, none whatsoever. I do believe that she knows exactly how to keep a meal warm for a few extra minutes." Caleb teases, causing Brian to give him a side eye that could kill the most hardened of men, which makes Caleb laugh harder.

"Come now, Caleb, you know how he is about his meals. Right on time or it's ruined!" Mary joins in the light-hearted teasing and this time I laugh quietly as well.

"Oh Leila, you've broken an old man's heart by joining in with these two!" Brian announces as we enter the dining room where Francine and Anita are already seated and another, older couple are seated beside them.

"I'm sorry but honestly, I'm laughing because I'm with you, Brian. I understand the importance of eating food when it's ready and at the perfect temperature."

"Of course you do! You're a trained pastry chef, how could I have forgotten?" Brian says, and all heads turn to us, making me wish I could crawl under a rock but as Caleb places his hand gently on my lower back, I feel comfort in his support. "I do hope that whatever we're dishing up for dessert tonight meets your very high standards."

"I have no doubt it will." I smile genuinely at him because if I've learned anything about our hosts, it's that they're all about the quality of the things they offer and I'm beginning to understand why Caleb wants to work with Brian for his brewery venture.

When we're all seated, Caleb and I are opposite the new couple, who we're both introduced to and I'm relieved that Caleb doesn't know them either. Francine and Anita are sitting on the other side of the table as well, which means I don't have to sit next to either one of them but I don't have to look at them directly either. The table isn't large though, so I can't exactly escape them either.

Anita keeps asking Caleb questions about Drake Wines, about him and I know that what she's really trying to do is show *me* that she knows him as well, if not better than I do. It's a pissing contest to her and beating her chest like some hyped up macho guy who is trying to take back his toy. I could answer the questions for Caleb and put her back in her box but it's so much more fun to just sit here quietly, knowing that he's not even telling her half-truths. I know his family well and I know that he's not telling her everything.

I smile to myself as we wait for dessert to come to the table and Caleb startles me by leaning over, his lips so close to my ear that they're almost resting on it.

"What's so funny, Darlin'?" He murmurs in my ear, the vibration of his voice travel over my skin, leaving goosebumps along it.

"Nothing, I was just thinking." I answer, turning my head slightly to look at him so he can hear me because I'm talking so softly.

"Thinking? About what?" He asks and if I'm not mistaken there's a little bit of hope in his eyes.

"Your friend over there was just reminding me how much I know about you and your family." I smile at him. "And I realise just how happy I am that I found Drake Wines and that I work at Vines."

"She's not my friend, in any sense of the word, Leila." He growls. Before I can respond, we're interrupted.

"Dessert is served." The head server announces as plates of a beautifully, decadent chocolate concoction is placed down on the table in front of us.

"This conversation isn't over, Darlin.'" Caleb announces, before pulling back from me, leaving my body feeling chilled in his absence. "Enjoy your dessert." He says so that the rest of the table can hear him.

"I do hope it meets up to your high expectations, Leila." Mary says with a smile.

"Nothing could *ever* live up to Leila's gorgeous, four layered chocolate cake but I'll give this a shot at impressing me." Caleb announces, causing me to blush.

"Oh, I've had that cake at Vines, is that one of your creations, Leila?" Mary asks.

"Yes, it is. I make it fresh every morning."

"You sell that many?" Mary asks, astonished and I can't help smiling at her.

"Well, we have a certain customer who eats a slice of it every day but yes, other than him we can actually go through two full cakes on busy days. It just depends on what else is on offer and if people want to try something new or go for an old faithful."

"Personally, I find trying new things very interesting and exciting." Anita comments, her eyes drilling a hole into the side of Caleb's head but he doesn't look up when he responds.

"*Personally*, I like knowing what I'm getting and what to expect but that doesn't mean you can't have something spontaneous and different every now and then, even with the same cake and flavours." He takes another mouthful of the dessert and turns to Mary. "Compliments to the chef as always Mary but it doesn't hold a candle to my favourite pastry chef's desserts. I'm not sure I could eat anything that could." He takes my hand, that was resting on the table in his and pulls it up to his lips, leaving a delectable soft kiss on my knuckles.

I don't think I need dessert after that sweet kiss and those sweet words. I also think I need to put the brakes on a little more because this heart of mine is due to break when we get home!

Chapter Twenty-three
CALEB

Once dessert is over and we've stayed at the table to join in the after dinner conversation for the appropriate amount of time, I excuse both of us from the gathering. If Leila's surprised, she doesn't show it, she simply follows my lead after thanking our hosts and telling the other couple that she was pleased to meet them, then says a quick goodnight to the Roberts ladies.

I lead her through the house, my hand resting lightly on her lower back, until we come to some French doors that open onto the garden that Mary has lovingly tended over the years.

"You navigate your way around this house so easily, I'm going to assume that you've been here a few times?" It's posed as a question that she already knows the answer to.

"A few, yeah."

I take her hand in mine and lead her around the beautiful gardens on the Weaver's property. Both of us quiet and in our thoughts for a few minutes. I don't know about Leila but I'm enjoying the quiet for a few minutes. Anita's constant nattering and questioning drove me insane but not answering would have been rude. I know what she was doing was the female equivalent to beating her chest and proving that she knew me better than my fiancée does and had this been my home, she wouldn't have gotten away with it. She would have been kicked out, in fact, she wouldn't have been invited to start with.

"I'm sorry." I say into the quiet night.

"About what?" Her question seems genuine but I'm not sure.

"You know what." I sigh, shaking my head. "I should have warned you about those two, especially Anita, before we encountered them but I'd hoped that Brian and Mary hadn't invited them, especially when I told Brian I was bringing you. On the other hand, I thought that *if* she was here, that when she heard you were with me, that she would back the hell off. I should have known better."

"It must be hard having beautiful women fall at your feet all day." She bumps her shoulder into mine and I know she's trying to lighten the mood but I'm not feeling it. What I *do* feel is like I'm an arsehole for putting her in this position at all. "Hey, I was joking."

"I know." I reply but I can't look at her.

"Women like them? They don't have boundaries, believe me, Caleb, I've encountered more of them than you could hope to imagine. Although, I do get now why you wanted, well needed, our arrangement." She whispers the last part like someone is skulking around listening to our conversation hoping to catch us in a lie.

"I'm sorry, Leila."

"So you've said but I'm still trying to work out what *you* have to be sorry about. Anita's behaviour is not on you, it's not your fault. If she had or even still *has* feelings for you, I get it, it can be hard to let go but as long as you never lead her on, then I don't see how her behaviour has anything to do with you. I also don't see why you'd need to keep apologising for someone else's behaviour. That's on her and her mother, not you."

"I never lead her on, I swear, Leila. I've never touched her in any kind of way that would have led her to believe that we had anything between us. I don't even have her phone number to call or text with her, I promise." I stop to think for a second. "We've danced a couple of times, at other events like this one but it was out of politeness, nothing more."

"You don't have to explain yourself to me, Caleb. We both have a past, who you did or didn't sleep with before me is none of my business." She says it with a smile but when I stop to look in her eyes I see a little bit of hurt. Perhaps that's just wishful thinking?

"I don't know about you but I don't want to think about you being with other guys before me. You're mine now and even though I know you have a past, that you're here with me is all that matters now."

"Same."

"I just wish *my* past wasn't getting in both of our faces this weekend." With my free hand resting on her hip, I pull her to fully face me, her free hand comes up to rest on my chest and I'm enjoying our closeness.

"Well, we are here so that your haunted past can move on, so I think we're on the right track." She laughs. Her laughter dies out as soon as she realises how close we are now and she has to tilt her head back slightly to look me in the eyes still. Our faces suddenly so close, that I can feel her breath on my lips.

"Just go with me, OK?" My voice so quiet I'm not even sure she heard me but when I hear her gasp, then feel a slight nod of her head, I know she did. I drop my lips to hers, not that they had to travel a huge distance and the second they touch, the world around us disappears.

My eyes close, my hand on her hip tightens and I drop her hand from my other to reach up and hold her cheek, keeping her lips on mine for as long as I possibly can. I have wanted this kiss, our first kiss for months and it meets every expectation I ever had and then overtakes them.

When Leila moans into the kiss, I drag my tongue along her bottom lip, encouraging her to open up to me. To give me more. I need more and when she gives it to me so freely, I can't help but take it. I push my tongue into her mouth and I'm greeted with her tongue, touching mine and matching me with every thrust, push and pull.

Her free hand runs up my side, sending shivers through my spine with every millimetre that she touches, goosebumps pebble my skin but when the hand she has resting my chest grips hold of my pec, I groan and deepen the kiss. Then she pushes her body closer to mine and it's like we can't get close enough.

This kiss is everything. It's everything I ever wanted, ever thought it could be and more. It's all consuming to the point that I've forgotten where we are. Both of us want more and I know, somewhere deep in my brain where it can still think in this moment, that this kind of want and chemistry can't be faked.

A cough in the distance registers but I ignore it. Until there's another one and then a louder one, followed closely by chuckling.

"Sorry to interrupt kids but I really want to talk to you both." Brian's voice permeates into my brain and I drag my lips from Leila's under protest.

I take a second to rest my forehead on hers before I grip her tight so that she can't get out of my arms, before turning to look at Brian. I hope he can see the frustration his presence is giving me, written all over my face.

"Brian." My voice doesn't even sound like mine, it's rough and gravelly.

"I'm sorry to interrupt you, Caleb, I can see you were busy." He chuckles, again and I wonder for a second if I can kill him and bury him in his own damned garden. "I can see those murderous intentions, Caleb and I can't say I blame you."

"Then why *did* you interrupt, Brian?"

"I told him not to." Damn, I hadn't even noticed that Mary was standing right next to her husband until she spoke.

Leila hasn't spoken and when I glance her way, I see that she's standing stock still in my arms, her eyes still closed and her breathing laboured, like she can't quite catch it. I did that to her and I feel my chest expand with pride.

"We should have let them be, Brian." Mary admonishes her husband. "Well, *you* should have let them be and walked away, just like I suggested but no, you decided your apology just couldn't wait!" I really wish that he'd taken his wife's advice.

"What is it you need, Brian?" I ask, sounding a little harsher than I probably should but I don't care right now.

"I just wanted to apologise again. About Francine and Anita." I feel Leila's body stiffen slightly against mine at the mention of their names but how do I tell her she has nothing to worry about? "I knew how Anita felt about you and I shouldn't have invited them but the invitations were done before you told us about beautiful Leila here and well."

"Don't finish that sentence, please Brian." I beg him, knowing the exact words that are hanging between the four of us now.

"So, now that that's out of the way, we'll let you two get back to, well you know." Mary says and I watch as she pulls Brian away from us.

"Oh my god, that was hot!" Leila says breathily. "And *so* embarrassing!"

"I'm sorry, I didn't mean to embarrass you." I go to step back, dropping my hands from where they've been resting on her hips while Brian and Mary were talking.

"No!" Her hands reach for mine and she places them back on her hips, then she puts her hands back on mine and pulls me back into her body. "Don't go. I didn't mean *you* embarrassed me, I meant it was like getting caught making out by our parents kind of embarrassing. I didn't say I wanted to stop!"

Laughter is bubbling up in my chest but I don't feel like laughing anymore when her eyes drop to my lips and then she licks hers. I don't know whether she can still taste me on her lips or whether it's the anticipation on having my lips on hers again, either way, I don't care.

"Are you sure?"

My question goes unanswered, my words at least because her lips land on mine half second after my question is asked. No words necessary, just touch.

One of her hands slides up my side, over my shoulder and her fingers tangle in my hair, holding my lips to hers so there's no escape from her. Doesn't she know that I have no intention of going anywhere. For as long as she'll let me, I'm sticking by her.

Chapter Twenty-four
LEILA

I could stand in this garden and kiss the life out of Caleb Drake all damned night and all tomorrow but we've already been interrupted once, by our hosts no less and I don't want to run the risk of anyone else finding us.

"Come on." I pull back a little bit, our lips still touching.

"Where?" He mumbles, his eyes still closed, not wanting to let go of the moment and neither do I, that's why we have to go.

"Back."

"Back, where?"

"To the room."

"Oh, OK. Absolutely." His eyes snap open, then he takes two too many steps away from me and I reach out for him, to bring him back to touching me.

"I don't want to stop, Caleb, I want privacy." I smile, hoping to reassure him.

His eyes dart between mine, obviously trying to read my thoughts and I let him. He must find whatever he was looking for and he takes my hand in his and leads us back towards the house.

"Caleb." The guy from the other couple at dinner says and I can't for the life of me remember his name right now.

"Sorry, Simon, I can't talk right now." Caleb says, walking right by the man and towing me behind him. Simon's laughter follows us as we reach the same French doors that we left through earlier.

"Caleb, Leila." Francine's voice says from somewhere that I can't see.

"Sorry, Francine, we'll catch up later." Caleb calls over his shoulder.

"I just wanted to apologise for earlier." She calls back.

"It's all good, Francine." He calls as we leave the room and start for the stairs.

"Mr Drake." Caleb stops in his tracks and I crash into his back. "Sorry, I can see you're busy, it's nothing important."

"If you're looking for me, it's important enough, Jeff." Caleb smiles, his entire demeanour changed.

"No, it truly can wait until later." Jeff smiles my way and it's a kind smile. "Or in the morning. You kids go enjoy your evening. Honestly, Mr Drake, it can wait." Jeff turns and walks away and Caleb stands still for a minute watching his retreating back.

Suddenly, he's walking again and we're both heading up the stairs.

When we reach our room, his hand reaches out for the door handle and then hesitates. I know what he's thinking, so I press my front to his back and reach around him to open the door. Then, I push gently against his back, urging him forward.

Caleb closes the door behind us, then rests his head on the door. His breathing is laboured but when I place my hand on his back, his breathing stutters.

"Leila." His voice is barely loud enough for me to hear and there is so much said in just my name.

"Caleb. Look at me." He shakes his head, rolling his forehead on the back of the door. "Please look at me, Caleb, I don't want to talk to your back."

"I can't."

"Caleb, I don't want to beg you to look at me but I will if I need to."

"Leila. If I look at you, I don't think I'll be able to stop myself from." He stops talking and lets out a shuddering breath.

"Look at me damn it to hell, Caleb Drake!" He spins around so fast, I stumble backwards in shock. He catches my hands and sets me upright, tight against his chest.

"You never have to beg me Darlin', you just have to ask. Ask for whatever it is you want and you shall receive. I can promise you that I will always give it you freely and willingly." He takes my face in his hands, so gently but then he kisses me. It's a deep, almost brutal kiss and I can feel it's touch right down to my soul.

I pull back after a few minutes, not because I want to but because I need to. Our lips are just millimetres from each other when I speak.

"Take me to bed, Caleb."

"Are you sure?"

"Make love to me, please." His hands to my arse, squeezing each cheek roughly before hitching me up and encouraging me to wrap my legs around his hips, my arms wrapping around his neck to keep us both steady.

He walks us back without looking, to the bedroom. The next thing I know, I'm flying! I land on my back on the soft bed, with a squeal of surprise. He stands between my feet that are hanging over the edge of the bed for a few seconds just looking at me. Suddenly, he's hovering over me and I see the hesitation in his eyes.

"Are you sure about this Leila? We can stop any time. Now, in five minutes, in ten minutes. You never have to do anything you don't want to and you shouldn't regret anything we do the next morning, either." How could I ever regret being with this man?

"Yes." It's simple and to the point. Not hidden messages or anything to interpret. "I want you, Caleb."

He searches my eyes for a split second, finding whatever he's looking for, he starts to undress. His shirt is undone, hanging off his shoulders, the button on his jeans is popped open, when I kick off my shoes and start to sit up. I can't watch him get naked any longer without joining in with the quest to get naked as well.

"No. I get to unwrap you."

"I'm not a present, Caleb." I giggle. Giggle! I never giggle damn it!

"Yes you are, you're a gift and I want the pleasure of unwrapping you, Darlin'." Who says those kinds of things? Caleb Drake, obviously!

"What about you?"

"What about me?" He cocks an eyebrow at me, obviously confused and completely adorable!

"Doesn't that make *you* my gift that I get to unwrap?" I send him what I hope is *my* version of his cocky smirk and start to sit up again, my hands reaching out to touch him.

"Darlin', you don't need to unwrap me, I am more than willing to get naked for you." He says, giving me that sexy, cocky smirk of his, as he gently pushes me back onto the bed.

"Then do it." I tell him, putting my hands behind my head and settling in to watch the show.

"Oh, we like demanding do we?" He says as his shirt drops to the floor at his feet.

"Sometimes." I shrug my shoulders, if he can't handle me liking to be in charge in the bedroom sometimes, then this is all over before we've even begun. "I'm not going to apologise for it."

"I wouldn't expect you to, Leila and I never said I didn't like it." He answers, as he draws the zipper on his jeans down. He moves so slowly, I feel like we're in quicksand. I want to tell him to hurry but I'm also enjoying the drawn out torture. "It's hot as fuck when a woman knows what she wants in the bedroom. I'm even willing to let you tie me up, if that's what you want." I gulp because I couldn't think of anything hotter than seeing Caleb tied to my bed and just waiting for me. He lets out a light, low chuckle. "I see you like that idea. Who knew there was a dirty girl under all of that sugar and pastry?"

"I still won't apologise." I raise my chin at him, I won't be talked into believing that what I like is wrong. Been there, done that.

"I never asked you, Darlin' but we probably shouldn't do that in someone else's home. We can certainly talk more on the subject on the way home and when we get home though, dirty girl and I can tell you, I am *so* fucking looking forward to it."

I swallow deeply again because I should have known Caleb Drake could handle anything I wanted to do. He's probably done more than I have or could even think of doing but that won't stop me.

"Are you just gonna talk all night or are we getting naked?"

"We're getting there, sassy pants." He smirks as he drops his jeans to the floor, leaving him in just his boxer briefs and I let out a gasp. He's still not naked but holy shit!

Is his body perfect? Maybe not to some. There's a hint of a six pack, he has defined pecs and his biceps are something else. I think he's the definition of gorgeous and that's all that matters to me right now and all I want is to be able to touch him. To have permission to run my hands all over him and learn every bump and divot with my fingers and my tongue. Yes! I want to lick him all over, taste him and get to know him.

"What are you thinking about, Darlin'?" He drops down to the bed, his body covering mine without touching it and I ache to reach up with every limb but I resist. I don't answer him, I can't. "Don't hold back on me, Leila, not now, not ever. Anything you want, you ask and if I don't want to or I'm not comfortable with it, I'll let you know. Same if I ask or try something, you have every right to say no, you're not comfortable or you don't want to. This is all about communication and everything between us is consensual. You understand? Leila?"

I'm searching his eyes, looking for even a hint that he isn't sincere and he lets me. It's like he understands that I need this, I need to know that we're equals even if one has the power at different points, we can both stop at any time.

"Yes." My voice is quiet but it's clear and strong in the otherwise silent room. It's his turn to search my eyes for the truth and he must find it.

"Are you sure you want to do this? This changes everything." He asks and I nod. "Words, Leila, I need to hear you say it."

"I want this, Caleb. I *need* you, please?" I see a flash of something I can't quite name in his eyes and then he's gone. I go to sit up to see where he went and to ask what the hell I did but before I can speak, my jeans are torn from my body.

"Up." He directs and I sit up. Seconds later I'm left in my pale yellow, lacey underwear. Are they a matching set? Hell yes, that's all I brought with me to wear all weekend. Did I do it because I planned on this happening? No but I thought that if he did see me in my underwear by some odd turn of events, I wasn't going to be caught in comfy granny undies again! "You. Are. Gorgeous. Even more beautiful than I imagined."

"You imagined what I'd look like in my underwear?" I'm shocked and not because he's imagining a woman in her underwear but that that woman is *me*.

"You have no idea." He runs a hand up the inside of my leg, from my ankle all the way up to my inner thigh. My legs spread to give him room and he groans. "So soft. So silky. So biteable." He drops to his knees beside the bed, hooks his hands under my knees and drags my body towards him until my legs are hanging over his shoulders, knees resting on the edge of his shoulders, keeping me spread open for him.

"Caleb." My voice is a deep, raspy noise that feels like I'm pushing it out over gravel. I feel like my senses are being overloaded and he's barely touched me. When he bends his head and kisses the inside of my knee and then slowly makes his way up my thigh with soft kisses and soft nibbles, I almost fucking die! "Fuck!"

"Not yet, Darlin' but soon, I promise."

"Caleb." His name is more of an exhale, than an actual word. My head drops back to the bed, I can't watch his progress anymore, he's barely touching me and I feel like I'm going to explode. I close my eyes, trying to hold back some of the sensations but it doesn't help because he hums his answer against my thigh and it sends vibrations up my leg, through my entire body and it feels like the vibration ends at my clit. That bundles of nerves is on high alert and is throbbing with need. The need to be touched, to not be touched but to come anyway.

"Are you attached to these?" He asks and I'm brought out of my relaxed state by his question because I don't understand it.

"What?"

"Your underwear. Are you attached to them?" I must give him a look that tells him I'm as confused as I feel. "Ahh fuck it, I'll buy you more, in any damned colour you want." Then he hooks his fingers into the sides of them and pulls. Then he pulls again and we hear a rip. Another pull and more ripping.

"Ohhh." I suddenly understand his question. "Well, they were a cute colour."

"They were sexy as fuck." He confirms, as he gives them another yank and he frees one side. "Fuck it." He repeats and pulls what's left of them off my leg, throwing them to the side.

"Well, that was. Different."

"That was harder than the movies make it look, that's for sure." We both look at the pile of lace on the floor for a few seconds, amazed that it held on so well. "Now, where was I?"

Seconds later, I've forgotten about ripped lace and torn up underwear. I don't care how many pairs he ruins if he can use his fingers and tongue like that!

"Fuck!"

"Soon, Darlin', really fucking soon." I'm not sure if it's a promise or a threat but either way, I can't fucking wait!

Chapter Twenty-five
CALEB

She tastes even better than I imagined and I imagined being here, between her legs more often than I should have.

I try to hold back, I don't want to scare her or bite her too hard as I nibble my way up her thigh. I nip here and there, then lick and suck it to take the sting away. With every bite, Leila sucks in a breath and relaxes when I lick it better.

"You like that, don't you Darlin'?"

"Yes." That one word is more of a hiss, than a word but I know what she means and I love that I've given her so much enjoyment even though I've barely touched her, that she can only hiss out a word. I smile against her thigh. "What are you smiling about mister? Don't you have things to do?" Damn I am *so* going to enjoy her bossiness in the bedroom!

"Yes ma'am!" I don't salute, instead I use my hands to spread her even wider for me so that I can see her pussy. That's where I want to be. I can see and smell how turned on she is and I'm excited to push ahead, instead I take my time, it will be better for both of us in the end and I know it. That doesn't make it easier to show some restraint, not when everything in me is begging me to skip the next few steps and get to the last one but I won't. I'm going to savour the time I have because who knows if this is my first and last time that I'll get this close to Leila.

Then my tongue touches her clit, her hips try to rise up off the bed but my grip on her thighs holds her still, so instead of lifting, she squirms.

"Hold still, Darlin' or I won't be about to make you come."

"I can't."

I release a thigh and smack the side of her arse and she groans. I just found something else my beautiful vixen loves.

"Move again and you'll get another one, only harder." I warn her and I hear her shocked intake of breath, just as I suck her clit into my mouth, making her moan again and her back arch off the bed, pushing her pussy away from my mouth. So, I follow through on my threat and smack her arse cheek, harder this time, seeing as how she very conveniently raised it up high enough that I could.

"Arghh! Fuck!"

"Are you going to stop moving?"

"No!"

"Well then, I look forward to watching you try to sit at the breakfast table in the morning." I don't give her the chance to respond because I suck her clit into my mouth again, hard and push a finger into her wet and pulsing pussy.

I drop my other hand from her thigh, to rub my cock through my boxers, feeling how ready for me she is makes my own need even worse. My cock just wants me to stop it already and let him in.

Or out? Ugh who cares?

Leila moves around a little but she still can't move too much with her legs up, over my shoulders like that. So, I change it up and push two fingers into her pussy, twisting them as I pump them in and out of her, working both of us up into a frenzy. I feel like I might lose my mind!

"Caleb!"

"Yes, Darlin'?" I ask with my lips resting on hers, the vibration of my voice on her now sensitive skin, making her shiver violently.

"Caleb. I'm going to." I pull my fingers from her pussy and push back from the bed. "What the? No! Get back here! Caleb, handsome, please?"

"Please, what?" She flings her arm over her face and growls, fucking *growls* in frustration at me. It probably shouldn't turn me on as much as it does but it makes my whole body hot and ready to jump. On her that is. Instead, I lower my body over hers, letting them lightly touch. "Move your arm."

"Arghh." She hesitates for a few seconds and just when I think she's not going to do as I ask, she flings her arm to the side so hard it bounces on the mattress. "Caleb, please, just let me come and then I promise, *I promise,* I will make you see stars!"

"Oh, you're right, you'll make me see stars, Darlin' but you need to learn some patience first." That earns me another growl and I kiss the tip of her nose. She growls again as she wraps her legs around my hips and pushes them down, making my cock nestle right where it wants to be, well close enough.

"I don't like getting so close to coming and then not being allowed to, Caleb, it's not much fun."

"That may be true, Leila but when you finally *do* come, you're not just going to be seeing stars, you'll be seeing entire solar systems." Her eyes are searching mine as I ask, "do you trust me?"

"Yes." She doesn't hesitate and I know without a doubt that she does in fact trust me, not just in the bedroom either. My cock twitches against her and she pushes up, grinding our hips together.

"Fuck!" I grind out between clenched teeth, my arms starting to shake from the effort of not just holding me up but because my entire body is just holding on.

"Yes, Caleb. Now. You said I didn't have to beg, I just had to ask, right?" I nod because I doubt that I can speak. "Then, what are you waiting for?"

I push myself off her body with such force that her legs drop to the bed and I can see that she's about to ask what's going on. I can see the panic in her eyes and the flash of anger. Stepping away from the bed, I walk over to my bag, only taking my eyes off her for a second at a time to make sure that I don't crash into anything or fall over. It wouldn't be a great look, when I'm trying to show her just how smooth I can be.

"What-?" She begins to ask, as I bend over to reach into my bag and when I stand back up, I have a box of condoms in my hand. An unopened, fresh box of condoms. "I guess you came prepared then?" Annoyance lacing her voice and I'm not sure what she's thinking but either way those thoughts could go, I'm pretty sure she's wrong.

"I didn't put them in there." I explain.

"You sure did find them fast enough though for someone who didn't know they were there. They didn't just magically appear, Caleb." She's sitting up, trying to find something to cover up her gorgeous body and I know I have to speak fast.

"I didn't put them in there, Jules did."

"What?"

"I didn't plan this, Leila and I sure as hell didn't plan on sleeping with anyone else this weekend."

"Oh." The anger is replaced with disappointment and I realise how what I said might have sounded to her.

"No, Darlin', you misunderstand me." I throw the box on the bed and crawl up the bed to lie facing the gorgeous woman who just moments ago was begging me to let her come, now she thinks I don't want her. "Jules put them in there somehow when he knew we were leaving Drake's together. He messaged me when we were at your mum's to let me know that he'd left a surprise in my bag. I found them and buried them under all of my clothes, that's how I knew exactly where to find them. It's also how they got in there to begin with."

"OK." She still hasn't relaxed though, so I run my hand up and down her thigh, trying to soothe her but also because I just want to touch her while she'll let me. Tonight, for now at least, I have permission, so I'm going to do it as often as I can.

"Leila, Darlin', what I meant when I said I didn't plan this, isn't what you assume. I meant that I wasn't going to push or pressure you into anything this weekend. I would have been more than happy to spend time with you, away from Drake Wines and Vines and all of the prying eyes that I feel watch our every move when we're together. Maybe I'm just paranoid."

"Oh, well I was looking forward to spending time with you too." I run my knuckles gently over her cheek, jaw line and then trace her bottom lip with the tip of my finger.

"I'm glad." I smile. "I want this, I want you but if you're not comfortable, Baby, I'm OK with stopping right here too."

"But you're still hard." We both look down to my crotch like I need to check that my cock is still hard and ready where Leila is concerned.

"I am but it won't kill me, Darlin'. It wouldn't be the first time I've gone to sleep with a hard-on and I doubt it will be the last."

"You'd really do that? Stop?"

"I told you earlier, you never have to beg me for anything, you just have to ask and this no different. If you want to stop, at any point, no matter when or why, then we stop. That's all there is to it." I reassure her. "I never want you to feel like you have to do anything with me, in the bedroom or anywhere else." I'm watching the finger that's still tracing her lip, as she sticks out her tongue and runs it over her lips and over the tip of my finger. We both know that she can taste her pussy on that finger and my cock jumps with the knowledge, as she wraps her lips around my finger and sucks it into her mouth. "Leila."

"I don't want to stop."

"Are you sure?" She doesn't answer me with words, she pushed on my shoulders and I fall onto my back.

"Lift." She demands, smacking my hips, so lift is exactly what I do. She pulls my boxers over the tip of my cock and pulls them down over my arse and down my legs, throwing onto the floor somewhere. "I want you, Caleb."

"If that's what you want, then that's what you'll get." I sit up, pushing her onto her back this time just as easily as she pushed me onto mine and in the same move, I pluck the box off the bed and open it, pulling out a string of condoms and throwing the box away. I tear one off the strip and tear it open, not once breaking eye contact with Leila, so I can read her and know this is exactly what she wants.

"Stop second guessing me, Caleb, I want this." She says, taking the condom out of my hand, reaching for my cock and rolling it on, but not before rubbing her thumb through the slit a few times first. My cock jumps and pulses from her brief touch.

"Fuck!" I close my eyes and roll my head back because her touch overwhelms my senses. I've wanted it for so long and now that she's finally touching me, I can't quite believe it. Her hand wraps around my neck and pulls my body down with hers as she lies back down. "Are you still ready for me, Darlin'?"

"God yes, Caleb!" I lean on one forearm and reach down to run my finger through her lips to check. "Stop teasing me, Cal." She's the only who has ever shortened my name, the only one I've ever *allowed* to shorten it and it does something to me. She watches, as I suck her juices off my fingers and a shudder runs through her body.

I line myself up with her and give her one last look, one last chance to change her mind and instead of pulling away, she pulls upwards. The tip of my cock enters her.

"More." But I'm worried that if I rush this, it might end up in bitter disappointment, for both of us. "Please." I can't resist her and I push in further and further until I can't possibly go any further and we both sigh.

"Fuck! You feel so fucking good, Leila. *So fucking good!* I want to move but I don't want to come too soon."

"Cal, please. I need you to move, I need more." Her hips start pushing against mine and my own need to move, overrules my head. Slowly at first, I move in and out, getting my bearings, working out our rhythm. "More." She begs, so I move faster but still use long strokes in and out of her pussy. "Harder. Faster."

"You want me to fuck you, Darlin'?" I grunt out between thrusts.

"Fuck. Yes!" She screams and I wonder for a split second if we should be worried about the noise and then I decide I don't give a fuck who hears us.

I push up to rest on the backs of my heels and grip tightly onto her hips, pulling her up to meet mine and then I start. Holding her hips to steady her, I start harder and harder. The only noises in the room is the sound of bodies slapping, my grunts and her moan and quiet chanting.

"Yes. Yes. Yes!" Her voice is hoarse and I feel a pride well inside me that I did that to her.

"You like that? You like it when I fuck you hard?"

"God yes! Cal! I'm gonna, fuck me!"

"You're gonna what?" I don't wait very long for her answer. "What are you gonna do, baby?" I ask through gritted teeth because I'm trying my best not to come before Leila does.

"Come! I'm gonna, fuck! I'm gonna come Cal!"

"Are you gonna come all over my cock, baby, is that what you're trying to tell me?"

"Arghh! Cal. Cal. Cal!" She screams the last one and then her pussy clenches around my cock, her fingers dig into the sheet underneath her and I can't hold on any more.

"Fuck!" I drop her hips to the bed and collapse on top of her, resting my head next to hers on the bed, trying to catch my breath.

After a minute, I pull out of her pussy, take care of the condom and pull the covers over both of us.

"That was -."

"Amazing." I finish for her.

"Yes!" She agrees and I pull her back into my front and get ready to settle into a well-earned and needed sleep.

"I need to pee." She wiggles her butt around and my cock takes notice. "Already, Caleb?" She sounds surprised and I don't know what jerks she's been with before but this woman only has to look at me and I'm ready for another round, so when she wiggles against my cock, yes, again!

"Go pee then, woman." I slap her arse to get her moving and it works.

"Uncalled for." She scolds me as she walks to the bathroom.

"But it got you moving, didn't it?" I call after her. I hear her mumble something but there's a closed door between us, so I have no clue what she's saying.

I hear the door open, so I watch her walk back towards the bed, drinking her in. I'm not letting any chance I get to watch her naked body slip by.

"Come here." I throw back the covers so that she can get in and as soon as her butt hits the bed, I pull her back into my body and cover us both back up again.

"We didn't even take my bra off." She mumbles as she snuggles in closer and I realise she has remedied that while she was in the bathroom.

"No, you didn't!" I agree with her, which earns me an elbow to the ribs but she barely manages to touch me, which pleases me no end because that means I did my job right! "Later, I'll lavish some attention on them, OK?"

"Sleep." She mumbles.

"But for now, you sleep." I chuckle as I hear her breathing change and her body relax against me even more. "You're going to need the rest, beautiful." I whisper.

Chapter Twenty-six
LEILA

I wake up with a smile on my face and the best dream on my mind. I probably shouldn't dream about Caleb Drake screwing my brains out but a girl's allowed to dream right? I reach for my phone on the bedside table without opening my eyes but when I can't find it, I have to open my eyes and *that's* when I remember.

I'm not in my bed.

Last night wasn't a dream!

I stretch and the evidence is right behind me. A warm body moves so that he's tight up against me and his arm comes around my waist. He murmurs something that I *think* might be my name but that could also be wishful thinking. If that wasn't enough to remind me, the ache between my thighs is.

My god the man knows what he's doing! I smile even bigger at the memory. He didn't even flinch when I admitted to liking being in charge sometimes or liking a bit of pain, in fact, he seemed to revel in it. My last boyfriend did *not*. Neither did the one before him, or the one before either, for that matter.

This is one of the many reasons that they're ex's and why there have only been a few. It never ceases to amaze me the amount of guys who *say* they're kinky, or they like a little kink *or* they're adventurous in bed and willing to try anything, when in fact they're actually not. Not even close to be honest.

I should have known that Caleb wouldn't be one of them. I think perhaps some corner of my mind knew it and that's why I was so hesitant to let myself sleep with him. I wouldn't even get close enough to kiss him prior to last night and I'm still curious as to why he kissed me to begin with. At this point it doesn't matter at all but I'm curious.

I try to pull out of Caleb's arm but it tightens around me like a steel band.

"Stay."

"I'm not a dog, Caleb."

"I know. Cuddle with me, please?" As far as I can tell, he hasn't opened his eyes and I know he hasn't moved at all. I give in, hoping that he'll go back to sleep.

Ten minutes later, I can hear his breathing slowing down and feel his body relaxing behind mine. I pick up his hand and slip out from under it. Standing next to the bed, I turn to look at him and that was a mistake, honestly. He looks so restful and almost childlike asleep. Usually he's got so much going on that he has little crease lines between his eyes. This morning, he looks completely relaxed.

"Leila." He mumbles out my voice and I freeze as his hand reaches out looking for me. I wait a few seconds until he sighs and stops moving, sleeping soundly again.

I walk as quietly as I can to the bathroom, closing the door behind me. I lean back on the closed door and take a deep breath. Holy shit, I slept with Caleb Drake last night and it was amazing! Everything I imagined and more. What do I do now? I mean, I can't run out on him while we're here. I couldn't bring myself to leave him to explain to the Weavers about why I left. Not to mention I don't want to leave him to that Roberts woman either.

Which means, we have to sort things out and soon.

I push off the door and do what I need to before turning on the shower. As part of the tour of the suite yesterday, Brian had to explain how to use the shower. Yes, of all things I needed a crash course in how and what to turn on to get water flowing and what temperature I could have it at. The answer is, any fucking temperature I want just as long as I tell it what I want. If I don't, then it just heats the water up to what the system is set at. Who knew there was so much technology involved in having a simple shower? Not me, I can tell you that! No bathroom I've ever used before had so many buttons, LCD screens and levers.

All of my toiletries are already in here thanks to that quick freshen up I had yesterday when we got here, so I plunge under the water that's just below the heat that it might strip flesh off your body and relax. There's nothing I enjoy more than my nice *hot* shower every morning. It's the thing I love the most about my house, the hot water is *hot*.

I shampoo and rinse, then put on the conditioner and while it's doing its thing, I soap up my body in the most delicious orange and almond milk body wash I've found. It smells amazing *and* keeps my skin silky soft as well.

"I hope you're getting everywhere on that gorgeous body." Caleb's early morning, raspy voice cuts through the steam, making me jump and let out a high pitched squeak.

"Caleb?" I wash the soap and water from my eyes and look towards his voice and almost swallow my tongue when I find him leaning a hip against the vanity. His arms are crossed over his chest, his legs crossed at the ankle and he looks so relaxed. *No* man should look that relaxed *naked!* No man should look that fucking lickable in a bathroom!

"Who else were you expecting, Darlin'? Brian? Maybe you were thinking that Jeff might pop in and offer to wash your back for you?" I know he's teasing me but I can't help getting defensive. I've had a couple of boyfriends in the past accuse me of cheating and it's never fun, especially because it was never true. Of me, anyway.

"I wasn't expecting *anyone* to join me in the shower, Caleb." My voice brittle.

"Not even me?" That smirk of his spreads across his handsome face and I almost falter.

"Not even *you*." I confirm and I see the hurt flash in his eyes and immediately I regret saying it.

"I'll leave you to it then." He uncrosses his arms and ankles at the same time, just as he pushes off the vanity I speak.

"You don't have to leave." I'm not sure if he heard me, until he stops moving. "I didn't mean it like that, I'm sorry, Caleb."

"How *did* you mean it then, Darlin'?" He stalks, yes that's the only word to describe how he walking, towards the shower cubicle.

"I just. Look, I've had guys in the past accuse me of cheating, so I get a little, defensive, when anything like it gets mentioned. Even when I know the other person is joking, it hits a spot that's still a little raw."

"Did you cheat?" I know he's not accusing me but I still bristle a bit more at the question.

"No, ironically, it never was me cheating."

"So, what you're telling me is, these arseholes blamed you, accuse *you,* of doing the exact thing they were doing, no doubt to deflect from their own behaviour and *you're* still carrying that with you?"

"I guess." I say, with a shrug of my shoulders, grateful that the hot water in this place never seems to run out. "Caleb, come in here."

"But you don't want company and I don't want to push you into anything." He says, stepping back from the shower screen. "You're not ready and that's OK."

"You must be freezing out there. You're naked and it's not warm." I shake my head at his stubborn streak. Makenna complains about her brothers and their stubbornness all the time but this is the first time I've seen it aimed my way and I can't say I'm enjoying it. The truth is, I want him in here with me. "I'm almost done if you want *your* space, not that there isn't enough space in here for another three or four people but have it your way."

I turn my face back into the water, soaking in the heat and peacefulness of the water cascading of my body. There's no door, just an open space to walk through to get into the shower but I still feel the air around me change when he walks into the space.

"I can use the other shower head." Yes, there are two showerheads in this shower, one at each end. I guess it gives everyone their own space.

"Don't bother turning on the other one, like I said, I won't be in here much longer, I'm sure we can share." I don't turn to look at him, in fact my eyes are still closed but I can *feel* his presence. My body is very aware of how close he's standing to me.

"You don't need to tell me twice." He says, his breath ghosting over the wet skin of my neck and shoulders, causing the skin to pebble and me to shiver. "Sorry, didn't mean to make you cold."

"You didn't." I admit as he steps further into the water.

"Holy hell, Leila! What the fuck woman, are you trying to melt all of your skin off?" He jumps back to escape the water and I can't help laughing, that is until he starts to lose his footing. I reach out to grab both of his hands in mine but he pushes me away. "No point in us both going down,

Darlin.'" But he doesn't go down, he manages to save himself from landing flat on his back somehow.

"Don't you know you shouldn't jump around in the shower, Caleb? That's dangerous!" I scold him as my heart starts beating normally again.

"It's dangerous to have the water hotter than Hades as well but here we both are!" He says, shaking his head. "I think I'll start up the other shower head but thanks for the invitation."

"Suit yourself." I say, haughtily because I'm tired of people, guys specifically, telling me how I should or shouldn't do things, even my shower. "It's not my fault you're not man enough to have a hot shower."

"Man enough? *Man enough!* Are you fucking kidding me? I'm *man enough* to know that I don't want to steam my bones clean of the flesh that I enjoy having on them. That's not normal, Leila."

"Who are you to decide what's normal, Caleb Drake?" I huff. "I'm tired of being told I can't like things the way I like them." I turn off my shower head and stomp over to his.

"I never said *you* weren't normal Leila, I said having the shower that *hot* isn't normal but if that's the way you like it, I'm not going to stop you."

"Good because I'm not going to stop having *hot* showers." I tell him, resting my palms on his very solid chest.

"Wanna wash me?" He says with a sexy grin and I reach behind me blindly, grabbing the bottle that my hand lands on. Happily, it's my body wash.

"If you want to smell like me all day, sure."

"If it means I get to have your hands all over me this morning, hell yes."

I squeeze some of the liquid soap into my hand, I hand him the bottle to do with as he pleases and then I rub my hands together. With our eyes locked, I place my hands on his chest and start soaping him up. I dodge his happy trail and his not hard but not quite soft cock, making him sigh but he holds out his arms so that I can get to them. He can do his armpits himself, I'm not going there. Suddenly he turns and I'm looking at his muscled back and his delicious butt cheeks.

"Soap." I demand, shoving my hand around his side so that he can squirt some into it, which he does without a word.

I soap him up and use it as an excuse to give him a light massage as well. His groaning does things to me though and I know I have to stop soon, when he drops his chin to his chest to give me access to his shoulders and neck. Who am I kidding? He doesn't have to do anything to make me want him, some days I just have to watch him eat my chocolate cake and I'm ready to strip him naked and do him on the table in the middle of Vines.

With that thought, I smack him on his cute derriere, making him jump a little and me smile.

"OK, you're done Mister and so am I. It's freaking cold in here!"

"That's it? Haven't you missed a spot?" He asks, turning around to face me and then looking down at his now hard cock.

"No, I think you're good, you can deal with that." I smile, as I step out of the shower and reach for a towel. I walk over to the claw foot tub, prop my foot up on the edge and as I bend over to dry my foot. I hear a groan behind me, without turning around, I put my foot back on the floor and lift up the other one. Another, louder groan sounds from behind me and I can't resist turning around and looking at him. What I find is the hottest thing I've ever seen.

Caleb is standing there, one hand resting on the glass wall as he watches me, the other hand rubbing up and down his hard cock.

"Caleb?" It's a question but I'm not sure what I'm asking.

"Don't. Just keep drying yourself."

I do as he asks, rubbing the soft cream towel all over my body, paying extra special attention to my boobs. I mean, the should be dried properly, right? I watch Caleb the entire time and I can feel my own arousal building as he starts to jerk off faster and faster.

"Leila." My name is said on a raspy breath out as he comes all over the glass wall and all I can do is stand there and watch. I never thought watching a guy come would be hot but I'm learning all kinds of new things this weekend.

"That was hot."

"Yes it was." He agrees.

Chapter Twenty-seven
CALEB

Leila's not wrong, that was fucking hot but I think we had very different perspectives.

"So, you enjoyed watching me come all over the glass, huh?"

"Uhuh."

"Are you turned on?"

"Uhuh."

"Do you need me to come help you?" I wait for her to answer but she's staring at the mess on the glass. "Leila?"

"What?" She looks up to meet my eyes. "What? Oh, no, thanks. I don't need any help."

"Are you sure? Cause I don't mind, really." I send a smirk her way and she shakes her head, even as she smiles.

"You need to shower."

"That's OK, I can come back."

"No. We need to get down stairs for breakfast. We're already running a little late." She opens the bathroom, then turns back to me before she walks out. "You don't want Brian to interrupt us because we're late, do you?"

I groan, loudly. I'm pretty sure the whole house could hear me and I can hear her laughing through the door she just closed behind her.

I quickly clean down the shower, no-one and I mean *no-one* should be left to clean that up, then wash myself quickly. Then I remember that Leila already did that for me and chuckle. That's what lead to one of the hottest moments of my life, I've never done that with anyone else before. I'm not even sure I've ever let anyone watch me come before, apart from when we have sex, that is.

I get out of the shower and grab a clean towel to dry myself off, then wrap it around my waist and open the bathroom door. As I step into the bedroom, I notice the door out to the living room is closed and I can hear voices.

I bet Brian or Mary, possibly both, have come looking for us so that we don't hold up breakfast.

I quickly get dressed so that I don't leave Leila out there on her own. Who knows what Brian and Mary could be attempting to talk her into right now. I'm smiling as I open the door but it drops when I see who is actually in the room.

"Don't, Caleb, it's OK."

"It's not even *close* to being OK, Leila! What the hell are you doing here, Francine?" My anger bubbling up and I know they can both hear it in my voice.

"Caleb, calm down, it's OK babe." Leila calling me babe distracts me for long enough for her to step between us and place her hand on my arm. "She came to talk to me and if I didn't want to, I wouldn't have let her in. Anita isn't with her, that's the only reason I let her in." She's searching my eyes to make sure I've calmed down enough to talk to Francine, so I nod slightly.

"I came to apologise, again, Caleb. I know Anita can be, let's just say, a lot to handle. She was hoping to see you this weekend and get a commitment from you, not that you owe her one." She rushes on before I can respond and I feel Leila tense up beside me, so I pull her in close to me. "I can see, *we* can see that isn't going to happen. I don't think it was ever going to happen but that girl can be stubborn when she gets something stuck in her head. You were her prize I think and I don't know why she thought that."

"Neither do I, Francine because nothing ever happened between us. We've danced a few times at these parties of the Weavers but it's never gone any further. Despite what she might have told you or anyone else, we haven't even kissed." I inform Anita's mother but I'm saying it for Leila's benefit just as much, I don't want her to think that I've had *any* kind of relationship whatsoever with Anita Roberts.

"I wasn't aware of just how little had happened between the two of you." Francine says, looking at Leila before looking back at me.

"Whatever you have to say, you say can in front of Leila." I bristle at the thought that this woman might think that I would hide anything from my fiancée, plus, I want Leila to hear everything first hand so that she knows what's been said. "We don't have secrets."

"Well, that's good but does she need to know everything about your past?" Francine says with a smile that can only be described as bland.

"She already knows about my *past,* Francine."

"As I already told you, Francine, everyone has a past and Caleb's no different. In fact, *I'm* no different and I don't judge people by their past, unless they show me that they haven't changed. Caleb loves me and I love him, otherwise I wouldn't have agreed to marry him, you can trust me on that one."

"His past is rather, *colourful* though, Leila."

"And how would you know that for certain, *Francine*? Because your daughter told you? Because other women have told you things? Because other men have told you? I wouldn't believe everything you hear and I believe Caleb when he says that nothing happened between himself and your daughter." My heart swells with pride and joy at Leila defending me. I know we're playing pretend this weekend but I also know she's telling Francine the truth. About her knowing my past, anyway and that she doesn't judge me on it.

"I already told you Francine, she knows about my past. No I didn't give her a list of people I've slept with but neither do I want one from her. She was also aware that we might run into a one, perhaps two this weekend, so, while we appreciate your time and apology, it is completely unnecessary." Just as I finish speaking, there's a knock on the door but the person on the other side doesn't bother waiting for an invitation, which makes me believe it could only be one person.

"Good morning kids, I hope you're decent, I'm just checking that you're coming down for breakfast." Brian enters the room but stops when he sees who else is here. "What the hell are you doing here?"

"Brian, just wait." Francine starts to protest.

"No, Francine, I told you! I told you to leave these two kids alone. I *told you* that the pair of you should mind your own god damned business.

These kids are *engaged,* Francine, they're going to be *married* and they do not need you and your daughter trying to put a wedge between them."

"I just came in to apologise to them, that's all." She looks to us, her pleading for us to agree with her, to save her from Brian but I'm not feeling generous. "Isn't that right?"

"By apologise, you mean trying to make Leila doubt my lack of relationship with your daughter? To make her question my commitment to *her?* Is that what you mean?"

"WHAT?" Brian roars.

"You know, Caleb, your fiancée is much more forgiving than you are. Perhaps because you know just how wretched your behaviour has truly been. You lead women along and then dump them without remorse!" I flinch at her accusation, I know it's not true but there are two other people in this room that I'm hoping don't believe a word of what she's saying. "See, you flinched, you know I'm right!" she screeches.

"OUT!" Brian screams and I look at Leila who kind of looks like a deer caught in headlights. I can't say I really blame her because I'm not sure whether Brian means us or Francine. "You're done Francine. You and Anita need to leave. Now! I won't take this anymore. Caleb doesn't deserve any of this and Leila certainly doesn't deserve to be treated to your bullshit!"

"What the devil is going on in here? I heard you yell in the entrance, Brian!" Mary walks in and stops in her tracks when she sees Francine standing in the middle of all the shouting. "Oh, Francine. Why are you in here disturbing these two?"

"She's leaving, with her daughter, right now." Brian informs his wife.

"What happened?" Mary asks.

"I'll explain in a minute but I think that Leila and Caleb certainly deserve a few minutes alone to talk." He looks towards us and I can see on his face just how terrible he feels about this situation but it's not his fault. "Come on Francine, out." Mary takes his hand in hers, as he uses the other one to wave Francine out of the room. The woman huffs but starts walking towards the now wide open door.

"I just wanted to apologise and Lila was very understanding until her *fiancé* walked into the room."

"It's Leila and you know it but you've given me another reason for asking you to leave." Brian says as he closes the door behind them but not before sending us another look of apology.

"Well, hasn't this been a weekend of joy and frivolity for you?" I ask, not looking at Leila. She might have known about my past and I might have told her we might run into that past this weekend but having it shoved in her face like this, it's mortifying.

"Their behaviour isn't your fault Caleb. What I told her was true, you've been honest with me about your past and you told me what we might come across this weekend. I didn't quite think the women would be so, shall we say, determined to get to you but I guess we're all learning new things."

"How the hell can you joke right now?" I ask, while pacing the floor in front of her.

"I'm joking because that's how I deal with life, Caleb. If we don't laugh, we crack and I refuse to let a woman, *women,* like that bring me or *you* for that matter, down." She rests her hand gently on my bicep, stopping my pacing. "What you did in your past doesn't make your present or your future. We're all capable of change, if that's what we want. With all of that aside, before us, before this, who you were before doesn't count. You don't treat me like I'm expendable, therefore we're good. Better than good, we're great."

"You're amazing you know that, right?" She smiles shyly and shakes her head slightly. "You agreed to come with me this weekend, knowing that we were lying, then you stood up for me just now and well, you were amazing last night." She blushes and I know we have to have a conversation about last night and this morning but I really just want to enjoy it for a little longer.

"Well, I don't have any issue helping you out and I don't have a problem defending to you anyone who thinks that you're not good enough, either. That includes your family, some crazy woman and anyone else who thinks they know you because I *do* know you and the Caleb Drake I know, loves with his whole heart. He's honest, he's kind and he's great in bed." She winks at me, as she wraps her arms around my neck and leaves light kisses along my neck.

Just as I'm about to say screw it to breakfast, I mean I don't need sustenance when I've got a beautiful woman in my arms, there's a voice behind me and I sigh. I'm not going to be taking anything anywhere just yet.

"I am so sorry about that kids. Truly sorry but it's nice to hear that you've got his back young lady. *That* I can truly appreciate." Leila pulls her lips off my skin and herself out of my arms, as for me, I want to *kill* Brian for the second time this morning. "Now, come and get some breakfast. Those two women have been escorted off the property and have been instructed to not return. Not this weekend and perhaps never. I just won't stand for behaviour like that." Brian shakes his head and turns away from us to walk back out the door. "Come on kids, let's put this behind us."

Leila stretches up on her tiptoes and I can feel her breath on my skin. "You know we're talking about the other thing later, right? We need to talk."

Before I can say a word, she takes my hand in hers and follows Brian out the door. They chat the whole way to the dining room but I can't concentrate on what they're saying. I know what I *want* to say later when we have this talk but I'm not sure she's ready for that just yet.

"Are you OK?" She asks quietly as we're seated. "You're very quiet."

"Yeah, I'm fine, Darlin'." I smile at her, hoping that it's reassuring and not showing the dread I feel. "I was just thinking. I guess the run in with Francine put me more off kilter than I thought." She looks at me and it's almost like she read my mind, while also diving deeply into my soul, so I smile bigger. I'm not sure what she finds but I don't think she's happy with it, either way, she doesn't say anything more about it.

The conversation flows around the dining table, coffee, tea and all kinds of food are served.

When the discussion moves to this evening and the dress code, I think Leila might just have a panic attack. After expressing that she doesn't think she has anything appropriate for the night, Mary tells her not to worry about a thing.

"Go get your things, Leila." Mary announces when we're all finished eating. "We're going shopping!"

"I'm sorry, wh-what?' Leila asks, looking at me for help but I have no clue what's going on either.

"Go get your phone and handbag, whatever else you need, I'm taking you shopping for a dress for tonight."

"Oh, n-no that's not necessary at all, Mary. I can make do with what I've got. If that's OK with you that is." Leila stutters out.

"No, that's not OK with us at all, young lady. Now, off you go, go get your things." Mary demands. "I won't take no for an answer young lady, so hop to it." Leila looks to me to rescue her and I shrug my shoulders, I think she should humour Mary.

"Fine!" Leila gets up quickly and leaves the room, leaving behind a chuckling Brian.

"I think she was hoping you'd save her, Caleb." Brian suggests.

"From what? Don't all women love shopping for new clothes?" I ask, earning myself a guffaw louder than anything I've heard before, even from Brian and that's saying something.

"I think she may have preferred to go with you, Caleb." Mary offers. "But I'm taking her because I know exactly what I want to get her and you won't choose it."

Leila returns before I can defend myself, even though I'm not even sure how I would defend myself in this situation. Instead, I pull my wallet out of my pocket and hand Leila my credit card.

"Here, use this. Please? I brought you away, so this is my treat." I know she understands what I'm saying and still she shakes her head no.

"Oh put that away, this is our treat." I start to protest but Mary cuts me off. "No arguing Caleb. Please let us do this. It's an apology for what the two of you have had to deal with since you arrived and because I don't get to take a beautiful young lady shopping very often these days. My kids are all self-sufficient and don't want my input very often. My card yes but rarely my input. It would be my absolute pleasure to take Leila on a shopping trip. We'll be back before everyone else starts arriving, I promise." Mary kisses me on the cheek and gives her husband a smacking kiss.

Leila comes over and gives me a kiss that is appropriate for the company and yet still, it gets me all stirred up, my cock ready to beg for more again.

"See you soon, Handsome." I slip my card into her hand and give her a look. If she can, she should use it.

The ladies say a last goodbye and then they're gone. I didn't realise that I watched them leave until Brian claps me on the shoulder and I jump.

"Come son, let's go play a round of golf to pass the time while they're missing."

"They won't be that long, will they?" My question causes Brian to let out another loud laugh.

"Of course they will, Caleb. We'll probably get in a few drinks afterwards as well." I know it's weird but as I look at the door where they left, I realise that I don't want to be away from Leila for that long. "Come on, they'll be back before we know it." I follow Brian to his gym and we get set up for a round of golf.

Chapter Twenty-eight
LEILA

Shopping with Mary today wasn't on my radar but the older lady has some stamina when it comes to dress shopping *and* she knows how to make it fun! I usually hate shopping for clothes, not because they don't fit or that I don't like anything but because it's so time consuming. I usually wear the standard uniform of black pants and a white shirt for work, which then gets covered up by an apron, so I don't really care too much.

Outside of work, I wear jeans with shirts or t-shirts with shorts or casual dresses in Summer. I rarely get dressed up and go dress shopping. Yeah, that's something that feels decidedly wrong to me. Especially with a woman old enough to be my mother, who I barely know and seems to be way too excited to be shopping with a woman *she* barely knows.

"I know what you're thinking, you know." Mary says, breaking into my thoughts.

"And what's that?" I ask curiously because she can't possibly know what I'm thinking!

"You're wondering why a woman my age, who you barely know, is so excited to take you out dress shopping." Well, maybe she *does* know what I'm thinking. "Don't look so shocked, Leila. I've been around a while now and I know people. Most people assume that I'm just the little woman, the one that keeps the home fires burning and support my husband. While all of that is true, I've also been around a *lot* of people who underestimated me because of it. I've had plenty of time to study people and discover how they think."

"I didn't mean to upset you." I sound pathetic even to my own ears and I blush because I'm so embarrassed. Reaching out to take my upper arm in her hand, she stops us both from walking and pulls me to the side out of the way.

"You didn't upset me in any way, Leila, honestly." She smiles and she reminds me of the friendly, if not hilariously full on, group of grannies that sit at a table in Vines. "I'm more than OK with people underestimating me, Sweetie. It makes no difference to me whatsoever what people think of me. I only care what the people I love think and how I *feel*. I know I'm a good human being, at least I try to be and I know when I find good people. You and Caleb, you're good people. Brian and I trust you both."

"Thank you." I say, gulping down the guilt that I now feel about lying to these two amazing people. I really need to talk to Caleb about a few things when we get back.

"Are you OK? You look like you just ate something sour." Mary laughs and I laugh with her because I can't confess what I'm really thinking. "Come on, let's go find you a dress that will make Caleb want to cover you up and make the other men jealous of him. Not that it will take much for either of those situations to arise." She laughs longer and louder at her own joke, the previous conversation not just dropped but completely forgotten apparently.

Without a second thought, Mary loops her arm through mine and leads me through a few shops, looking at dresses that I might be able to afford, if I had a chance to save for them. I know that Caleb gave me his card and even though I'm here doing him a favour, I don't feel comfortable using it.

"Mary." I lean in close to whisper in her ear because I don't want to embarrass either one of us. "I can't afford any of these dresses." Mary pulls back to look me in eyes and she searches them for a few seconds before throwing her head back and laughing loudly, causing everyone in the shop to look our way.

"Oh sweet, sweet girl. I wasn't joking when I said that I was buying you a dress. I'm not expecting you to pay for it. This is a gift from Brian and myself."

"I can't accept that kind of gift, Mary!" I'm embarrassed not only because she's caused everyone to look at us but because I'm not comfortable having other people pay for anything for me, just ask Sara!

"You can and you will sweet girl. I want to do it and I know Caleb slipped you *his* credit card but we won't be using that one either." She nudges me with her shoulder like we're sharing secrets. If only she knew I hadn't planned on using Caleb's card either! "Please, Leila, let us do this for you? We both see how happy Caleb is and we just want to do our part. Not to mention, that young man of yours should have explained tonight's dinner event to you much better so that you were better prepared. Men, they never quite understand how much thought and preparation goes into these kinds of things for us women, do they?"

"Not really." I mumble out because I don't disagree with her but I'm also still trying to get my head around someone else buying my clothes. Does this mean I now have to give up control over what I like and want to wear?

"Don't worry so much, Leila. I'm not going to force anything you don't want to wear on you, I promise." She laughs again, much quieter this time thankfully. "No, you didn't say anything and no, it wasn't written all over your face either, I just know what I'd be thinking if I was in your position. I'd be wondering what kind of crappy dress I'm going to be left wearing because I had no say in it as I'm not paying for it. That's not me, if you don't like a dress, say so and we'll move the hell on. Life is too short to wear uncomfortable underwear or clothes you're not happy in."

"OK." I nod my head, quietly agreeing with her. I mean, I'm the queen of comfy undies, right? I wear granny undies at work because they're just more comfortable in the warmth of the kitchen and I don't have to pluck a wedgie out of my butt all day long!

"Speaking of, do you need some lingerie? Oh, we'll wait and see what dress you choose and decide from there if what you brought with you suits it. How does that sound?"

"OK." Mary takes that one word and decides that I'm all in. We walk in and out of a few more stores until I come to a stop in front of a cute little boutique with the most gorgeous dress I think I've ever seen. Before I know what's going on, Mary is pulling me inside and asking the shop assistant for the dress in my size and I'm being lead into a changeroom. "Mary, I can't." I start but Mary just waves her hand at me.

"You can and you will." She smiles happily back at me as the curtains close in front of me.

"If you need any help, just let me know. That one can be a little tricky to do up."

"Thank you." I cough because my voice doesn't seem to want to work but I don't repeat myself, I know they both heard me. Instead I take the time to really take this gorgeous dress in before I can even think about putting it on.

I'm not usually one for sparkles or glitter, I'm more understated than flash but there's just something about this dress.

"Are you OK, Leila? Do you need some help?" Mary asks, pulling me out of my daydream.

"No, I'm good, thanks." I tell her loudly enough that she can hear, then I start taking off my clothes. I don't quite feel good enough for this dress but I'm still going to try it on. The shop assistant wasn't wrong, I'm going to need some help doing it up but I take a minute to check myself out in the mirror before I draw back the curtain and step out. "Would you mind helping me do it up please?" When neither Mary or the sales assistant answer me, I look up to see them both staring at me, mouths hanging open, making me think that the dress doesn't look as great as I thought and I start to step back into the dressing room.

"No!" Both women say at the same time.

"Here, let me help you do it up." The sales assistant offers.

"That's OK, I think I'll just go take it off." Not wanting to embarrass myself or Mary, any further.

"Don't you dare!" Mary says loudly and I can't help looking around to see if there's anyone else in the store. "We're buying that dress."

"I thought you didn't like it." I say, as I feel the dress tighten slightly as the small zip and few buttons are done up.

"That dress was *made* for you, Leila." Mary insists.

"Absolutely." Kirsty, according to the name tag on her shirt, agrees.

"Caleb is going to swallow his tongue when he sees you in this tonight." She turns to Kirsty and says, "Shoes, we need some shoes to go with it and a small clutch."

"I have the perfect match, I'll be right back." Kirsty rushes off.

"Mary, that's not necessary, honestly." I try to tell her but she brushes me off.

"Oh rubbish. This is my treat and I'm telling you, new shoes and gorgeous little clutch will be perfect." Before I can argue, Kirsty is back and I'm trying on the most gorgeous pair of shoes I've ever seen. "See, I told you." Mary smiles at me and I can't help smiling back.

"I feel like I've got my very own fairy godmother." I laugh, as Kirsty hands me the beautiful clutch that matches perfectly with the dress and the shoes. These women *know* how to shop!

"I've been called a hell of a lot worse things than a fairy godmother." Mary laughs and I laugh with her because I can't imagine this woman being anything except gracious, wonderful and loving. "Go take it all off so that we can get it packed up and take it home." Mary instructs, as I step out of the shoes and hand them and the clutch to Kirsty.

I can't imagine how much all of this is going to cost and I can't even check. Kirsty took the tag off the dress before she put it in the dressing room at Mary's request and I didn't even get the chance to look for the tags on the clutch or shoes.

"Let me help you." Kirsty says through a small gap in the curtain. I nod and she steps in without letting anyone see in and makes quick work of the buttons and zip.

"Thank you." I smile at her.

"My absolute pleasure. Pass the dress through the curtain when you're done and I'll get it wrapped up for you." She smiles back and I know that if I had come in here on my own, there's no way she would have been anywhere near as gracious as she has been with Mary by my side. I smile to myself as I pass the dress through a split in the curtain to Kirsty, I'm glad I had Mary with me.

I pull my clothes back on and walk back out into the store to find Mary. I feel out of place once again until I spot the woman who I now consider my fairy godmother at the counter.

"Ready?" She asks as I get closer and I nod. "Let's get out of here and get back home, I can't wait for you to put this on tonight. I'm going to bring you over to our wing, so that my hair stylist and makeup guru can get you ready as well."

"That's not necessary, Mary." I say, as we head towards the car waiting for us.

"I know sweet girl but indulge me, I want to do this."

"OK." I smile back, my guilt at the lie that Caleb and I have told these two amazing people, making me give in to her.

The drive back to the house is full of chatter and excitement. Mary has this way of making you feel like you're part of her happiness.

We walk into the house smiling and laughing. Even in all of that distraction, I can feel Caleb nearby and when he speaks, his voice sends a shiver through my body at the anticipation of him seeing me for the first time in this dress.

Chapter Twenty-nine
CALEB

"Did you ladies have fun today?" I ask, trying not to go to her. I shouldn't want to run to her and take her into my arms and tell her I missed her, should I? It's only been a few hours for god's sake but I see her hesitate slightly, obviously deciding against coming to me, so I take a few long strides to her instead. Then I pull her into my arms and I sigh. "I missed you." I whisper in her ear and it's the truth.

"I missed you, too." She says softly in my ear and I feel my body relax as she relaxes into me, snuggling her face into the crook of my neck.

"I knew it was a good idea for me to carry the bags." Mary says with a chuckle. "Why don't you two kids go spend some time together. Go for a walk around the garden or head back to your suite. I'll come and get you, Leila, when it's time to get ready."

"Are you sure?" Leila asks, Mary who shoos us away.

"Ahhhhh, young love hey, Darling?" Brian says behind us as we walk away and into the garden.

"We can go up to our rooms too if you like, I can show you what I bought on our little shopping trip." Mary squeals behind us and we hear them leave.

"Do I want to know what she bought while you ladies were out?" I ask Leila as I drop her hand and wrap my arm around her shoulders.

"I don't think you do." She giggles.

"So, you two ladies had fun?"

"Yes. Did you?"

"We played a round of golf and then had a few beers." I tell her.

"But did you have fun?" She asks with a laugh and I can't help joining in.

"I did, I guess."

"Why didn't you enjoy yourself?"

"The truth?" She nods and smiles at me. I stop us at what I now consider our spot in the Weavers garden. "I was wondering what you were up to."

"Oh." She steps out on my embrace. "I didn't spend any of your money, Caleb. Mary insisted on paying for everything, despite my protests." She starts looking in the bag hanging off her shoulder and I stop her.

"That's not why I was thinking about you, Leila." I take her hand in mine and lead her over to a bench nearby. "I wouldn't mind if you'd used my credit card, Leila, it's what I gave it to you for." I smile at her as I gesture for her to sit and then I sit next to her, her hand still in mine.

"I don't think you'd say that if you saw how much that dress cost." She snorts. "I didn't even get to see all the price tags because Mary insisted they didn't matter." I don't even want to think about how much that shopping trip just cost Brian!

"After last night, I think we need to talk." I wish we didn't have to but we do.

"After last night?"

"Don't you think we need to make new ground rules?"

"Oh, you mean you want to go back to friends only? That's OK with me." She rushes out and I realise she's as nervous as I am. "I was thinking while I was out shopping with Mary that I would suggest a 'friends with benefits' arrangement for the weekend but if you don't want to, that's OK."

"Do you regret it? Last night I mean?" I ask, wanting to make sure that I'm heading in the right direction.

"Do I regret it? No!" She shakes her head vigorously then suddenly stops, looking me in the eyes. "Do you? Oh god! You regret it, don't you? You wanted to keep this all easy, simple and we muddied it up last night, didn't we?" She gets to her feet and starts pacing in front of me. "I'm sorry Cal, I didn't mean to change things, I don't *want* things to change. I like you, a lot and I value our friendship. I don't want to lose that, not for anything."

"Leila."

"We've stuffed it all up, haven't we?"

"Leila." I say again, trying to get her attention but she's still pacing. This isn't the Leila I know and I can't help wondering what else is going on here. I stand up, grab her shoulders and turn her to face me. "Leila, are you sure you're OK with 'friends with benefits' kind of arrangement for *just* the weekend?" I ask because I *know* I'm not happy with it and not because it means I get more of Leila but because in the end, I get less of her.

"If you are, I definitely am. I enjoyed last night, Caleb and I sure don't regret it!" I can't say I'm not happy with the arrangement but I'm also disappointed that's all I get. This weekend.

"Deal." I smile.

"Kiss me." She commands and I lean in and take her lips with mine. "Let's go back to the suite." She mumbles against my lips and even though I know I shouldn't because she thinks it's for show, I deepen the kiss because fuck it, I want to.

"Are you sure?" I feel like I'm always asking her this but I don't want her to regret me, us. She doesn't say a word but she takes my hand in hers and leads me back towards the house. We manage to reach the door to our suite without seeing a single person and I'm relieved.

I close the door behind us and as soon as I turn around, Leila pushes me back into the door. "I've been thinking about doing this all day!" Then she pushes her lips to mine and she kisses me, deeply and passionately just like when we were outside.

Her hands slide under my t-shirt and I worry for a second that I'm sweaty and gross but I'm distracted when she tweaks my nipples, making me groan.

"You like that?" I groan again because how to I tell her I *love* anything that means she's touching me. Her hands run up my chest and start trying to push the bunched up t-shirt up over my head.

"Why don't I give you a hand?" I ask, without waiting for her reply, I pull it up over my head.

"Do guys go somewhere to learn that one-handed top off move?" She asks with a smile against my lips.

"It's in our DNA." I reply with a smile of my own, before taking her lips with mine again. I can't get enough of having her lips on mine, of kissing her and having her kiss me. "Your turn."

"I can't do that one-handed trick." She says while taking a small step away from me but I don't want any distance between us.

"Here, let me help." Within seconds her top is dropping down to join mine on the floor and her hands are reaching for the button on my jeans when there's a knock on the door, startling the both of us.

"Leila, Caleb, are you in there? I couldn't find you in the garden." I rest my forehead on hers and she starts to laugh.

"Give me a minute, Mary." She steps back, plucks our tops up off the floor and throws mine to me. "Get dressed, Caleb." She smiles, as she pulls her top back on and straightens herself up and I do the same. I love Mary but she has some really awful timing this weekend.

"Hi Mary." Leila says, as she open the door to let our host in and I stand behind Leila because Mary doesn't need to see the results of our hot and heavy session just now and she will if I don't use Leila as a shield.

"I hope I didn't interrupt anything." Mary says, a distinct sparkle in her eyes like she knows exactly what she just did.

"No, not at all. We were just talking about tonight." Leila graciously says but I stay silent.

"Good, I'm glad. I hope you didn't tell him anything about your dress?" Mary asks and I can certainly answer that one for her because I didn't even ask much about it.

"Not even a hint. She won't even tell me the colour." I answer with a smile.

"Good. Good." Mary says just as happily. "I just wanted to let you know that we're going to start getting ready a little earlier than I expected. So, if you can be in my rooms in about half hour, that would be excellent."

"OK. I'll have a shower to freshen up and then head over." Leila tells her with a huge grin.

"Perfect. I'll see you soon." Mary turns to me with a glint in her eyes. "You're going to fall in love with this young lady all over again when you see her in this dress tonight."

"Not possible." I tell Mary, as I pull Leila's back to my front and hold her close. "I couldn't love her more than I do right now." Leila's body relaxes against mine and it feels nice, natural to have her in my arms.

"That's lovely to hear, Caleb." She smiles so big, it hits me right in the chest because I hate lying to her, even though I know I couldn't love Leila more than I already do. "You, I will see soon. Sorry to break up the mini reunion." She grins as she walks out the door, closing it behind her.

"So, tell me all about this dress then?" I prod Leila, not letting go of her.

"No." She shakes her head. "I promised Mary I wouldn't tell you a thing, she wants to see your reaction the first time you see me."

"No fair." I pout as I turn her around in my arms to face me. "How about I come help you freshen up in the shower, that way I'll at least know everything about what's underneath the dress."

"You already know what's underneath the dress *and* if you join me in the shower, I won't get to Mary's rooms in time and we both know it!" She says while wiggling out of my grip and laughing.

"I can be quick." I waggle my eyebrows at her as she looks over her shoulder at me, disappearing into the bedroom. The bedroom where I could have been having my way with her if Mary hadn't interrupted us yet again!

"That, kind sir, is not an incentive to let you join me. I've never understood why men think telling women they can be finished quickly, would ever end well for them. I mean, there's a time and a place for a quickie for sure but when you're trying to convince a woman to have sex with you, speed is rarely a turn on. Just so you know."

"Duly noted, Darlin'." I salute her as she smiles at me and closes the door behind her, closing off any chance of me getting an invite to join her.

Instead, I decide to sit down at the small table and pull out my laptop, I might as well get some more work done in my down time. I don't understand why women need so many hours to get ready but I'm not going to argue with them. I'm concentrating on my work and I don't hear the bedroom door open quietly, nor do I hear Leila walking towards me, so I jump when her hands touch my shoulders.

"Sorry, I didn't mean to startle you, I thought you heard me." Leila apologises and I settle my hand over hers.

"I was engrossed in these numbers, sorry and didn't hear you come out here, Darlin'." I look up and see her standing there in one of the pale blue robes that were hanging on the back of the bathroom door, a turban like towel wrapped around her hair and a pair of matching pale blue fluffy slippers. She looks freaking adorable.

"Sorry again but I just wanted to let you know, I'm heading over to Mary's rooms now."

"Not like that you're not." I say without thinking.

"I'm sorry?"

"You're not walking through this house, while there are a hundred odd people milling about putting the night together, with just that robe on."

"I have underwear on!"

"No, that's not acceptable."

"It's the same amount of clothing I'll have on under my dress tonight, Caleb!" She sounds amazed and yet soothing at the same time.

"True but the robe advertises that you just got out of the shower and every man you pass will be thinking about that. You being wet, in the shower and urghh!" I don't even want to *think* about what other men will be thinking!

"Caleb, they won't." She tried to reassure me but I know men, I am one for fucks sake!

"They will. Please, for me, at least put on another dress or something. Jeans and a top would be even better."

"You're serious?"

"Deadly." With a huff she stomps back to the bedroom and closes the door behind her. At least she didn't slam it shut! She walks back out a couple of minutes later in jeans, a t-shirt and the fluffy slippers again, the towel turban still wrapped around her hair.

"Better?"

"Thank you." I say, getting up and kissing her. "Have fun." She mumbles something about men and their stupidity that I choose to ignore and she gives me one more kiss before she leaves.

Now, I have a couple of hours to kill before I need to have a shower and get ready for the night as well. I might as well get some more work in before then. So, that's what I do and when the alarm goes off to remind to me to get ready I'm glad because I could do with the break.

I have a shower, shave and clean myself up, dress in my suit and tie then head down stairs to meet Brian. After about fifteen minutes there's a crowd of people in the ballroom and then there's a small commotion and when I look up to see what the cause is, I almost swallow my tongue because coming down the stairs is the most gorgeous sight I've ever seen and I get to call her my fiancée.

Chapter Thirty
LEILA

Caleb's reaction to seeing me in my dress doesn't disappoint. Him standing there staring at me? That kind of does disappoint.

"Give him a minute, Sweetheart, his brain has to kick back into gear." Brian says from beside me as he loops Mary's arm through his and guides her the rest of the way down the stairs. "You look gorgeous."

"Thank you." I reply without taking my eyes off Caleb, who is still not moving. It takes for Brian and Mary to walk by him, to jog him out of the trance he seems to be in.

"Go get her son, before someone else decides he wants her." Brian laughs a warning at Caleb, which jolts him into action.

"You look *amazing*, Leila. Absolutely gorgeous." He says as he stops in front of where I'm at the bottom of the stairs and I reach out and smooth my hands over his lapels.

"You look pretty handsome yourself, Caleb." The smile that spreads across his face at my compliment is so bright and happy, I can't help smiling widely back at him. He moves up to the step below the one I'm standing on, making us the same height and gently places his hands on my cheeks, pulling my forehead to his.

"Thank you, Leila. Thank you for doing this for me, thank you for being my friend and thank you for being you." Then, he's kissing me, he's kissing me like he's drowning and I'm the air he needs to breathe. He kisses me so soundly that I forget where we are and that I just had my makeup done. When he breaks away from me, I'm breathing deeply and my mind is scrambled. "You're amazing."

"You're pretty amazing yourself." I tell him, as I run my hands up his lapels, shoulders and up to cradle his face in my hands. I love having the

217

freedom to touch him, to feel him like I've wanted to from the moment we met.

"Isn't young love grand?" I hear from behind Caleb and he sighs.

"We're not so old you know, Brian." Mary says, sounding annoyed but when I look over their way, I can see the twinkle in her eyes that shows she's enjoying teasing her husband.

"I don't know, Mary my sweet, I think some days I'm getting too old for most things." Brian answers her.

"Don't be ridiculous." Mary laughs.

"You're only as old as the woman you feel, Brian." I counter and we all laugh.

"In that case, I just aged a year or two." Caleb jokes and I can't help laughing at him. "Come on, let's show you off to the rest of the party." He says, offering his arm for me to take.

"I'm not a trophy you know, Caleb." I tell him and instead of taking his arm, I step around him and down the steps myself.

Brian roars with laughter and through his laughter he says, "She's a fire-cracker, Caleb. I love her!"

I swear I hear Caleb mumble, 'me too' but he takes my hand in his to lead us into the dining room as he talks to Brian and it all happens so quick-ly, that I'm sure I was hearing things. He smiles at me as he pulls out a chair for me to sit down and I decide it was wishful thinking because he doesn't show anything more than affection.

We sit through dinner and conversation flows between all the diners. I notice that there aren't any empty place settings at the table and can't help wondering where Francine and Anita would have fit if they'd stayed.

"Mary had the settings changed so that you wouldn't notice." Caleb leans in and says quietly. I look at him and wonder how he knew. "I noticed you looking up and down the table, almost counting the seats. There are definitely two missing but no-one else here would notice the difference."

"If the two Roberts women are always guests at these things, surely *someone* is missing them, Caleb?"

"No-one here is missing those vapid Roberts women, Leila, believe me." The man, Jeff, sitting beside me answers, earning a very dirty look from

Caleb. "Sorry, I couldn't help overhearing part of your conversation." He holds his hands up in defence.

"Thank you, Jeff." Caleb says, but I don't think he's truly sincere and I'm not sure what he has against Jeff because he's been nothing but pleasant to me this evening.

Brian announces that we're moving to the ballroom for drinks, dancing and fun, before anything else can be said between the men on either side of me.

Caleb takes my hand in his, his grip not quite crushing but it's certainly firm.

"I didn't even know there *was* a ballroom." I lean in and say quietly to him and he chuckles, which relaxes him immediately.

"There are a few rooms in this house that you don't know about, Darlin' and I doubt you'll be able to find this particular room by yourself either." I look at him surprised. "Yes, I used the word house very loosely because let's be honest, it's more of an estate than anything else but somehow, Mary and Brian have made it *feel* like a home and for that alone they should be celebrated."

"You're absolutely right on all accounts." I agree with him and he smiles at me again and it lights me up.

"I'm not sure how they do it but they do." I open my mouth to respond to him but then Brian sweeps open a set of double doors to the most magnificent room I have *ever* seen. It's seriously like something out of a fairy tale.

"Wow!"

"Do you like it?" Mary asks, suddenly beside me.

"Like it? Mary, this looks *amazing*!" I face Mary and give her a warm hug. "It is utterly incredible."

"We thought that perhaps you two might like to have your wedding here? Well, the ceremony out in the garden and the reception in here. I was trying to make it look as magical as I could." Mary smiles warmly but hesitantly.

"Oh Mary it *is* gorgeous. Magical is definitely how I would describe it and any bride would be thrilled to get married here but, Caleb and I haven't even discussed it yet. Neither of our families are close by and it would be such a small affair that I think this room might be wasted on us, Mary."

"There's no such thing as a wasted room, Leila. Promise me you'll think about it." She looks by me to Caleb. "Both of you. It would be an honour to host your wedding here. It would give us both great pleasure to do so and I promise it wouldn't be a waste, nor would you have to lift a finger."

"Come on my love, let the kids talk about it. Not tonight though because there will be no decision on it this evening. We're here to celebrate and have fun." He steers Mary away into the crowd but not before turning back to us to say, "There truly is no pressure at all." Before he disappears behind his wife into the small crowd.

I turn to look at Caleb to see what he thinks about the whole thing, only to find him staring at me with a strange look on his face.

"Are you OK, Caleb?" I ask concerned, maybe something at dinner didn't sit with him very well.

"What? Oh no, I'm good, Darlin', just thinking, that's all." He smiles at me and it's the kind of warm smile that makes me melt a little inside. He's such a handsome man but he's also loving, kind and very attentive. "Let's dance." He says holding his hand out to me, as some beautiful soft music plays in the background. I place my hand in his and let him lead me to what I hope is an actual dance floor and he pulls me into his arms. The music is slow and soft and we move in time with it, he has one hand resting on my lower back and I've got one hand resting on his shoulder, our other hands are clenched together in between us. When the first song blends into the next, I rest my head on his shoulder and he rests his chin on the top of my head and we sway together on the dance floor for another song, before heading for a drink.

Caleb heads to the bar and I make for the ladies room. There's no-one else in there, so I make quick work of dealing with this amazing dress and then head back out to find Caleb. I don't find him immediately and a few people stop to talk to me as I keep looking.

"Well, hello there gorgeous, could I have this next dance?" A guy dressed nicely asks me as I step away from a conversation with Jeff and start looking for Caleb again.

"No, thank you." I answer with a smile.

"Come on sweetie, it's just a dance. One dance won't hurt anyone, will it?" Ohhh he's slimy and I just want him to go away.

"It might if my fiancé sees us." I tell him, flashing my engagement ring to bring home the fact but it doesn't stop him.

"What he doesn't know, won't hurt him, right? I mean, you're not married yet, are you?" He suggests with a sleazy grin and I take a step backwards, only to step into a brick wall of a man but as I turn to apologise, I hear the man speak and I relax.

"What her fiancé *does* know, is that other men should respect a woman's boundaries, engaged to be married or not. Married or not. *My fiancé* said no thank you and she was very polite about it, much more polite than I feel like being right now, so why don't you back the fuck off."

"Cal, honey, it's OK." I say, trying to diffuse the situation because can I see the anger in Caleb's face.

"Yeah, *Cal,* no harm done." The sleaze says and I can't help wondering if the idiot has a death wish.

"Simon, that's enough." Brian's booming voice says as he approaches our little group. We haven't garnered a lot of attention just yet and I'm hoping to keep it that way. Simon looks at Brian and he looks like he's going to keep arguing but then seems to think better of it and just walks off into the crowd. "Oh kids, I'm so sorry for that, you're not having the best of weekends with us, are you? There seems to be a test for you at every corner! I am *so* dang sorry about all of it. Simon is harmless, mostly but he does get a bit handsy and creepy when he drinks. I try to limit his intake when he's here but sometimes, I just can't. He will not harass you or anyone else this evening, I promise, Leila."

"Keep him away from us, Brian." Caleb says, the tone in his voice is nothing I've ever heard before.

"I promise, Caleb. I think we need to find some new people to invite to our events." He says it with a chuckle but the amusement doesn't reach his eyes and I can tell he isn't finding any of it funny. "Please, enjoy the rest of the evening. I can't promise it won't be eventful but I'm hoping that we can at least give you some time to relax tonight." This time he does give a genuinely warm smile and I smile back at him. Caleb seems to still be lost in thought though.

"Thank you, Brian, we will I'm sure." I watch him walk away before turning back to Caleb. "Are you OK?"

Chapter Thirty-one
CALEB

"Yeah, I'm fine, Darlin', let's enjoy our night." I smile at her, hoping that it hides how much I want to deck that guy.

I noticed that guy watching Leila at dinner and I did everything to mark my territory without actually bending her over and fucking her there at the table in front of everyone. In between courses, I draped my arm over the back of her chair, I leaned in to whisper in her ear and when others were talking to her, or me, I let my hand rest on her knee. Yet, that idiot *still* decided to shoot his shot when he saw the opportunity!

I can't say I blame him because she looks fucking amazing. I might have to pay Mary some kind of finder's fee because this dress they found, it fits her curves without being so tight that she can't breathe or move with me as we make our way around the dance floor. The emerald green material of the dress makes her gorgeous green eyes sparkle. Combine that with her deep red hair, wavy and loose around her shoulders, making her look like a cross between Jessica Rabbit and the Little Mermaid come to life.

Sexy and innocent all at the same time and any man's wet dream. Mine included and that's why I don't leave her side for the rest of the night. Mostly, anyway.

"Caleb, I need to go to the bathroom and I don't need your help for that, despite your kind offer." She laughs and her eyes light up with amusement. I want to be the reason she smiles that kind of smile more often. Every damned day if I can get it.

"Are you sure? I can be pretty handy you know." I bounce my eyebrows up and down suggestively, hoping to make her laugh again and I succeed.

"Stop it or I'm going to make a mess here and that will all be your fault."

"Oh well, we can't have that can we? My offer of a helping hand is still there." I wink at her this time, even as I let her go and she drops her hand to her side, then walks away with one last look over her shoulder. I want to follow her, make sure she's OK but that's pure insanity. It's not like Simon is going to corner her in the ladies room for fucks sake!

"She'll be fine, Caleb." Brian's voice behind me startles me and I laugh as I turn around to look at him.

"I know that Brian but it doesn't stop me from worrying about her *or* watching her walk away in that amazing dress!" I quip. "I think I owe your wife more than I could ever earn."

"By all accounts, that was the only dress that Leila tried on and Mary didn't even let her look at the price tag, she just bought it." Brian laughs like that's the most natural thing in the world to do, but buying something without knowing how much the damn thing costs. I mean, Drake Wines does really well but not *that* kind of well! "Don't look so shocked, Caleb. We're honoured that the both of you are here and we wanted Leila to look amazing tonight and I think that was achieved."

"That was definitely achieved, Brian and we both thank you for your generosity."

"You're both more than welcome." The rest of whatever Brian might have said, is cut off by a woman's voice that I know very well, yelling.

"I've told you, it's not happening! Engaged or not you creep, I wouldn't go out with you!"

My feet are moving before I can even think about what I'm doing and I can feel Brian right behind me but I don't stop, I couldn't even if I wanted to.

"Leila." My voice doesn't even sound like mine, my anger is rolling off me in waves. Her head snaps up from the hand that is gripping her upper arm and I don't see a woman who is scared or needing to be rescued. Oh no, I see a woman who is about to lay a guy she doesn't want touching her out! Her hand is balled into a fist, ready to strike.

"I think your girl has it covered." Brian says beside me but I don't look his way to either confirm or deny his comment, my eyes are firmly fixed on Leila and if she needs me, I'll be right there.

"Come on honey, he doesn't have to know." The guy, Simon, drawls.

"This has *nothing* to do with Caleb, other than the fact that he would knock you out for touching me. *This* has everything to do with *me* and I'm telling you, *you don't get to touch me. You don't get to touch* anyone *without their permission and I sure as hell don't give you permission to touch* me!"

"Of course this has everything to do with your *fiancé!* If it weren't for him I'd have already fucked you against the wall by now!" There's a collective gasp in the room as Brian and I both take another step forward but before we can step in, Leila raises her fist and punches the guy square in the nose! He screams as blood pours out of it! "You broke my nose! *She broke my* nose! You all saw that, you're all witnesses to her assaulting me."

"I think you got what you deserved and we're all witnesses to exactly *that.*" Brian roars as he grabs Simon by the upper arm and a security guard appears from nowhere, taking his other arm, holding him up and marching him out of the room.

"I'm suing you, bitch!" I step in front of the three men as they pass me and get in Simon's face.

"Call her or any other female that again and see what happens."

"If it weren't for you, I'd have already had her and this would have never happened." He screams in my face, spitting blood over me.

"Sue her, we have more than enough witnesses here to back up *her* story."

"Fuck *you!*" I don't give him the satisfaction of saying anything else, I step out of the way to allow Brian to keep walking him out. He starts yelling something but all I hear is Brian.

"You should shut up now and count yourself lucky that I didn't let Caleb take you out because it would have given me great pleasure." Then they're gone and I've already pulled Leila into my side.

The silence that settled over the room, is now filled with music and low talking again.

"Well, this has been quite an eventful weekend for the pair of you, hasn't it?" Mary says as she walks up next us.

"I'm sorry Mary, I shouldn't have hit him." Leila apologises quietly. "I've ruined your evening."

"You've done no so such thing young lady and you're not the one who needs to apologise. I think that might be something that Brian and I owe the pair of you if anything! I mean first the Roberts' and now Simon! This was supposed to be a party, a celebration of your engagement and simply just a gathering of our friends. What it's ended up being is the catalyst for a few people to be unceremoniously dropped from our guest lists and a little bit too much excitement."

"I'm sorry about that, Leila, Caleb. I want you to know that he won't be making any more trouble for you or anyone else, not tonight or any other night." Leila's eyes widen in shock and Brian laughs. "Not like *that*! I meant that he's not welcome here anymore and any contracts we might have had are now in the hands of my lawyers to retract. That behaviour is unaccept-able."

"I shouldn't have made such a scene, I'm sorry." Leila apologises to them both again and before I can speak, Brian does.

"Nothing to apologise for young lady. You are safe here and deserve to not be harassed no matter where you are! Never apologise for defending yourself against fools like that. Ever!"

A woman approaches us and takes Leila's hand in hers. "Thank you! That guy has hit on just about every woman here at some point. Not all tonight, I promise." She says looking at Brian and Mary. "But at some point, we've all had to fend him off over the years. Thank you for doing what I should have done last week. If you need someone to look at your hand, please, let me know." She smiles and then walks away.

"Let me look at your hand." I pick it up and inspect it. "Let's go get some ice on it, just in case."

"You know where to go, Caleb." Mary says with a smile that is so warm I can't help smiling back.

As we make our way to the kitchen, we ask one of the bustling staff in there for an ice pack, we're stopped multiple times by both women and men. All of them telling Leila that they're glad she hit the jerk and by the time we make it to the kitchen, she's smiling again.

I sit us both down in a quiet corner of the kitchen, placing her hand on my knee and then the ice pack on top of her hand, when she flinches, I feel bad for not thinking about icing it sooner.

"I'm sorry." I say quietly, wondering if she even heard me over the hustle and bustle in the kitchen at the moment.

"What for? You didn't make that idiot feel he had the right to touch me or anyone else. He's a jerk and there are plenty of them around and I think you'll find most women have been in similar situations and have had to deal with jerks like that who think they have the right to do whatever they want." It makes me mad that anyone has to go through anything like this but to be so blasé about this guy's behaviour is infuriating. My anger isn't directed at Leila or any other woman who has dealt with this but at Simon and guys like him. I can't help wondering if Makenna has had to deal with this kind of bullshit as well.

"So when you say *most* women?" I ask.

"I mean almost *every* woman has had to deal with something similar to that in their life. At least once." I hate that it's such a casual response, I change the subject because I know I'm getting angry all over again.

"You broke his nose, Leila." I say choking back my laughter.

"Yeah, well I didn't mean to do *that* but I'm not upset about it either." She says with a shrug. "I won't apologise for that. I feel like he paid the price for every other guy who hasn't taken no for an answer and I guess that's unfortunate for *Simon*."

"Well, I'm glad you did it. If you hadn't, I would have and I think Brian would have been right behind me."

"I don't think Mary was too far away either." We're both laughing and I feel my anger disappear. I have nothing else left to say about what happened, I have no way of explaining just how proud of her I am, so instead, we talk about stupid things that mean nothing.

Chapter Thirty-two
LEILA

Sitting in the kitchen just talking about nothing much with Caleb is relaxing. This is us. This is the thing I love most about us, this easy friendship that we have. We can spend time together without the pressure of trying to find something to talk about.

"Do you want to go back out there?" He asks, nodding towards the kitchen door.

"Not really. I feel like everyone is going to be looking at me now." I admit, staring down at the ice pack still on my hand, even though I don't need it anymore. "But if *you* want to go back in there, you should go. In fact, this weekend was supposed to be about you networking, so we should get back out there." I pull my hand out from under the ice pack and start to stand up, until Caleb rests his hand on my shoulder and gently pushes me back into my seat.

"Sit down, Leila." He chuckles. "We most certainly do not have to go back and join in the party, especially if you're not comfortable and yes, I do mean *we* because if you don't want to, then neither do I." His smile is so sweet and kind, it just makes me feel even more guilty about ruining his evening.

"But this is about the Brewery, Caleb and I want you to succeed at it." I tell him, taking his hand in mine and squeezing it. "Come on, let's go." I say trying to pull him out of his seat.

"Your wellbeing means more than any kind of networking I could be doing in that room, Darlin', I promise." I look deep into his eyes and I know he's telling the truth, he wants me to feel comfortable and the rest, well it can wait.

"I'm feeling fine and you need to get back out there." I repeat.

"No, I really don't." I know he's trying to reassure me but I won't be deterred.

"Caleb."

"Leila." His voice is deep and the look on his face does things to me it shouldn't when we're in public. "Stop it. I don't need to be out there. We were here for fun and to see Brian and Mary. The Brewery and the deal can wait."

"Yes, they can young man." Brian says as he enters the kitchen, closely followed by Mary and I can't help wondering if there are many places these two go where they're alone!

"Don't you guys have other guests to talk to?" I ask, only half joking.

"Of course but we wanted to check and make sure your hand is OK. Are you sure you don't want to see a doctor?" Mary asks, concern all over her face.

"I'm fine, honestly." I say, showing them that I can make a fist and move all of my fingers. Does it hurt? Yes, yes it does but that's to be expected, I punched a guy but everything still moves and I feel like that's a definite bonus.

"Caleb is right, he doesn't need to be in that room to network or show me that he's serious about his business. You kids should go up to your room or go for another walk in the garden. You've got a long drive home tomorrow and you, young lady, need to rest that hand so that you can go back to work. If you go back out there, I think you'll have too many people wanting to shake that hand and you'll have to take a couple of days off to recover." Brian laughs but suddenly I feel exhausted.

"Come on, I think it's time to get up upstairs." Caleb says, helping me to stand up as he does, then rests his hand on my lower back, ready to guide me out of the room.

"Good idea!" Brian agrees. "You look exhausted, Leila and I'm sure that has a lot to do with the pain."

"Did you get some pain relief?" Mary asks, concerned.

"It's OK, Mary, we'll get her sorted up in our room, if you don't mind?" Caleb says it with that charming smile of his and see Mary swoon right in front of me, even as Brian rolls his eyes at his wife.

"Go on, take your girl up to your suite and take care of her but if you need anything, anything at all, you come find one of us, OK?" We all say our goodnights and Mary gives me a tight hug.

"I'm so sorry, I kind of wasted this dress didn't I?" I whisper in her ear and lean back, amusement clear in her eyes.

"No, you did not." She leans in to give me another quick squeeze. "Caleb most certainly doesn't think it was a waste." She whispers and then she takes her husband's hand and they disappear back into their party.

"What was all of that about?" Caleb asks, as he guides me towards the stairs.

"What?" I ask, innocently as I can.

"The whispering, Darlin', the whispering." He says, a smile creeping across his handsome face.

"Well, Handsome, I was apologising for wasting such a beautiful dress. It doesn't feel like I gave it the night it should have enjoyed." I explain, as we reach the top of the stairs.

"That dress is *not* wasted, maybe on that douche canoe Simon but believe me, it was *not* wasted on me, Darlin'. Not. At. All. I can promise you that." He takes a step back from me as we reach the door to our suite but doesn't drop his hand from my lower back, as he sweeps his gaze up and down my body, very much admiring the dress.

"It *is* a pretty spectacular dress, isn't it?"

"The dress is only half of the appeal, Darlin'." Caleb declares, as he steers me past the bed and into the bathroom. Before I can ask what he means, he spins me around, finds the zip and eases it down, then silently lets the dress fall to the floor. Mary didn't need to buy me any lingerie, thank the lord for that because I couldn't wear a bra underneath the dress and I already had plenty of underwear to wear. "Definitely only half of the appeal, Darlin'." He rumbles out.

"Caleb." I start but he shakes his head.

"Get in the shower and wash the night off." He gestures to the shower, while picking the dress up off the floor and heading for the door.

"You're not joining me?" I ask, coyly hoping that I can change his mind but when he turns back to face me, I can see by the stern look on his face that isn't going to happen.

"No. I have something to take care of but I'm not leaving the suite, so if you need anything, yell out."

He disappears out of the bathroom, closing the door quietly behind him and I strip out of my underwear, then step into the shower. I wash my face, knowing that I should really get some makeup remover instead but really, I can't be bothered, all while trying to not get my hair wet. I'm not one hundred percent successful but I'm not really in the mood to care.

I step out of the shower, dry myself off and wrap the pale blue fluffy robe around me and walk out into the bedroom just in time to hear Caleb end a conversation on the phone.

"Thank you, I would appreciate that. I don't want to see him again." He's quiet, obviously listening to the person on the other end of the call and nodding. "Goodnight Brian and thanks again."

"Is everything OK?" I ask, even more concerned when his head whips around to where I'm standing and I see the look on his face. He softens the second he sees me standing there, all it takes is three strides, until he's standing in front of me.

"How are you feeling, Darlin'?" He asks with a warm smile.

"I'm fine." I think for a second, then say, "Tired but fine."

"How's your hand?" He asks, gently taking my slightly bruised hand in his, bringing to his lips and kissing it softly. I shouldn't melt inside but I do, this man is killing me!

"It's fine. I've done worse damage in the kitchen, believe me!" He raises an eyebrow at me in question. "Ask Sara when we get back, she'll tell you all about it." I laugh, then I realise I mentioned home and I stop laughing. Reality is hitting us tomorrow and I don't want this to end. I want to have the freedom to touch him if I want to, to kiss him and have him kiss me but that ends tomorrow when we leave here.

"Why don't we go to bed. We've got a long drive tomorrow and you need to get some rest."

"Why? I'm not driving, am I? I mean I *can* if you want me to, obviously but I assumed I wasn't."

"That's not what I meant." He chuckles as he leads me across the room to the bed. "I meant, there's been enough excitement for one night and it's time for sleep."

"Oh, OK." He lifts my feet off the floor and starts to turn me around so that I can lie down. "Ummmm I'm not sleeping in this, Caleb." I say, pointing to the robe, as he pulls back the covers.

"Of course." He says and I start to undo the tie around my waist and stand up, dropping the robe to the floor. "Oh." I didn't think that through because now I'm standing there in the same underwear I had on before the shower and nothing else. I didn't get the chance to change after my shower.

"Here, arms up." Caleb demands, quietly and for some reason, I obey. He takes the t-shirt he was wearing off in one quick movement, then drops it over my head and lets the hem drop to my mid thighs. I didn't even notice that he'd changed out of his suit and into pyjamas. I never imagined Caleb sleeping in pyjamas but with the way the Drake siblings walk in and out of each other's homes, I shouldn't be overly surprised with the revelation. "Come on, Darlin', let's get some sleep."

Gently, he pushes me back onto the bed, walks around to his side of the bed, climbs in beside me and turns off the lights.

"Goodnight, Caleb." I whisper into the dark.

"Come here, Darlin'." He pulls me into his arms, my back to his front, settling his chin on the top of my head, his arms firmly around my waist. I have no doubt he's going to wake up with a dead arm at some point but I'm too selfish to tell him to move.

"I'm sorry, Caleb, this weekend hasn't worked out the way you planned at all, has it?" I laugh quietly into the darkness.

"As long as you're OK, I don't care what else happened."

"But your deal with Brian." I try to roll over to face him but he holds on tighter so that I can't move.

"Doesn't matter. If Brian doesn't want to deal with me after all of this, then so be it. Now, go to sleep." He kisses the top of my head.

"Yes but this whole thing."

"I know. Now shush and go to sleep, Darlin', the rest will either sort itself out, or it won't." I breathe in getting ready to speak again. "No, that's enough."

He pulls me impossibly closer into his embrace, leaves a soft kiss on the back of my neck and goes silent. I feel his breathing even out and realise he's literally told me to go to sleep and fallen asleep himself.

Being in his arms feels so warm and comforting, almost normal, I find myself drifting off to sleep moments after he does.

When I wake up the next morning, we're not snuggled up together. I open my eyes to find Caleb on his back, one hand on his chest that is rising and falling with his even, steady breathing, his other hand stretched out and holding onto my hip, like he needs to know I'm still here and I can't help smiling to myself. I take a minute or two to just watch him but then I don't want to wake him, so I look over my shoulder at the old fashioned digital clock on the bedside table and see that it's still early. My body clock can't help itself, it rarely lets me sleep in these days because it's used to getting up to get into Vines to start the baking for the day.

Not wanting to wake Caleb up, I gently remove his hand from my hip and when he stirs, mumbling my name, I lean in to whisper in his ear that I'm just going to the bathroom. He mumbles back, 'hurry up' but he's more asleep than he is awake and he settles back into bed easily.

I make my way to the bathroom, brush my hair and put it up in a ponytail, then walk back into the bedroom and quietly pull on some pants and the first hoodie I see. I grab my socks and shoes, then quietly tiptoe out of the room. I sit down on the couch and slip on my shoes, then as quietly as I possibly can, I slip out of the door. I breathe a sigh of relief that I didn't wake Caleb up as I make my way down the stairs and out the backdoor, into the garden. I smile and nod to the few people that I come into contact with, as I put my earbuds in and open my music app on my phone.

After half an hour out in the fresh, crisp morning air, I make my way back to the suite and quietly slip into the bedroom, tiptoeing into the bathroom without checking to see if Caleb's still in bed. My mind fully focused on not waking him up and having a shower to clean up after my morning walk.

I've still got music playing loudly in my ears as I strip out of my clothes, it's not until I turn the music off to put my earbuds and phone on the vanity, that I realise the shower is already running. I look up to find Caleb standing there, leaning against the shower wall, water and soap all over his body and his cock in his hand. It takes me a few seconds to realise he's not simply washing his cock but he's actually got his eyes closed and he's moaning.

I *know* I should probably look away, leave the room to give him some privacy but I just can't bring myself to move. I stand there, frozen to the spot, drinking in the very sexy sight of a wet, soapy, naked and *very* hard Caleb.

Suddenly he stands up straight, leans back against the wall and runs his other hand over his chest, down his stomach, down his happy trail, around his cock and squeezes his balls. I make a small squeak sound that I try to hide but obviously don't because his eyes snap open and catch mine.

"Sorry." I squeak out.

"Don't be." His voice is rough.

"I'll ummm, leave you to it." I mumble and *try* to leave but I'm still rooted to the spot, my legs don't seem to want to move.

"Where are you going?"

"Oh, out." I jerk my thumb towards where I think the bathroom door is. "You know, to give you some privacy."

"You've seen me naked before, Darlin' and I promise you, I don't need privacy." His hands haven't stopped moving the whole time and he's still maintaining eye contact with me. "Just in case you haven't noticed, you're naked too."

"I am." I agree.

"Why don't you come and join me?"

"I could." I really could, couldn't I?

"You should." Fuck it. I don't wait for him send out a written invitation, my feet walk towards him without me telling them to and then I'm under the steamy water as well. The water isn't as hot as I like it but it's hotter than hell watching Caleb jerk himself off right in front of me.

I swear, even with all the weirdness that happened this weekend, it's the best weekend of my life!

Chapter Thirty-three
CALEB

Did I mean for Leila to catch me jerking off in the shower? No. Am I sorry she caught me in the act? Hell fucking no! Watching her watch me jerk off, is hot as fuck. She must know that my morning glory was totally because of her? My dreams for months have been filled with Leila and I've woken up with a rock hard cock. Having access to her and her gorgeous body this weekend, while amazing, hasn't really helped relieve my need for her. In fact, I would hazard a guess that it's made it worse now that I know what she feels like under my hands and around my cock.

My hand reaches for her as she joins me in the shower but she shakes her head, no.

"Don't stop." Her voice is a soft rasp, eyes are wide and her attention fully on what my hands are doing.

"You like watching, Darlin'?" My voice rough with my desire.

"Yes. No." I watch her blink slowly and then refocus on my cock. "I didn't think so but watching *you* is hot."

"Fuck." I ground out. "You haven't? Before?" I ask between breaths.

"No." She shakes her head, making her tits bounce slightly. "Never wanted to before, never caught a guy doing it before."

"Really?" I can't imagine a guy not needing to give his cock a few pulls just to give himself a little relief when he got naked with her. Then again, I'm not a huge fan of thinking about Leila being with another guy, so I push the thought out of my head.

"Really." I watch as her hand slides between her breasts, over her ribs, down her stomach and her fingers tangle in the small patch of tight curls just above her clit. "God Caleb, what the fuck are you doing to me?"

"Nothing, Darlin', I'm not even touching you." She moans as she lifts her leg and rests her foot on the small step that seems to be conveniently placed for just such occasions and slips her middle finger in to her pussy. "Are you wet, Darlin'?"

"Yes." That one word is more of a groan than an actual spoken word. "Caleb."

"Yes, Darlin'?" I ask, watching her play with her pussy and clit, knowing that I'm not going to last much longer, no matter how fucking hard I try to.

"I can't wait."

"What are you waiting for gorgeous girl?" I'm pretty sure I know what hearing her say it, is going to do to me.

"For you."

"For me?"

"To come."

"You want me to come?"

"Yes!"

"A gentleman makes sure the lady comes first. Every. Single. Time."

"Not today, Caleb. I. Need. You. To. Come."

"You want me to come first, gorgeous girl?"

"Yes!" She screams and I can't help wondering who can hear her. Just the thought makes me come in my hand and all over the shower wall.

"Fuck!" I want to close my eyes and rest my forehead on the wall to recover for a second but I can hear Leila's breathing getting quicker and she's making these noises that I've learned mean she's about to come and I can't not watch her.

Watching Leila bring herself to orgasm is one of the hottest, sexiest things I have ever witnessed. Her eyes are close, her head stretched backwards, resting on the wall and I can feel my cock getting hard again, I don't think there will ever be a moment where I'm not hard when this woman is around.

"Look at me, Leila. Let me watch you come, Darlin'."

"You are." She complains but she pulls her head up and her eyes snap open, looking deep into my soul. "Caleb?"

"Yes, Darlin'?"

"I'm going to come." My cock twitches and even though I came myself just a few beats ago, I have no doubt I could go again but this time, it's all about Leila.

"Come for me then." I command. I glance down at her fingers and her pussy, I can't help the groan that escapes me. "So fucking sexy, Leila. Watching you make yourself come is the hottest thing I've ever seen."

"Caleb." She breathes out, her hand reaching out for me and I can't deny her a damned thing, so I move closer enough for her to touch me. "I need."

"What do you need gorgeous?" I mumble into her neck, as she pulls me in closer to her with one hand and moans.

"Fuck. Fuck. Fuck!" She chants and then as she starts to shout out her release I take her lips with mine and swallow her scream. It's for me and me alone. "Caleb."

"Leila." I want to tell her. I have a sudden and overwhelming desire to tell her exactly how I feel. That I don't want this to end when we leave here. That I've fallen head over heels in love with her and I can't see a future without her.

"Caleb."

"Mmmmm." I can't move. I don't *want* to move. It's not like the hot water is going to run out and I just want to enjoy the moment with her. The peace, the privacy. A time where we can just be us and enjoy each other without having to put on a show. A few minutes when I don't have to wonder if what she feels is real or not. A few minutes not hiding, one way or another, from anyone.

"Caleb? We have to get out of the shower."

"It can wait a minute." She lets out a low chuckle.

"It really can't. There's someone at the door!"

"Fuck!" It's only then that I can hear the faint sound of knocking on the door. "I'll go, you clean yourself up."

"Caleb, you're naked and wet!" Leila laughs as I step out of the shower and grab a towel. I quickly run the towel over my hair to soak up most of the water, then quickly run it over my body, before fastening it around my hips.

"Not anymore, Darlin'." I smirk and leave the bathroom as my phone starts rattling across the bedside table. "Where's the fire?" I ask as I answer the phone, Leila's laughter following me out of the bathroom and I can't help smiling myself.

"Caleb!"

"What can I do for you Brian?" My voice is full of laughter.

"You can open your damned door, that's what you can do."

"Why would I do that? Is something wrong?" I ask suddenly concerned for Leila's safety, so I make my way to the door.

"What? Oh no, I just want to talk to you." I open the door, my phone still at my ear and a startled Brian on the other side. "Why are you in a towel?" He seems shocked.

"Why do you think Brian? I'm in a towel because I just got out of the shower." He moves to walk into the room but I block him. "What do you need, Brian?"

"Oh well, Mary was wondering if the two of you are joining us for breakfast before you leave?"

"Of course. Did you think we'd leave without saying goodbye? We did tell you we'd see you this morning."

"Well, you know, Mary wanted me to check in to make sure." Sure she did.

"We'll be down as soon as we're ready." I smile at the man who may or may not hold my future plans in his hands. "If you don't mind, I'm getting a little chilly and I want to go check in with Leila. You know, to make sure she's OK."

"Good morning, Brian. Isn't it a beautiful morning?" Leila's voice almost sings behind me, as she wraps her arms around my waist from behind me, placing them on the knot at my waist and resting her chin on my shoulder. "I hope you and Mary aren't waiting on us for breakfast? We'll be down just as soon as we pack up. It's my fault if we're running a little late, I went for a walk around your beautiful gardens this morning and only got back a little while ago and needed a shower." Her smile is radiant and genuine. I rest my hands on hers and smile at Brian, knowing that he can't misunderstand exactly what just happened here.

"Oh, yes of course, Leila, take your time, Sweetheart, there's no rush. No rush at all." Brian rushes out, a smile on his face. He's charmed by Leila, without a doubt and I'd love to admit to him that he's not the only one.

"Thank you, Brian. Again, I'm sorry if we've held up your breakfast." She steps away from my body and I feel the loss immediately, until she takes my hand in hers. "We'll get packed up now and be down there to join you and Mary in about fifteen minutes."

"I'll let Mary know." Brian smiles at her, completely ignoring me.

"See you soon, Brian." I tell him, as I close the door in his face and make sure to lock it.

"That was a bit rude, Caleb." Leila admonishes me, even as she smiles broadly.

"Maybe, Darlin' but necessary." She laughs loudly, throwing her head back and giving me amazing access to her neck, which I of course, take full advantage of and kiss along it, with a few nibbles here and there, causing her to moan softly. "Keep making that noise and breakfast will be postponed for a while longer."

"Keep doing that with your mouth and I won't mind at all."

"Brian can wait." I tell her while walking her back into the bedroom and trying to get her out of the fluffy bathrobe she's wearing.

"Maybe Brian can but Mary can't. I for one don't want to explain to *her* why we were late." The blush that creeps up her neck and onto her cheeks is fucking adorable.

I want to make them both wait but only because I don't want to leave the weekend behind us. I wish we could stay here, in this little bubble of bliss that we've created. I sigh because I know I'm just trying to delay the inevitable.

"You're right, Darlin', we can't keep Mary waiting." I drag myself away from her body, knowing that if I stay too close to her, I'm going to want her, again.

We both move around the room silently gathering up our things and packing them back into our bags, leaving out the clothes we're wearing today. I take both of our bags in my hands and nod for Leila to lead the way.

She opens the door for me to walk through first, then hesitates and looks back into the room for a few seconds, like she's trying to remember every detail for later.

She's not the only one. The memories of being happy with my fake fiancée are going to stay with me for a while.

Chapter Thirty-four
LEILA

Taking a few minutes to look back into the room as we leave, I can't help thinking this is the best weekend I've had in a long time. Even with all the craziness that happened, I've never felt more at ease, relaxed or happier.

"Let's go to breakfast." I smile as I turn to look at Caleb who is waiting in the hallway for me to close the door behind us. He insisted on carrying both of our bags, that means both of his hands are full and the least I can do is open and close some doors for him.

"Let's go." His smile is almost as sad as I feel.

"We shouldn't keep Mary and Brian waiting any longer." I blush at the memory of Brian knocking on the door while we were in the shower. Together but not touching. Each other, anyway.

"Are you OK?" Caleb asks as we head towards the dining room.

"Yeah, why?" I ask, as I walk beside him.

"You look a little, flustered." He smiles, it's an almost knowing smile, which makes me blush even more. "I hope you're not coming down with something, Darlin'?" The bastard tries to hide his smirk but I know and he *knows* that I know he thinks he knows what I'm thinking!

"I feel perfectly fine, thank you for your concern though Mr Drake." I send him a sweet smile to highlight exactly what I said. Even though I'm not quite sure what I'm thinking or saying.

"If you say so, Ms Phillips."

"Miss."

"Hmmm, what's that?"

"Miss. It's *Miss* Phillips, not *Ms* Phillips."

"Oh, my apologies, *Miss* Phillips." The corner of his lip quirks up and I have an overwhelming desire to kiss that smirk right off his sexy mouth but just as I begin to lean in, we're interrupted. Again.

"Leila, Caleb, I'm so glad you could join us this morning for breakfast before you leave."

"We wouldn't have it any other way, Mary." I say, as I walk in to her open arms for a warm embrace. Is it strange that I'm going to miss this woman? I only met her just over day ago and yet, I feel this warm attachment to her. "Would we, Caleb?" I smile at my fake fiancé for another hour if I'm lucky.

"Absolutely not! How could we not enjoy another meal with you and your husband, Mary?" Caleb drops the bags to the floor, holding his arms out for his own warm hug from Mary. For her part, she doesn't hesitate for a second. Honestly, I wouldn't hesitate if I was on the receiving end of one of Caleb's embraces either.

"I would hope not." Mary laughs quietly. "Let the guys take your bags to your car while you join us." The 'guys' she speaks of, quietly move closer and take our bags, as we follow Mary into the dining room. There, we have an amazing breakfast, the likes of which I might have to try and emulate at Vines for special occasions because it's just delicious.

"Well, it's time for us to hit the road." Caleb smiles at me, taking my hand in his as he stands up from the table. Breakfast is well and truly over and even though we've all managed to have another coffee to hold off saying goodbye, it's inevitable that we're leaving and I'm glad that it's Caleb that makes the decision because the fact is, I don't want to leave this bubble we've created for ourselves. A place where we can be together without his family's eagle eyes watching our every move or touch. Where we're *expected* to behave as if we're in love. "We've got a reasonably long drive ahead of us."

"I wish you could stay longer." Mary says, as she follows to the door. "I want to spend more time getting to know Leila and helping you two organise the wedding."

"Don't push them, Love. They set a date when they set a date." Brian says with a smile, taking his wife into arms and mouthing a 'sorry', to us.

"Don't apologise for me Brian Weaver!" Mary exclaims as she extricates herself from his arms and then envelops Caleb into a tight hug instead.

Mary says something in his ear and his eyes dart up to meet mine and I make a note to ask him what she said that made him look at me like he regrets his decisions, when we get in the car.

Then, I'm wrapped up in her arms and I have to hold onto her so that we both don't end up on the ground. The funny thing is, I didn't even realise that she'd let Caleb go, I was too busy trying to read the look on his face.

"You my girl, are very special. I want you to take great care of this young man, he's very special, not just to us but he's an amazing young man." She says quietly in my ear.

"Yes, he is." I tell her just as quietly and when I open my eyes that I didn't even realise that I'd closed, Caleb's still staring at me.

"Now, you two take care of each other and if you need anything, anything at all, you don't hesitate to call us, you hear?"

"We will." Caleb promises as he takes Brian's hand in his and the two men shake.

"Thank you both for having us this weekend." I lean in and leave a light kiss on Brian's cheek.

"I hope you enjoyed yourself, Leila, despite everything. I promise things are normally much quieter around here." The smile on his face is filled with warmth and I can't help returning it.

"Well, it's fair to say, that it wasn't a boring weekend, Brian but even with all of the, shall we say extra events, I had a wonderful time." I look over to Caleb and step into his side, revelling in his touch when he wraps his arm around my waist, pulling me even closer into his side. If I didn't know better, I'd think it was more because he wants me close than for show. "Any time I can get Caleb away from Drake Wines and have him to myself is a good time." I tell them as I snake my arm between us and hug his waist.

"It doesn't happen often enough." He replies, leaving a light kiss on my temple that I wish was longer.

"No, it doesn't." If eye contact could burn a hole in a person soul, my soul is ashes. I'm not sure how long we stand there, gazing into each other's eyes but a cough, then a second one, which is then followed by laughter, breaks the spell.

"Oh, sweet girl, there's no reason to be embarrassed. It's nice to see two young people so in love."

My blush burns my cheeks even harsher at Brian's comment and it's embarrassment that causes it, it's the knowledge of our lie to these two amazing, loving people.

"Come on Darlin', let's get moving." Caleb says, patting my hip.

"Alright, Handsome, let's hit the road." With a last kiss on both Mary and Brian's cheeks, I let Caleb lead me towards the car. He opens the door and waits for me to get comfortable before closing it and walking around the front of the car to the driver's seat. We put down the windows and wave to our hosts as we drive out of their gorgeous, winding driveway.

The car is silent, except for the radio playing quietly as Caleb steers us quickly through town and out to the highway. It's not an uncomfortable silence as such, it's just that I don't know quite what to say to him and I figure he might need to concentrate on driving for a while before we talk.

"Are you OK there, Darlin'?" His voice startles me out of my own thoughts, making me jump a little. "Sorry, I didn't mean to make you jump."

"That's OK." The few minutes of silence that follows is awkward this time and I think it's because we're both trying to work out what to say next. "Thank you for the weekend." I smile at him, hoping that he can see I mean it.

"That's OK, Darlin', it was my pleasure. One hundred percent my pleasure." He turns his head to look at me for a few seconds, that dangerously sexy smirk that shows off his dimple, on his lips. Lips I've kissed. Lips I want to kiss again. Lips I want to kiss *me* again. Lips that I want to feel kissing me all over, again. I can't help wondering if I'll ever have that chance again. I also can't help missing him already.

The pleasure wasn't his alone this weekend.

"It was definitely a pleasure for me too." I return his smile, probably with less brilliance than his but happy all the same.

"Are you sure? Because that was the most eventful weekend I think I had, ever and there were some pretty wild weekends while I was in University and my big bro and sis weren't around."

"It was certainly-." I pause for a second, then continue. "Shall we say, interesting." This time it's my turn to smirk at *him* because interesting doesn't cover even half of what happened this weekend.

"That's one way of describing it, Leila but I'm not sure that covers everything that happened." The chuckle that rumbles through his chest is so damned sexy, it's hard to take my next breath. "Between the Francine and Anita debacle and then Simon getting handsy, I'm sure it was the best weekend away you've ever had!"

"Don't forget to mention, that I slugged that creep and broke his nose." I remind him and watch him wince. "Now, I have to say, *that* makes it probably my best weekend ever. I can't say I've ever punched a guy like that before, I usually just walk away."

"When you say, you've never hit a *guy* like that before, what exactly do you mean? Have you hit another woman like that before?" His eyebrows are almost up in his hairline and I can't help laughing at him.

"Yeah, I have. I don't mess around with slapping or pulling hair my friend, oh no. You want to fight me? I'm going to fight you and I don't care what gender you are."

"Well, consider me warned then." There's a few seconds of silence. "I promise to stay on your good side." Then he cracks up laughing and I can't help joining him.

"I only do it when I feel like I need to defend myself, Caleb. I doubt I'll ever feel like breaking your nose."

"Well, that's reassuring. I've seen what you can do slugger, so I'm going to behave myself." I look out my window and mumble, 'don't behave on my behalf'. "What was that Darlin'?" He asks, his head snapping to look at me and then back at the road so that we don't crash.

"Nothing." He darts a look at me, one eyebrow raised in question. "No, nothing."

"If you're sure?"

"Positive." I smile sweetly at him. He doesn't look too convinced that I didn't mumble something under my breath but he *does* accept, after looking at me for far too long, that I'm not going to repeat it. "Eyes on the road." I tell him, pointing out the windscreen and smiling.

The next couple of hours are filled with periods of comfortable silence, listening to the radio and idle chitchat.

"I'm going to stop for fuel here. We can get some drinks and something to eat as well if you want?" He nods towards the petrol station.

"I do need a bathroom stop and I wouldn't mind a coffee." I say with a smile, which he returns in his normal, sexy way. He pulls up and I get out to find the bathroom and by the time I come back out, Caleb has filled up, paid *and* bought us both coffee's and some snacks. I take a sip of the coffee and I'm surprised when it's exactly how I like it.

"We can stop later for dinner if you want?" I nod yes because I don't think I can speak. I'm squealing like a teenage girl at the fact that he's trying to stretch out the time we get to spend together before we have to go back to reality.

"I'd like that." My voice isn't quite normal but if he notices, he doesn't mention it.

"Me too." He nods once and pulls back out onto the highway.

"It sounds like a plan then."

We drive along in that comfortable silence again for a while, with me quietly singing along to the radio before I notice he's restless. He's tapping the steering wheel with his fingers, and squirming in his seat.

"Leila?"

"Hmm?"

"I don't want this to end." He says in a rush.

"What?" He can't mean what I think he means. Can he?

"This. Us." He takes a hand off the wheel and points a few times between himself and me. "I don't want this to end." Holy shit! He can't mean what I think he means.

Chapter Thirty-five
CALEB

I don't know how to ask her for more. More time. More us. More *every-thing.*

So, without thinking about the consequences, I blurt it out and put my heart on the line.

"I don't want this to end."

"What?" The surprise on her face kills me. Is she surprised because she doesn't feel the same way or does the surprise stem from me just spilling it all out in a rush?

"This. Us." I wave my hand between us, trying to make her understand what I mean. "I don't want *this* to end." I repeat.

"And by *this,* you mean our arrangement?"

"Arrangement?" I ask, confused.

"Friends with benefits. That's what you mean, right?" Fuck! That's not what I mean but if that's what she's offering, I'll take it. For now.

"Yes."

"I don't want it to end either." Her smile is wide but it doesn't reach her eyes. I want to ask why so that I can put that sparkle back in her eye but I don't. "I've really enjoyed our weekend."

"Me too." And because I want to hear her laugh, I can't help adding, "The sex *was* amazing, wasn't it?" My self-congratulatory statement does exactly what I wanted it to do and she throws her head back, as her laughter fills the car.

"You're something else, you know that?" She's shaking like she can't quite believe I went there but her smile is so wide, I can't help returning it.

"I do know that Darlin'." I send my flirty smirk her way and she shakes her head again but the smile is still on her face and now her eyes are sparkling as well. "It's always reassuring when your woman feels the same." I wink at her

"Is that what I am?"

"What?"

"Your 'woman.'"

"If you want to be, yes." I take my eyes off the road to look at her, I need to see her when she responds. "I want you to be."

"Would that make *you* my man?" Her question makes my stomach churn but it's not in panic, no it's in anticipation and delight. In the past, if someone had asked me that same question, I definitely would have been sent into a spiral of panic.

"I guess so. Yes, yes it would, Leila." I reach over and take her hand in mine, needing her touch and wanting to reassure her at the same time.

"As friends with benefits?" I want so much more but I agree with her.

"Yes."

"Would we tell people or -?" Fuck! I don't want to tell Kenna and Logan because they won't just give me a hard time, they'll give Leila a hard time as well and I don't want that. "You're right, we should keep it quiet."

"Leila." I growl as she tries to pull her hand from mine. "That's not what I said. It's just that, Kenna and Logan are going to be, I guess you'd say, in our business if they know."

"No, that's OK, I understand. No, Caleb, I do. It's not like we're together, you're not my boyfriend or anything, so we should keep it on the down low. I mean, I don't want to lose my job and you need to have your siblings on side for the brewery. I get it."

"Just for now." I say because she really *doesn't* 'get it' at all.

"I understand." She's agreeing with me but she won't look at me.

"I don't think you do, Leila." She doesn't reply and a silence that isn't as easy as before settles between us but she doesn't pull her hand from mine, so I grip it tighter, hoping that she can understand what I can't say. Yet.

That's how we stay for the rest of the drive and I take comfort in the fact that she doesn't try to take her hand out of my but instead lets it rest there, between us, our fingers twisted together. I don't know why she hasn't let go but I know that I need her touch and that's why I don't move my hand.

While she's comfortable touching me, even just my hand, I'm going to take it.

"What are you doing? Why are you stopping? Is there something wrong with the car?" Leila asks each question one after the other, I'm not even sure she's taken a breath in between them. What I *do* know is it makes extremely difficult to answer any of them.

"Everything is fine, there's nothing wrong with the car and I'm pulling over so that we can talk before we get to Drake Wines." I wait until she stops looking at where we've stopped and she looks at *me*. "I think we have a few things to set straight before we face the onslaught of questions we're going to get in there." I nod my head in the direction of the vineyard.

"You're right." She slaps her forehead with the hand not holding mine. "Of course we should get our stories straight before we talk to anyone else. We don't want them to know that we spent the weekend together or about our arrangement." She rolls her eyes like she's an idiot.

"Not quite what I meant but yes, we need to talk." I say quietly. "Leila, Darlin', I want to keep seeing you."

"You mean, you want to keep being friends with benefits?" I close my eyes and sigh. I want to agree with her but also explain that I want more. I want to build this stupid arrangement into a relationship. A *real* relationship but I don't think she's ready to hear it.

"Yes."

"And to keep it between us? A secret?"

"No. Yes." I sigh again. "For now, yes. I don't want anyone else, namely my siblings to stick their nose into our *arrangement*." Just saying the word leaves a bad taste in my fucking mouth. This woman is more than an arrangement to me.

"For my job and your brewery." It's not a question, it's a statement.

"That too." She raises an eyebrow at me and cocks her head to the side. It's the cutest fucking thing I've ever seen. "The truth is."

"The truth is what, Caleb?" she asks after I hesitate for way too long.

"The truth is, I want to keep you, us, to myself for a while, Leila. I don't want everyone else's opinion or thoughts to intrude on us. I know we don't technically have to get to know each other but I want to get to know you. You *know* what my siblings and Jules are like, Darlin', they're going to have something to say *all* the time. They just can't help themselves." This makes her laugh, which is what I was hoping for.

"Yeah, I do know what you're family are like." She agrees with a smile.

"I mean, even Savvy's becoming just like her Dads, Aunt and Uncle! We both know that she'd never stop asking questions either!"

"And you don't want to answer those questions." She says quietly. Once again, it's a statement, not a damned question. "I get it because Sara will be the same and I don't have the answers for her questions either."

"It's not that I don't want to, Leila, it's more that we don't quite have the answers to their questions that they're going to ask." She nods in agreement but she's real quiet and it's making me nervous.

"So, what do you want to tell them about this weekend, if anything?" She brings her eyes up to meet mine finally, a steely determination in them that is sexy as fuck.

"The basics and no more? If we keep it simple, we can't screw it up, right? If we tell them that I dropped you at your Mum's for the weekend and you had a wonderful weekend catching up with her. Which we both know that you did, I stayed to meet your Mum and then headed into the city. Then, we reversed all of that and drove home."

"You're still not going to tell them about Brian and your plans to add a brewery?"

"Soon, yes but Brian still hasn't agreed to be my supplier. I think I'm going to have to start seriously looking into the other couple of suppliers that I shortlisted as well."

"Brian won't let you down, Caleb, Mary wouldn't let him, she likes you too much." That makes me smile.

"We're friends, sure but that doesn't mean that Brian will do business with me and I don't want him to if he feels uncomfortable about it. That's not me." I shrug my shoulders. "So, what do you say? Are you OK with all of that?"

"So, you met my mum hey?" She nudges my shoulder with hers, making me realise that we somehow moved close together while were talking. If anyone was to drive by right now, they might be excused for thinking we were getting very close!

"Of course! I wouldn't let that opportunity slip by and this way, if your Mum comes out for a visit and mentions meeting me, we're covered."

Chapter Thirty-six
LEILA

I know I shouldn't be hurt by Caleb asking to keep our friends with benefits relationship going but I am.

I'm not complaining, I was just hoping for a little ... more.

"Right. If Mum comes out to Drake Wines and Vines, we're covered." I smile at Caleb, trying to show him the same enthusiasm but it kind of hurts my heart. "As an added bonus, my job is safe as well." I add as he turns to keep driving us home.

"They would never fire you, Leila." He hesitates, his hand resting on the gear shift, staring at the road ahead, not meeting my gaze. "They'd rather I didn't work at the Vineyard, believe me."

"I don't think that's true at all, Caleb." I reach out and rest my hand on his bicep. "They love you Caleb and they wouldn't choose me, a worker, over you, their flesh and blood."

"Yes -." I don't let him finish.

"No, they wouldn't. You know it and so do I and that's OK. That's how it's *supposed* to be Caleb." He doesn't say anything before he puts the car in drive and continues along the short distance to the gate that announces we're arriving a Drake Wines.

I don't take my hand off his arm until we're close to Vines, where someone might see us but I give it a gentle squeeze before I drop my hand to my lap.

I expect him to pull up outside Vines so that I can drop my bags in my car but instead, he keeps driving until we reach his place. We sit in the silence as the garage door opens so that he can pull the car inside. This silence isn't as comfortable as the ones before and I find myself trying to find words to say as we sit in the darkening garage. As the door closes behind us and he turns the car off.

"They would keep you, you know." He announces quietly into the silence after a few minutes, before getting out of the car and slamming the door, leaving me in shock. It's not until he opens the door into the house, bringing brightness into the dark, that I finally pull myself together and get out of the car, slamming my door behind me.

I storm into the house behind him, not even checking to see if he grabbed my stuff out of that car as well as his own. I follow him inside, slamming the door to garage behind me, earning me his attention. The scowl on his handsome face makes me want to kiss him.

"What the hell, Leila?" He shouts, making me jump. I've never seen Caleb mad before. Logan? Yes. Caleb? Never.

"What do you mean, what the hell?" I demand, hands firmly on my hips.

"You can't go slamming doors in my house, Leila!"

"You're pissed because I slammed a door?" I ask, a little taken aback by his words and his anger.

"Yes! No!" He runs his hands over his face in frustration. "No, I'm pissed because you don't believe me when I know it's the truth. They wouldn't fire *you* if we got found out, Leila, no they'll take Drake Wines from *me*."

"You're being ridiculous, Caleb!" I tell him sharply, I know he's wrong. "You're family and I'm not. They love you, I'm an employee. I know that you *think* they don't want you around and don't value, you but you're wrong. *So* wrong that I don't even know how to make you believe it!" My voice gets louder with every word I say.

"You. Are. Wrong." He enunciates every word clearly, concisely and with a freaking growl.

"I'm not and you know it!" He takes four giant steps and before I can react, his front is pressed to mine but he's not forceful enough to knock me off balance.

"You are." His nose is almost touching mine.

"I'm not wrong." I whisper, resting my hands on his cheeks and touching our foreheads together. "I am right and you know it. It's OK, I don't want to share this with anyone either." My voice is barely above a whisper.

"Why not?" His voice is a raspy whisper too.

"I don't want to break the spell." I can't explain it to him in words because I don't know how. All I know is that I don't want to tell anyone about our arrangement because I don't want to hear the negatives. "I don't want anyone to tell me I'm doing the wrong thing." Because I know without a doubt, Sara will tell me that I'm setting myself up to get my heart broken. She may not be wrong but I'm still going to take Caleb in whatever way I can have him right now. I can get over the heartbreak later.

"Who would tell you you're doing the wrong thing?" He asks, running his hands through the length of my hair. He's barely touching me and yet, it feels like heaven.

"It doesn't matter because I won't tell them." I smile and push my lips out a little so they just touch his. "This is just for us."

"Just us? Are you sure you're OK with that?" He pulls back so that he can look into my eyes, obviously making sure that I'm telling him the truth.

"Just us." I smile and give him a slight nod. He kisses me, softly, tenderly and when he pulls back, I say, "You're still wrong though." Then, before he can respond I take his lips with mine in a kiss that is almost bruising, even more so when he returns my passion. "Just us."

He drops his hands to my hips, his fingers digging into the softness of the cheek of my butt and lifts me up, encouraging me to wrap my legs around his hips. He doesn't once break our kiss, as he spins us around slowly, carrying me to his bedroom, barely managing to step over our bags that he dropped to the floor when we got inside. I can feel his cock getting harder as it rests against the seam of my jeans and I moan into his kiss.

He pulls back and I prepare for my feet to connect with the floor but the next thing I know, I'm flying through the air for a few seconds and then my back hits the mattress, making me squeal.

"Caleb!" I can't believe he just did that! It was enough that he carried me to his bedroom but the fact that he threw me onto the bed like I was nothing and is *still* moving towards me like a sexy, prowling tiger. He is so sexy and I can't quite believe this is real, even after our weekend together.

He reaches behind him and does that sexy as fuck one handed trick to pull off his t-shirt and I sigh.

I can't wait to touch him.

He drops to the bed, and crawls up my body, lifting one hand to push my own t-shirt up over my boobs. I suddenly realise that he needs some help removing my top, so I move my hands to the hem and raise up off the bed just enough to pull it off. Caleb takes the opportunity of me being raised up a little to undo the clasp on my bra, before I lie back on the bed. Smart man. He slides the straps off my shoulders and I pull my arms out of them, dropping my bra to floor beside the bed.

Bending down, he takes a nipple into his mouth and sucks. Hard.

"Fuck!" I swear, somewhere in the back of my mind, I hear someone speaking but with Caleb's hips pressed into mine and his mouth sucking my nipple, it doesn't register properly.

Until Caleb drops my nipple with a popping sound and sits up between my thighs, resting back on his heels to listen and that's when I hear her.

"Caleb? Is that you? Are you home already? Is Leila with you? She left her car here, so I assume you didn't drop her home yet." Makenna's voice breaks through my sex haze.

"Oh my god! She can't find us like this, Caleb." I start to panic, searching for my bra and top.

"Leila, Darlin', relax." He says, as he springs up off the bed, pulling on his t-shirt. How can I relax? If his sister finds us in here, like this, we're screwed. *I'm screwed.* "I'll go out there and distract her. All we have to tell her is that it was a long drive and we both needed the bathroom."

"But we're going to look like we were." I motion to the bed that's now a rumpled mess, while I stand there looking for my top still. I found my bra and I'm struggling to put it back on while I talk.

"You weren't properly screwed and you know it." He smirks at me and I don't know how he can be so cocky in this moment.

"Caleb? Leila? Are you here?" Makenna yells out.

"Yes, Kenna! For fuck sake, can't a man pee in peace in his own home? Do I still need you to supervise my every move, big sister?" Caleb smirks at me again as he walks out of the bedroom, closing the door quietly behind him.

"Do you have to be so crude, Caleb? I'm sure Leila doesn't want or need to hear you talk like that!" I hear Makenna say through the closed door and I can't help smiling.

"She's heard me say worse, much worse, big sister, I'm sure she's OK with it." A quiet giggle escapes me before I clamp my hand over my mouth. He's right, I've heard him say a lot worse and not over this weekend when we started our arrangement either.

"Hallelujah!" I whisper yell when I finally find my top. I don't know how it worked its way to the foot of the bed but that's where I find it.

I run my fingers through my hair, then smooth my hands over the top of it and wish that I had a hair tie with me so that I could tie it back. That way, it wouldn't look as messy as it probably does now.

Taking a deep breath, I walk over to the door, cracking it open slightly to see where they're standing and work out how easy it's going to be for me to get out of here without her noticing I'm walking out of her brother's room! When I look through the gap, I see that Caleb has managed to work it so that he's facing the bedroom, with Makenna's back to me. I can hear their voices still but I can't make out what they're saying.

I open the door and slide out, quietly closing it behind me. I cough quietly so that they both know I'm there and join them.

"Leila." Makenna gives me a warm hug, giving me no choice but to hug her back. I look over her shoulder at Caleb, who raises an eyebrow at me and I know what he's trying to say without words. "It's so nice to have you back. How's your Mum, did you have a nice time with her?" She asks, as she pulls out of the embrace to look in my eyes, her hands resting on my shoulders.

"Mum is great, thanks for asking." I smile and step away from her to stand next to Caleb.

"I hope he wasn't too annoying on the drive there or back?" I know that her question has more than an underlying question to it and I smile at her.

"Caleb was great, although I doubt he would want to do that trip with me again. I think I fell asleep and started snoring on the way there." I laugh. Caleb drapes an arm around my shoulders and instinctively, I move into his side. Until Makenna raises that damned eyebrow at us again and I pull away a little.

"She did snore but I found it endearing. What's a little buzz saw action between friends on the long, lonely highway?"

"Rude!" I say, pushing him away to get some distance from him.

"Are you driving home tonight, Leila?"

"No, she's staying here again. That is, if unless us *adults* need your permission for a sleepover between friends?" Caleb says before I can respond.

"That's OK, I can drive home."

"No, you're not driving home now, it's not safe." I look between the siblings and I can see the silent conversation going on between them and decide to excuse myself.

"OK, I'll just grab my bag then and take it to the spare room. Maybe use the bathroom."

"Didn't you already do that?" Makenna asks, not taking her eyes off Caleb's.

"Well, yes but now that I'm staying the night, I wouldn't mind having a shower to freshen up. I'll see you tomorrow Makenna." I don't wait for her to answer, I pick up my bag and hot foot it to the spare room faster than a flash of light.

I'm not sure what's going on between them but that's for them to sort out, I'm staying out of it. Far, far away from whatever that was.

I drop my bag in the room and pull my pyjamas out of it and some clean underwear, then head to the bathroom. I can hear the faint rumble of voices as I move from one room to the other but I can't understand what they're saying. Nor do I really want to. I turn on the shower to let it warm up while I strip off. Standing under the steamy water, I feel all the coiled up energy and stress leave my body.

There's nothing in the world better than a nice hot shower. Well, almost nothing.

Chapter Thirty-seven
CALEB

"You're both looking a little rumpled." Kenna says, one eyebrow raised like she's suspicious and trying to wheedle an admission of guilt out of me. Us.

"It was a long drive, Kenna, of course we look a bit rumpled. We only walked in the door about ten minutes ago, if that and you're already here harassing us!" I whine, hoping to get my sister off my back. No such luck.

"But didn't you pick Leila up from her Mum's place? Which means she wasn't that far away, an hour at most. *You've* been driving for a few hours." She frowns at me and I can see wheels spinning in her head but before I can try to head them off at the pass, she continues. "Unless of course you were together the entire weekend. That's not the case though, is it, Caleb?"

"Of course not!" I scoff. I have no idea how the hell to get her off the scent but I know I need to do *something*. "You know, Leila doesn't think of me other than her employer, thanks to your fine self and Logan drumming it into *both* of us that's she's off limits. I offered to drive her to her mum's because that car of hers is a clunker and we all know what a shitty car on the road means. She's a valued employee, that's it." I tell Kenna with a straight face, hoping like fucking hell that Leila doesn't hear me and if she *does* happen to be listening, she understands what I'm doing. I do *not* feel like Leila's boss and I sure would like to get back to what we were doing *before* my sister arrived to check up on me.

"If you say so, Caleb, I trust you." And there's the knife twist that she's hoping will get me to cave and admit to some kind of wrong doing. It might have worked on me when I was a kid and even as a teenager but not these days.

"Thank you." I say simply, resting my hands on her shoulders and directing her towards the door, not subtlety telling her to leave. "I appreciate you saying you trust me, now you can go home to Brady and call Logan to tell him everything is fine."

"I might wait. I need to talk to Leila about something -." I cut her off as I open the door for her.

"It can wait until tomorrow when she's back at work. Enjoy your evening, Kenna." I drop a kiss on her cheek as she reaches the front step, then I close *and* lock the door behind her. I smile and wave at her before turning around and walking back towards my bedroom, when I hear the shower running in the main bathroom, I quickly change direction, making a beeline for what I hope is an unlocked door.

I rest my hand on the handle and take a deep breath, before twisting it. The door quietly and slowly swings open to reveal a bathroom filled with steam, warmth and Leila.

I take a few heart beats to just watch her, to take her in and then I step into the room, quietly closing *and* locking the door behind me, just in case. I strip out of my clothes in less than a minute but to be fair, I only had on jeans and t-shirt, after being interrupted by my sister earlier.

"Hey there, Darlin'." I say quietly as I step into the shower cubicle and circle my arms around her waist.

"Caleb?"

"Who else were you expecting, Darlin'?" I ask, smiling against her neck.

"Honestly? No-one, not even you." The laughter in her voice takes the sting out of her comment. "Did Makenna leave?"

"No, she's waiting out in the living room for us. I said I'd come in here and get you." The sound of her gasp and the slap of her hands on mine was well worth it. Before she can take her hands off me, I take them in mine and rest them on her stomach. "Of course she's gone, Leila,"

"Caleb!" She might be scolding me but I can feel the laughter shaking her gorgeous body even as she says my name in that school teacher tone that makes my blood heat up and my cock stand to attention.

"Leila!" I stretch her name out as long as I can. "How about we finish what we started before we were so rudely interrupted." I mumble against her neck, as I kiss and suck along the skin there and along her shoulder. She stretches her neck to give me better access even as she starts to protest my suggestion.

"What if she comes -." She begins. "Oh wow!" I drop my hand to cup her between her legs and run my thumb over her clit.

"The only one coming in the next few minutes is you, Darlin'." Her head drops back onto my shoulder, her eyes closed, mouth slightly open like she's gasping and the most gorgeous look of bliss on her face. "How long do you think you can last?"

"Until the water runs cold." She answers, a ghost of a smirk on her lips.

"It's endless hot water, Darlin'. The water gets heated as it's used." I tell her as I push a finger into her pussy.

"Well, fuck." Her voice is barely a husky whisper and I can already feel her tightening around my finger.

"Exactly." I push a second finger into her and rotate them so that I can push on the front wall of her pussy, rubbing that spot that makes her shake. it's not the most natural position for my wrist but I can deal with it for the few minutes it's going to take to get her to come all over my hand. "That's it Darlin', come for me. Come all over my hand." I tighten my hold around her waist to hold her up as her knees start to buckle and she grips on tightly to my forearm.

"Caleb." If my ear wasn't so close to her lips, I doubt I would have been able to hear my name.

"Leila. Are you ready? Do you want to come?" She nods her head slightly. "Yeah? Right now? All over my hand? Or do you want to come all over my tongue and my lips? Which would you prefer?"

"Now." She sighs as a full body shudder rushes through her. "Please." The word is more of a groan than a word. I nip at her ear and she moves her head just a little bit, giving me access to her shoulder, just like I wanted. I bite down on her shoulder, while pumping my fingers in and out of her pussy relentlessly, bringing her right to the edge. "More." She demands, so I add another finger and within a couple of pumps of my hand and another bite on her shoulder, her voice is ringing out in the bathroom and she's coming all over my hand.

"You are gorgeous when you come, Darlin'. I mean, you're beautiful any time but I just love to watch you fall apart in my arms." I admit, putting more of myself out there than I truly intended but in this moment, I can't bring myself to care.

"Caleb." She hasn't moved a muscle, she's relaxed back into my chest and I do not want to let her go. Ever.

I reach around her for the soap and start lathering her up. Running my hands over her body and even though it's not with the intent of being sexual, I can feel her body reacting to my touch and a sense of pride blooms in my chest. Suddenly, she pushes off my chest and spins in my arms. I take hold of her hips in my hands, worried that her movements are too quick and she's going to fall over. Instead, her hands land on my chest with a slap. Her eyes, still shining from her orgasm, meet mine and she smiles broadly.

"Your turn." She says, as she slides a hand down my stomach but I catch her wrist before she reaches my cock. "You don't want me to make you come?" She asks, an adorable frown creasing her face.

"No. I mean, yes but not in here." I shake my head, she makes it hard to think when she's touching me.

"I thought the hot water wouldn't run out?" She asks with a smirk on her beautiful face.

"It won't but I won't be able to stay standing if you give me a hand job and I don't want to take us both down." I reach around her again and turn off the water, take her hand in mine to lead her out of the shower. I quickly wrap a towel around my waist and before Leila can reach for one, I do and just as quickly rub it over her hair and then her body, wrapping it around her and tucking the corner between her breasts.

"You're an expert at that." She states, not really asking the question about how I might know how to tuck towels between breasts that well. The truth is, I've never done it before and it was dumb luck.

"Not at all, Darlin', just motivated." I smile, taking her hand back in mine, I lead her to my bedroom without another word.

"Are you sure, Caleb?" Her question stops me in my tracks.

"Sure about what?" I turn to look at her because wanting to be with her, hand job or not, isn't a question and notice she's looking out the door towards the living areas. "I locked the door behind Kenna, Darlin' and no-one has a key to the place. Believe me, I made sure of it." I chuckle and pull her into my arms.

"What do you mean?" She asks, staring at her fingers that are playing with the hair on my chest.

"What I mean is, they *think* they all have keys but they don't. They're fake keys. In fact, the only one who *has* an actual key that will work, is Jules and I know he won't use it unless there's an emergency."

"What you mean by fake keys?" I untuck the towel from her breasts as I answer.

"Not fake per se, they're their own house keys."

"How do they not know?"

"I rarely lock my door, I haven't had any reason to." I shrug.

"But won't they find it weird if you start now?"

"No because they're *all* locking their doors now." I laugh, mainly because I'm the reason they're locking their doors.

"And you trust Jules not to let himself in?" She asks, as her hands find the knot in the towel at my hip and untucks it, letting the towel drop to the floor.

"Yes. Plus, if he *does* let himself in, I trust him to not tell anyone else you're here and why." I explain, as I run my hands from her hips up to her gorgeous breasts and palm them, giving them a couple of squeezes.

"How can you be sure?" She moans as I pinch both of her nipples.

"About Jules?" I ask and she nods as she moans.

"For one, he owes me and two, he likes me and he likes me with you."

"But."

"No. More. Talk, Darlin." I don't give her the chance the say anything else because I cover her mouth with mine and kiss the breath out of both of us, until she pulls back.

"This isn't about me, it's about you." She pushes me back and I let myself fall back on to the bed.

"If you want to have your wicked way with me, have at me Darlin', I'm not going to complain or fight you. Not for a hot fucking second. Do whatever you want with me." I stretch my arms out to my side, letting her know that I am up for anything she wants to do.

She smiles at me as she prowls up the bed, between my legs and I spread them as wide as I can to give her all the access she wants.

"Anything I want, hey?"

"I am all yours." Now and forever, I say in my mind because saying it out loud isn't going to do me any favours tonight. One day soon but not tonight.

No, tonight I'm just glad to have her here in my house, in my bed until morning and she didn't argue with me about it. *That* in itself feels like a miracle to me. I can't wait to hold her all night and wake up with her tomorrow, before we both head out to work.

I don't want to get ahead of myself but I could *really* get used to having her here and making this *our* house.

Chapter Thirty-eight
LEILA

Having free range to do whatever I want to Caleb is exhilarating and at the same time completely nerve wracking. I also can't deny that it's making me hot ... all over! I can feel my entire body heating up with the anticipation of having my hands all over him.

His declaration of, 'I'm all yours', almost makes me implode with desire. I crawl up the bed, hoping with every part of me that it looks sexy because it feels kind of awkward and stupid but the smile on his face and the heat in his eyes tells me he likes it. He likes it a lot!

He's spread out and vulnerable in front of me. He's like a smorgasbord of delicious that I could only dream of. I never could have imagined what he was hiding underneath his clothes and believe me, I have definitely imagined! My imagination has fuelled so many sessions of bean flicking that he'd be horrified and here he is, in all his glory, trusting me to give him pleasure.

"Whatcha waiting for, Darlin'?" He asks with a smirk, dragging me out of my daydreaming.

I rest my hands on his hips and I feel the muscles twitch underneath my touch but his face gives nothing away.

"Did you want me to wrap my lips around you or my hands." A low growl escapes him but still, he doesn't move.

"Darlin', you can do whatever the fuck you like with me. You can wrap that gorgeous mouth around my cock. You can use your tongue to lick me like an erotic lollypop. You can wrap your hand around my cock and fist me until I come all over my stomach. You can do a combination of all of the above and more, I just want you to touch me and make me come."

"Any way I want?" I ask while running my hands up and down his sides and chest, just missing his nipples that almost seem to be *begging* for my touch.

"Anything. You can bite me and leave your mark. I'm up for anything once Darlin'." He smirks.

"Wow!" His low chuckle tells me that I said that out loud. With permission like that, who am I to say no? To anything.

Without thinking, I lower myself down to his chest and take a nipple between my teeth. The hiss as he draws in a breath drives me on. I love that sound! So, I move over to the other side and give his other nipple the same treatment, resulting in the same hissing sound. I run my tongue around them, one at a time to take away a little of the sting.

I kiss down his chest, over his stomach and take great pleasure in licking and sucking on his abs, making them jump, hopefully in pleasure!

When I reach his cock, I run my tongue through the slit, cleaning the precum off the tip and licking my lips. I look up Caleb's body to meet his eyes, I find fire and ice all at once.

"Leila." I rest my hands on his thighs, my thumbs rubbing the crease between his legs and pelvis. It's my favourite stretch of skin on a guy. It's smooth, silvery and as close to untouched as it can get.

"Caleb." I say his name in the same low tone that he says my name. At least, I try to anyway.

"Are you mocking -?" He looks down his body to ask me but doesn't finish as I suck the head of his cock into my mouth and he drops his head back down to the pillows. "Fuck! That feels so fucking good, Leila."

I wrap my hand around the base of his cock and start slowly drawing my hand up and down, twisting a little bit every now and then. The groaning and mumbled curses coming from Caleb's lips push me on. I've never been a big fan of giving blowjobs, therefore I don't have much experience but hand jobs? Those I know how to do and I do them *very* well even if I do say so myself. Caleb doesn't seem to be complaining about either right now though.

His hips come up off the bed as he tried to push harder into my fist but I don't let him have his way. I stop my movements and he groans.

"Leila, Darlin', please don't stop." Caleb begs me and I can't help the thrill that runs through me. It feels like my blood is on fire. Having a man like Caleb begging *me* not to stop and to give him pleasure is more of a turn on than I could ever explain.

"You want me to stop?" I ask, with a grin and start to pull my hand off his hard cock.

"Don't you dare stop, Leila."

"What are you going to do if I stop?" I ask, curious to know and wanting to push his buttons some more, just to see how far I can get.

"I'll make you watch me." I feel my eyes go round and I lick my lips, just thinking about watching him make himself come. Again. It's the hottest thing I've ever seen and I'd love to watch it again. "But you don't get to touch. I'd get myself off without any help from you whatsoever." I see the glint in his eyes, the teasing in them and I smirk.

Leaning forward, I run my lips up the column of his throat, when I reach his ear, I take it between my teeth and nip gently. "But we both know, you *want* me to touch you. You want me to keep jerking you off. You want me to wrap my lips around your cock and suck you dry." I say softly in his ear. It's not quite a whisper but I'm not being aggressive either.

"Fuck!" I can feel his Adam's apple bob against the side of my cheek, as he swallows deeply. "You trying to beat me at my own game there, Darlin'?"

"And what game would that be, Handsome?" I ask him as I pull my face back up until I can look into his gorgeous blue eyes.

"Dirty talking until you're ready to explode." He doesn't hesitate or mince words. I didn't expect him to, he hasn't since we tumbled into bed together this weekend and we both know, his dirty mouth makes me just as hot as his touch does.

"I'll always win." I tell him, sounding a hell of a lot more confident that I feel, as I bite his bottom lip to drive my point home.

"You have no idea how right you are, Leila." I don't get the chance to ask him what he means by that because he runs his hand through my hair and drags my mouth down to meet his in a scorching kiss. It's the kind of kiss that a girl remembers for the rest of her life, it's that damned good!

I pull out of the kiss before he can distract me from what I was doing and he groans, reaching out his hands for me when I move away from his lips and back down his body.

"Come back here." He gasps loudly before he can finish his demand because I wrap my lips around the head of his cock and suck. Hard. "Fuck!" I release the pressure and run my tongue through the slit, licking up the pre-cum.

I don't give him the chance to move or say anything else. Instead, I take as much of him as I can into my mouth, running my tongue around him as I go. Both of us are lost in the sensations as I bob my head up and down, taking more of him into my mouth until the head of his cock hits the back of my throat and my lips rest at the base. I hum and his hips shoot up off the bed, making me pull up, releasing his cock from my mouth.

"I'm sorry, Leila -." I run my hand up and down his cock, taking whatever words he was going to say, away. "I'm going to come if you keep doing that."

"Isn't that the point, Caleb?" I smile at him when his eyes catch mine.

"I guess so." He agrees through gritted teeth. I can tell he's trying to hold on for as long as he can. Is it because he wants to prove he can last or because he wants to draw out the pleasure?

We keep eye contact as his hips start to move, matching the movement of my hand and he grunts as he releases all over his stomach.

"Fuck!" He relaxes into the bed and I smile. It feels good to make a man lose himself like that. It feels good to make *Caleb* lose his self-control if even for just a few minutes.

"I'm going to go clean up." I say, nodding my head towards the bathroom.

"Mmmhmmm." Is all Caleb manages as I get up and my smile getting even broader.

I wash my hands and walk back into the bedroom. I walk slowly back to the bed so that I can admire Caleb sprawled out on the bed. He's pulled up the covers to his waist and he's lying back, hands under his head, with his eyes closed and smile on his face.

"Come here." He says, as he stretches out his arm in invitation, without opening his eyes.

"How did you even know I was back in the room?" I ask, as I crawl into the bed and straight in his arm, to rest my head on his chest, his arm pulling me in impossibly closer.

"I just did." He shrugs his shoulders. "And I heard the water turn off and took an educated guess." I smack his chest lightly and he chuckles.

"Don't you need to get cleaned up?"

"Nah, already done."

"But I was in the bathroom."

"That's what tissues are for, Darlin.'"

"Oh." I didn't even think about it. "I should have let you use the bathroom first."

"I don't mind either way, Leila." He squeezes me tighter. "Now, come here and get comfy so that we can get some sleep."

"Are you sure I should stay here?"

"You're not driving home now!" He says, his eyes suddenly wide open.

"No, I meant that perhaps I should sleep in the spare room. You know, just in case we get an early morning visitor."

"They know better." He grumbles, settling back into the bed and pulling me with him. "You're not going anywhere. I want you here, with me."

"OK." I whisper

"Good. Sleep now, we've got an early start."

"I do, you don't have to get up."

"We've got an early start. Don't argue with me, Leila." He moves his head to the side so that he can kiss my forehead. It's the sweetest gesture and I find myself sighing with happiness. "Goodnight, Leila."

"Goodnight, Caleb."

I smile against his skin and drift off to sleep.

Chapter Thirty-nine
CALEB

The next morning, we don't get a visit from any of my siblings or their spouses, which I take as a win. If any of them noticed that I walked Leila to work this morning, none of them mention it and I'm grateful. We got to Vines before Sara, so even she didn't have anything to say because I was long gone before she arrived.

Even though I spend a lot of time in Vines doing work, I also have an office that I have to show my face in every now and then, just to keep Kenna and Logan appeased. Also, most of my files and paperwork are in there and even I know that I can't take those things over to Vines. That would be insane but don't think I haven't thought about it. If I thought I could get away with having my office in the tasting room, I would, make no mistake.

"What's got you smiling so early this morning little brother?" I startle as I open my office door, I wasn't expecting company this morning and finding someone already in my office waiting for me, was completely unexpected. Not to mention, it's pretty rare that either of my siblings show up here, they usually summon me to them!

"Good morning *big brother*, what can I do for you this fine Monday morning?" I ask with a smile and an emphasis on the big brother because I wish they would *both* cut out the little brother bullshit when they address me. I move around to sit behind my desk, glad that he chose to sit in the visitors chair instead of mine. That's something I suppose.

"I take it you had an enjoyable weekend then?" He asks, with a look on his face that tells me he's assessing every movement I make and word that I say. He's an amazing businessman and when he looks at you like that, you can see why but he's still just my brother to me.

"I had a great weekend, thank you for asking." I tell him truthfully.

"So, what was her name this weekend?" He's got a sour look on his face, like he knows what I got up to and he's disgusted.

"I spent the weekend with friends, Logan and we did actually have a great time. I didn't find a woman whose name I don't know or won't remember, in fact that's rarely what happens. I'm not in school anymore and I take my job seriously." Logan studies me intensely and most other people would probably crumble under his scrutiny but I've lived with it for years, I'm as close to immune as I can get. I hope. I've seen it make the toughest of businessmen and women crumble though.

"I'm not calling out your ability or commitment to the job, Caleb. Despite what you may think, I'm proud of everything you're doing and have done around here. You've taken up every challenge we've given you and you've made it a success. I just worry about your reputation and what that could mean for you."

"You mean, you're worried that my supposed reputation might have a detrimental effect on Drake Wines but I can assure you that despite what *you* might have heard, I'm not that guy." I raise my hand to stop him from speaking as he opens his mouth to either deny what I said or defend himself. "I know what yourself and Makenna think you know, Logan but you're wrong. I might be your younger brother and maybe you've decided you know what I am but you don't know me. Neither of you have taken the time to get to know me properly since Mum and Dad died. You both just jumped in feet first to be parents and while I understand it to a degree, you're not my father, you're my brother. No-one can replace Dad, not even you. I don't need either of you to treat me with kid gloves or as your stupid younger brother who needs his hand to be held at every turn. I earned my business degree just like you did and just like Makenna did. So, while I appreciate your concern about my 'reputation', it's not required."

"I never meant to insult you or make you feel like we didn't trust you, Caleb. You're still a young guy, you're allowed to be 'having fun', it's just that -."

"It's just that we're running a business, well you and Kenna are, right? I'm just the hired help. I mean, it's not like I'm contributing anything to the bottom line, is it?" I cut him off, my good mood after leaving Leila at Vines completely destroyed now.

"Caleb. You know that's not what I mean. I'm worried about you, that's all. I don't want you to get into something that could hurt you and that you might not be able to repair."

"So, now what you're saying is, '*Caleb, I think you're screwing a member of staff, one that is respected and admired by all. You're not both adults, capable of making your own decisions, so I've made it my mission to make sure you don't screw it up or make her want to leave Drake Wines. If it comes down to it, you go before she does.'* We both know that's the truth." I tried to imitate his stupidly deep, serious tone but I know I failed.

"We would never choose a member of staff over you, Caleb, ever and I hope you know that."

"But?"

"*But* that doesn't mean that Leila isn't more than a member of staff here. She's family, Caleb and we just want you to be careful."

"So, let me ask you this, Logan. Did you pull the short straw or did you choose to be the one who came and spoke to me about the dangers of dating a staff member? I think we both know that this conversation is happening because Makenna barged into my house last night and discovered that I invited Leila to stay the night so that she didn't have to drive home."

"You're right, Kenna and I did talk last night and I did choose to come over and talk to you but it wasn't just because Leila stayed with you last night or that you gave her a lift to her mum's. We're just concerned, about you *both*, Caleb."

"Right, you're worried about Leila because nothing good could possibly come of the two of us spending more time together, could it? It will inevitably end in disaster as things can with me, thanks for the vote of confidence! Now, can you get out of my office so that I can get some work done please? Thank you. I'm sure you have more than enough of your own work to get done, so see you later."

"Caleb."

"I'll talk to you later."

"I didn't mean to upset you."

"Well, then I guess you'll have to learn to live with the fact that you did. Bye." I don't look up from the papers I'm looking at on my desk, tapping my pen on them while pretending to read them but not actually seeing a fucking word.

I hear him sigh and the door open and then close as he leaves. I wait for another minute before I look up to make sure he's actually gone.

I watch out of the window as he disappears back to his office right next to Makenna's and sigh. This visit this morning proves my point. This is why I want to keep whatever is happening between Leila and I between us. At least for now. She thinks they will get rid of her if this goes wrong and even though Logan just confirmed that they'd keep me no matter what, I wouldn't let that happen. I'd rather walk away from the family business and branch out on my own with my brewery, than have Leila end up without this job.

I shake my head to clear it and start working on the numbers for that brewery of mine. I need to fine tune a few things before I present my idea to Makenna and Logan and that means putting my head down and working.

"Knock, knock." I look up at my office door and smile. "You didn't come over to Vines for your usual mid-morning coffee and slice of chocolate cake, so I thought I'd bring them over for you." Leila smiles and places both items on my desk, in front of the paperwork I'm looking at.

"Thank you Darlin'. I didn't realise the time, otherwise I would have come over." I was concentrating so hard on what I was doing, I didn't even see her walk by my window.

"You looked pretty engrossed in those papers." She smiles at me. "I figured you could do with the break. I, umm, saw Logan leave here before. Is everything OK?"

"Yeah, everything's fine. He was just being a big brother." I shrug like it's nothing but I can tell she knows that's not how I really feel about his visit.

"He was warning you off me again, wasn't he?" When I don't answer her, she continues. "I had a feeling this would happen after leaving here together for a weekend and then Makenna catching us last night."

"Hey." I say getting up to move around my desk so that I can take her hands in mine. "Kenna didn't catch us doing anything last night, Darlin'. Everything was innocent in her eyes and that's the way it's going to stay. They can have their suspicions but until one of us confirms that something's going on, they don't know anything." I want to tell her that I'd leave before

I let them take her job from her but I know that she wouldn't agree to that, so I shut my mouth for a change.

"I don't want to get you into any trouble, Caleb." I laugh at her choice of words.

"Leila, Darlin', I'm a grown arse man and they're not my parents. Even if they were, getting into trouble with them isn't something that I'd care about. I want to spend time with you, to get to know you. Plus I kind of like having you around and I want to keep you around." I smirk at her, hoping that I can ease her mind.

"I just don't want to cause any tension between you and your family." She mumbles into my chest as I pull her into a crushing embrace. I just love having her in my arms and any time I can, I'm going to take it.

"There's no tension between us, I swear. Well, no more than there was before we went away for the weekend and their suspicions got even weirder." I laugh and kiss the top of her head as she tried in vain to get away.

"That's not funny, Caleb. I'm worried about causing a rift between you and your siblings and you think it's a joke."

"I don't think it's a joke, Darlin' but neither do I think it's anything to worry about." Not yet anyway but I don't say that out loud. "I promise, if anything happens that makes life difficult with Makenna and Logan, to talk to you about it and then tell them about us. Until then, can we just enjoy us, please?"

"OK. I should probably get back before Sara or anyone else decides to come looking for me."

"Didn't you tell anyone where you were going?" I ask, as she slips out of my arms and makes her way to the door.

"I'm sure Sara and Georgie had a pretty good idea considering what I was delivering but no, I didn't confirm or deny where I was actually headed." She smiles at me and it warms my insides. I know I shouldn't but I can't stop myself from taking the couple of strides to her. I take her cheeks in my hands and pull her lips to mine and kiss her until we're both struggling to breathe.

"I'll see you at lunchtime." I say, pulling just far enough away from her lips so that we can breathe and I can talk.

"Mmmm. OK." I kiss her forehead and open the door for her. "See you then." Then she's gone.

I watch her until she disappears and then I sit back down at my desk. I open the takeaway cup and discover my favourite tea to go with a slice of the best chocolate cake I've ever tasted.

As I take the first bite of cake, I shake my head. I don't know how the hell I'm going to be able to keep my hands off her while we're here. Shit, I don't know how I'm going to keep what I feel for Leila in check when other people can see me.

I adore this woman beyond belief and I'm not sure how long it's going to be before this all blows up and I have to make a choice. Who am I kidding? There is no choice.

I choose Leila every time.

Chapter Forty

LEILA

Walking back to Vines, I can't help the grin that spreads across my face. Somehow, over the weekend, I became addicted to his kisses and the one he just gave me was amazing!

"Are you OK, Leila?" Sara asks as I float into the kitchen, not even realising that I was back.

"Hmm? Yeah. Yup. Perfect." I smile at her and walk by her without stopping.

"So, the bossman is happy with his office delivery then?"

"Huh?" I stop and turn to look at her, only to find her smirking at me knowingly.

"Caleb? I take it he was happy that you took him his morning tea? Did he say why he couldn't make it over here today? I mean, he's always here in time for cake and coffee. The natives are getting a little rowdy without their weekly vision of Caleb eating your chocolate cake." She nods her head towards the table that the ladies we affectionately call 'the granny's' sit at and all four of the women are there. "They've been asking after him, wondering where he is today. Do you have an answer for them?"

"He's just busy working, Sara, no secret there." I shake my head and go to start some paperwork in my makeshift office in the corner of the kitchen. It was planned this way so that the manager could supervise the kitchen at all times but today, I would have really appreciated walls and a door.

"Sure." She smiles at me wickedly like she knows exactly what happened in Caleb's office. "That's why you're blushing and on cloud nine, right? Because nothing happened?"

"Sara!" There are a few people milling about in the kitchen and I don't need anyone hearing Sara's teasing me about Caleb. "Cut it out! This is neither the time nor the place to talk about our boss." I whisper yell at her but she just laughs at me, making me angry.

"Oh come on, Leila, you'd have to be blind, deaf and completely ignorant if you couldn't see the sparks that generally fly around the place when you two are together." Her laughter and cavalier attitude to my privacy really pisses me off. I'm not sure whether I'm embarrassed that there's a chance everyone sees it or that she's teasing me about it, either way, I *am* pissed.

"Sara, it doesn't matter what anyone *thinks* they know. The fact is, this is a workplace and I am the boss. *Your* boss and I think I deserve a certain measure of respect. I don't tell everyone here anything about your personal life and we both know that I could."

"You wouldn't." Her eyes widen and her voice is just above a whisper.

"You're right, *I* wouldn't, so how about you afford *me* the same respect and decency." I don't like to pull the boss card because I'd rather have an environment where people feel comfortable and can have fun at work but sometimes, well sometimes you just have to put your foot down. Sara and I are friends outside of work but we met here before I was her boss. I thought she was OK with that but perhaps she's not?

"You're right. I'm sorry, Leila."

"You should be, you're feeding into the gossip about us, Sara and most people would believe you *because* we're friends." I sigh because I know she didn't mean to hurt me or put any added pressure on me. "I know you're not doing it maliciously or to make my life difficult but the truth is, you're putting me in an awkward position."

"You're right and I'm sorry." She walks over to where I'm sitting and pulls me up into a hug. "But he was good, wasn't he?" She whispers in my ear and I can't help laughing. I push her away and shake my head without answering her.

"Now, get back to work you lazy cow." I laugh as she clasps her hands on her chest and gasps in shock.

"And you're complaining about me being unprofessional! Listen to the way you talk to your staff!" Her mock indignation is hilarious.

"Uhuh. Get back to work!" I turn back to my paperwork and let Sara get back to what she was doing when I got back. I'm not sure what she was doing but I rarely keep tabs on her, she knows what needs to be done and she does it all without needing my supervision. Which is why I could go away for the weekend with Caleb to start with because Sara can run this place just as well as I can. It's also one of the reasons I agreed to keep our friends with benefits deal just between the two of us. Despite what Caleb thinks, I know I can be easily replaced because they have Sara. She may be a bit more abrasive and not quite as customer or staff friendly but she knows her job and she does it well.

Thinking about the weekend with Caleb makes working on orders, kitchen plans and spreadsheets a lot more fun and I find myself smiling.

"I didn't realise the paperwork was that much fun." Sara teases as she rests her hip on the edge of my desk a little while later.

"I enjoy my work." I reply without looking up her. I know she'll read me like a book if I meet her eyes.

"There's a certain Drake in the dining room for lunch." She waggles her eyebrows at me when I glance up at her to frown.

"What would you like me to do about that? The Drakes own the business, Sara, they're allowed in here any time they like." I shake my head and bury my nose back into my work.

"Are you hiding out in here so that you don't have to see him?"

"You haven't even told me who is out there, Sara, so how would I know?"

"So, if it's Logan out there, you'll go out and say hello?"

"If *any* of the Drakes are in Vines, I'll go and say hello, Sara. They're my bosses and it's respectful."

"Well, there's a Drake in Vines, so I guess you should go say hello then." She pushes her butt off my desk and leaves the kitchen before I can respond. Honestly, she leaves before I can find the words to respond to her because we both know who is out in the dining room and if he wanted to see me, he would simply walk back here.

I know I shouldn't let her bait me but I get up from my desk anyway to look out that small portal window to check whether it's Caleb who has come in for lunch or not.

When I look out, I confirm that it is in fact Caleb and he's laughing with Georgie about something and I feel a twinge of jealousy. I start to move away from the window but Caleb suddenly looks up and makes eye contact with me immediately. Almost like he sensed that I was watching him and he knew exactly where I was. Our connection sends a shiver of desire through me, especially as he doesn't break eye contact with me as he answers Georgie's question. She touches his shoulder to get his attention and that finally breaks our connection.

I don't wait to see how long they talk, instead I head in the opposite direction to the staffroom and into the ladies room. After Sara giving me grief about my relationship with Caleb, I'm nervous about interacting with him in Vines. It shouldn't be any different to before but everything feels like it's changed and it has, therefore, it *is* different.

I know what he tastes like. I know what he looks like when he orgasms. I know how his tongue feels on my pussy. I know what his cock feels like in my pussy. Fuck! Now I'm hot, wet and ready for him!

I close my eyes to get my body back under control, I can't allow myself to get all hot and bothered every time Caleb comes into Vines.

My phone dings loudly with a message, the quiet of the bathroom making it feel louder than normal and it makes me jump slightly. I pull it out of my pocket and look at the screen.

Caleb: *Is everything OK?*

Of course he noticed that I slipped away without talking to him, how could he not?

Me: *of course*

Caleb: *So you're not avoiding me then?*

Me: *Nope*

Caleb: *Are you sure about that? Because I feel like I've done something wrong*

Me: *You haven't but we need to talk*

I hate to send those words to him because I know what I'd be thinking if he sent them to me. Nothing good can come of being that you need to 'talk'. I can feel his eyes burning into the side of my head as I walk back out to the dining room and immediately catch his eye. I smile at him and I hope it's reassuring but I don't want to linger too long on him because I don't want to draw any more attention to us but it would be strange if I *didn't* go over and talk to him.

As I walk by the coffee machine (I gave it a name and now I can't remember it lol) there are a few drink orders ready.

"Is one of these for Mr Drake?" I ask Georgie and she smiles as she hands me the freshly made cup she just finished. "Thank you." I smile and walk towards Caleb's table, placing the hot drink in front of him.

"Thank you, Georgie." He looks up at me with the most devastatingly handsome smile on his face that makes my heart skip a beat, until I remember that it was meant for someone else. "Leila." He says my name and it sounds sexy, silky and smooth.

"Caleb." I say, as I sit in the chair opposite him and watch as his eyes heat up with desire.

"So, you're not avoiding me then?" He asks with a knowing smirk. "After you visited me this morning to drop off my morning tea, I thought we had an understanding of sorts."

"Of sorts." I agree, his smirk getting deeper and his eyes twinkling with mischief. If we were anywhere other than my place of work, I'd definitely find out exactly what kind of mischief he was after.

"Oh, we definitely have an agreement, Miss Phillips."

"Caleb." I warn him.

"Yes, Darlin'?" he asks, as he lifts his mug to his lips and all I can think about is how they feel against *my* lips as he wraps them around the edge of the mug.

"We can't do this here, you know that." I warn quietly.

"Do what exactly, Darlin'?" He raises an eyebrow in question and I have hold back a laugh.

"We can't flirt here, Caleb."

"Is that what we're doing?"

"Don't act innocent with me, Mr Drake, you know *exactly* what you're doing." I drum the fingernails of my right hand on the table top.

"I'm sure I have no idea what you mean, Leila, I just came in to get some lunch like I do any other day. If anyone's acting weird, it's you." I can't handle sitting here with him any longer. I want to kiss that smirk right off his face, which means I can't stay.

"Of course it's all me." I say with more attitude than I'm feeling, as I stand up and take a step away from the table. He reaches up and grips my upper arm, pulling me down as he stretches up until his lips are against my ear.

"We'll finish this later, Darlin', I promise." Then he suddenly lets me go, it takes me a second to get my balance but when I do, I walk back to the kitchen without looking back.

"Ohhh dear. Looks like Leila and Caleb have had a lovers tiff." I hear Betty say in a loud whisper as I pass the granny's table.

"I guess that means you're still in for a chance then, Beryl." Martha jokes and their laughter follows me into the kitchen.

I know they mean no harm but that doesn't stop the jealousy that threads through me at their teasing.

I can't lay claim to Caleb Drake, perhaps I never will and logically, I know he won't date any of those older ladies but today, I wouldn't mind telling them that yes, Caleb and I are together. I can't help but wonder if they'd be shocked or happy for us. The thing is, I would tell those ladies today that we're together because they're not the ones I'm worried about finding out.

Makenna and Logan on the other hand, I'm terrified of what they'll think if they find out. When they find out.

I don't know how I'm going to survive the next few hours of being around Caleb without anyone knowing about us, how the hell am I going to cope with the next few weeks or months? How am I going to be able to keep this a secret from Sara? How can we keep what we're doing quiet when we see each other every day?

"You worry too much." Sara says in my ear, making me jump again today! "Things have a way of working themselves out, Leila." She drops a kiss on my cheek and then she's gone again.

I hope she's right because I don't want to give up working at Vines but I don't want to give up Caleb either. I don't think I could make the choice if it came down to it. Let's hope I never have to make that choice.

Chapter Forty-one
CALEB

I watch as Leila walks back to the kitchen without a backwards glance, although she does hesitate next to the table of my favourite bunch of older ladies. I can't help laughing because I can just imagine what those four ladies are saying to each other, especially if it gave Leila pause.

I turn my attention to my laptop and my coffee while I wait for my lunch to arrive.

To anyone looking on, I'm sure I look like I'm reading something on my laptop but in reality, I'm thinking about Leila and how I'm going to manage to keep my hands to myself. Having the freedom over the weekend to touch her whenever I felt like it, within reason of course, is something I don't think I can give up easily.

"What are you thinking about boss?" Sara's voice says way too close to my ear to be comfortable as she places my lunch down on the table.

"Work?"

"Is that a question or your answer, Mr Drake?" She asks with a smirk that I know she wouldn't give my brother.

"Sara!" Leila's voice rings out behind her friend, causing Sara to straighten up and walk away from the table, still smiling. "I'm sorry about whatever she said, Caleb, I'll talk to her."

"It was nothing, Leila."

"The look on your face tells me otherwise." Before I can reply she turns and walks away from me. Her abruptness with me isn't something I'm going to get used to or let slide. I'm also not going to call her out during business hours, so I eat my lunch and continue working on my brewery proposal.

The hours pass as my dishes get cleared away, more coffee comes my way and the granny's pass by my table and have a chat as well. I have to laugh as they try to wheedle out of me if Leila and I have had a fight or if we've had sex. That Betty is an absolute firecracker who doesn't hold back with her questions. That woman is capable of leaving *me* blushing!

I look up and realise I'm the last one sitting at a table and the sun is starting set. I didn't even realise that the customers had left and only Leila, Sara and Georgie were left to do the end of day clean. So, I finish off what I was working on, save it and turn off my laptop.

"Goodnight, Caleb." Sara says as she walks by me with Georgie. "Don't forget to lock the door behind us." Both women laugh as they reach for the door to leave.

"He won't need to, I can lock it behind him when he leaves."

"Oh, someone's in trouble!" Sara quips, earning her a dirty look from Leila and cracking Georgie up as the door closes behind them.

"Have I done something wrong, Leila?"

"No." Her answer is short but by no means, sweet.

"If you say so." I reach out for her hand as she turns to walk towards the door and she stops when my hand wraps around hers. "Leila, Darlin', I don't want to argue but I do want to know what's wrong. You've barely spoken to me all day." She sighs as she takes a deep breath, before she turns around to face me.

"Look, I think we need to watch our behaviour here, at Vines. My *workplace,* where I'm the boss. I know you're *my* boss but I'm the boss *here.*" She explains without looking me in the eyes.

"Leila, look at me." She shuffles her feet and looks everywhere but at me. "Please?"

"What?" She asks sharply as her eyes dart to mine and then look away just as quickly. My hand is only holding onto her wrist loosely, she can break away if she really wants to but she doesn't. So, I reach out slowly, giving her the chance to move away from me, to gently take her chin in my hand and guide her eyes back to mine.

"Leila, what happened? Did Sara or Georgie say something to you?" My eyes flick between hers, trying to get a read on what she's thinking.

"No, of course not." She hesitates for a second and when I don't relinquish my hold on her, or break eye contact, she sighs. "Sara gave me a little bit of stick about our 'weekend away' but she doesn't know the truth.

I swear, I didn't tell her about anything that happened this weekend, not even about my mother having a male 'friend'." She shudders and I can't help laughing.

"Then what's the matter?"

"Nothing. Well, I felt a little – strange. I wasn't sure how to behave around you now that we're back here, at Drake Wines and Vines because I can't touch you, I can't kiss you and I guess I got used to all of it." She says in a rush.

"Come back to my place and we'll order dinner. We can decide how we deal with all of this and you can stay again."

"You know, using the excuse that I'm working too late isn't going to last for long before both Makenna and Logan start asking more questions. Even Sara will start asking questions seriously if I keep staying with you, Caleb."

"Well, we won't let them know or even guess. We can even go back to your place every other day but Leila, I don't want to not see you. I don't want to stop." I never want to stop! "I know you feel like you're the only one with something to lose here, the only one with your job on the line but you're not and I want you to know that we're in this together, no matter what."

"I don't want to argue with you, Caleb." She finally gives a sweet smile, it's almost hesitant but it's a smile, nonetheless.

"Come on, let's go get something to eat and relax for a while. Please?"

"OK." She agrees and I release my loose hold on her so that she can go through with her closing routine and we lock the door behind us.

When we reach my place, I insist that she go have a shower while I cook us something to eat. It's nothing fancy but it will do and we sit on the couch, watching ridiculous TV until she almost falls asleep sitting up. Then I take her to bed, wrap her up in my arms and fall asleep feeling more peaceful than I have in what feels like forever.

This is how we spend the rest of the week and after talking about it that first night, we also decide that we won't do things any differently than we were before we started our arrangement. We're friends, we're allowed to laugh, joke and talk to each other and I'm going to keep working at my table in Vines. Not to mention I want my slice of chocolate cake on the daily.

That slice of cake is also the reason I have to keep working out in the gym I put in at my house and why I go for a daily run as well.

After a week of navigating our new normal, we get back to my place after closing down Vines once again. The minute we walk inside, I get the feeling that something isn't right and I tell Leila to stay behind me or at the door so that if there's an intruder, she can escape quickly and easily.

Instead, she sticks to me like glue as I stalk through the kitchen, living areas and into the hallway that leads to the bedrooms and bathrooms. There are lights on that I don't remember leaving on and that confuses me. I'm not confused at all once we reach my fucking bedroom though!

"What the fuck are you doing here?" I ask Anita, who happens to be making herself very comfortable in my bedsheets!

"I'm here because that's what you wanted." She smiles at me like she's the sane one in the room?

"Who is it?" Leila asks from behind me and I flinch at her voice. It's not like I forgot she was here with me, her hand is in mine but I don't know what she's going to make of this fucking mess.

"What the hell is *she* doing here, Caleb? I thought you would have gotten rid of her by now!" Anita squeals, not really trying to cover herself up as Leila moves around to stand beside me.

"Anita?" Leila's voice is filled with disbelief. She's not the only one who can't believe her eyes. "What the hell?"

"I didn't invite her here, Leila, I swear. I don't even know how she got *in* here because I know I locked up when we left this morning."

"I know you didn't and I know the door was locked." The fact that she believes me gives me a sense of relief I didn't know I needed but it makes me wonder how the hell she *did* get in.

"How *did* you get in, Anita?"

"I used my key, silly!" She says with a small wave of her hand, a quiet giggle and a strange sense of entitlement.

"I never gave you a key." I say slowly.

"I got one cut myself, silly." More giggles and another wave of her hand like it's nothing at all to get a copy cut of someone else's house key when they didn't ask you to and yes, I understand the irony here.

"Wow!" Leila says quietly.

"Wow isn't what I would say, Darlin' but you're on the right track." I look from Leila back to Anita and I can't help comparing them and wondering what the hell I ever saw in Anita. Honestly, I know what I saw in her and it isn't even close to complimentary to her. Perhaps even less so to me. "Where is the key now, Anita?"

"On my keyring of course!" Of course that's where the wrongfully gotten key would be. Like a woman who thinks she should be comfortable in my home, she's left her handbag and keys on the coffee table. I don't even know how I missed them when we walked in, except for the fact that I was looking for an intruder, not a crazy woman and her luggage.

"What are you doing?" She asks from behind me, as I pick up her keys and start removing my key from her collection.

"Is this the only one?" I ask, as I check the rest of the keys to make sure it's the only copy she has on her.

"Yes."

"Anita."

"It's the only copy I have."

"On you or at all?"

"At all." I stare her down, barely noticing that she's wrapped herself up in our sheets. "I swear, it's the only one I have, here or at home. I only made one copy, I swear."

I nod as I pocket my key and make to walk by her to my, *our* room to find her damned clothes but Leila's beaten me to it.

"Here you go, Anita. We'd like our sheet back please and thank you." Leila says as she hands over the other woman's clothes and I struggle to hold in my laughter.

'Is that what you want, Caleb?" She asks, fluttering her eyelashes at me and not for the first time in the past week, I wonder what in the hell I ever saw in this woman.

"Do I want our sheet back? Yes but I think it might end up getting burned or put in the trash after this." I watch in horror as Anita drops the sheet to the floor right there in the middle of the living room in front of Leila and myself. I turn my back to her, not having any desire to see her naked now or ever again.

"You truly are desperate, aren't you?" Leila asks, as she hands the other woman her underwear. "I have some advice for you, Anita, you should find someone who respects you and who loves you as much as you love them. Mutual respect and admiration is something we should all aspire to. This kind of behaviour will only make you sad and unhappy."

Anita gets dressed in record time and as she collects her things she says with venom in her voice, "When you get sick of this one and dump her like all the others, you know where to find me, Caleb, darling."

"The only way Leila's getting rid of me is if *she* leaves me, Anita, so I wouldn't hold my breath if I was you." She stomps towards the door, flinging it open so hard, I worry about my door hinges.

"You'll get sick of her, you always do but I might not be waiting for you."

"Please, Anita, don't wait for me, it would be a waste of your time."

"Don't wait around for any man, Anita. You're worth more than that." Leila advises and if I hadn't already fallen deeply in love with this woman, tonight has sealed the deal for me.

Not only did she trust me and believe that I hadn't invited Anita here, let alone into my bed, *our* bed now but she was giving the woman some solid advice as well.

"If you don't think Caleb is worth waiting for, then he's definitely making a mistake." Anita quips, looking at me hopefully.

"No mistake here, Leila is the only woman for me and *she's* worth the wait, however long that is." I say truthfully. Leila leans her body into mine and I wrap my arm around her shoulders and pull her in even closer, kissing her temple. "When you find love, Anita, you realise nothing else in the world compares." Leila sighs beside me and I hope she can tell by my tone that I'm speaking the truth.

"Goodnight, Anita. Have a safe trip home." Leila says sweetly and Anita stomps her foot and slams the door behind her as she leaves. "How did we miss her car sitting in front of the garage?' Leila asks, pulls out of my embrace and picks up the sheet that Anita dumped on the floor.

"I have an idea, I think I was too busy talking to you to notice." I tell her, pulling her back into my arms and kissing her, she pulls away before I take it too far.

"Do you want to wash these?" She holds up the sheet and laughs as I screw up my nose and shake my head no. "Burn them?" She laughs.

"Hell yes! Let's get the other stuff off the bed and pile them at the laundry door ready for the sacrificial burning in the morning. Tonight, we get fresh sheets that haven't got the scent of lunacy on them!" I only half joke.

We make quick work of getting the other sheet off the bed and Leila makes her way to the laundry to dump them, when I reach out and take her hand in mine.

"Thank you, Leila."

"For what?" she asks, genuinely seeming confused.

"For believing in me." She raises an eyebrow, so I continue. "For believing that I didn't invite Anita here and that she let herself in. I wouldn't ever do anything like that to you, we agreed while we're together, we're exclusive and I will honour that one hundred percent of the time."

"I know." She kisses my cheek and leaves the room.

I can't believe how lucky I am. Maybe it's because she assumes this isn't a real relationship but for me, this is totally real.

I am truly one lucky bastard!

Chapter Forty-two
LEILA

I'm not going to lie, coming back to Caleb's place after a hard day at Vines and desiring nothing more than to sit back and relax with the sexiest man alive, was all that I wanted. Finding Anita freaking Roberts naked in his bed wasn't something that I expected, nor really wanted but I also trust him. Despite what she tried to hint at, I know Caleb didn't invite her into his home and especially not his *bed*!

I shake my head as I put the sheets at the back ready to be thrown out tomorrow.

"I wonder how she got in." I wonder out loud as I walk back into the bedroom where Caleb is remaking the bed with clean sheets.

"What do you mean? She cut herself a copy of my key." He says without stopping what he's doing.

"No, I mean onto the property because the front gates are usually closed by now. They get closed at the end of business every day and you have to open them with a remote, which only a few of us have or get someone to let you in." I have the remote because of the early starts I have at Vines.

"You're right. That means she either got someone to let her in *or* she's been here for a while. Dear god how long was she sitting in here waiting like that for me?" A full body shudder runs through him and I stifle a laugh. "Imagine if you'd come in here alone and found her like that? Imagine if Kenna or Logan had walked in on that! They both already think I'm some kind of filthy manwhore."

"No, they don't *but* maybe one of them let her onto the property?" He looks at me like I'm crazy. "It's possible, she could have told them that you were expecting her. Lori walked right up to Logan and Jules' door the day she arrived here."

"That was different, it was business hours *and* I messaged him to warn him. It's not my fault he didn't read it." He shakes his head as he finishes putting the bed back together. "Anyway, I might have a few issues with my siblings but neither of them would let some random woman onto the property and into my house without first calling me to ask if she was expected."

"Are you sure about that?" I ask, as we walk out to the kitchen to organise some food. "I can see how Logan might call you but I can also see both of them deciding to let this one slide just for the hell of it." Caleb thinks on it for a few minutes, I can see his brain working, considering every option, as we work together to prepare dinner.

"If you said Jules or Brady, maybe. I mean, I've walked in on them having sex with their other halves and played a few practical jokes on all of them but I don't think they would let a woman they didn't know, had never seen before, onto the property after hours just on her say so."

"That's definitely something I'd do to Matt."

"Really? You'd let a strange woman you'd never met into his house without checking in with him?" He looks up from the stove with a shocked look on his face and I laugh again.

"Yeah, it wouldn't be the first time either. He's done it to me too, so paybacks a bitch!"

"Wow, you guys are mean!" Caleb laughs.

"You have no idea." I mutter but I know he hears me because he smiles and shakes his head some more.

"We give each other a lot of grief but we're close. I don't know what I'd do without my brother and sister, not to mention their significant others. Since our parents died, well obviously, they're all I've got." He smiles at me but it doesn't really reach his eyes and he looks a little sad at the reminder that his parents aren't here. Unfortunately, this conversation serves as a reminder to me that I shouldn't get too attached to him and the other Drakes because despite what he says, I *know* I'm dispensable to them. They'd never get rid of one of their own for sleeping with a staff member.

I shake myself out of my dark thought and resolve to enjoy our time together while it lasts. That's exactly what I do as we sit down to dinner and a movie, then head to bed later that night.

I enjoy every single inch of Caleb's body with my tongue and then I enjoy his tongue on every single inch of *my* body.

It's exactly what we do over the next few weeks too. If we think we can't get by his brother and sister, or Jules, that man is a nosy bastard let me tell you, we head to my place. The only issue with going to my house, is we then have dodge Sara, as well as my brother on the odd occasion.

Matt is reasonably easy to dodge. He's seeing someone, he thinks I don't know but he has a few tells when he's seeing someone new and he's got them in spades right now.

Sara is a little more difficult to get off our tails but it can be done, I just have to go out with her on a semi-regular basis so that she's not feeling unloved but I get the feeling that she's seeing someone new too, she just doesn't want to share anything about him at *all*. Which is highly unusual but not completely unheard of. It does however mean that she likes this guy a *lot* or she doesn't think I'm going to like him. Either way, I'll find out one way or another when she's ready.

"What do you want to do tonight?" Caleb asks as we finish cleaning up after dinner one night at my house, pulling me out of my thoughts and back to the present.

"You." I smile and throw the cloth into the empty sink. "Always you." I step closer to him and run my hand up his sides, drying my hands on his t-shirt, all while managing to drag the material up so that I can touch his skin. He throws what's in his hands onto the bench with a loud clang and then his lips are on mine in a brutal kiss.

In a move that makes me want him even more, he places his hands on my butt cheeks and hauls me up onto the kitchen bench.

"Right now, here?" He murmurs against my lips.

"God yes!" Without further invitation, he pulls my top up over my head and dumps it on the floor, my bra following shortly after. He pulls his own t-shirt up over his head and dumps that on top of my clothes, the he starts on getting my pants undone when there's a knock on the door.

"Ignore it." Caleb murmurs and I do because nothing could be more important than the man in front of me right now.

"Lei, are you home? I can see the lights on. Why have you locked the door?" My brothers voice breaks the silence and I shake my head.

"Fuck it. Now I know how Brady feels!" He grumbles as he lifts me off the bench, picks up our clothes and hand me mine to put back on. "I'll go to your room and close the door behind me." He says quietly with a sigh.

"You don't have to hide away." I tell him. "It's just Matt, who's he going to tell?"

"Everyone at Vines? Sara? I don't know, Leila." He looks and sounds frustrated but he still rushes into my room and closes the door behind him. I start to follow him as I put my top back on and throw my bra onto the couch. If my brother wants to show up unannounced, then he has to deal with finding my things around my house. That's when I spot Caleb's phone on the coffee table. I run to my room, open the door and pass it over with a small smile.

"Leila, are you OK?" I rush over to the front door and open it with a flourish.

"What? I'm not allowed to be in the bathroom? I mean, you expect me to be just sitting around waiting for your arse to show up unannounced and uninvited?" I scowl at him, hoping against hope, that I can make him not want to come inside but just my luck, he storms by me and sits his arse down on my couch with a thump.

That can't be good and it only means one thing. Girl trouble.

I close and lock the door and make my way over to sit next to him.

"What's wrong?" He doesn't answer, he just sits there, on my couch, scowling and behaving like a little kid. "What's her name and what did you do?"

"What makes you think there's a girl?" I raise my eyebrow at him and he sighs. I don't know who he thinks he is but it's *always* a girl! "I like this girl. We've seen each other for a while but she doesn't want to make our relationship public."

"And you do?" Well, doesn't that hit a little close to home? Apparently the Phillips siblings are prone to private people.

"Yes. Well, I don't know but I'd like to have a real, proper conversation about it."

"Can I suggest that you work out exactly what it is that you *do* want and then go talk to her. Tell her that this is what you want and it's a deal-breaker. If she can't give a timeline that you find satisfactory, then perhaps it's time to think about moving on, Matt." I hold my hand up to stop his protests. "No, you and I both know, that only makes for a one-sided relationship where neither party is ever truly happy. You have to choose happiness, Matt. Yours and hers."

I sound and feel wise but I'm the one hiding a boy in my room!

"You're right, I know you are but it's a difficult, complicated situation."

"Well, uncomplicate it and make it less difficult."

"Easier said than done." He grumbles and boy, I so understand that sentiment.

"Can we watch a movie?"

"No!" I said too fast and in a high-pitched voice that pretty much tells him of my anxiety. "I have a really early start in the morning and I know that's my life daily, tomorrow is earlier than most."

"OK. Thanks for talking me down, Leila. You're the best sister ever." He kisses my cheek and stands up. "Get some rest and we'll catch up when you're not as tired."

"Absolutely." It's all I can say in response and still I feel like a complete bitch.

"Goodnight, Leila. I love you."

"Love you too." I say and then he's gone and I lock the door again behind him. I rest my head on the door, as I listen to his car disappear and breathe out a sigh of relief.

"Is he OK?" Caleb asks, as he comes up behind me and wraps his arms around my waist.

"Yeah. Sounds like girl trouble. I don't think she wants to commit to him."

"Her loss. Hopefully he can see that eventually."

I'm tempted to ask him if we're a lost cause as well but I can't bring myself to do it.

We have an agreement and while I know that can change at any time and has the possibility of going either way, I'm not brave enough to bring it up just yet. Even though we spend almost every day together and most nights in recent weeks. It *feels* like a real relationship to me. I always assume friends with benefits arrangements were so that you had a lover or companion on call when you wanted it, not that you saw each other every day and spent most nights together.

But, I have no intention of bringing it up right now because for one, his lips are back on mine and my brain explodes and two, because I don't want to have that conversation.

"He'll be fine, he's an adult." I smile against Caleb's soft lips. "Now, where were we?" I ask and within seconds my top half is stripped of clothing again and he's starting on undoing my pants once again.

The 'talk' can wait for another time, tonight I'm going to enjoy being with Caleb just like I want to be.

Chapter Forty-three
CALEB

Hoping like hell that Leila's right about her brother and he won't return, I strip her and myself out of our clothes as quickly as I possibly can. We fall naked, onto the bed in a tangle of limbs and lips.

"I need you now, Caleb." She murmurs against my lips, barely pulling out of our intense kiss.

"Let me get you ready, Darlin." I murmur back, knowing I'm ready but wanting to make sure that she is.

"Caleb, I *am* ready." She declares as she pushes her hot pussy against my hard cock. "I couldn't be more ready for you, Handsome." I reach between us and run my finger through her lips and find her ready for me.

"Are you sure?" I ask, while pushing my finger into her and curling my finger forward a little, making her hips push harder up into me.

"Yes! God yes!" She says as she throws a condom at me and I laugh. I don't even know when she had the time to grab that out of her drawer but I'm not complaining. Apparently, I take too long to do what she wants me to because she pushes on my chest and I fall over onto my back willingly with a chuckle. My laughter doesn't last long though, as she wraps a hand around the base of my cock and rolls the condom on with the other one.

"Leila." My voice is a hoarse whisper full of want, need and red fucking hot desire. I can see all those feelings reflected back at me in her eyes as she crawls up my body to line herself up so that she can slide her pussy down my cock.

"Caleb." Her voice sends a shiver through my body, as she pauses for a few seconds, her eyes closed, as she adjusts to the feeling of me being inside her again. "I need ..."

"What Darlin'? What do you need from me?"

"Everything."

"You've got it." I promise her and pull her lips to meet mine as I sit up with her still in my lap, then I flip us so that her back is on the bed and I'm back on top. Leila sighs and her eyes snap open, the smile on her face makes my heart flip.

Moving my hips slowly, I start making love to her. I hold her head in my hands and kiss her, telling her everything in that one kiss that I can't tell her with words. Not yet. Her hands run up and down my back, caressing me. I know we both feel it, we're not fucking tonight. It's more than that, way more.

Leila's hands skim lightly up my sides, skim up the front of my shoulder, run along my collarbone and she takes my face in her hands. We stare deeply into each other's eyes as we rock back and forth with each other, our rhythm perfectly synced and it feels extraordinary. I've never felt anything like this with anyone else and I know she feels it too.

"Leila, Darlin', I'm going to come. You need to-." I groan and drop my head into the crook of her neck. She wraps her arms around my neck, running her hands up and down my back.

"I'm so close, Caleb. *So* close. Come for me, Handsome. Come for me, now." She whispers in my ear.

With her words ringing in my ears I can't hold back, we come at the same time and I know it's unusual and probably won't happen again. It's an intimacy that I've never felt before and I couldn't explain it if I was asked to. I'm falling in love with her, that I know for sure.

"What did you say?" Leila mumbles against my shoulder. I didn't realise I'd said that last part out loud.

"Nothing that meant anything, Darlin'." It wasn't nothing but I'm not brave enough to repeat it so that she understands me yet. "I'm just going to go, you know, clean up." I pull away from her and manoeuvre around limbs so that I can get off the bed and walk to the bathroom. I do what needs to be done and then lean against the basin, close my eyes and take a deep breath.

"Is everything OK?" I startle at Leila's quiet voice behind me.

"Of course, I'm just trying to catch my breath." I walk towards her, pull her into my arms and kiss her.

"Wow."

"Now, go do what you need and come back to bed." I slap her on the arse as I walk back into the bedroom, making her squeal in surprise and I can't help laughing as I get comfortable in the bed, only half pulling up the covers so that Leila can get back in easily.

"Thank you." She says as I hold up the covers so that she can get into bed. I drop them down and pull her back to my front.

"You're welcome, goodnight, Darlin.'"

"Goodnight, Caleb." She hesitates, like she wants to say something else but instead she wraps her hand around mine and kisses my bicep that her head is resting on.

I feel both the most relaxed and happiest I've ever felt while being in someone's bed and nervous for some reason as well. Perhaps my gut knew that the next day things were going to blow up in spectacular fashion. I'm grateful that I had no premonition of what was to come because if I had, I might have kept Leila as a sex slave in her own home for the next decade.

LEILA IS UP AND SHOWERED before I'm even fully awake the next morning. When I finally have my own shower, I go to join her in the kitchen for breakfast. Her front door slams open and her best friend breezes in without a care in the world.

"Is that Caleb Drake's car out the front?" Sara asks loudly, taking a seat at the bench and reaching for what I think may have been a morning coffee for me.

"Yes, it is Sara." I say as I pull up a stool beside Leila and watch her out the side of my eye to see what her reaction is to this revelation.

"I knew it!" Sara exclaims.

"You knew what, Sara? That I would make an early trip out to see a supplier I'm talking to, only to discover they're no longer in business? Or perhaps you knew, like I do, that Leila's car is a piece of shit that barely gets her to work every day and so I thought I would swing by and ask her if she wanted a lift back to Drake Wines? Is that why you're here this morning, to give her a lift to work?" I ask with an raised eyebrow.

"It's very early, Caleb." Sara states with a raised eyebrow all of her own. "Plus, you just came walking out of Leila's bedroom, buttoning up your shirt."

"It is quite early but I had a very early meeting." I tell her without breaking eye contact. "I came walking out of Leila's bathroom, where I used the facilities so that I didn't piss myself on the way back home, if that's alright with you? Which was the other reason I swung by, hoping that Leila was home, I knew I wouldn't make it back to my place. Also, I'm not *buttoning up my shirt,* as you put it, I'm rolling the sleeves back down after washing my hands. Have I explained myself enough or do you need more?"

"What's with the coffee?"

"Leila's polite, unlike her best friend who likes to interrogate her boss first thing in the morning and thought I might need something to keep me awake on the drive."

"So, you don't need a ride from me then?" Sara asks Leila and I take the opportunity to look at Leila to see how she's feeling about this whole thing.

"You're not even working today, Sara! It's Sunday, I always start later on Sundays because Georgie goes in early instead. Go home, get some more sleep before you turn into a grumpy bitch that no-one wants to talk to."

"Well, that's just rude!"

"That may be but it's the truth." Leila laughs at Sara's scowl and I have to admit, it's fun watching the two of them when they're not at work.

"I'll give that to you this morning but only because I found you with a hottie in your house so early in the morning." Leila mutters something as she pushes Sara, who is struggling only for show, out the door.

"Bye Sara." I say with a smile and a short wave of my hand.

"Bye Mr Drake." I laugh again, that girl is crazy. I hear whispered mutterings before the front door opens and closes and Leila makes her way back into the kitchen looking sheepish.

"Did she get you to confess that I stayed the night?" I ask, pouring myself a fresh cup of coffee. Tea is definitely my hot beverage of choice but that first drink in the morning is always coffee.

"No but she made me promise to try to seduce you while you were here." Her answer makes me laugh all over again.

"That best friend of yours is crazy, good crazy but crazy all the same, I feel for any guy who tries to keep up with her!" I kiss Leila on the cheek, wanting to push for more but knowing we don't really have time. "You don't need to seduce me gorgeous, you can have me any time you want me."

"Any time?"

"Any damned time. I've already told you, I'll give just about anything a go once." I pour both of our coffees into travel mugs as she stands there trying to get her head around that idea. "Come on, let's get this show on the road, otherwise you're going to be late and then you'll be mad at me for it."

"Will not!" She protests.

"Will too, now move that gorgeous arse of yours and let's get out of here."

I go quickly back to the bedroom to pick up my duffel bag, glad that I didn't bring it out with me earlier when Sara showed up, otherwise there would have been many more questions.

I press my hand into the small of Leila's back and direct her out to my car, open the door for her, then dump my bag in the back. The drive back to Drake Wines is filled with music, singing and talking about everything and nothing.

It's easy, like we've driven into work together a hundred times before and it's just normal. If only we knew then that the day was not going to end in the same peaceful, 'normal' way.

Chapter Forty-four
LEILA

Sara showing up unannounced at my place this morning really threw me off balance. I had no idea how to explain Caleb's presence to her and even though I hated to lie to her, I hated that Caleb came up with that lie so easily. I was also pretty impressed with his quick thinking.

It also made me realise that I needed to gather my thoughts about this situation and work out some reasons that we're spending so much of our time together. It was inevitable that someone was going to notice that we're spending a lot time together, even for us. I mean, we kind of spent all day together before this, so it might not come as too much of a surprised to anyone.

Maybe that would help to hide this for longer than I thought it might.

"Hey, is everything OK?" Caleb reaches over and rests his hand on my thigh. The warmth from his hand touching me warms my entire body. How the hell does he manage that with one touch? He hasn't even moved his hand and I can feel his touch all over. "Darlin', what's wrong?" The concern in his voice brings me back to the present.

"Of course, everything is fine." I smile at him, hoping that he can't see what I'm thinking.

"Are you sure?" I nod. "Because you've been awfully quiet on this drive."

"Just thinking."

"About?" He keeps taking his eyes of the road to look at me.

"Eyes on the road mister." I tell him, pointing to the road in front of us leading towards to the gate at Drake Wines, then I glance down at the hand he's resting on my thigh.

"I'd rather look at you, Darlin'."

"Well, as flattering as that is, Caleb, I would much rather you watch where you're driving. I'd like to make it to work today in one piece." I see him flinch and look back at the road, staring straight as he takes his hand off my thigh and I realise what I've said. "Plus, I'd really like to keep seeing you and your handsome face around." I tell him, as I take his hand in mine and bring it to my lips, kissing each of his knuckles before placing it back on my thigh.

"You want to keep seeing me?" He asks quietly, almost shyly and this isn't the Caleb Drake I know, I know him to be ballsy, bordering on arrogant and sexy as fuck because he's just so strong.

"Of course I do." I smile at him.

"Good." He removes his hand from my thigh again so that he can steer the car into Drake Wines and I feel the loss of his touch immediately.

"That's it? Just 'good'." I'm a little confused and without a doubt, a little hurt as well.

"Yes. Good." He looks at me, confused. "Did you want me to park at Vines or did you want to walk back from home?"

"Home?"

"Yeah, you know, where I live." His smirk that usually I find endearing and sexy is really annoying me, so much so, that I want to punch him.

"Why don't you drop me at Vines and then you can go can do whatever you want?"

"You don't want to come to the house?" His eyebrows pull in, in confusion as he slows the car down.

"Not really, no. I've got a lot to get done at work this morning, so it's probably best that you stay at your house and do, well whatever it is you do on the weekends."

The car pulls to a stop out the front of the bistro that I've helped build up from almost nothing when the last chef left and I can't help the twinge of panic that sets in like a swarm of butterflies at the thought of losing it all.

"Is there anything I can help with?"

'No, thank you." I open the car door and jump out, then reach into the back to grab out my stuff.

"Leave that there, I'll take it into the house."

"That's OK, I think I might get Matt or Sara to come pick me up later."

"Did I do something wrong?"

"No." I shake my head. "Nope, I just think it might be good to spend the night apart. You know, have a break."

"Leila, what's wrong?"

"Nothing, I just want, I want to go home tonight that's all. A girl's allowed to change her mind isn't she?"

"Of course you can but this just seems really sudden and I want to see you tonight."

"We're not dating, Caleb, we're screwing remember?" I slam the car door closed and stomp into the bistro without looking back. I hear the wheels skid in the dirt as he takes off and the door closes behind me as I enter the bistro. It's only then that I turn back to look at him. The car has kicked up a shitload of dirt and dust.

"Everything OK?" Georgie asks from beside me, making me jump. "Sorry, didn't mean to sneak up on you."

"That's OK and yes, everything's fine. Caleb just gave me lift this morning." Georgie smiles, looks at the bag slung over my shoulder and nods, knowingly.

"It's not what you think."

"Of course, I don't think anything. I just want you both to be happy." Before I can correct her, she walks back to the coffee machine with a knowing smirk on her face. I decide to not let her bait me and instead ask her how the bistro has been this morning.

"Running smoothly as always, Leila." She smiles and tells me to go put my stuff away. "Everything out here is good."

I thank her and head back to my office, wishing once again for the privacy that walls and a door would afford me. I might have a talk with either Makenna or Logan about getting one put in. Decision made I sit down and text Matt, asking him to come in to have a late breakfast with me. It takes a while for him to respond but when he does, he says he'll see me in half an hour. Sara should be in soon as well, so that we can go over some recipes we're trying to develop, which means two of my favourite people will be able to distract me from all the stuff that's going on with Caleb.

I get lost in paperwork until I hear Matt say good morning to Georgie and I rush out there, expecting a nice warm embrace, only for my little brother to brush me off with the excuse of really needing the bathroom. The excuse of the long drive is ridiculous but he really does seem to be in desperate need of said bathroom, so I let him scurry away without my hug.

While I wait for my brother, I walk around and check in with all the customers, most them regulars but there are a few new faces as well.

When Matt comes back, he wraps me up in a huge bear hug, just like I wanted him to and I feel instantly better. He kisses my cheek and takes my hand in his, leading me to a table, where Georgie almost immediately places coffees down in front of us with a huge smile. She takes our order and then leaves us in peace.

We sit and catch up but I don't tell him about Caleb and I feel like he's holding something back as well. I know he's seeing someone but he won't tell me her name or anything else about her.

Sara enters and says good morning, Matt barely acknowledges her which is unusual for him but I don't really get the chance to ask him about it because when I look up at Sara I see the tears in her eyes and follow her to the kitchen when she takes off.

I talk Sara down from her meltdown about this new guy she's seeing that is apparently the biggest arsehole on the planet and while I tell her to tell him how she feels, I feel like it might be a lost cause. I can't quite believe it when Matt is discovered listening in to our conversation which results in some pretty harsh words spoken between him and Sara. Not wanting to cause more of a scene than we already have, I push Matt back out to our table, where Georgie has already put our food.

I realise that we're sitting with our heads almost touching, talking about everything and nothing all at the same time. He's still got my hand in his when Caleb appears at my side.

"Matt, it's nice to see you again!" Caleb says as the two men shake hands but not before Matt notices the possessive hand Caleb has resting on my shoulder and when I don't shake his touch off, Matt raises his eyebrow at me in question.

"You too Caleb!" They have an entire conversation, until Caleb excuses himself to go get something to eat.

"So, you and Caleb huh?" Matt asks, his eyebrows bouncing up and down in some weird way that makes me want to smack him and laugh at him at the same time.

"He's my boss, Matt."

"Uhuh. Just your boss, no worries. He's pretty possessive and protective for a boss."

"No, he's not. He knows you Matt, I doubt he thought you were a threat."

"So, there's something to threaten?" I knew I'd screwed up the minute the words were out of my mouth!

"No!" I roll my eyes, trying to make him believe he's reading too much into what I said. "I'm his employee and he's my boss, Matthew!"

As he opens his mouth to respond, I hear my name and freeze in my seat. I close my eyes and hope like hell that when I open them that I just thought I heard that voice. Oh fuck!

"Leila, sweetheart! I'm so glad we caught you working today, we weren't sure if you would be here or not. Where's Caleb, is he here as well?" I look around Vines frantically, wondering where the hell Caleb disappeared to so quickly. Did he see them arrive and slip out the back door or something? He wouldn't leave me here alone to deal with Brian and Mary, would he?

"Mary. Brian! What are you two doing here?" I ask, rising up out of my chair to greet them, only to be engulfed in a tight hug from Mary and then a bear hug from Brian. "I wish you'd let us know you were coming, we would have had you over to the house." I grin tightly, trying with everything I have to ignore my brothers gaze burning a hole into the side of my head right now.

"We were just in the area and thought, we were this close that we would drop by and surprise you." Brian chuckles. "I haven't been out here for a while and I wanted to talk to Caleb about where he plans on putting-." I stop him from talking by talking over him because no-one here knows about Caleb's brewery plan.

"Well, you're both welcome any time. Why don't we head over to the house, I'm sure Caleb's over there." I say, trying to usher them out of Vines but Matt takes this opportunity to stand up and introduce himself.

"Hi, I'm Matt, Leila's brother." He shakes both of their hands.

"Oh we're delighted to meet you, Matt. It's lovely to meet Leila's family, she's told me so much about you." Mary informs him and I have to try to remember exactly what it is I told them because I don't really remember saying much about my family at all.

"Mary. Brian. What are you two doing here?" Caleb asks from behind me, I feel some of the stress drain out of me at the sound of his voice, then I relax a little more when he rests his hand on the small of my back.

"Here he is. Caleb, we were just telling your beautiful fiancé here that we were in the neighbourhood, so we thought we'd surprise you and say hello."

"Well, you've certainly surprised us."

"Did he just say fiancé? You two got engaged?" Matt queries.

"Fiancé?" Logan's voice booms out in the bistro and I cringe.

"Fiancé? You guys got engaged? We didn't even know you were dating!" Makenna's voice joins in, adding to the confusion and stress.

"So, you didn't know either?" Matt asks Makenna and Logan.

"No." They respond together.

"Congratulations, that's amazing!" Brady says, shaking both of our hands.

"We're not. We haven't." I can't get out any words that make any sense and when I look behind Logan, I see Jules standing there, Savvy's hand in his and he's smiling like a lunatic. "Caleb." I look at him but he looks just as bewildered as I feel.

"Oh boy, I'm so glad we decided to come in for brunch today ladies." Betty says excitedly. "This is going to be something else!"

That's just what I need, the granny's sitting at their table witnessing my life, personal and professional, implode upon itself.

Fuck my life!

Chapter Forty-five

CALEB

Everyone starts talking over each other and it's unnerving.

"It wasn't public knowledge yet? Your engagement? I thought your family would have known. I'm sorry Caleb, Leila. I guess I should have kept the conversation strictly business and talked about the brewery venture then?" Brian.

"Brewery? What brewery?" Logan asks.

"Fiancé? When did you get engaged?" Kenna demands.

"I knew it! I knew something was going on between the two of you!" Sara shouts.

"You got engaged? When? Does Mum know?" Matt asks, confused. All while Brady, Jules and Savvy stand back smiling at the chaos.

"OK, let's all calm down!" Logan bellows and everyone stops talking at once. "Let's take this into the tasting room, so that we can have this discussion in private." He says, nodding towards the room at the back of Vines.

"I'll stay out here and help Georgie" Sara says to Leila, giving her a tight hug. "But you and I? Yeah we're talking once this mess is done, got it?"

"We can be quiet, Logan. You don't need to take this into the other room." Betty smiles at my brother and doesn't flinch when he directs his very well-known glare at her, she just shrugs her shoulders at him and with a wicked grin. "Just saying."

I try not to laugh because this really isn't the time for it but those ladies always amuse the hell out of me and today is no different. They've got such a zest for life and they give no fucks about what anyone thinks about them, it's pretty amazing and inspiring.

"Caleb, what are we going to do?" Leila, who is pressed up against my side, asks me quietly. I'm not sure what the fuck we're going to do but I can't

305

tell her that, so instead I smile at her reassuringly and guide her in the tasting room with everyone else.

"It'll be fine, I promise, Darlin'." I hope I can keep that promise as I kiss her temple and look up to see everyone watching us.

"Well, don't you two look cosy together." Jules smiles at us. Leila starts to pull away from me but I don't release her. If we're facing the firing squad, we're doing it together. I am not letting her take the fall for this, not even a little bit.

"OK, Caleb, explain what's going on here, please?"

"When did you two get engaged and why didn't we know?" Kenna asks.

"Yeah, I want to know that too!" Matt chimes in.

"I want to know about this brewery first." Logan says sternly. Business always comes first with him and I can't help rolling eyes at him.

"I'm not sure where to start." Leila says, pulling everyone's attention her way. "To start with, we're not engaged. Sorry Mary and Brian." She faces them, her apology written all over face.

"That's OK, Sweetheart." Mary waves her apology off. "I had a pretty good feeling that you weren't."

"Oh." Leila says, blushing.

"Not because you two don't belong together or that you don't love each other, just because it all seemed very sudden and new."

"We're not in love." Leila stutters out and I can feel my heart breaking. I knew that my feelings were stronger than hers but her stating out loud that she doesn't love me stings. I'm not going to lie, it stings a hell of a lot.

"Ouch! That's got to sting." Brady mumbles from next to Kenna and I can't look his way without him seeing the hurt in my eyes. I don't want anyone to see the hurt in my eyes so I close them for a few seconds to gather my thoughts and then take a half a step away from Leila. I need the distance for now.

"Look." I hold my hands up to stop everyone from talking, the added bonus is that I'm now not touching Leila. "If you'll all quieten down, I'll explain."

"We're waiting." Jules pipes up from behind Logan somewhere and I wonder why the hell he's still here.

"Thanks for that, Jules." Leila moves to stand in front of me, her hands resting on my chest, drawing my eyes to them and then to her eyes.

"You don't have to do this alone." I smile sadly at her because I know now that I actually do.

"It's OK, Darlin', I dragged you into this mess, I'll make sure they know that." I step back from her, causing her hands to drop to her side. I'm pretty sure I see hurt flash in her eyes but it's gone as soon as it appears, so I can't be sure. "OK, let's start with, none of this is Leila's fault. She was doing me a favour and being a good friend." I flinch at the word friend because I believed we were becoming more.

"OK but *what* did you drag her into?" Matt demands and I can't fault him for looking out for his sister, I would do the same thing if it was Kenna in her position.

"I've been putting together a proposal for a brewery, here on Drake Wines. Brian here, with his lovely wife Mary, is the supplier of the hops I was hoping to use to brew said beers." Brian and Mary both smile at the rest of the crowd that look their way. "When Leila and I went away a few weekends ago, we were together, at Mary and Brian's for a party. We went as an engaged couple."

"Why did you choose to fake an engagement?" Kenna asks.

"I think I might be able to answer that." Brian pipes up and steps beside me to face the crowd. "I called Caleb to check in and see if he was coming. I think I put him on the spot when I asked if he was bringing someone with him and I might have given him the impression that I only did business with clients that were settled. You know, with a wife and a family." I look at him and he smiles sheepishly at me but before either of us can say anything Mary steps up to stand on my other side.

"And I may not have helped the situation he found himself in either." Mary pats my bicep and continues. "Caleb has been to a few of our parties and well, I always set him up with someone. I just wanted to see him happy and I can admit, especially after the mess of the last one, that wasn't the best move. I'm sorry Caleb, without setting you up with unwanted dates, including the horrible Anita, I feel like you wouldn't be in this mess but I'm also glad to have helped you and Leila get together."

"Who the hell is Anita?" Logan asks in his booming voice that makes most people shrink back but no-one in the room does, except Leila.

"Anita doesn't matter." I tell him dismissively. "The point is, I lied to Brian to get him to work with me and I lied to you guys about my relationship with Leila. I'm sorry that happened but it's out in the open now and we can move on. Leila agreed to help me out as a friend and that's that. She hasn't done anything wrong. If you need someone to blame, it's all on me." I say to the whole room, while also ignoring Leila who takes a step closer to me.

"So, you guys *did* go away together that weekend?" Kenna asks, as she pushes the stroller filled with babies back and forth absentmindedly.

"Yes, Kenna." I confirm, not sure why she's stuck on that particular detail. "Now, why don't we let Leila get back to work. Matt, you can leave with her because everything else is between my family and myself." I take a breath and realise I've forgotten someone. "Mary, Brian, why don't you guys go with Leila and she can get you set up with a drink and food of your choice."

"Caleb." Leila starts but I cut her off.

"No, you take your brother and the Weavers back out into Vines. I'll deal with the rest." I don't give her the chance to argue with me because I don't look at her, I smile apologetically to the Weavers though. "I'll come and talk to you when I've spoken to my siblings."

Brian nods while he directs Mary towards the door, he also takes Leila's arm gently to guide her out of the room as well. "I'm really sorry Caleb, it would seem that I've dropped you in it in multiple ways today, son." He pats me on the shoulder as he passes by me.

"You've got nothing to apologise for, Brian, this is all on me." I smile and he nods again. The door closes behind the four of them, then there's awkward silence for a few minutes before Jules speaks up.

"Well, this is fun but I think Savannah and I might go back and take Jaspa for a walk." He guides Savvy out of the side door which means they won't have to walk through Vines to leave.

"I'm going to join you." Brady says in a rush, kisses Kenna on the cheek, sends a smile my way, then quickly follows Jules out the door.

"So." It's all I can manage to say. I have no fucking clue where to start.

"So, you have an idea for a brewery?" Logan asks.

"Yes."

"How long have you been working on it?" Kenna asks.

"Since I got back home but I've been thinking about it for longer than that."

"Why didn't you tell us, discuss your thoughts with us?" Logan asks.

"Because he wanted to prove that he could do this on his own. He wanted to prove to us that he's not just our baby brother anymore." I look at Kenna and emotions I rarely let out stir in me.

"Is that why you didn't tell us?" Logan asks. "You think we wouldn't take you seriously? That we wouldn't believe in you and back you?"

"Partly, yes."

"Fucking hell." Logan mutters under his breath and Kenna gives him a one arm hug. "Tonight, dinner at Kenna's, then the three of us will sit down and go over your plans and business proposal."

"We don't have to, Logan."

"Do you have everything ready?" He asks.

"Yes, yes I do if I can get Brian to still agree to be my supplier. If not, then I do have a couple of back up suppliers as well."

"Good. Tonight then." Logan demands and that's it, business is done.

"Which brings us to, why did you pretend to be engaged to Leila?" Kenna asks.

"Because Brian made it seem like he wouldn't partner with me if I couldn't show him that I had stability. A family, an anchor and a reason to make this a success. Apparently you two and your families, plus the family wine business wasn't enough. When he called and asked me if I was bringing someone to their party, I panicked. It was the morning after Leila stayed over and she was there, sitting at my kitchen bench. We're friends and I asked for a favour."

"But you want to be *more* than friends with her, don't you?" Kenna asks. I know I could lie but I just don't want to anymore.

"It doesn't matter what I want Kenna, you heard her just now, we're friends and that's all she sees me as." I shrug.

"You've been seeing each other since that weekend away though, haven't you?" Logan asks and I'm shocked that he even noticed. "It's hard not to notice that you're not at my house or Kenna and Brady's as often as usual. It's also hard to miss how you look at each other."

"If even our blind as a bat brother with everything except work, Jules and Savannah can notice, then we've all noticed, Caleb." Kenna jokes, then comes over and pulls me into a tight hug. "We've watched you two dance around each other for months. You two getting together was inevitable."

"Well, you heard her, we're friends. It doesn't matter what I want."

"What *do* you want, Caleb?" Kenna asks gently.

"What do you want me to say, Kenna?"

"The truth, Cal."

"Do you want me to tell you that I've wanted her since the day I met her? That I haven't gone out with or slept with anyone since I got back home? That I work in Vines every day just to be near her and eat her delicious food?" I throw my hands up in the air. "Is that what you want to hear?"

"Is that the truth?" Kenna asks.

"Kenna, stop," Logan cautions her but I'm on a fucking roll now and I don't think I can stop. It's like a valve has been released and it feels fucking good to let my feelings out.

"Yes, it's the truth! It's also the truth that I've fallen for her. I thought I'd already done that but since that weekend and in the time we've spent together since, I've fallen in love with her!" I say loudly, forgetting where we are. I throw my hands up in the air in exasperation. "That's right, I've fallen in love with Leila Phillips and she stood here and told me and everyone who would listen that we're just friends."

"You love me?" Leila's voice is soft, hesitant from the doorway into Vines.

"I told you to stop Makenna! Why couldn't you let the two of them work this out for themselves?" Logan growls at Kenna. "They would have gotten there eventually."

"They were taking too long." My sister smirks, fucking smirks at me, even as I drop my head into my hands. I didn't want Leila to hear that I love her for the first time said to someone else, in frustration.

"Fuck you Makenna." I grumble at her.

"Caleb." Leila's voice is soft and feels like a caress over my wounded heart. "Was all of that true?"

"Right, that's our cue to leave. Come on Makenna." I hear their footsteps retreat and then the door close behind them. I still can't look up and meet Leila's eyes though.

"Caleb." I jump when her hand lightly touches my arm but I'm grateful when she doesn't pull way. "Is that all true, what you just told Makenna?"

"Which part?" Knowing that I'm being an ignorant jerk.

"All of it, honestly." She walks around until she's standing in front of me. "Look at me, Cal, please?" I can't resist obeying when she calls me that.

"Leila, you said yourself, we're friends. So, how about we don't do this? If we don't do this, if you don't ask me if what I said was true and I don't answer, then perhaps we can go back."

"Back?"

"To being friends because the last thing I want to do, is lose your friendship."

"Is that what you want, for us to be friends?"

"It doesn't matter anymore, Leila, don't you see? You've already said how you feel and the truth has already been spilled. The Weavers know I lied and I have to face Logan and Kenna tonight with the plans for the brewery. That's if I even have a hops supplier anymore and I just can't lose you as well, Leila." I shake my head and close my eyes, I don't want to look at her anymore, it hurts. "So, let's just call it what it is and move on. Friends with benefits has run its course and we're friends, only friends."

"No." My eyes snap open and my eyes meet hers.

"What do you mean, no?" I'm confused.

"I mean, no. I want you to answer me. Did you tell Makenna the truth when she asked you how you felt about me?" Her eyes are flicking between mine, trying to get a read on what I'm thinking, what I'm feeling. "Please Cal, I need to know the truth." I can see the pleading in her eyes and I know that this is my chance. I need to tell her everything.

Chapter Forty-six
LEILA

I watch him close his eyes and take another deep breath. I know, I *know* I could make this easier for him but I'm being selfish. I *really* need to hear him say it first, I couldn't take it if I heard what he said wrong or that he was saying it just to get Makenna and Logan off his back.

"Caleb?" My voice is quiet but demanding.

"Yes." His voice is a hoarse whisper that I can just hear and he doesn't look me in the eyes.

"Yes what?"

His head whips up and his eyes meet mine, I see in them the steely determination that I love about him. Yeah, he's not the only one feeling the feels here.

"Everything I said to Kenna was true." His words are strong, clear and concise. He means every word. "I have wanted you since the first day I saw you here at Vines and I've never felt any different. Why do you think I work in here rather than in my very quiet, granny free and boring office?" The smirk that spreads across his face is almost my undoing. Almost.

"You also said something else." He raises an eyebrow at me, that smirk firmly in place and I know he's going to make me ask. "You said you love me Caleb."

"I did, yes." He takes the half a step that brings him chest to chest with me and stares into my eyes, daring me to ask the question I so desperately want the answer to.

"Did you mean it?"

"I very rarely say things I don't mean, Leila."

"But it can happen? I mean, it's possible you said it in the spur of the moment to get Makenna and Logan off your back, right?"

"It's possible, yes." He's really going to make me ask, isn't he? Fuck it!

"Is it true, Caleb, do you love me?"

"Yes." His voice is raspy, as he reaches a hand up to caress my cheek with his thumb. "I just wish I'd told you before I told my family, you deserved that much and for that, I'm incredibly sorry. That doesn't make it any less true though."

"Did it happen while we were at the Weavers?"

"No." I'm surprised because that's when I knew I was in love with him.

"No?"

"No, Leila, I've been half in love with you for months. Absolute fucking months, that weekend at the Weavers was the nail in the coffin for me but I already knew, I just hadn't admitted it to myself. I couldn't."

"Why not?"

"Because I didn't want to start something with you and ruin it all. Our friendship, your job, my job the whole thing. I wanted you in my life however I could get you and you didn't seem to want more than my friendship."

"So you didn't even try?" I ask, pressing my hands into his chest and gathering his shirt in my fists.

"You didn't either."

"You're right, I didn't and I wish I had."

"You do?" He sounds surprised but I don't know why, not after I agreed to be his fiancé for a weekend or our beneficial arrangement afterwards.

"When you asked to make this a friends with benefits arrangement, I wanted to tell you then but I just didn't know how to. I didn't think you wanted more from me but I knew then, in that moment that I didn't want what we had to end. I didn't want a friends with benefits arrangement though either, I just couldn't say no to more time with you. I figured I could work out the rest of the stuff at another time." I explain with a shrug of my shoulders.

"Darlin', are you saying you want more? No more friends with benefits?"

"Oh, I want the benefits, Handsome, I just want to be your girlfriend."

"Not fiancé?" A grin spreads across his face and it's infectious.

"Not yet, no but one day, absolutely." Then I stretch up and kiss him. He hesitates for a second, like he can't quite believe it's happening and then he takes charge. My grip on his shirt tightens and I moan into his mouth, as he kisses me until I can't breathe or remember where the hell I am. I pull back slightly and his lips chase mine like he can't get enough. "I love you too, Caleb." I say against his lips.

His hands grip my face and his eyes dance between mine, looking to see if I'm telling the truth and I smile.

"Fuck!" He kisses me, deeply and thoroughly. "I love you too, Leila. So fucking much Darlin'." There's a cough from somewhere in the room and we're both startled.

"Hi, yup, sorry to interrupt guys but apparently because I'm related to one of you, I'm the one who gets to break up your little confessional and ask you to come back into Vines. Sara needs your help, Leila and Brian wants to talk to you, Caleb. I just want to be anywhere but here, honestly." I look at my brother standing just inside the door and laugh, while I smooth down the front of Caleb's shirt, trying to make him look presentable again.

"We'll be there in a second, I promise, Matt."

"Don't make me come back in here, I don't want to walk in on anything other than what I just did. That was more than enough, thank you very much!" He shudders and he turns his back to us and walks back out the door, closing it behind him.

"So, I guess he's not mad?" Caleb asks.

"I really don't know. I doubt he'll be mad that we're together, he might be annoyed that I hid it from him for a while though."

"Well, you can blame me for that one, I'm more than happy to take the hit." He runs his hand down my cheek as he speaks. It's tender, I can feel myself melting into him and pull myself away from his body.

"Come on, before one of them comes looking for us again. If it's Sara, we'll never live it down. Plus, you need to talk to Brian and see if he's still going to supply your hops so that you can discuss your proposal with Makenna and Logan."

"You heard that part too, huh?"

"Yes, I did and you're not backing out of it."

"I'd rather spend the night with you, celebrating that you're mine." He says as he wraps his arms around my waist from behind, while we're both walking towards the door and kissing my neck.

With my hand on the door handle, I hesitate. "We can't do this, you can't do this while I'm at work, Caleb. I need these guys to still see me as their boss and not as your girlfriend."

"You're not going to tell them we're together?" He sounds wounded but he's misunderstood my intentions. He steps away from me and I feel the loss of his touch immediately.

"They already know, Caleb, that I know without a doubt but no, that's not what I meant. They can *know* that we're together but I don't want to be obvious about it at work. I am still their boss and you are still effectively *my* boss whether you see it that way or not. I do and so do they. Let's just give people the chance to get used to there being an us first, OK?" I smile at him, hoping that I'm reassuring him, then give him a quick kiss before opening the door back into Vines.

"So, you expect me to keep my hands to myself after finally getting you to agree that we're together?" I look over my shoulder to find him pouting, actually pouting and it shouldn't be attractive.

"For now, yes."

"She's giving you the, 'keep your hands and lips to yourself', lecture isn't she?" Sara asks from behind me.

"She is, yes. You don't agree?" Caleb asks with a glint in his eyes, he can smell an ally in my friend but before I can warn her to keep her opinions to herself for now she answers him.

"Generally speaking, I would agree with her but in this case, we all knew you two had feelings for each other and were taking bets on how long it would take you to see it *and* act on them."

"Sara!" I don't know whether her name is a warning or because I'm embarrassed but Caleb just laughs.

"I'm glad we've been entertainment for the rest of you but I have to ask, who won?"

"Caleb!" I say *his* name in shock.

"I want to know, Darlin'."

"See now, you can't be calling someone Darlin' without feeling there, at least not in my mind anyway. I'd like to say I won because I had the inside edge, what with knowing Leila as well as I do but I didn't. I honestly thought you would have given up by now, Caleb, so I lost a few months ago."

"You were betting on my sister's love life?" Matt pipes up next to me. I'm not sure where he was before he spoke.

'It was a bit of fun, Matthew, relax." I watch as my brother bristles and scowls at Sara using his full name. It's unusual and I never introduce him to people like that, only as Matt. I don't have time to think about what that might mean because Sara announces who won the staff bet. "Congratulations Georgie. I should have known you'd win, you've got this knack of getting these things right."

"Georgie? I can't believe you'd actually participate in something like this!" I tell her, as she bows at Sara.

"Thank you, Sara and what can I say boss? I have a keen eye and a real talent for seeing when people are either hiding their feelings from each other or the people in their lives. With you two, it was from yourselves, with others, it's a different story. Isn't it Sara?" she asks pointedly, before looking towards my brother and then walking back to her coffee machine.

I don't have time to ask any questions because Brian interrupts and asks to speak to Caleb and myself before they have to leave.

"We'll talk as soon as we're done." I point at Sara. "You can stay until we're done too." I look at Matt but give neither of them a chance to respond. There's something going on between those two and I don't know whether I'm happy about it or not.

I can't think about it now though because we sit down with Mary and Brian. This chat isn't going to be awkward at all! We lied to them and now we have to explain ourselves. I just hope that it hasn't ruined Caleb's chances of doing business with them. Considering this whole mess started because he *wanted* to do business with Brian, I hope we can work everything out.

Chapter Forty-seven
CALEB

Facing Brian and Mary isn't something I'm comfortable doing and I sure as hell don't want to be doing it in Vines but here we are. I wondered for a red hot minute if I could get them to come over to the house but then I decided that perhaps a public place would be better after all.

"Mary. Brian." I nod at them and shake Brian's offered hand.

"Hi Mary." Leila smiles as she sits down in the seat next me. "Hi Brian." They both smile at her warmly which relaxes me slightly.

"I just wanted to start by saying I'm sorry." I look at Leila and she takes my hand in hers. "We're *both* so sorry that we lied to you."

"We didn't mean any harm, honestly." Leila adds.

"We understand why you did it." Mary assures us and reaches across the table to take Leila's other hand in hers. "I'm sorry that we made you feel like you had to put yourself in that situation. Especially you, Caleb." Her eyes meet mine and I can see that she means what she says.

"Mary is right, Caleb. We never should have put you in the position where you thought you had to lie to us about your relationship status. The truth is, your relationship or lack of one, never had any bearing on whether or not I was willing to supply you with hops and I'm exceptionally sorry that I made you feel like it did."

"And I'm sorry that I made you so uncomfortable trying to find your perfect match that you felt like you needed to fake having a fiancé to make me back off." Mary says sheepishly. "Although, you *did* choose a very beautiful young lady for your fiancé and if it's not too bold of me to say under the circumstances, I think it pushed the two of you together."

I look at Leila, squeeze her hand and smile. "You're right Mary, it has made us see what was right in front of our faces." Leila's beaming smile warms me from head to toe. If we didn't have a mess or two to clean up after this revelation, I would be taking her back to my place and celebrating all damned night. Like she can read my mind, a blush creeps up her cheeks. Perhaps she *can* read my mind after all.

"We don't want to keep you for too long, I think we can all see that you have other things to take care of." Brian smiles knowingly at us and Mary laughs. "What I mostly wanted to say to you, Caleb is that I was always going to do business with you and I regret making you feel like I wouldn't. You're a man of integrity and worth, Caleb Drake and I wish I'd told you that before that call checking in if you were bringing someone with you."

"Thank you, Brian."

"I want to do business with you, Caleb, if you still want to do business with me that is." I don't think I've ever seen Brian Weaver unsure of anything but he sits across from me this afternoon, at Vines and looks like he's honestly unsure of whether I'll do business with him.

"We just wanted the best for you, Caleb. We wanted to see you happy and settled." Mary adds.

"I know that Mary." I smile at her. There's a lot of smiling going on at this table and I realise that we're all so fucking tense we don't know what to do or how to speak. "Look, let's just say it's all water under the bridge, what do you say?" I look between everyone at the table. "We all made some mistakes and we all regret them. If you're willing to do business with me after all this mess, then I'm more than happy to move forward as well, Brian. That's if I can get Logan and Makenna onboard with building the brewery here."

"What if they don't get onboard, Caleb?" Brian asks.

"I've taken that into consideration as well and I've been working on other options. I have a couple of other avenues that I could go down, if it comes to that. I guess what I'm saying is, I want to make this brewery a reality and I'm determined, one way or another to get it up and running. I would love to have you beside me along the way, Brian."

"You've got a deal, son." Brian stands up and holds his hand out for me to shake. I stand up and take his hand in mine. Without warning he pulls me around the side of the table and into a bear hug. "They'd be crazy if they passed up this opportunity, Caleb but I'll work with you either way. With or without Drake Wines, I'm behind you one hundred percent of the way."

"Thank you, Brian." We shake hands and there are hugs. Leila and I walk the Weavers to their car and watch them drive away.

"Well, their surprise visit certainly shook everything up!" I say, as I gather my *girlfriend* up in my arms and she rests her head on my chest as she circles her arms around my waist.

"If I'm being honest, Caleb, I'm kind of glad they showed up."

"You are?"

"Yeah. I mean, I know we have a lot of stuff to deal with from the fall out but I'm actually grateful they showed up and forced our hand. I hate lying to anyone and that includes myself. I wish that we'd been able to admit our feelings for each other sooner without someone playing a hand in it but the fact is, we might never have confessed to each other. We both had our reasons for not speaking up. Let's face it, it could have been easier to never say a thing."

"But then I wouldn't be able to do this in the carpark of Drake Wines." I say, then I take her lips in a scorching kiss that I never want to pull out of but I know I have to. "I would love to stay here and kiss you all day, Darlin' but I have a meeting with Mr Drake and Mrs Harris this evening about a brewery and I need to get my proposal in order."

"You've got everything you need, Caleb, you just have to show up and tell them the work you've already done, with all the passion you show me when you talk about making Drake Brewery a reality."

"Will you come with me?"

"To your business meeting?" Her eyebrow wrinkle in confusion.

"We're having dinner first." I say, as if that explains everything. "*Family* dinner where the events of today will no doubt be discussed among other things but business will be discussed afterwards. Jules will probably take Savvy home and Brady may go to work."

"So, you want me to join you for family dinner?"

"Yes but I want you with me when I present my proposal to Kenna and Logan too. You know this as well as I do and I could really do with your support. You've believed in this and me since I told you about it when it was just an idea of what I might like to do here." I search her eyes for a hint of her feelings. "Please?"

"Of course." She smiles. "Let me get back to Vines to talk Matt and Sara down from the excitement this afternoon and to sort everything out in the kitchen, then I would love to join you."

"Are you sure? I can come and talk to Sara and Matt with you. You don't have to do it alone."

"They'll be fine." She waves away my concerns. "As for dinner, I wouldn't miss it."

I kiss her deeply, needing one more before we go our separate ways. Me to my office so that I can work and Leila back to Vines to do everything she needs to do. I can't contain the smile that spreads across my face as I sit behind my desk. Not only did I get the girl but I'm one step closer to getting my brewery up and running as well.

I SPEND THE REST OF the afternoon and early evening making sure I've got everything for my brewery proposal set and ready to go. In the back of my mind, I know I'm being stupid. I mean, I've worked the numbers, I written it up and talked it over with Leila I couldn't even count how many times but I'm still nervous. This is something I really want and if Kenna and Logan can't get behind me and this venture, then I'm going to have to look at places that aren't Drake Wines.

I wonder what they would think if they knew that I would do to go through with it. Not to mention the fact that I have actually scouted out a few local properties that I could potentially purchase and branch out on my own.

"Are you ready?" I jump at Leila's quiet question. I didn't notice her standing in the doorway to my office. Before I get the chance to answer, my phone chimes with a message.

Kenna: *You coming for dinner still, aren't you?*

Another one coming in hot on its heels.

Kenna: *You're bringing Leila too, aren't you?*

I can't help laughing as I respond.

Me: *yes & yes*

Logan: *Bring Leila and your plans to dinner. See you in a few minutes.*

I frown at that message. He can be such a demanding arsehole, so much so sometimes I can't help wondering how the hell Jules and Savvy put up with him.

"Everything OK?" Leila is still standing in the doorway, looking beautiful as always but nervous as hell.

"Everything is perfect, Darlin'." I stand up and gather my paperwork neatly into a folder. If nothing else, my brother will appreciate the fact that I'm organised. I'm just hoping I've got the answers to everything he could possibly ask me tonight. "Kenna was just making sure that I was bringing you along." I smile, rounding my desk and draping an arm around her shoulders.

"So, they want me there?" The hesitation in her voice is something I'm not really used to.

"Of course! They probably want you there more than they want me there because, let's be honest, I'm a pain in their collective arses." When she laughs, I feel the tension leave my body.

"Siblings are *always* a pain, no matter how old you get." I want to ask her what Matt said when she went back to Vines and what the story is between Sara and her brother but we don't have time to get into that conversation. The walk is short between my office and the main house that is Makenna and Brady's house. "Are you nervous?"

"Honestly?" She nods. Of course she wants honesty, she always does. "Yes."

"Do you think they'll say no?" We're nearing the house, so we slow down our pace a little so we can keep talking.

"Not really. I think they'll *want* to say yes but I think them saying yes terrifies me *more* than them saying no. I have a backup plan if they say no, so there's a safety net there but if they say yes? What happens then? What if it fails, what if *I* fail them, Leila? What happens then? They've put their trust in me and backed me, then I screw it all up?"

"You won't screw it up, Caleb." I snort at her over confidence in me. She stops walking and because I have an arm around her shoulders, I have to stop as well otherwise we'll both fall over. "Caleb, look at me." I turn to face her, not knowing what she's about to say and concerned by the look on her face but when she catches my eyes and holds them, I relax. "You forget, Mr Drake, that I've watched you every day, working on this project. Working out the numbers. Working out the how to and the where to and the what to. I know you've worked out all the details. I *know* you've put in the hard work, Caleb. If anyone can make this brewery and a Drakes craft beer brand work, it's you. If Makenna and Logan can't see that, then you'll work your arse off to prove it to them on your own. You'll show them that they were wrong, that they said no, when they absolutely should have said yes!" After that impassioned speech, I pull her into me, smashing her chest to mine and I kiss her. Deeply, possessively and tenderly all at once, until neither of us can remember where we are. When we finally break apart, we're both breathing heavily.

"What would I do without you?" It's a genuine question because I have no fucking clue what I did without Leila Phillips in my life.

"Wank?" Her quick and witty response cracks me up, my laughter carrying across the now empty property.

"Are you kids joining us for dinner or should we start without you? The kids are hungry!" Brady's voice carries the short distance between his front porch and where we're standing. I rest my forehead on Leila's and we both laugh.

"We'll be right there Brady!"

"Don't stress. It's not like Kenna and Jules have been cooking all afternoon or anything." He smirks and walks back inside, leaving the front door open for us.

"Wow! He's got that Dad guilt perfected, doesn't he?"

"He sure does." I slip my arm around her waist, pulling her as close as I can get her to my side so that we can still walk, to the steps that then allows us to follow behind Brady and close the door behind us. I'll never hear the end of it if one of the kids gets out and runs amok. It happened once, once I tell you and I've never fucking lived it down!

"Good evening. Nice of you two to join us." Brady smirks, as Kenna walks by him, slapping his arm, before pulling Leila into a warm embrace but taking her out of my arms.

"Stop it Brady! I promise to give her back in a minute, Caleb." I don't get the chance to pull Leila back into my arms, Jules pulls her in for a hug and they're quickly joined by Savvy.

"I'm here too you know!" I grumble and Savvy throws herself at me, I catch her just in time but I stumble a little.

"Be careful with our daughter, Caleb." Logan grumbles as he takes his fucking turn to embrace my girlfriend! "If he gives you any trouble, any at all, you call me and I will kick his arse for you. Understand me?"

"I'm sure I won't need your assistance but thank you for the offer." Logan just grunts and takes Savvy off me, then leads us all to the table.

Brady brushes by me and drapes an arm around Leila's shoulders. "That goes for me too. In fact, put Logan and myself in your speed dial and if this guy screws up, you know who to call."

"What? Because I couldn't come to her rescue as well?" Kenna asks sounding offended. "Put your paperwork in the office, Caleb, we'll look at it after dinner." It only takes me a few minutes to drop the folder on her desk but when I return, I find Kenna rolling her eyes at her husband.

"You so could baby but you don't need to." He drops his arms from around Leila, to take my sister into his arms and kiss her almost indecently.

"I'm right here! Leila can deal with me on her own, thank you very much but thanks for the vote of confidence that eventually I'm going to screw up." I complain. "Nothing like your family having your back." I mumble.

There's laughter and too much talking as we eat dinner. These are the kinds of messy, noisy and fun dinners we used to have when our parents were still alive. I sit back and watch everyone. Kenna and Brady with their toddlers, Logan and Jules with Savvy and I've got Leila sitting beside me.

I'm happy I realise as I sit there watching everyone interact. Even if Kenna and Logan don't like my plans to start up a brewery on the Drake property, I suddenly realise that Leila's right. I can do it without them, I'd rather not but I know that I can if I need to and that takes all the pressure off the meeting we have planned for after dinner.

Chapter Forty-eight
LEILA

I was nervous about joining Caleb for dinner with all of the Drakes but I shouldn't have been. I know all of them, including Brady, Jules and Savannah, pretty well because I work at Vines and they're all in at least a few times a week. Knowing them in that environment is one thing though, I'm employed by the family, I'm not a member of the family. That makes it sound like they're a mafia family and while it can sometimes feel that way, they're so far from what I'd expect from a mafia family it makes me laugh.

"What's so funny?" Caleb leans in and quietly asks in my ear as everyone finishes the chocolate cake I brought over from Vines. It's Caleb's favourite but it's also one of Logan's as well, so I thought I might be able to soften him up a little bit.

"Nothing. I just had a funny thought, that's all." I look away from Caleb to see Logan watching us with a frown on his handsome face. I know he's concerned about his brother being in relationship with me and the fallout if things don't work but as intimidating as I know Logan can be, I also know he's as soft as a marshmallow inside. I think he's as worried about Caleb as he is me and despite what Caleb thinks, I don't believe that Logan is worried about Vines. The man is well aware of the fact that I'm replaceable if it comes down to that. I think he understands that I would leave too.

Once we've finished eating, Jules pushes the three Drake sibling towards Makenna's home office with the promise of clearing everything up, if they just get the business side of the evening done and dusted. I hear him whisper to his husband to 'be kind' before kissing him.

"You can stay here or go home, if you like. You don't have to stay here, I'd like you to but I'll understand if you want to leave." Caleb tells me, bringing me out of my thoughts and back to the present. "You have the real key remember." He says against my lips, making me laugh.

"I'll save her from the hard questioning that Jules has planned, Caleb, go!" Brady tried to reassure him.

"Go. I'll stay and help Jules and Brady clean up." I kiss him back. "You go win Makenna and Logan over with your brilliant idea for a brewery *and* remember what I said before we got here."

"I love you."

"I love you too. Now go, go get your brewery!" He gives me another kiss and just when I think he's going to deepen it, Logan speaks.

"Are we having this meeting, Caleb? Or are you too busy tonight?" Caleb rolls his eyes at me and I have to stifle a laugh after he turns to follow them. I smile and start to clear up the cake dishes.

"You make him happy, you know that don't you?" I look up and see Jules grinning broadly at me from across the table. "Logan is just worried about you both and not for the reason that Caleb thinks either."

"So, he's not worried because if we break up I'll leave Vines?" I probably shouldn't ask but Jules brought it up. "Or that I might break his little brother's heart?"

"Well, we'd all be exceptionally sad to see you leave Vines no matter the reason, Leila but I think you'll find that he simply wants to protect you both from heartache."

"OK, so what you're saying is, he assumes that we're not going to last and the worst will happen?"

The smile disappears from Jules' face. "No, that's not what I said." He stammers out and I don't think I've never seen Jules stutter over words in the whole time I've known him.

"Give up Jules, you're not saying it right?" Brady advises.

"You try then." Jules bites back.

"Nope. I think they're good together. Actually, I think it's awesome that they finally got their shit sorted and saw what the rest of us have seen for months. Months and months. They're adults and they can make their own decisions. They both know and understand the consequences of their relationship, which means none of us have the right to judge them."

"Thank you Brady."

"You're welcome, Leila but know that those two in there with your man, they're judging you both and not because they're not happy for you both or because they expect the worst. No, they're worried about you both because they love you *both*. That's not going to change but they *will* get past it eventually. You just have to give them some time."

"Well, that's what I said!" Jules protests.

"No, you really didn't." Brady cracks up. "It *is* however what you were *trying* to say."

"Whatever!" Jules says with a wave of his hand before picking up some dirty dishes and taking them into the kitchen.

"I promise, they'll get over it and quickly. Just don't let them get to you before they get the chance, OK? You and Caleb are happy, that's all that matters." We gather up the rest of the dirty dishes and follow Jules into the kitchen.

"Do you think Makenna and Logan will give Caleb a hard time over his brewery?" I ask them as we clean up. "He has everything in order. He's been over the details a million times to make sure they're right and he spent this afternoon making sure there were no mistakes."

"If he's got everything in order and can answer the million questions that Logan will undoubtedly ask, I think he's a shoe in. They want him to succeed, Leila and they'll do whatever they can to help him."

"I agree." Jules says. "As long as he can answer Logan's questions and he has his ducks all in a row, they'll back him. Don't you worry honey."

"Uncle Brady, the twins are starting to get a little edgy." Savannah says as she walks into the kitchen and hugs both her uncle and her dad. "Hi Leila." She smiles shyly at me from beside Jules.

"Hi Savannah." I see Brady hesitate. "Go look after the twins, now that Savannah's here we can get finished up in here while you put them to bed."

"She's right, off you go daddy." Jules teases, flicking Brady with the tea towel in his hand, making his daughter laugh and Brady to flip him off before going to tend to his kids. "You're going to fit in just fine, Leila. Perfectly fine, honey."

We work together to get everything cleaned up and by the time we're done you wouldn't know that a meal had been eaten in the house, much less prepared and cooked here.

The four of us are laughing and chatting a while later when the three Drake sibling join us in the kitchen. Silence falls across the room, even Savannah seems to understand that something is going on.

"Let's go home, Darlin'." Caleb says, reaching out and taking my hand in his.

"No, you can't just leave without telling us what the deal is?" Jules exclaims. "I won't let you walk out before you tell us, is there going to be a brewery on the property?" Jules, Savannah and Brady are all looking between the three siblings but I'm only looking at Caleb. He looks at me and our eyes catch and I know what the answer is before he speaks, I can see it in his eyes.

"It's your news, you tell them." Logan says with a curt nod.

"Yes, Caleb, tell them." Makenna does not have a poker face at all.

"Drake Brewery is going ahead." Caleb announces and I can't help the squeal of excitement that escapes me and jump into his arms.

"I knew you could do it! I'm so proud of you Handsome!"

"And *that* right there is why she's perfect for him. She believes in him and she's right beside him when he makes those big and small plans." Jules announces to the room.

"Alright you big softy." Logan says to his husband. "Now that the news has been shared, let's get Savannah home and in bed."

"Dad! I can stay up and help Uncle Caleb celebrate." The young girl groans.

"Another day, Savvy, I promise." Caleb promises as I drop my feet to the floor and he releases me so that he can go give her a tight hug.

"Chocolate cake tomorrow at Vines?" She asks hopefully.

"I'll save you both a piece for after school, I promise." I say and Jules coughs not so subtly. "I'll save a few pieces for after school tomorrow." I laugh as Logan rolls his eyes.

"Congratulations man, I'm super proud of you!" Brady says, giving Caleb a one armed man hug, slap on the back, thing.

"It's wonderful news, Caleb but I never doubted that it was a great idea." Jules says as he gives him a hug.

"I can't wait to see you make this work, Caleb." Makenna smiles, Brady's wrapped himself around his wife from behind.

"I'm looking forward to helping you get this off the ground." Logan agrees. "But, for tonight, that's it."

There is another round of hugs of which I'm a part of and that kind of freaks me out because now I'm hugging my employers! It's going to take some getting used to, that's for sure. We leave with Logan, Jules and Savannah but split up to go in opposite directions home.

Caleb and I don't say a word for the short distance to his house. I don't know about him but I'm thinking about all the things that changed today.

"You're quiet. Is everything OK?" Caleb asks as he closes the door behind us. locking it and tossing the folder in his hand on the bench. Then he pulls me in to his arms and I relax against him with my arms around his waist.

"It's been a big day." I admit.

"It has."

"A lot of things have changed."

"How are you feeling?"

"A little overwhelmed if I'm being honest." He tries to pull away from me but I hold on to him tighter. "I'm so damned proud of you Caleb. I knew your plans for the brewery were solid but I'm just so glad that Makenna and Logan saw it too and are behind you." I feel his smile on the top of my head.

"I had answers for every question they threw at me. When we were done, Logan told me that he was impressed with how thoroughly I had done my research and worked out what I wanted to do and what timeline I had. He told me it was very realistic and acceptable."

"And Makenna?" I ask, not moving.

"She said the same and added that our parents would be proud. That my dad would be over joyed that I was going my own way but keeping it in the family still. He believed in working together but having our own pursuits. Kenna thinks that he'd be behind my brewery without a second thought."

"That's amazing, Caleb." I lean up and kiss him. The kiss turns heated and deep quickly but then he pulls away.

"And us? How do you feel about us?" His eyes are shut, making me believe he's actually nervous about what I might say.

"Us? You mean, the two of us? About us being a couple?" I tease him and his eyes snap open. I take his face in my hands so that he can't look away. "I am so in love with you Caleb Drake. I couldn't be happier about that development today, believe me."

I squeal as hands grip my butt and he lifts me up off my feet. "Wrap your legs around my waist, Darlin." I do as he asks and he carries me through the house, into the bedroom, tossing me on the bed. "I'm going to do dirty things to you all night to celebrate."

My body heats at his dirty promise and I feel the need pooling between my legs.

"Let's celebrate then." That's exactly what we do, maybe not *all* night but close.

Chapter Forty-nine
CALEB

My meeting with Kenna and Logan couldn't have gone better. I knew what I wanted to say, I had all the answers to Logan's questions, as well as the few that Kenna threw at me.

"I'm impressed, Caleb. You've really thought of everything." Kenna smiled at me.

"You've got an amazing idea here, Caleb. My only question is, is it the right thing for Drake Wines?" I knew that's what it would come down to with Logan.

"I wondered the same thing, so if you don't want to put a brewery on the same property as a vineyard and winery, I understand. I've got my eye on a couple of properties nearby that would be perfect."

"Would you have to move?" Kenna asked softly.

"I wouldn't *have* to, Kenna but yes, I would want to. It would make my life easier to live on the property so that I can keep an eye on everything. Just like we do here." I know Kenna doesn't like the idea of me moving away. "It could be a reality at some point anyway Kenna. It may not always be practical for me to stay here." While Kenna looks like she might cry, those hormones of hers really play some games with her, Logan's been quiet, too quiet.

"We could change the name."

"What?" I'm pretty sure I didn't hear him right. "Change what name?"

"Drake Wines." He looks at Kenna, who nods her agreement. "We can change Drake Wines to something else." He shrugs his shoulders like it doesn't mean anything.

"But dad-."

330

"Dad would be proud of you for stepping out on your own, even if you do stay here." Kenna assures me.

"Dad would be more than proud of you, Caleb." Logan says with a catch in his voice. "I'm proud of you. You've thought everything through, you presented us with a clear and concise plan, with projections of when you'll start making money. I'm telling you, Caleb, you've done an incredible job and I can see that you're really passionate about building up your brand and the brewery. Having your brewery included in the family brand isn't in question, not for me anyway. It belongs here, just like you do."

"So, that's a yes?"

"No." Logan shakes his head and Kenna has a smile spread across her face. "That's a fuck yes, Cal. Drake Brewery is a fucking go ahead." I can't believe it and I have to make sure one more time.

"And you're sure?"

"Don't be an idiot, Caleb, we mean it! I'm more upset that you didn't tell us about this sooner. This is brilliant and the perfect fit for you. I think I speak for Logan as well as myself, that we knew the Vineyard and Winery weren't a fit for you, we just didn't know *where* you fit." Kenna engulfs me in a hug. "For a hot minute we thought about putting you in Vines to manage it but Leila is doing an amazing job there and while I know she'd rather have more time for baking and cooking, I think it suits her. Don't tell her but I'm thinking of hiring her an office assistant so that she can hand off a few of the more menial things and free up her time a bit."

"You know, Sara and Georgie would be a perfect fit for that position." I laugh.

"Yes, I know and I was thinking I might offer the position to Georgie. I think Sara prefers the kitchen than the paperwork. I did feel her out and she seemed extremely happy to *not* have to do all the paperwork but Georgie has an admin background, so I think she might be the perfect fit."

"I think you're right. As always."

"OK, with all that sorted, let's get out of here. Kenna and Brady need to get the kids to bed and enjoy a little bit of peace and I want to get my family home too." Logan says, ushering us out of Kenna's office. "You have to get Leila back home too, I'm sure you have a few things to discuss after your eventful day." The smirk my brother sends me tells me he knows *exactly* how I want to celebrate.

"Ewwww. I do *not* want to know." Kenna's disgust tells me she understood exactly what Logan meant too.

Telling our family that the project is going ahead is more entertaining and enjoyable than I thought it would be but the best part was the absolute happiness for me on Leila's face. While Brady and Jules were all hugging me and congratulating me, I looked over their shoulders to find Leila. I catch her eyes and she mouths, 'I'm so proud of you'. Having my brother and sister behind me is amazing and I'm grateful for their support but having Leila tell me she's proud of me? That warms something in me I didn't even realise I had.

After everyone doles out what feels like a million hugs and handshakes, we leave Kenna and Brady to enjoy some peace before they go to bed. Leila and I part ways with Logan, Jules and Savvy to head to our place and my heart warms more because Savvy and Logan's laughter fills the quiet air of the vineyard. I'm overjoyed that he finally found that happiness for himself.

When we get inside, I make sure to lock the door behind us. I don't want anyone interrupting us tonight or in the morning. I know Leila has questions about what went down in the meeting tonight but I really want to celebrate with her.

I plan on licking, biting, nibbling and sucking on every inch of skin that I can.

I grip her amazing arse in my hand and lift her off her feet, making her squeal. "Wrap your legs around my waist, Darlin.'" She does what I ask without hesitating. Which is awesome because it makes carrying her into our bedroom and tossing her onto our bed that much easier. "I'm going to do dirty things to you all night to celebrate."

"Let's celebrate then." She gives me this look that sends a tingle all the way down my spine. She thinks she's in control tonight but she's not. I am.

"Do you want me to tell you what I'm going to do to you, Darlin', or do you want to just float on the cloud of orgasmic bliss I'm about to deliver?"

"Confident much?"

"You know it! I haven't let you down yet." I tell her as I strip out of my clothes until I'm left in my boxer briefs. I love watching the desire light up her face. Her eyes get a little dark, a slight blush creeps over her cheeks as she heats up and she licks her lips like she's imagining licking *me*. I would be more than happy to let her have her way with me but later, right now I'm going to give her everything she didn't realise she wanted until me. Until tonight.

"Prove it, Handsome. Show me what you've got." It's a dare, a light-hearted hit to my ego but I don't feel it. All I feel for the woman lying on my bed, looking up at me with challenge in her eyes, is love.

Slowly, I start to undress her and as I remove each piece of clothing, I tell her exactly what I plan on doing.

"First, I'm going to strip you bare." One shoe drops to the floor. "One slow step at a time." The other shoe drops, then I peel off her socks. "Then do you know what I'm going to do?" I ask, sitting her up a little bit so that I can pull the Vines hoodie she's wearing over her head. "I'm going take turns pulling each of your nipples into my mouth. Do you know what I'm going to do to them?"

"No." Her voice is rough and husky with need.

I undo the few buttons on the polo shirt with the Vines logo on it and gently pull it up over her head as well before I continue. "I'm going to lick those rosy nipples, I'm going to nibble on them and suck on them until you're writhing underneath me and those nipples of yours are hard and begging me for more." I slide the straps of her bra off her shoulders and reach behind her to unclasp it. The lace and satin land on the floor with the rest of her clothes and I gently push her to lie back on the bed. "Do you want that?"

"Yes." She nods without breaking eye contact with me and I smile.

"Good." I drop my head to her chest and do exactly what I promised, until she's writhing underneath me, begging me to stop, while also begging me for more. More of what, she's not sure but she wants more of it and she wants it now.

"Caleb." My name is more of a breath, than an actual word. I unbutton and unzip her jeans. I have to sit up , leaving her nipples behind, to pull them down over her hips and down her legs but in the end, they end up in the same place as the rest of her clothes and she's left in a pair of satin and lace briefs.

"Play with them, Darlin', tweak those nipples and keep them happy until I can get back to them." Her eyes widen in surprise at my command but she only hesitates for a few seconds before she rolls both nipples in between her finger and her thumb, causing her to moan. It's the sexiest sight *and* sounds I've ever fucking heard.

I bend down and run my tongue from between her breasts all the way down her ribs and stomach, kissing, sucking and biting along the way, making her squirm, squeak and moan as I do. When I reach her lace covered pussy again, I push them aside and push a finger into her pussy.

"Fuck, you're so wet for me already!" I hiss.

"Yes." I drag her briefs down her legs and throw them somewhere behind me, not caring where they might land.

I settle myself between her legs, she needs to spread them wider to accommodate me and it couldn't make me happier. Why? Because it gives me the perfect access to her pussy.

I run my tongue through the lips of her pussy, from bottom to the top, licking up her sweetness and settling on her clit. I push two fingers inside her and start pumping them in and out, slow and steady, as I circle her clit with my tongue, over and over until she's begging me to make her come. I bite gently down on her clit and she fucking explodes. She screams out my name, as she rides my fingers until her orgasm starts to fade.

"Caleb." She reaches down and takes my head in her hands, guiding me up her body until my lips meet hers. Then she kisses me until I can't see straight. I reach over to the top drawer of my bedside table and pull out a strip of condoms. "Let me." She smiles against my lips, as she tears one off the strip, then pulls the condom out. I use the time to strip out of my boxer briefs.

When she takes my cock in her hand to roll on the condom, I don't how long I can hold on. My breath hisses out between my teeth and I have to close my eyes so that I don't embarrass myself.

"Leila."

"Let me take care of you, Handsome." She pushes on my chest until I give in and lie back. She straddles my hips and uses a hand to guide my cock into the opening of her pussy. Slowly, too fucking slowly, she slides down the length of my cock and I have to hold on to her hips to ground me. I close my eyes again and grit my teeth, because the sensation of her surrounding me is incredible.

Just as slowly she starts moving, up and down. Slow shallow movements. They're not enough and too much all at the same time.

"Fuck!"

"That's the plan." I reach between us to use my finger to rub her clit. "Fuck Caleb! I'm not going to last long if you. Fuck! Keep. Doing. That!" I need to make her come again and soon, because I'm not going to last much longer.

I'm completely done in when she falls down, pressing her hands into my chest so that she can leverage herself better to slide up and down my cock in longer, faster strokes.

"Leila." I grit out.

"Caleb! I'm going to come." Good!

"Come for me, Darlin'. Ride my cock, make yourself come, Darlin'." And that's exactly what she does and I follow close behind her. She collapses onto my chest, resting her head in the crook of my neck. I can feel her heavy breathing against my neck.

We lie there like that for a few minutes, maybe ten who knows, before I gently lift her up and place her back onto the bed. I get up, walk to the bathroom and take care of the condom. I'm in a daze as I walk out of the bathroom and I almost bump into Leila, who is going to do what she needs to do in the bathroom.

I get back into bed, lie back and close my eyes, waiting for her to join me again. I feel the bed dip beside me and pull the cover up over both of us as Leila snuggles in next to me.

I pull her in closer, kiss the top of her head and shuffle down a little until I can look her in the eyes.

"I am madly, deeply and totally in love with you, Leila Phillips."

"I am madly and deeply in love with you too, Caleb Drake."

"Tell me you're mine, Darlin'."

"So bossy and possessive." She teases me and I smack the butt cheek that was resting in the palm of my hand. "I am yours Caleb, if you're mine too." She looks unsure but it's only a flash so I'm not sure I saw it at all.

"I've always been yours, Leila." I know I always will be but that's for another day. First, I'm going to get the brewery up and running, *then*, Leila Phillips will become Leila Drake. Maybe not right away but someday soon.

EPILOGUE
LEILA
6 MONTHS LATER

A few months ago, Caleb and I decided that I should move into his house, now *our* house. The simple fact is, with Caleb working so hard to get the brewery up and running, I spend most of my time here anyway. It just seemed like the natural thing to do.

It took that long for Logan to realise that I'd moved *in and now* I'm headed over to his place for what I imagine is going to be a long conversation about my relationship with his little brother but the thing is, this 'meeting' seems pointless to *me* but it's important to Logan, so I'm going.

Caleb's ropable and wants to tell his brother to mind his own business, only not so politely but I understand where Logan is coming from. He's not only protecting the family at large and the business but also his brother.

"None of us butted into his relationship with Jules." Caleb stormed, about twenty minutes before my scheduled meeting and I just raised an eyebrow at him as I got changed out of my Vines uniform and into something a little more casual. I didn't want to blatantly remind Logan that I worked for him while he worried about my intentions towards his brother!

"You and I both know that isn't quite true, Cal." I use the shortened version of his name on purpose, hoping that it will calm him down.

"Well, we only told him he was an idiot for *not* telling Jules how he felt and that he shouldn't let what he *thinks* other people think, dictate how *he* should live his life. That, Darlin', is the *exact* fucking opposite of what he's doing here!" OK, so he didn't calm down. "I'm coming with you!" He stomps to the door to put his shoes on.

"Caleb? Hey, Handsome?" He looks up at me, his emotions written all over his face. He's angry at the audacity of Logan thinking he can dictate how we live our lives. He feels guilty that I'm being put through this. Then he's pissed that Makenna hasn't told Logan to mind his own business. Then the guilt reappears because he wants to fix everything for me, for us. "You're not coming with me." I rest my hand gently on his shoulder.

"But I *want* to come with you, Darlin'. Logan can be a real dick when he wants to be and you shouldn't have to deal with that bullshit on your own." I don't say a word, I *know* he knows that he's being ridiculous about this. I deal with Logan day in and day out about business, I'm pretty sure I can deal with his overprotective arse when it comes to the man I love. Caleb's shoulders sag in resignation when he realises that I'm right *and* I'm not going to give in. "Fine! I'll stay home but if you need me, call me. I don't care what he says, if he upsets you, I *will* kill him!"

I cradle his face in my hands and kiss him. "I know, Handsome but I'm pretty sure I can handle your brother. We both know that he has a tough exterior but he's as soft as a marshmallow on the inside. As long as I tell him the truth and he knows that I'm not going anywhere, he'll be fine." I drop my hands to his shoulders and give him an awkward hug.

"I know." He sighs. "I love you Leila." He mumbles into my stomach and pulls me in tighter for a cuddle.

"I love you too, Caleb." He gives me one more tight squeeze and lets his hands drop to his lap. "I'll be back soon and I promise I'll be in one piece." I laugh but Caleb just sighs and shakes his head.

I probably should feel nervous as I walk over to Logan's office. I'm amused that he wanted to talk to me here, rather than at his house or ours. I'm guessing though that he didn't want Jules or Savvy to interrupt us or for Jules to tell him he's being ridiculous.

"Knock , knock." I say as I actually knock on the door.

"Come in, Leila. Shut the door behind you and take a seat." I do as he says and try to look at ease. "I'm sure you know why I asked you here today?"

"No, not really. I *think* I know but I'm not sure." He doesn't say anything else, he's waiting for me to bring up the subject. Any one that I think he might want to talk to me about. *This* right here is why he's a brilliant business man but I know he's not as intimidating as he might appear to most people. Instead of answering him, I wait him out. It's all about not showing him any weakness and I know he respects me for my work but I also know that he understands I'm not going to hurt Caleb intentionally as well.

"Vines is doing well?" He sits back in his chair, hands clasped together in his lap.

"Is that a question or a statement? Because I think we're both more than aware of the fact that Vines is not *doing well,* it's thriving." I smile at him, knowingly and I see his lip twitch slightly, like he *wants* to smile but he won't allow himself just yet.

"You're right. Sara and yourself are a great team and we're more than pleased with the job you, specifically, have done."

"Thank you." A compliment from Logan is usually hard earned, so I'm happy to be on the receiving end of one. He gives them out often but you definitely know that he means them *and* you've earned it.

"You and Caleb? It's serious?"

"Yes." I swear I just got whiplash he changed the subject so quickly but I don't falter.

"You've moved in?"

"Yes. A while ago actually." I confirm and he nods.

"I guess Jules wins that bet then." He nods his head like I just confirmed something they've debated for a while and I can't help laughing.

"Jules knows more than he lets on. That man sees everything!"

"That he does." Logan shakes his head but he's also smiling. "So, you're happy? You're both happy?"

"I am. We are." Neither one of us speaks for a few minutes but neither do we break eye contact. "Logan, can I just say, that as an older sibling and one that's taken on some of the adult responsibilities of her family, I understand you're just being protective but honestly, I love your brother. I'm in love with him and I can't imagine my life without him. I know that yourself and Makenna are worried that we're moving too quick but the fact is, we've been dancing around our feelings and each other since the day we met. Just between you and me, I'm grateful that Brian put Caleb on the spot that day and that I was the one that was there because he pushed us together that weekend. So, while we might have started our relationship under false pretences, I think we both wanted it to be real."

"But even after that weekend at the Weavers, you didn't really have a relationship per se, did you?"

"Well, that depends on your definition of a relationship." I want to say that he's the last one to hand out advice or reprimands about 'real' relationships but I know it still hurts him that Jules felt like he didn't love him. "Look, the truth is, I stopped Caleb from coming with me today because I wanted this to be between just us. I know you have reservations about me, about us and I want to assure you that I will never hurt Caleb, not on purpose, anyway."

"I don't have reservations about you, Leila." Logan starts and my anger boils over and I get to my feet.

"Well, then this discussion is over because if it's your brother that you have reservations about, then you're an arsehole. That man loves me. He's kind, generous, sweet, giving and he loves me and your family. All of them, without *reservation*. That love includes my mum and brother, as well as my best friend." My chest is heaving with the emotions I'm feeling. "How dare you call Caleb's integrity or love into question."

"I wasn't but it's nice to know that you'll fight for my brother so passionately." He stands up and rounds his desk, when he reaches me, he engulfs me in a tight bear hug. "Welcome to the family, Leila."

"What?" He steps back and drapes an arm around my shoulders. "How about a slice of your famous chocolate cake to celebrate?" I don't speak as he leads me out of his office, towards Vines. I can't, I have no fucking clue what just happened.

I'm still in a state of shock when Logan opens the door to Vines and waves me in first with a giant smile. I take a few steps inside and realise that something isn't quite right but I can't put my finger on it. Then I realise it's quiet. Dead quiet even though it's full.

The granny's are sitting at their table watching me walking in the door. So are Makenna and Brady, each of them holding a toddler. Jules and Savvy are standing beside them, Savvy barely standing still. Mum, Matt, Sara and Georgie, Brian and Mary are all standing with them as well, just gawking at me with goofy grins on their faces.

"What the hell is going on here?" I notice Caleb standing there, an enormous grin on his face. "Caleb?" I'm confused.

Caleb nods at Sara, who taps something on her phone and then Bruno Mars starts crooning about it being a beautiful night.

CALEB

The minute Leila is out of sight, I finish putting my shoes on and rush over to Vines, while hoping that Logan can keep Leila in his office long enough for me to put everything into action.

Pushing open the door, I can hear the noise of a lot of people talking all at once.

"I'll ask Caleb when he gets here." I hear Sara say with a certain amount of irritation in her voice. Matt steps up beside her and gets everyone to quieten down.

"Caleb will be here any minute, he can answer any of your questions then, OK?" I decide to speak up before anyone can give them any more trouble.

"I'm here now, what the hell's going on?" I continue walking towards the group of people, some of them my favourite human beings on the planet but right now, they're annoying me. They're all talking at once and I can't understand a word of it. I put my thumb and finger in my mouth and whistle, loudly, causing everyone to stop. "Now that I've got everyone's attention, Sara, what's going on?"

"Why are you asking Sara?" Kenna asks, pouting like she's hurt.

"I asked Sara because she's the one who's helped me set this up. Now, if the rest of you don't shut up and just do what you've been told, you can all leave." I warn them, looking at everyone individually. "Except you of course, Kim." Leila's mum beams with happiness and I hear Kenna grumble again but she cuts it short when I give her a dirty look and Brady pulls her back against him. Well as much as he can with a toddler in his arms.

"Thank you, Caleb. Handsome and smart, I can see why my daughter loves you." She smiles wickedly at me. She caught me walking around the

342

house naked recently and keeps giving me these weird looks and waggling her eyebrow at Leila, which causes her to blush and me to laugh.

"Logan just sent me a text, Leila is on her way back to Vines." Then Kenna starts laughing uncontrollably and Georgie takes Beau while she gets herself under control. "She's perfect for you, Caleb and she's going to fit into the family perfectly. She just read Logan the riot act, defending you and your relationship to our brother. Man, I wish I'd been there to see that, there's few people who would dare give Logan a mouthful and tell him he's arsehole all at once!"

"She didn't?" Brady asks, starting to laugh as well.

"She *did*. Can you imagine? I would have loved to have seen Logan's face!" Then Jules is laughing as well.

"He doesn't like it when people call him an arsehole. I would have loved to have seen his face too, given the fact that he loves Leila and respects the hell out of her, that would have made for interesting viewing." Jules says as his laughter dies down.

"Shut up! All of you, Leila will be here soon and you're going to ruin this for me."

"We won't, we promise." Kenna promises and they all calm down. She takes Beau back from Georgie with a thank you and then the door to Vines opens and in walks the love of my life. The woman that I don't want to live without.

"What the hell is going on here?" She makes eye contact with me after she's noticed everyone else standing behind me, including her mum. "Caleb?"

I nod and Sara plays the song I asked her to queue up for me, as the first words boom out of the sound system, I watch as the realisation of what's about to happen play over her beautiful face. Her eyes widen, her mouth drops open and she uses her hands to cover it up.

I don't know what comes over me but listening to Bruno Mars sing about looking for something dumb to do and how it's a beautiful night, I step up unto the closest chair and then up onto the table it sits next to. Leila rushes over but stops short of touching me as I sing at the top of my lungs about how I want to marry her.

As the songs fades away, I jump off the table, by some miracle, I land right in front of Leila and I drop to one knee.

"It's not a dumb idea but I'm ready if you are, Darlin'. " I smirk at her, the love of my life and I hope that I did this one right. I pull the ring out of my pocket and hold it up to her. "Wanna get married? For real this time."

"Caleb." Her voice is barely above a whisper.

"What do you say, are you going to marry me?"

"For real?" There are tears sliding down her cheeks and she drops to her knees in front of me.

"Absolutely. I wouldn't have gathered the ragged bunch of humans behind us for just any reason you know." I take her left hand in mine. "I love you Leila Phillips and I have no intention of ever letting you go, not now that I've got you."

"I love you too!"

"Oh my god Leila, answer the man!" Sara demands.

"Put us all out of our misery." Matt groans and everyone else starts mumbling and wondering why she's hesitating but I know that's not what she's doing.

"You're the only one for me, Darlin'."

"You're the only one for me, Handsome." She smiles and I my heart melts. "Of course I'll marry you."

The bistro erupts into cheers and congratulations but I only have eyes for my fiancé as I slide the ring on her finger.

Kim is the first one to come over and hug us both, tears in her eyes. "Thank you for asking me this time, Caleb." She says, patting my cheek gently.

"You didn't?" Leila asks, her surprise written all over her face.

"He did and even asked me too." Matt confirms, joining us and giving his sister a tight hug, then holds his hand out to me, which I gratefully take and we shake.

"I can't believe you did that. That you asked my mum is one thing but to ask Matt, that's ridiculous." Leila shakes her head in amazement.

"Hey, I appreciated the sentiment. Even if I do agree he didn't need to ask my permission, it was a nice gesture. He only needed to ask *you* and I told him as much."

Tears well in Leila's eyes but she doesn't get much of a chance for more emotions because Sara engulfs her with a hug and they start talking about how she went behind Leila's back for weeks to organise everything and I roll my eyes. It was days but Sara's not one to let the truth get in the way of a good story sometimes. I hope Matt knows what he's doing with that one.

Then everyone is surrounding us, congratulations and hugs are given and received way too many times. When Logan announces that everyone gets a free slice of chocolate cake and a drink of their choice to celebrate our engagement, the crowd disperses. Leila and I take the opportunity of everyone being distracted to sneak out through the door into the tasting room and then outside. We hurry back home, close the blinds and lock the door. We added a deadbolt a few months ago so that no one can get in if we don't want them to, after Jules walked in to see something he hopes to never see again!

"This is the same ring? Your Mum's ring?"

"I hope you don't mind. I always wanted the woman I spent the rest of my life with to have it." I didn't doubt the decision until now.

"Then why did you give it to me back then?" She's curious and I can understand why.

"Because even back then, I knew I wanted to spend forever with you."

Don't miss out!

Visit the website below and you can sign up to receive emails whenever Chelle Pimblott publishes a new book. There's no charge and no obligation.

https://books2read.com/r/B-A-FGVL-HRJSB

BOOKS 2 READ

Connecting independent readers to independent writers.

Also by Chelle Pimblott

Built for Love
Built to Last
Built for Trouble

Drake Wines
Vineyard
Sandy Cove - A Drake Wines Novella
Winery
Lori's Memories - A Drake Wines Novella
Brewery
Sara's Forever

Sneaky Love
Sneaky
Sneaking Around
No More Sneaking Around

Standalone
Barefoot & Dumped!

www.ingramcontent.com/pod-product-compliance
Lightning Source LLC
Chambersburg PA
CBHW070050120726
47909CB00002B/344